ALL
GOD'S
CHILDREN

ANNA SCHMIDT

ALL GOD'S CHILDREN

THE PEACEMAKERS BOOK I

BARBOUR
PUBLISHING

"This is a call to the living,
To those who refuse to make peace with evil,
With the suffering and the waste of the world."
Algernon D. Black, former senior leader,
New York Society for Ethical Culture

PART I

MUNICH
OCTOBER—DECEMBER 1942

CHAPTER I

Beth Bridgewater rushed into the cramped foyer of her uncle's third-floor apartment. Her uncle was a professor of natural sciences at the Ludwig-Maximilians-Universität München, and his collection of files and notebooks for his research projects cluttered every available space. Beth moved a stack of books so that she could shove her feet into the slippers tradition required her to put on the minute she entered the house. "I'm home," she called.

Of course, this wasn't home. Not really. This was Germany—Munich, the capital of Bavaria and headquarters of the Third Reich. Home was half a world away in Wisconsin. Home was a farm where her parents lived just outside of Madison. Home was the Quaker meetinghouse where she and her friends and family gathered for all of the important and mundane events of their lives. Home was certainty and safety where at any time day or night she would not have to scurry for the protection of the cellar beneath the ground-floor bakery should the air-raid sirens sound.

Home was where she should be—should have been ever since Germany had declared war on the United States. But Germany might as well be the Land of Oz for all the good it did her to think of returning to the United States. She would never forget the day she arrived in

9

Munich and stepped off the train. Everything she saw or smelled or heard was as foreign to her as the language. But at the same time it was all so exciting. She truly began to believe that living in Germany could turn out to be a grand adventure. Little did she imagine that a few months of summer would stretch into eight long years.

As an American still living in Munich in 1942 after America had joined the war against Germany, she kept a low profile. She helped her aunt with the cooking and cleaning as she cared for her eight-year-old cousin, Liesl. She chose her associates with care. She could not afford to come to the attention of the authorities, although more than likely they already were well aware of her presence in their midst.

As if being American were not enough, she and Uncle Franz and Aunt Ilse—who, like Beth's mother, were also natives of Bavaria—were members of the Religious Society of Friends, or *Freunde* as they were known in Germany.

"I'm home," Beth called out again as she unpinned her hat and fluffed her wispy blond bangs. She heard movement in the room just off the foyer that served as her uncle's study and assumed that Uncle Franz was within earshot. "Such an incredibly lovely day," she gushed as she set her shoes aside. "It reminds me so much of autumn in Wisconsin, and I have to admit that on days like this I find it impossible to believe that..."

She had been about to say that surely on such a day there could be no place for war and discord, but the door to the study opened, and a stranger stepped into the hall. In the early days after she'd first arrived from America to live with Uncle Franz and Aunt Ilse, she might have finished her statement without a thought. But that was before.

She was so very weary of the need to always measure everything in terms of *before*....

Before a friend had been interrogated and then fired from his job and evicted from his apartment because he had dared to make some derisive comment about the Third Reich.

Before Ilse had begun taking to her bed, a pillow clutched over her ears whenever the jackboots of the soldiers pounded out their ominous rhythm on the street below their apartment or passed by in perfect lockstep while the citizens of Munich cheered.

Before an apartment in the building two doors down the block had been raided in the night and the occupants taken away.

Year by year—sometimes month by month—things had changed but oddly had also stayed the same. Other than the matter of people being rousted from their homes and simply disappearing in the dead of night, Munich was little different than it had been the summer she arrived. Neighbors went about their daily shopping and errands, chatting and joking with one another as if those people who had vanished from one of the shops or apartments on the block had never existed. Children who had once attended school and played together with no thought for ethnic heritage now flaunted that heritage by wearing the brown shirts of the Hitler Youth or, in some cases, forcing others to wear the crude yellow star that marked them as Jew.

Beth's first reaction on seeing this stranger in their apartment—this stranger in uniform—was alarm. Was he here to question them? Uncle Franz had been called in for questioning several times—mostly because he had refused on religious grounds to sign the required oath of allegiance to the government. He was also under scrutiny because he taught in one of the more outspoken departments at the university. Every time he was summoned for an interrogation, Beth's aunt suffered. The debilitating nervous anxiety that Ilse Schneider had developed shortly after giving birth had not improved with time and was only exacerbated by the uncertainty they lived with day in and week out.

Had this man come to deport her? The Nazis had a well-deserved reputation for being sticklers for detail—people who left nothing to chance. Even with the war raging, it was not unthinkable that the presence of an American in their midst might draw their attention. Or perhaps something else had happened. Were they all to be arrested? In these times such thoughts were natural—even automatic.

"Hello," the man said in accented English. He wore a medic's insignia on his military jacket and held his military cap loosely in one hand. Although he was several inches taller than she was, he seemed to be looking up at her from beneath a fan of lowered lashes. She was pretty sure that he wasn't more than a year or so older than she was.

"Elizabeth, this is Josef—Dr. Josef Buch," Uncle Franz explained as he came to the door and stood next to the soldier. "I found the citation we were looking for, Josef." He held a book, his forefinger marking a page, his wire-rimmed reading glasses balanced on his forehead. His hairline had receded a little more every year since Beth had first arrived to answer his plea for help with his sickly wife and overactive daughter. His shoulders were a bit more stooped, and he looked a good deal older than his fifty years. He hid his worrying about his family, his job, the future as well as he could, but it was taking a toll. Although Beth had offered repeatedly to return to America, her uncle would not hear of it. "I need you here," he always said as he cupped her cheek with his palm. "We all do."

As she waited for him to explain the doctor's presence, she studied him closely for warning signs that she should be concerned or remain silent. But he looked more relaxed than Beth had seen him in weeks. Clearly something about this stranger had put her uncle completely at ease—had even lifted his spirits. Once again Beth turned her attention to their guest.

"*Grüß Gott, Herr Doktor*," she said. She kept her curiosity about why the man spoke such flawless English to herself, having been admonished repeatedly by Ilse to say as little as possible in the presence of others and never to ask questions. Instead she took a moment to examine him while her uncle read aloud a passage from the book he carried.

The doctor's hair was close-cropped and the color of real coffee laced with real cream—neither of which Beth had enjoyed since her last visit to America five years earlier. His eyes, spotlighted by the sunlight pouring across the polished wooden floor of the cramped study, reflected the green of a Northern Wisconsin pine forest. But there was something more than the startling color. An underlying and indefinable intensity belied his polite reserve.

And as she studied his features, she realized that although Josef Buch was listening politely to her uncle, he was also studying her in return.

"Josef was one of my students, Beth," her uncle explained when he'd finished reading aloud the passage. "I'm afraid whenever he's around he challenges me to prove my point in any discussion."

"My uncle has so many former students stopping by these days," she said, speaking in German as she always did in the presence of visitors, especially ones in uniform. "Former and current. Our home is a regular café for his students. We are always pleased to welcome someone new." She wondered if the man had come because word had gotten out about the meetings for worship held here for the small group of Quakers still living in Munich or perhaps about the literary soirees her uncle held for students and fellow faculty members from time to time. In spite of the need to maintain a low profile, Uncle Franz insisted that some things could not—should not—be changed.

She gave up trying to guess why this man in uniform had come. She had worked hard to fight the natural paranoia that came with all the changes and uncertainties they'd had to endure over the years. Why not consider that perhaps the man had simply stopped by for a visit or to bid a favorite teacher farewell before leaving to take up his military duties? "Are you on leave, Herr Doktor?" She blurted the first thought that came to mind.

"Josef has served on the western front in France and has now been given permission to return to the university to complete his medical training," Uncle Franz explained. "You two should have much in common, Beth. Josef studied in Boston. I expect that explains his command of English. You were there, what, Josef? Two years?"

"Three."

"And now here you are back home again in Munich, albeit after a small detour to perform your military duty."

"I'm afraid that I was asked to leave your country, *Fräulein*. But I

13

did enjoy my time there." His tone revealed no anger or disapproval regarding his deportation.

"Will you stay for dinner, Josef?" Franz invited. "Afterward we can get you properly settled."

"I don't wish to intrude, and I do not expect *Frau* Schneider to prepare meals for me as part of our agreement," Josef replied.

They were all speaking German, but somewhere along the way Beth felt as if she had missed some key piece of information. *What agreement?*

"Josef is going to board with us for the time being, Beth," her uncle explained as if he'd recognized her confusion. "We're going to set him up in the attic."

It was not uncommon for people to make room in their home for a *Studentenbude*. Franz and Ilse were fortunate to have the top-floor apartment and the extra space of the attic above, but there had been no discussion of such an arrangement in their home. "I see," Beth said when in fact she did not understand at all.

"These are hard times for everyone, and Josef has agreed to pay rent and share his rations with us."

"That would..."

Her uncle turned to the doctor. "Beth moved here to stay with us several years ago after my wife took ill following the birth of our daughter. A nervous condition that is chronic, I'm afraid. I don't know how we would have managed had she not agreed to come and stay. Our daughter, Liesl, would be lost without her."

Beth studied her uncle closely. He was talking more than he usually did, interrupting her before she could speak. Perhaps he was nervous after all.

"You live here then?" the doctor asked, his intense gaze still focused on her.

"She shares a room with our daughter." Uncle Franz's laugh was a little forced. "And I may as well tell you right now, young man, Frau Schneider will not tolerate anything less than strict chaperoned visits

14

between you young people."

Beth blushed and wished that her uncle would just stop trying to explain everything. There had to be more to the story of why Josef Buch had suddenly appeared in their house than her uncle was admitting. She cast about for some way she might learn more without appearing too inquisitive. But before she could come up with some offer to help, a door slammed at the far end of the corridor, and her always-boisterous cousin Liesl came running down the hall.

"You're finally back," she cried as if Beth had been gone for days instead of an hour. "Can we go to the park?" She hopped up and down. "*Bitte, bitte, bitte!*"

Liesl had been born when Beth's aunt and uncle had given up any hope of ever having children. To complicate matters, Liesl had always been an unusually high-strung and active child whose mood swings and short attention span were more than Aunt Ilse could manage. As Aunt Ilse's struggles to cope with her child and the world around her had increased, so had the scope of the responsibilities Beth now shouldered in the household.

She placed a calming hand on Liesl's shoulder. "I am here, and we will go to the park tomorrow after the meeting for worship."

Again Uncle Franz was quick to explain. "Our family regularly holds meetings for worship here on First Day—what you refer to as Sunday. We are members of the local Religious Society of Friends—Quakers, Freunde." Beth was stunned to hear her uncle offer such information so freely. For so many reasons they had become increasingly cautious about revealing anything related to their personal lives or religious beliefs to those they did not know. And student of her uncle's or not, this man was certainly not someone they knew well.

"We have a guest, Liesl," Franz continued, nodding toward Josef. Beth was glad for the diversion, knowing that the stranger in uniform would claim Liesl's full attention.

"My name is Liesl, and I am eight," the girl announced as she took a step closer and gazed up at the doctor.

Beth was moved to see how Josef immediately seemed to grasp that Liesl was not a typical eight-year-old. He crouched down so that he was more on a level with her and offered her his hand. "And I am Josef Buch. I am twenty-six. I am pleased to meet you, Fräulein Liesl Schneider."

Liesl frowned as she studied his outstretched hand. "You are a soldier," she reminded him. She snapped her heels together and offered him the salute of the Third Reich. "*Heil*, Hitler," she bellowed, her right arm stiff and raised to the prescribed level.

In the stunned silence that followed, Beth heard a glass shatter in the kitchen and realized that her aunt was no doubt listening to everything they were saying. Beth took hold of her cousin's outstretched arm and guided her through the sitting room across from the study toward the closed door that led to the kitchen. "Come. Your mother needs our help."

The one thing about life in a German home that Beth thought she would never become accustomed to was the way doors between rooms remained closed at all times. She understood such vigilance at this time of year when the days turned cool and the nights could be quite chilly, but closed doors regardless of the season only added to the atmosphere of isolation and a certain undercurrent of fear that these days permeated every facet of their lives. Once inside the kitchen, she realized that Josef Buch had not returned Liesl's salute—a detail that only added to her confusion about the true purpose of his presence in their home.

She swept up the broken glass while Ilse settled Liesl at the kitchen table with a saucer of apple slices. All the while, Beth's aunt whispered warnings that Beth should say and do nothing in the presence of this man that might give him information he could use against them.

"Why is he here?" Beth asked.

"How should I know? The point is—"

"Beth, tell me a story," Liesl begged as she popped the last of the apple slices into her mouth.

"Not right now," Beth replied. She was determined to return to the study and learn more about this sudden change of events. She handed Liesl a piece of paper and the stub of a pencil. "Draw me a picture," Beth said, "and I'll tell you a story about it before bedtime." Liesl loved to paint and color and draw, and the activity always calmed her. The little girl bent to her work.

"Perhaps I should take them some tea," Beth suggested.

"I suppose. He might think it odd if we aren't hospitable in the usual way," Ilse replied, casting furtive glances toward the closed door beyond which they both could hear the murmur of male voices. "Use the good tea cups," she added.

Beth made the tea and placed the pot on the tray with the cups and saucers. Ilse poured a little milk into the cream pitcher and got spoons for stirring and the sugar bowl. Then she opened the door and watched as Beth carried the tray back to the study and tapped on the closed door.

"I brought you tea," she said when Uncle Franz opened the door and stood aside to let her pass. The doctor was sorting through a stack of books, setting aside one or two that seemed of interest to him. He placed the rest in the limited space available on the already-overcrowded floor-to-ceiling shelves.

"May I help?" She avoided looking directly at her uncle's former student. While Beth had been preparing the tea, Aunt Ilse, through whispered comments, had made clear her view that the man was surely a government spy. Her aunt's litany of fears and anxieties—for her child, herself, and most especially for her husband's career as a professor at the university under this new regime—was ceaseless these days.

"*Danke, Liebchen, aber* I think perhaps there is something you might rather do," her uncle said with a twinkle in his eyes. "If you check under that stack of books there, I believe you will discover a letter from home."

Beth gave a yelp of delight as she set the tray on the library table that also served as her uncle's desk and foraged through the mail, all thought of their new boarder cast aside. "It's been weeks," she said, hugging the envelope to her chest. "Please excuse me." She stepped into the hall, and as she turned to close the door, she added, "It was nice to meet you, Herr Doktor."

"Josef," her uncle corrected. "He's part of the family now, and there's no need to stand on ceremony, right Josef?"

"I don't wish to make anyone uncomfortable," the doctor replied.

"Josef then," Beth said. "And I am Beth." She gave him a polite smile. Her uncle's insistence on the informal use of the man's given name was odd in a society where a bit of reserve between new acquaintances was more the tradition.

"Now don't get all caught up in replying to that letter," Uncle Franz called out to her. "You'll need to set an extra place for supper and help your aunt. Josef has agreed to join us, although he insists that there be no special attention given to him."

Beth understood the underlying message. Any slight change in their routine could upset Ilse to the point where she would take to her bed for the remainder of the evening. It had happened before. And having the doctor share their meager evening meal was just the sort of thing that could send Ilse over the edge.

"I'll just go read this. I can answer it after Liesl is in bed," she promised.

In the small bedroom that she shared with her cousin, Beth kicked off her slippers and slid her thumbnail under the flap of the envelope. Using her toes, she pulled the straight-backed rocking chair closer to the late-afternoon light streaming through the single window that overlooked the small courtyard in back of the apartment building. She smiled as she settled into the creaky old chair for a long-anticipated taste of home.

The letter had already been opened and crudely resealed. When she removed the thin pages, she saw several places where her mother's words had been blacked out—censored. Was nothing sacred to these people? Not even an innocent letter from mother to daughter?

She held the pages up to the daylight streaming through the window, trying to recover the words some government person had decided were threatening or seditious.

Dearest Beth,

    Your father and I hope this finds you well and _____. Your letters are always so full of _____ and good cheer, ___ we read _____. We are quite certain that circumstances _____ here. _____ _____ your father and I _____ to leave as soon as possible. _____ _____ _____ Franz and Ilse to _____ as well. After all there is Liesl to _____. If only. . .

    _____ we must constantly seek God's guidance _____. And who knows whether coming back here is the answer? Here in America there is growing animosity toward people like us—people of German heritage. Even those of your generation are not immune to the taunts and snubs of some.

    _____ back home with us, but _____leaving Munich_____. I know that my brother is well-respected _____ . . . .

Beth let the letter dangle from her fingers as she stood and stared out the window. The sun reflecting off the autumn leaves that had seemed so glorious earlier was blighted now by gathering clouds. She had so longed for news of life at home—of her father raking leaves and her grown brothers leaping into the pile, then helping him to repair the mess they had made. She had longed for images of the neighborhood—Bertha Dobins walking her poodle down the country lane that connected their farms, old Mr. Remington leaning out the window of his rusty pickup truck as he offered Beth's mother advice on putting up the last of the tomatoes. She wanted to hear of the pot roast her mother had prepared and of friends from her high school days who had stopped by to ask how she was faring and when she might return. She wanted gossip and news of what had been said at the meetinghouse that week. She was desperate for that taste of home.

In the years since she had come to live with her aunt and uncle, she had gone back to Wisconsin only once, and that had been barely two years after she had first arrived. These days Beth had to wonder if she would ever be able to leave. More than just the need to stay and care for Liesl—and her aunt—kept her from leaving. A year or so earlier in a moment of impulsive reaction to the unfairness of life for many of her neighbors, Beth had given her visa to a friend who was frantically trying to leave the country. At the time, she had naively thought that as an American it would be easy to say she had lost her papers and get the precious document replaced. But that had been before the American consulate had been closed and the consul—a friend of her parents from Wisconsin—had been reassigned to Berlin. She had had no choice but to tell her uncle what she had done. She knew that he had tried everything he could to get the visa replaced—even making a trip to Berlin—with no success.

So if Beth wanted to leave Munich—and she did more than anything—without the proper papers, how could she? Her eyes widened in shock as she considered that perhaps this was why Dr. Josef Buch had come. He knew.

~≋ CHAPTER 2 ≋~

Are you certain that inviting me to live here is a good idea, Herr Professor?" Josef handed the older man a stack of books. "Your niece seemed a little reticent."

"Everyone will adjust, and I thought we had an understanding."

Josef paused in his work and looked at his former mentor. "Still, Herr Professor. . ."

"I am Franz, and you are Josef," Franz reminded him. "Now suppose you tell me why you have decided to accept my offer to room here when you could just as easily—"

"I do not wish to live with my parents during this time. There are too many—distractions. And besides, I have a shorter distance to travel between the university and the hospital if I am here. But of course if you should ever change your mind. . ."

"Not at all. I've been outnumbered by the females in this house long enough. It will be so pleasant to have another male point of view." He chuckled, and for Josef it was a taste of the days when he had been a carefree university student savoring Professor Schneider's lectures in natural science. That had been such a wonderful time in Josef's life. He and his friends had naively complained of the long hours and difficult coursework, never once understanding that they had been happier than at any time in their young lives—happier than Josef suspected they would ever be again. He thought of the one friend he missed the most.

"I saw Willi Graf at the train station last summer when we all left for our assignments," he told Franz as the two of them continued sorting and cataloguing the professor's library of journals and texts. "Do you remember him?"

"Quiet young man with blond hair. *Ja?*"

"Blond *thinning* hair," Josef said laughing. "We were joking about that. He and some of the others from my class were sent east to Russia." He flipped through a book of medical terminology, and a folded paper fell out.

"I'll get that," Franz said, his voice sounding slightly panicked as he bent to retrieve the slip of paper and stuff it into the sagging pocket of his cardigan sweater without looking at it.

The two of them returned to their work, but the mood in the room had undoubtedly shifted. Something about that paper had unnerved the professor. More to the point, Josef suspected that his simply seeing the paper had contributed to Franz's sudden reserve.

They worked in silence for several minutes. Despite the closed door, Josef was aware of cooking odors and the muffled sound of female conversation coming from the kitchen. He thought about the paper the professor had been so anxious that he not see. The brief glimpse he'd had of it showed it to be something printed on a mimeograph machine. Something about the layout of the printing had felt familiar.

Then he remembered why the paper had triggered a memory. That summer, a flurry of leaflets had appeared, calling for Germans to rise up and take a stand against Hitler and for their country. The leaflets had not been signed except for the title on each: "*Flugblätter der Weissen Rose,*" Leaflets of the White Rose. As far as Josef knew, they had been distributed primarily at the university throughout the summer. Yet just as suddenly as they had appeared, they stopped. Josef had assumed that the authors had been caught and arrested.

But the words of that first leaflet had stayed with him during the weeks and months he had spent serving in France:

> *Nothing is so unworthy of a civilized nation as allowing itself to be governed without opposition by an irresponsible clique that has yielded to base instinct. It is certain that today every honest German is ashamed of his government... ashamed of his government.*

It was precisely what Josef felt every time he saw the black swastika and heard the ranting of Adolf Hitler broadcast across the land. Germany was Josef's homeland and had always been a place of culture and refinement that set a standard for the rest of the world. But no more.

He considered whether he could ask the professor if he had ever seen the leaflets from the group known as the White Rose. Surely Franz would be in complete agreement with their cause. Perhaps he even knew what had become of them.

But these were unusual times, and friends did not ask friends about things that might be controversial. Friends showed their friendship by respecting the silence, the caution that permeated daily routine. There was no longer the luxury of casual conversation—not in Germany.

Clutching her mother's letter, Beth stood at the window and stared down at the bustling street below, tears of disappointment leaking down her cheeks. Earlier she had seen workers leaving their jobs for the day to gather at the café on the corner. Across the street was the bookstore that had been owned by the family taken from their apartment. The shop was dark and closed now, although the window still featured a display of books gathering dust.

Through the open bedroom window, she could hear the jingle of the bell on the bakery that occupied the ground floor of their building. On mild October days like this one, the baker opened the rear door to get more air circulation in the hot kitchen. She and Liesl so liked waking to the aromas of fresh bread and pastries baking. A streetcar passed. The wind rattled through the trees, scattering their brilliant red and gold leaves. In the distance she heard the piercing siren of an ambulance.

She settled her gaze on a woman entering the rear courtyard of the building next door, a straw shopping bag in each hand. From the looks of her parcels, she hadn't gotten much at the market. Beth recognized her as the woman who, with her husband, had moved into the apartment that had been suddenly abandoned. This new couple had been taken into the camaraderie of the neighborhood without question. She watched the woman greet another resident of her building who was sitting on the rear steps, smoking his pipe. The man gestured broadly as he apparently relayed some news. The woman's shoulders sagged a bit more, and then she shrugged and shook her head before continuing on her way.

Turning away from the scene below, Beth's thoughts returned to the letter she held. She stared at the blacked-out lines, then smoothed and folded the thin sheets of stationery and placed them back in the envelope. How she longed for some positive news—at least something that might make her heart lighter. How she longed to return to a place where she didn't have to censor her words or thoughts.

But even if Beth could return to Wisconsin, then what? How would Aunt Ilse cope? How would Uncle Franz be able to concentrate on his research and teaching so that his position at the university remained secure? No, her place was here—not just because she had no exit visa, but because everything told her that this was the right thing to do—this was God's plan for her at this time in her life. She had prayed about it in meetings for worship over the last several months, asking God to show her His way, and in the end she had come to the certainty that she was meant to be where she was. She could only hope that in time she would be able to go home.

She turned her thoughts back to the immediate situation. The arrival of the doctor presented a new puzzle. He was here—as apparently he would be tomorrow and for days to come—his sudden presence only adding to the confusion and uncertainty that roiled through the house these days. Oh, what did it all mean?

Beth sighed, for in their faith there was only one answer to such a state of inner turmoil.

"Be still and know that I am God."

She should wait for the following day when the few remaining Friends living in Munich would gather in her uncle's simply furnished sitting room for the weekly meeting for worship. But as her mother often told her, at times a person could not wait for the gathering of others to seek God's guidance. So Beth sat in the rocker, folded her hands in her lap, closed her eyes, and waited for the calming beacon of that inner light that Friends around the world believed dwelt in every person—even Chancellor Adolf Hitler.

After several moments she was able to shut out the sounds that floated up to her from the street through the open window. She was less successful in shutting out the sound of Uncle Franz's laughter, which found its way to her like a whiff of the rationed and treasured pipe tobacco he smoked. Determined to find the calm and comfort of silence and to have all thoughts focused on God, she pushed away each concern that plagued her—her mother's censored letter, the unexplained presence of the doctor, her nonexistent documents for going home. . . .

But her efforts to find inner peace were short-lived as she was startled back to reality by Liesl's howl of distress and Ilse's strident and impatient attempt to settle the child. Her prayer would have to wait.

At supper Josef sat on the bench across the kitchen table from the professor's niece and the child, Liesl. The professor sat at one end of the narrow table and his wife at the opposite end. He tried to concentrate on his food and the conversation—stilted as it was given that the professor's wife was decidedly uncomfortable in his presence.

But again and again, his attention returned to Beth.

In his presence she appeared nervous, never meeting his eyes directly, maintaining her silence unless spoken to directly. No, not nervous. More cautious. From what he had observed on the battlefield, caution was something to be admired. He far preferred to be in the company of soldiers who considered their options rather than those who rushed headlong into the fray.

Earlier she had burst into the house as if the crisp autumn wind had driven her there. Her chatter had been filled with the unmistakable vibrancy common to Americans. During his time in Boston, he had never gotten accustomed to the way his American friends had of simply blurting out their thoughts and feelings without any attempt at censoring them first. But once she had seen him—or more to the point seen his uniform—she had assumed the guarded reserve that was commonplace throughout Germany these days.

"Do you live near Munich, Herr Doktor?" Beth asked, apparently as unsettled by the strained silence as everyone else.

"My parents live in Harlaching—in the southern part of the city." He saw the professor's wife glance at him for the first time. Harlaching was less than two kilometers from the professor's cramped apartment.

"That's quite a lovely area," Beth continued. "The homes are quite... stately."

"They are larger," Josef admitted.

"And yet you have decided to—"

"Josef wishes to take a room with us to be nearer his work at the university," Franz said, and the look he gave his niece was a warning for her to stop probing. "You must tell us what your mother had to say, Beth."

Beth's answer was surprisingly blunt. "Everyone appears to be fine." She darted a quick glance in his direction. "Once the censors had their way with it, I'm afraid there was much in the letter left to the imagination."

Earlier when Franz had given her the letter, Josef had been

taken aback by her unadulterated joy. Clearly as she ran off to savor the contents, she was anticipating news of friends and family. In that moment he had actually envied her, for he well recalled the letters that his father had written to him while he served his first tour of duty as a medic. They were brief missives of instructions and curt reminders of the honor he could bring to the family name. He was quite sure that it had been his mother who had lobbied for his father to use his influence to get Josef back to Munich to complete his studies.

Now as he observed the professor's American niece helping Frau Schneider serve the meal, he wondered if perhaps her news from home had been as disappointing as the letters from his father had been. Certainly when her uncle had inquired about her letter, Beth's answer had been surprisingly curt.

"Beth, that's too much mustard," Liesl said testily.

"I thought you like lots of mustard," Beth replied as she scraped off part of the condiment, added a slice of sausage, and handed the half sandwich to the girl. Josef could not help but notice that Beth attended to the child's constant needs as if she—not her aunt—were the parent.

"It's too much," Liesl fumed. "Papa?" She turned to the professor for support.

"Liesl, we have company," he said quietly.

Liesl's face got very red, and Josef feared she might be about to cry—or worse, launch into a tantrum. From the look of Frau Schneider, Josef believed that she was anticipating the same thing.

"What did you learn in school today, Fräulein Liesl?" Josef asked, wanting to do his part to ease the situation and spare his hostess any embarrassment.

It worked. The child gave him her full attention, her voice filled with the excitement of her report. "Oh, our teacher told us all about *der Führer* and what a great and good man he is. He came to Munich last spring, you know. He passed right by our house here."

It was evident that the child's comment had not eased the strained atmosphere around the table but rather worsened it. "Did you see him then?" Josef concentrated on his food even as his curiosity overruled his reason. Speaking of Hitler would certainly do little to ease Frau Schneider's anxiety.

Liesl frowned and toyed with her food. "*Nein.* Some soldiers came that morning and made us all stay in the kitchen, and then some other people came into our house. They had little flags, and they were all dressed up and everything."

Josef looked to the professor for an explanation, as he had never heard of such a thing. But it was Beth who provided the answer.

"Because we are Quakers, the authorities have some doubts about our enthusiasm for the Reich," she said, obviously measuring each word. "Apparently they felt that occupying the apartment with cheering strangers for the occasion was preferable since they felt they could not rely on us to be quite so—enthusiastic."

"Liesl, drink your milk," Frau Schneider said. She reached for the glass of cider beside her plate, and her hand shook so badly that she nearly spilt the amber liquid. Josef noticed her send her husband a pleading look—one that clearly begged him to change the subject.

Josef cast about for a way he might help and turned his attention to Beth. "Professor Schneider tells me you came to Munich to learn our language while you helped Frau Schneider with Liesl's care," Josef said.

"Ja. My mother was born and raised here in Munich but moved to the United States when she and my father married. Once they moved to the United States, she insisted that only English be spoken in our home. As a girl I became fairly adept at reading and understanding the written words, but my spoken German needed work." Her eyes met his, challenging him to question her presence in a country that was at war with hers.

"I must say that after eight years with us our Beth speaks like a native," Professor Schneider added with a wink at his niece. "She's even managed to pick up much of our Bavarian dialect. *Net woar*, Beth?"

"Of course, because her mother is a native," Ilse added, "some would agree that this gives Beth the right to…to…." She looked at her husband.

"To live here as well," he finished quietly. "And certainly after eight years. . .well, she's become a treasured member of this family—like a daughter to Ilse and me and a sister for Liesl."

Josef focused on cutting his sausage into bite-sized pieces. Perhaps it would be best if he allowed the professor to guide the conversation. Certainly his attempts to ease the strained atmosphere that surrounded the meal had failed. He glanced up and was surprised to see that Beth was smiling at him. It was a sad smile but lovely nevertheless.

"My brothers do that," she said, nodding toward the way he held his knife and fork in a position that Americans would consider the reverse of how it should be. Her tone was soft and wistful, and Josef felt a flicker of pleasure at having given her some reminder of home.

"Your mother brought some of her ways to you and your brothers then?"

"She has. I never really thought about it, but yes."

Josef set his knife on the edge of his plate and took a bite of the meat. "Your brothers are younger?"

"By two years. Twins, although they look nothing alike. Fred is married. He and his wife are expecting their first child in the spring. Theo is a farmer in Wisconsin like my father."

He took a bite of his supper and then turned his attention to Frau Schneider. "This is the best meal I have had in some time," he said. "Thank you for inviting me to dine with you and your family."

"It is our pleasure," she replied without meeting his gaze. "The professor tells me that you were one of his best students."

Every word was measured before she uttered it. The woman was definitely a bundle of nerves.

"I am flattered to hear that he thought as much. Your husband had many gifted students. He was one of—"

"Herr Doktor," Liesl said, tapping her fork against her plate to gain his attention, "do you know what else my teacher told us today?"

"What?"

The girl lowered her voice and leaned toward him as if about to share a secret. "She told us that there could be some of us whose parents might not follow all the new rules so we needed to be sure that if we saw them doing something that wasn't right, we should tell them about the rules. And if that didn't make them do right, then we needed to tell our teacher or the *Blockwart*."

"Liesl!" Frau Schneider hissed. "The doctor was speaking. Do not interrupt."

The girl frowned, slouched back onto the bench, and took a bite of her sandwich. Josef glanced at Beth, who was looking down at her barely touched plate of food.

"They are in the military—your brothers?" It was an impertinent question, and Josef regretted it the moment he heard the shocked intake of Ilse Schneider's breath.

"We are Quakers, Doctor," Beth said, reverting to English.

Silence pervaded the room, making the scratch of forks on crockery all the more pronounced. Josef felt compelled to say something that might ease the tension. "I have always wondered why the name Quakers."

"Members of the Religious Society of Friends—Freunde," the professor explained, clearly relieved to have moved on to this topic. "Our faith is rooted in the tenets of silent prayer and individual inner searching rather than those of ceremony and sermon. As for being called—"

"We're different," Liesl announced. "My teacher says being different is not a good thing."

Professor Schneider cleared his throat, and the child gave a shrug and drank her milk.

"But why Quaker?" Josef asked.

"In the past, some early worshippers were said to have developed a habit of being so overcome by the spirit within that they were said to 'quake.'"

Josef had to hide a smile as he recognized the voice his mentor used when he lectured.

"For some time it was a term of contempt, as people of our faith were persecuted for their beliefs," Franz continued. "These days..."

Ilse Schneider's fork clattered to her plate, and Josef saw that she had suddenly gone quite pale. Her husband ducked his head and continued eating without completing his sentence.

Beth stood up and began gathering the serving dishes. "To answer your original question, Herr Doktor, my brothers are required to register for military service, but they have the option to refuse to serve for religious reasons. We do not believe that war is an answer," she explained without looking at him. But then she paused in her clearing of the table and met his eyes defiantly. "We will not do battle either for the kingdom of God or the kingdoms of men."

In spite of the charged atmosphere around the table, Josef could not seem to control his curiosity or his tongue. "Your government allows such a thing?" It was well known that in Germany refusal to serve on any grounds was punishable by imprisonment—or worse.

"Dessert?" Ilse Schneider's voice was high-pitched with a warning that they should cease this dangerous discussion at once. "Why don't you take our guest into the sitting room, Franz? We can have dessert in there."

But Beth ignored her. "My country was founded on the very principle of religious freedom."

"I baked an apple kuchen," Ilse persisted, her voice every bit as shaky as her hands were.

"So that's what smells so wonderful," the professor said as he stood and indicated that Josef should follow him to the other room. But Josef was aware that just before closing the connecting door between the kitchen and sitting room, the professor laid his hand on his niece's arm.

"Sorry," she murmured, blushing at her uncle's silent rebuke.

"Josef, I expect that you are wondering why Beth is still here," the professor said as soon as they were seated in two overstuffed chairs positioned at either end of a worn sofa. "No doubt she should have gone home to America some time ago—certainly once Germany declared war on the United States. But she chose to stay and help us. As I mentioned earlier, after the birth of our daughter, my wife's health deteriorated. I'm afraid that it has only worsened in the years since. Surely you observed that she is not at all well, and as you may also have noticed, our daughter can be quite challenging."

"But in these times, Professor. . .I would think that your niece would wish to be with her parents. Furthermore I would have thought that the authorities. . ."

Franz sighed. "So far the authorities have elected to overlook her presence. Perhaps over eight years she has become so ingrained in the community that everyone thinks of her as one of our own. Nevertheless, as you may well imagine, her presence here draws attention. My wife worries about that."

"Have you been harassed?"

Franz shrugged. "Who hasn't these days? You've been away serving with your unit. On the surface things probably appear the same as before. But beneath that surface? Well, Liesl was right in saying that being different is not something the authorities encourage." At the sound of female voices, he went to open the door for his wife and niece.

"Ah, a delectable treat to celebrate your moving in with us, Josef," Franz said in a voice that was too loud. "Just smell that cinnamon."

Josef could not help noticing that Franz's smile was forced. His true expression—concern for his wife, apprehension about the state of things in his household—could be read in the sadness and strain that lined the rest of his face.

They ate the apple kuchen and sipped cups of ersatz coffee in silence interrupted only occasionally by Liesl's whining plea for a second helping of the rich vanilla cream that topped the dessert and Ilse's repeated refusal. Finally the child started to blubber, prompting Franz to take her on his lap and suggest that they sing a song for their guest.

To Liesl's delight Josef joined in the singing, even going so far as to add some of the hand movements associated with a Bavarian folk dance. Before the song was finished, Beth had joined in. Even Ilse was humming and lightly clapping her hands in time to the music.

"I like you, Herr Doktor," Liesl announced, her tears forgotten.

"Enough that we can be on a first-name basis, Fräulein?"

Liesl looked to Beth for a translation.

"He means he would call you by your first name," she explained.

"I am Liesl, and you are...?"

"Josef," he said, grinning at her. He stuck out his hand for her to shake. "Friends?"

She giggled and pumped his hand up and down several times. This time there was no mention of showing proper allegiance to Hitler with a salute.

After Josef and Franz had climbed the narrow enclosed stairway from the kitchen to the attic to finish getting Josef settled into his new space, Beth sent Liesl off to change into her nightgown and prepare for story time.

Over the years that she had lived with her aunt and uncle, she had learned to read her aunt's frequent mood shifts almost as well as she knew how to calm her cousin's tantrums. As the two women washed the dishes, Beth was well aware that something beyond the conversation at dinner had caused her to become so upset—perhaps something that had occurred while she was out shopping earlier. Whatever the reason, Beth had learned that it was best to address the situation directly rather than allow it to fester overnight.

"I apologize for upsetting you earlier," she said, taking a freshly washed serving dish from her aunt and wiping it dry. "I know that sometimes I say things that—"

Aunt Ilse wheeled around and glared at her. "You must mind your tongue, Beth. These are troubling times—dangerous times. We know nothing of this man—this Josef Buch."

"I thought he studied with Uncle Franz."

"As have any number of such young men, but is that enough? Is that all we need to know to take him in, to have him living here, taking meals with us, engaging us in conversations that might ultimately be reported?"

Ilse was whispering, although she and Beth were alone in the kitchen. They could hear the men walking around the bare boards of the attic above them. "Reported?" Beth asked.

Her aunt heaved a sigh laden with frustration. "Sometimes you are as distracted and dense as Liesl is. This man's father works for the government—has quite a high position in the Gestapo right here in Munich. His mother entertains regularly, and word has it that some of the highest ranking politicians have sat at her table—perhaps even Herr Hitler himself."

"Uncle Franz explained his reasons. I don't understand. . . ."

Ilse shut off the water and wiped her hands on her apron. "Of course you don't understand. What do you know of the way things are here? The way everything has changed?"

Beth struggled to control her bent toward impatience when it came to her aunt's hysterics. Sometimes Ilse still treated her as if she were the newly arrived teenager instead of a twenty-five-year-old woman. "I understand more than you may realize. I've lived in this country for eight years, after all, and in that time—"

"Ha! 'My country was founded on the principle of religious freedom,'" Aunt Ilse mocked, practically hissing the words. "Well, I must remind you that you are not living in *your* country. You are living in *this* country, where things are very different. And as an American living in the very birthplace of the Nazi Party, you bring all of us under scrutiny. There are things that you—" She bit her lip as if to stop her tirade and turned her attention to scrubbing a pot.

"Auntie Ilse," Beth pleaded, "tell me what has upset you so."

The scrubbing slowed and finally stopped as Ilse let the pot sink into the suds. "This morning I was on the telephone with Gudren Heinz and heard a clicking sound on the line. She professed not to hear it, but she certainly got off the line quickly. What if the government has tapped our telephone? What if they have taken notice of the meetings for worship we host and these so-called literary soirees? What if they have decided to watch us because we are harboring an enemy—an

American? What if that young man's father sent him here to spy on the professor—on you?"

"Surely Uncle Franz—"

"Your uncle is a good and decent man who believes in the goodness and decency of all men. He is, in these times, a fool." Ilse pressed her fist to her lips as if she would take back those harsh words. "And I can't protect him—or Liesl," she whispered, her voice cracking as she turned away. "And you. . ."

Beth folded her dishtowel into precise thirds and then folded it in half and in half again while she considered her next words. "Shall I move out?"

"Of course not," Ilse snapped. "You are the daughter of my husband's beloved sister. Liesl adores you. You are family."

"Then what do you want of me?"

"I want you to keep your distance from this doctor—this Josef Buch. I want you to keep your thoughts and comments to yourself whenever he tries to engage you in conversation. I want you to be as invisible as possible to this man. Can you do that?" Aunt Ilse's previously sarcastic tone had settled into a plea.

"Yes. You have my word."

Her aunt surprised her by cradling Beth's face in her still-wet hands and kissing her on both cheeks.

"Danke," she whispered as she turned away and wiped her eyes with the hem of her apron.

CHAPTER 3

Later that night after making sure that the front door was secured and the blackout shades properly in place, Franz trudged down the corridor that led to the bedrooms after stopping briefly in the kitchen for a glass of water. The truth was that he needed some time to consider how best to ease Ilse's fears about the presence of Josef in their home.

Earlier after Josef assured him that he had everything he could possibly want to be comfortable in the attic space, Franz had insisted that the young doctor join him in the study to share a cup of hot cocoa made with the chocolate that Josef had given them. They were listening to a recording of Schubert's "Trout Quintet" when Beth tapped lightly on the door and entered the room.

Franz had been glad to see her as he patted a place on the sofa, inviting her to sit. But she did not stay as she normally would have, and Franz accepted her excuse that she wanted to answer the letter from her parents. He had not missed the way that she had barely glanced at Josef as she paused at the door and bid them both good night.

Now after glancing up the attic stairs and seeing that Josef's light was out, Franz headed for the bedroom he and Ilse had shared for over thirty years. He had expected to find her curled on her side, her breathing deep and even. Instead she was sitting at her dressing table, her hair—still golden in spite of streaks of gray that seemed to have appeared almost overnight—loose from the austere bun she wore it in these days.

"Ilse?" There was something about her posture that raised an alarm for him. Her shoulders were rigid under the thin fabric of her satin robe, and she was so still that she might have been a statue. *A prelude to one of her nervous attacks,* he thought and sighed heavily as he closed the bedroom door and moved to stand near her, their images reflected in the mirror.

"I cannot do this again, Franz," she said. Her voice was devoid of emotion. "I don't think I can survive another war...at least not this war."

"What has happened?" Franz knew his wife so well. It was evident that more than Josef's arrival had upset her so. When they'd first married shortly before the last war—the war that was supposed to end all wars—had begun, Ilse had been a rock, moving through difficult times with the certainty that this, too, would pass. But lately...

"When I went to the butcher's today, Herr Schwarzhagen was not there."

"He is ill?"

"He's been arrested, Franz, and sent to Dachau."

"What is the charge?"

Ilse did not turn to face him but continued to stare at his reflection. "The charge? There doesn't need to be a charge, Franz. If anyone should know that, it is you. From the day the Fuhrer's People's Court began, there are no rights...."

It was true. Never could Franz have imagined there could ever be a place like Dachau in his Germany. Located only a few miles north of Munich, the concentration camp had opened just six months after Hitler took office, one of a network of such camps for imprisoning anyone deemed a threat to the Reich. In March of that year the government—citing the need to be granted extraordinary powers—had passed the Enabling Act suspending civil rights for all citizens and effectively demoting the Reichstag or governing body to the position of little more than a sounding board for Hitler's pronouncements.

The incredible thing was that most Germans had gone along with these extraordinary acts, had even applauded them as true leadership. Franz was well aware that the butcher had been one of the most outspoken when it came to praising the new government. So if he could be detained, then. . .

"There must be some cause," Franz said. He placed his hands on Ilse's shoulders and felt her soften as she surrendered to his touch. Then she was shaking, her sobs coming in choking waves.

"I am so very tired of always being afraid," she managed.

Franz sat beside her on the small upholstered bench and wrapped his arms around her. "I am here, Liebchen. I will make sure you are all right. There is nothing for you to fear." But he knew it for the lie it was. Every day he went to the university half expecting to find a letter from his superiors relieving him of his duties because of "political unreliability." That was usually the reason given these days, no further explanation required. Once given, Franz would have no recourse. And then there was the matter of Beth living with them—an American in their house only added to the danger for them.

"We should go away," Ilse was saying.

"Where would we go?" Franz asked as he stroked her hair and kept his voice light as if they were discussing plans for a holiday rather than contemplating fleeing their homeland.

"Marta and Lucas have talked of going to Switzerland," she said, nodding toward a framed photograph of her sister and brother-in-law and their three children that she kept on her dressing table. "We could go with them. You could find a teaching position at the university in Geneva. I could care for Liesl and their darlings while Marta finds work perhaps in a flower shop. And Beth could go home."

"You must consider your health, Ilse. That is why Beth has stayed with us all these years. Besides, Munich is our home," Franz reminded her. "Our friends are here. My work is here."

"But if our closest family moves to Switzerland. . ." She broke down with fresh tears.

"Shhh," Franz crooned. "You know your sister. She is a dreamer—not easily satisfied. It's talk, Ilse, nothing more."

"But if we all went, then we could be safe."

"We are safe here." But the words stuck in his throat. How safe were they really? How safe was anyone these days?

The brilliant sunny days of October settled into the more somber gray days of November, and although their boarder had been in residence for nearly three weeks, Beth barely saw him. He left early in the morning and did not return sometimes until everyone else was in bed for the night. Beth always heard him when he came back, the key in the front lock followed by silence while he removed his shoes and coat and hat and left them in the foyer. Then she would hear the tread of his steps moving through the front hallway to the kitchen and from there up to his room above the one where she and Liesl slept.

She lay awake making sense of the sounds she heard as he prepared for bed, the squeak of the single bed's metal springs, the click of the lamp. Only once she felt certain that he was settled for the night could she finally get to sleep. For some reason she felt as if he were a buffer against the constant foreboding that a knock would come in the night and she would be arrested as an enemy of the State—they would all be arrested for harboring her. To her surprise, with Josef in the house, most nights she could sleep without the underlying apprehension that dominated so much of her waking hours.

During this time they were all awakened for several nights in a row by the whine of the air-raid siren. There was no telling whether the siren signaled a practice drill or the real thing. But ever since the British had bombed Cologne in May, they took no chances. Beth wrapped herself in her robe and roused Liesl, who slept easily through the sound, and led her down the back stairs of the building to the courtyard and the entrance to the cramped, dank cellar beneath the bakery. Behind them came her aunt and uncle and the other residents of the building. Usually Ilse was crying hysterically, her hands clamped firmly over her ears as Franz tried without success to reassure her. Josef was always the last to join the group that crowded into the tight space of the cellar.

Each family had fallen into the habit of taking up the same place in the underground bunker. Beth and others in her family squeezed together inside the small room where the baker stored extra bags of flour. The floor where they huddled had once held burlap sacks bulging with the staple, but these days the space was almost empty. Lately Beth had noticed that only a couple of empty flour sacks and a half-dozen glass canning jars filled with the baker's special spiced peaches were all that remained.

One night late in November and after more than a week's reprieve from the ritual of moving to the cellar, they were jolted awake by the shriek of the sirens. Silently—except for Ilse's sniffling—they made their way down from their apartment and took their places, as did their neighbors in the cubbyholes each of them had marked as a reasonably safe haven. Once Ilse and Franz were settled under the bottom row of shelving toward the back of the closet-like space, Beth sat on the floor and pulled Liesl onto her lap.

"Mama, don't cry," the child said sleepily. "It's just the planes. They can't hurt us here, can they, Papa?"

"That's right, Liebchen," Franz replied as he held Ilse, rocking her as if she, not Liesl, were the child.

Beth watched as Josef positioned the light he carried so that he could see that the others from the building had all made it down safely; then he helped one of their neighbors close the heavy cellar doors. After that he crouched next to her in the only space remaining and flicked off the light. In the dark and silence of their hiding place, they could hear the now-muffled sound of the siren followed by the steady and ominous drone of a fleet of airplanes. This time the warning had been real. When the echo of the first wave of bombs finding their target reached them, the glass jars rattled on the shelf above their heads, and Ilse cried out.

Beth covered Liesl's ears by cradling the child closer to her chest and sang to her. She could feel Josef's shoulder pressed against hers, and she was surprised to realize that she took comfort in that. On the one occasion when he had not been with them during the air raid, she had missed his nearness even though that had been only a practice.

Another wave of bombs struck their target—this time much closer—and Beth could not help but give voice to her own fear. Immediately she felt Josef's arm come around her shoulders. "It's all right," he said, his mouth so close to her ear that his breath was like a warm breeze. "They aren't as near as it sounds. Keep singing."

They stayed that way until the all-clear signal reached them. "There," Franz said to Ilse, as he clicked on his flashlight. "You see? It's all over."

Ilse blinked in the sudden light and focused her attention on Josef's arm still around Beth's shoulders. "We can go back to our apartment now," she said as she stood and reached for Liesl.

"I can take her," Beth said.

"You seem to be otherwise occupied," Ilse replied with a curt nod toward Josef. She lifted Liesl into her arms and waited for Franz and a neighbor to open the cellar doors so she could pass. Beth and Josef followed Ilse from the tiny room with Josef lighting the way up the back stairs of their building until they reached the door to their apartment.

"We should all have a cup of tea," Franz suggested. "Calm our nerves so we can get back to sleep."

Ilse made no reply as Beth watched her aunt continue down the hall to Liesl's bedroom.

"Ilse?" Franz followed his wife down the hall.

"I did not mean to upset your aunt," Josef said as he stood at the foot of the stairs to the attic.

"You didn't. It's all of this that upsets her—the uncertainty of everything." She folded the coverlet she had used to wrap around Liesl and clutched it to her.

"Ja, my mother is the same. Sometimes I think it is harder for their generation because they have been through so much—the war before and the struggles after that and now again."

It was the first time that Josef had spoken of his parents.

"And your father?"

"My father is. . .my father will always do what he thinks necessary to survive." There was no mistaking the resignation and disappointment in his voice, but he recovered quickly and smiled at her. "Now perhaps we might talk about your singing voice," he teased.

Beth blushed. "My brothers have always said that I could not carry a tune in a bucket," she admitted. "You have a very nice voice."

He bowed to her. "Why thank you, Fräulein."

"I dance better than I sing," she added and immediately wondered why she was pursuing this conversation.

"Prove it." He held out his hand to her, and when she placed her hand in his, he guided her into a pirouette. "Very nice," he said. "Very nice indeed."

Late into the night and all of the following day Josef thought about his father. It was true what he had told Beth. His father would do whatever he thought necessary to make certain that his family was safe and that they came out of this war unscathed. *As if anyone could,* he thought as he recalled the sirens and the panic and the sheer exhaustion of being emotionally spent that came along with the all-clear signal.

He thought about the things he had heard about and witnessed firsthand during the months he'd served as a medic in France. There had been the time he'd been taking the train from one assignment to another. The train had stopped briefly at a small town, and Josef had gotten off to stretch his legs. He'd lit a cigarette—a rare vice he allowed himself now and again—and started walking along the platform.

He heard a commotion in the village square behind the station and followed the sound. Several other soldiers had gathered around a crowd of townspeople to watch whatever was happening in their midst. There was laughter and cheers, and when Josef was able to work his way into an opening so he could see the source of the crowd's entertainment, he could not believe his eyes.

An elderly man—Jewish given his skull cap and beard—was on his hands and knees, crawling around on the hard cobblestones and barking like a dog. Standing over him was his "master"—a brawny, red-faced man wearing the insignia of a German lieutenant and shouting out orders. If the old man did not obey the commands quickly enough, the lieutenant kicked him and struck him with a riding crop. Nearby another soldier held his pistol to the head of a white-haired woman.

Josef was paralyzed with shock. This was happening in broad daylight, in full view of anyone passing by, in full view of the shops that lined the square. It was incomprehensible. Whatever the man's crime might be, this was intolerable. It was obscene.

He made a move toward the soldier with the pistol but felt a hand grip his shoulder and pull him back. "Leave it," whispered a burly bearded man with the saddest eyes that Josef had ever seen. He glanced at those around them—all laughing and pointing and enjoying the spectacle. Fathers had hoisted children onto their shoulders to give them a better view.

"You'll get them both killed," the man added.

"But..."

All around them the crowd groaned with disappointment, and Josef turned to see what had happened. The old man lay on the ground, unable to respond to his master's kicks or commands. The soldier lashed him with the riding crop, and when the man did not respond, he looked up at the crowd and shrugged. "Show's over, folks. We've got a train to catch."

The other soldier released the woman, shoving her onto the ground next to the inert body of her husband, and joined his buddies as they headed back toward the station, laughing as they lit their cigarettes and mimicked the man's barking.

Josef turned to tell the man in the crowd that he was a doctor, but the man had disappeared, swallowed up in the throng of people now going about their business as if nothing had happened. "I'm a doctor," he repeated quietly as he edged his way to where the woman covered her husband's body with her own and murmured words of comfort to him.

She glanced up, and the hope that filled her eyes turned instantly to hate. "You have killed him, so why not shoot me as well?" she said, and Josef understood that in his uniform he appeared no different to this woman than the man who had tormented her husband or held the gun to her head. "Go on," she growled, her eyes bright with loathing. She pointed to the center of her forehead. "Here—shoot me here, you monster."

Behind him the train whistle sounded. Around him people kept their distance from the old couple in the street. Across the way he saw the man who had stopped him, sweeping the sidewalk outside a floral shop. The man signaled that he should go, and it suddenly occurred to Josef that this was not a one-time event. The people in this village—those who were not Aryan—had been through similar humiliations before.

Slowly he backed away, and when the train whistle blasted a second time, he turned from the couple and ran for the train. He had just settled into his seat when the train began to move away from the station, away from the town, away from the shopkeeper who was now lifting the old man's body high in his arms.

The scene haunted Josef for days, and when he returned to Munich, he told his father about what he had seen. "These things happen in times of war," his father said without a trace of shock or reproach.

"But these were soldiers—*Deutschland* soldiers—a ranking officer among them," he had protested. "This is not who we are, how we conduct ourselves. Why we..."

His father had looked at him with something akin to pity. "Again in time of war... Do not go stirring the pot, son. There will be time enough once the war ends to set things right. There always is."

"And are the actions of Hitler and his government a way of setting things right, Father? By blaming others for what happened in the past, for the losses and hardships suffered?"

His father's eyes had flashed with anger. "You know nothing of what we suffered. You were a boy, and blessedly I was able to keep you and your mother from having to—"

"And that man in the street made to kneel in the hot sun and bark like a dog for the amusement of others? What about his family? His right to—"

"You do not know what crime this man was guilty of."

"Whatever that old man's so-called crime, we have laws and courts and such to determine his guilt and set his sentence, Father. Or at least we used to."

Josef had left the house that day and stayed with a fellow student until the professor had extended the invitation to come and board with his family. And he had made the decision to find some way that he might fight to restore the Germany of his youth—the homeland that he loved.

~ミ CHAPTER 4 ミ~

By December, Beth was more worried about Aunt Ilse than she had ever been. With each passing day, her aunt seemed to grow more anxious—and frail. She barely ate, and what nourishment she did consume was quickly spent in pacing and in her compulsive need to rearrange the apartment furnishings. Beth hesitated to say anything to her uncle. He had so much on his mind already—her missing visa, his job, the fact that two more families from the Friends group had left the country.

But things could not go on as they were. Aunt Ilse's irrational outbursts and hours spent sitting alone in the dark of her bedroom were affecting Liesl. Beth decided she needed to do something. To her relief, her uncle was obviously already aware of the deterioration in his wife's health.

One December morning after Beth had walked Liesl to school and returned to help with the housework, she heard her uncle remind Aunt Ilse that his winter break was fast approaching. "We could go to Lenggries. Your sister and her family could join us there. It's been over a year since we were all together."

"Someone has to be here in the house," Aunt Ilse replied, her hands cradling her coffee cup as if seeking warmth from it. "There have been

break-ins in the building across the street, and someone has to manage
the blackout curtains, and. . ."

"I can stay here," Beth offered as she came into the kitchen and
began washing the breakfast dishes. It would be foolhardy for her to
even attempt to travel without the proper papers. But her aunt knew
nothing of that. "Unless you need me to help with Liesl, I mean," she
added, not wanting Aunt Ilse to think she was trying to shirk her duties.

"I can care for my own daughter," Aunt Ilse snapped.

Uncle Franz laid his hand on his wife's. "Then there is our answer.
Beth will stay here while we take Liesl and go to the mountains for a few
days. It will do us all good. We can eat at that café you like so much in
Bad Tölz, maybe ski some. Beth will have some time to herself, and—"

"That man is not to be in this house with you when you are alone,"
Aunt Ilse instructed with a jerk of her head in the general direction of
the attic.

At least twice since the night of the air raid, Ilse had come into
the kitchen or sitting room when Beth had been talking to Josef and
laughing at something he'd just said. Beth had given up trying to explain
that with Josef living under the same roof there were bound to be times
when the two of them might find themselves alone. "There is nothing
between us, *Tante* Ilse," Beth said softly.

Her aunt's eyes filled with tears. "I know—it's not that I don't trust
you. It's just all too much, and I am so very tired of. . .of everything," she
admitted. "Forgive me, Beth. I don't know what we would do without
you." She turned to her husband. "Yes, let's go to the mountains. Let's
all go," she added, glancing at Beth. "It will be nice."

"If it's all right with you, I would like to stay," Beth said. She knew
that her uncle's mind must be racing to find some reason to leave
her behind. "It will give me some time to do some shopping in the
Christkindlmarkt and, with all of you gone, I might even have time to
give the apartment a thorough cleaning."

Aunt Ilse frowned and glanced toward the stairway to the attic.
"Still, that man. . ."

"I'll ask Josef to find other accommodations for a few days," Franz assured his wife. "So, my darling Ilse, shall we take this opportunity to go to the mountains and see if your skiing has improved at all?"

The smile that Beth saw pass between her aunt and uncle touched her deeply. For the first time in years, Aunt Ilse looked lovely—almost girlish, the way her eyes sparkled. "A holiday before the holidays," she whispered, and then she laughed.

Hearing her aunt's laughter was like listening to what had once been the sound of normal in this closed and cramped apartment.

"Yes, let's go to Lenggries, Franz," Aunt Ilse whispered as she wrapped her arms around her husband's neck and kissed his bald forehead.

A few days after she'd seen her aunt and uncle and Liesl off at the train station, Beth hurried across Stachus, one of Munich's busiest squares, her head bent against the sleety mist. The puddles that were starting to glaze over with ice crystals caught the reflection of the enormous red banners hanging from the Palace of Justice on one side of the square. Indeed these banners draped every official building, flags branded by the omnipresent black swastika that these days looked to Beth like some mockery of the cross.

When she'd first come to Munich in the summer of 1934 and seen the banners, they had been impressive—even festive. The flags had snapped and fanned almost playfully in the breeze, energizing the entire city with a fresh sense of vivacity and hope for the future. Adolf Hitler was Munich's adopted native son, and the city was bursting with pride. But so much about her feelings toward the government had changed.

Beth had once heard a nurse describe the sound a dying patient made when the end was near as a death rattle. Now as she stared at one banner that hung from what she had come to think of as the Palace of *In*justice and listened to the sound it made as it slapped against the building, she shuddered.

Just a year earlier the wet street, the cold mist, the hint of red that shimmered in the puddles might have lifted her spirits. She might have seen the banners as harbingers of the coming holidays. How she loved spending time wandering through the fir-covered booths that filled the marketplace. How she savored the scent of roasting almonds and mulled wine. It was all part of what had for her become the magic of the holiday season.

But on this night, she found herself shivering as much from the uncertainty of her future as from the cold. How long could she continue to live here before someone complained to the authorities about the possibility that she was not only American but also a spy living in their midst? It had happened to others.

A year earlier when Germany had declared war on America, Beth had gone to her uncle's office at the university, terrified at what might happen to her—and to them for having her in their house.

"I must leave at once," she had announced.

"We will take it up with the others," Uncle Franz had said.

The others meant those Friends still living in the area—at that time twelve families. At the next meeting for business—a monthly routine among Quaker groups around the world—Uncle Franz had told everyone about Beth's concern that she needed to continue to care for Liesl and help Ilse, but that in doing so she was placing the family in danger. He had left out the part about her not having proper documents for being in the country at all or for leaving to go back to America.

Ilse had taken Liesl to the park and not attended the business portion of the meeting. One by one Friends spoke openly of their concern for Ilse's health and the way Beth's presence had positively affected Liesl's development. One woman raised the concern that a change in routine would only call more attention to the family. In the end after hours of silence and prayer, the clerk for the meeting announced his belief that they had reached consensus that Beth should stay in Munich.

But just a day earlier as she had helped Aunt Ilse pack for their holiday, Uncle Franz had called her to his study, where an agent of the German government was waiting to question her about her intent to leave the country.

"Now?" she had whispered. "It's been over a year since our two countries went to war."

"Who can say why the authorities have chosen today but—"

"My papers," she had gasped.

"We will try and reason with the officer," Franz assured her. "We just need more time. I had intended to speak with Josef about your missing papers," he admitted. "I thought perhaps he could help."

"Uncle, no," Beth protested. "He is. . .his family. . ."

"We have to trust someone, Beth."

But she did not miss the way Uncle Franz could not meet her gaze as he said this. She knew that he had to be wondering if Josef had told his father of the situation, prompting the visit from the agent. "Get dressed," Uncle Franz said. "I will offer this man some tea."

Beth tried reasoning with the government representative. "My mother was born here and lived here until the age of twenty-two," she told him, making sure to speak in flawless German as she served him the last of their ration of sugar for his tea.

"My wife is quite ill," Uncle Franz confided. "Our niece has lived with us for the last eight years, caring for our daughter and helping my wife to manage the house. She was little more than a girl herself when she arrived. She has practically grown up here."

"We have nothing to do with politics," Beth assured the man. "We are peaceful people—Freunde."

"You are Quakers?"

"Ja aber. . ."

The man's entire demeanor shifted. He stood and actually smiled at Franz. "After the last war," he said, "my family had nothing—nothing to eat, nowhere to sleep, nothing to wear—nothing. If it had not been for the *Quäkerspeisungen*, we would surely have starved." He focused all his attention on Beth, his brow furrowed in frustration. "You have no papers, do you?"

Beth opened her mouth to protest—to lie—but the man stopped her with a dismissive wave of his hand as he collected his hat and gloves and walked to the door. "Do whatever you need to do to replace them, Fräulein. The next person who asks for them may not have owed your people the debt that I do."

Of course, Beth knew exactly what had become of her papers. One glorious June day when she had been walking Liesl home from the park, they had come upon a crowd gathered outside the American consulate on Lederer Strasse. It was immediately evident to Beth that the gathered people were trying to leave the country. It was a common sight in those days, as arrests for no cause and strange disappearances of entire families escalated. From time to time, news got out that a limited number of exit visas would be handed out on a certain day, and the result was always a scene like the one she and Liesl were witnessing.

On the edge of the crowd, Beth had recognized her friend Siggy, a young woman who worked as a helper in the bakery. The bakery clerk had recently confided to Beth that she was Jewish. Because of her Aryan looks, she had been able to hide that fact from her employer and—so far—from the authorities. But recently a customer—their neighborhood Blockwart who came regularly to the bakery—had spoken to her more than once in veiled threats, seeking her agreement to meet him after work. His intentions were clear in the way he watched her and found ways to touch her arm or hand whenever she waited on him.

"I have to get away," she had told Beth.

So on that June day, seeing her friend being jostled by dozens of others all seeking the same prize, Beth had made a decision. The authorities checking papers and deciding who would get exit visas would never allow Siggy to leave. She had no ties in America, no job waiting, no family there. Beth had seen the woman's forged papers, easily identifiable in the light of day as fake. She fingered her visa and other identification papers—always available in a deep pocket of her dress or coat since at any moment someone might demand that she produce them.

Siggy was the same height, the same weight, and they looked enough alike that they had been mistaken for sisters on more than one occasion. She steered Liesl along the edge of the sidewalk as Siggy glanced up and saw her. Her lovely face was lined with fear and desperation. Siggy had told Beth that her parents and siblings had all been taken away and she had no idea if she would ever see any of them again. "There are such horrible stories," she had whispered.

The man charged with inspecting papers and deciding who would be admitted to the consulate and who would be sent away was moving closer.

"Siggy," Beth called, smiling and waving. "I came to say good-bye." She pulled the young woman into an embrace and pressed her own identification papers into her hand.

"No," Siggy whispered as she realized what Beth was offering.

"Yes," Beth assured her. "My uncle has influence, and I am American. I'll come back here tomorrow and get them replaced. I'll play the dumb female and say I lost them."

"Papers," the bored consulate employee demanded.

Siggy hesitated, then handed him Beth's identification papers. Beth faded back into the crowd, afraid the man might look from Siggy to her and realize what had happened—or worse, ask for her papers as well. She hurried after Liesl, who was skipping down the street. "Liesl, wait," she called even as she glanced back and saw her friend waving to her as the man stood aside and indicated that she should go to the short line of people accepted for going inside.

That night Beth had told her uncle what she had done. He looked at her with a mixture of admiration and fear. "Replacing your papers will not be so easy," he had said. "But perhaps. . ."

The following day the consulate had been closed for good, and in spite of everything her uncle had tried over the last year, it was clear that any opportunity she might have had for replacing the precious documents had disappeared. Every time she left the apartment, Beth ran the risk of being discovered, of being arrested and taken to who knew where. The least that could happen would be that she would be deported back home to America. The worst? She did not wish to consider the worst.

Now as the sleet turned to snow, she wrapped her arms tightly across her body and walked quickly across the plaza. This holiday season would take more than the scent of roasted nuts or evergreen branches to lift her spirits. She passed a young couple, their arms around each other as they stumbled out of a beer hall. The man was in uniform, and although that was his only resemblance to Josef, Beth found herself thinking of the handsome doctor, recalling how he had coaxed her into that pirouette and how he always wrapped his arm around her during the air raids.

As Franz had requested, Josef had gone to stay with a fellow student, and Beth had not seen him but was aware that he had been back to the apartment only once since her aunt and uncle had left for their holiday. He had left a note to say he was missing a certain book and if she found it would she call his friend's landlady and leave a message for him. She had also noticed that a heavy wool scarf he favored in the colder weather was missing from its usual hook in the foyer.

And on this cold, silent night as she stood in the city center— Mariensplatz, so named for the large statue of the Virgin Mary in the middle of the square—she realized that she missed Josef. She pulled the pale blue, cable-knit woolen scarf her mother had sent as an early Christmas present higher around her chin and tried to ignore the hollow mocking sound her leather boot heels made on the wet cobblestones as she continued on her way. That sound had been amplified a thousand times over by the passing parade of soldiers routinely marching in lockstep through the streets and into this very square. Day after day and sometimes in the dead of night, they pounded the message of Hitler's omniscient power into the very soul of Bavaria's capital.

Beth forced her thoughts to focus on more pleasant images. She was only a few blocks from home, and for once she would not need to face her aunt's condemning silence. With no one else at home, there might be enough hot water left to wash away the damp chill that seemed to have found its way into the very marrow of her bones.

She had spent the evening celebrating a friend's birthday at the famous Hofbrauhaus beer hall, and in the relief of mindless conversation, good food, and beer she had lost track of time. She had missed the last streetcar, and if she didn't hurry, she would be out past the government-enforced curfew. She longed for the sanctuary of silence that she knew awaited her in the empty apartment, for the peace she always found in taking the time to look deep within herself and seek God's guidance.

She turned a corner and heard male laughter. Half a block away, she saw two soldiers sharing a cigarette break under the shelter of the arches of the Neues Rathaus or New City Hall. In spite of dating back to the late nineteenth century, the building was called *new* because the original city hall—still standing—dated to 1310. There had been a time when such amazing historical facts had intrigued Beth, but on this night she entertained no such thoughts. Instead she focused on searching for an alternate route back to the safety of the apartment. If the soldiers stopped her. . .

She had one thing in her favor. Her long golden hair worn this night in fashionable braids pulled back from her face, her sky-blue eyes, and her willowy athletic body were all in keeping with the Aryan features so prized by the regime. More than once her looks in combination with her passable command of the local dialect had gained her the tentative smile or trust of a shopkeeper or passerby. More than once she had talked her way out of showing her identification by playing the role of the empty-headed female.

Still it had been foolhardy to take such a risk as she had taken this night. Had her aunt and uncle not gone away, she never would have agreed to join her friends. But the temptation to finally escape the pervasive undercurrent of fear that the city wore these days like a second skin had overwhelmed her good judgment.

She glanced around for some source of shelter and saw that she was within steps of a small gated park where she sometimes brought Liesl to play—the park where she used to meet up with her friend Siggy.

Knowing the soldiers would continue their rounds sooner or later, Beth sought sanctuary in the park. She made her way to a half-hidden concrete bench in a far corner, a favorite hiding place for Liesl when they came here to play.

Determined to contain the fear and panic that threatened to overwhelm her, Beth concentrated on positive things. The bench was stone but plain enough that it reminded her of the simple wooden benches in the meetinghouse back in Wisconsin. That Wisconsin meetinghouse floor was constructed of wide wooden planks oiled and waxed to a mahogany patina. The ground here was black earth worn down by the shoes and boots of others who had sat in this same place.

Missing, of course, was the silent support and comfort that came with the presence of other Friends in an actual meeting for worship. From the time she'd first begun attending meetings with her parents, Beth had found such solace and assurance in that spiritual family that every Quaker relied upon to help in challenging times. That circle of fellow Quakers in Munich had dwindled to a mere half-dozen souls over the last few weeks as more families had left the city. Now there was just Beth, her uncle and aunt, and one other elderly couple and their widowed daughter.

In the darkness of the park, Beth bowed her head and willed herself to find the stillness. She closed her eyes and concentrated on the scent of the cedar tree that sheltered the bench, the hard-packed earth beneath her feet, and the surprisingly refreshing coolness on her skin of the sleet that had softened into snow. In her solitude she prayed for the Inner Light that all Friends sought to guide their thoughts and actions.

But a rustling to her right brought her alert. Streetlights were not permitted in keeping with the blackout, and she blinked several times as she adjusted her sight to the shadows surrounding her. Huddled in the corner behind the bench like stumps of a tree was a woman clutching two small children. Her eyes having grown accustomed to the darkness, Beth realized that the woman was watching her. She also caught a glimpse of the crude yellow felt star that Jews were required to wear.

Beth motioned for the woman to remain silent. Meanwhile she crept back to the gate, hoping the soldiers had decided on a different route.

But half a block away, two cigarettes hit the street, glowed briefly, and went out as the soldiers readjusted their uniform caps and started walking in her direction. The woman was now standing next to her, and had Beth not put a hand on her shoulder, she surely would have tried to make a run for it.

What was the right thing to do in this situation?

She longed for the gathering of her Quaker family or at least her aunt and uncle so that they could pray silently until some discernment of the circumstances made God's will clear for them all. *Waiting* was their way. Certainly when she had decided to hand over her papers to Siggy, she could have done with the counsel of others. "We do not act alone, Elizabeth," Uncle Franz had gently chided her.

But this woman was in grave danger, and there was no time to seek the counsel of others—no time for waiting. For the second time she was going to have to make a choice without the traditional regimen of taking the matter to an appointed clearness committee or even her closest family members. Quakers simply did not make such momentous decisions as she was now facing on their own. The gathering of the community to come to consensus on matters of such importance was central to their faith, yet she felt that she was being led to help this woman and her children.

She squeezed her eyes closed and prayed for guidance. *Show me the way.* She had done no such praying when she'd handed over her visa to Siggy, and look where that had gotten her. She certainly could not afford to make a mistake here—a choice that not only might endanger this woman but could also place Beth and the rest of her family in further jeopardy because of her rash actions.

Please! she pleaded silently. *The soldiers are almost here, and I don't know what to do.*

The woman gripped Beth's arm and motioned toward a fence at the back of the park. Apparently she was trying to say that she and the children would scale that enclosure and escape. Beth found herself focused on the woman's ugly felt star, and in that instant she knew she had been given her answer.

"*Schnell*," she whispered, urging them to hurry as she herded the woman and her children back toward the corner bench. "Take off your coat and turn it inside out." She knelt and began helping the oldest child—a boy with wide, dark eyes—to do the same. "Put this around you and the baby," she instructed, handing the woman her scarf and thanking God that her mother had made it wide enough to serve as more of a shawl. "Hurry. They're almost here."

She could hear the two soldiers talking as they slowly made their way up the block, pausing here and there to peer into a darkened alley or doorway. As soon as the woman and her children were changed, Beth motioned for them to sit on the bench.

"If they come in," she instructed in German, "we were here earlier and I dropped my key." She took the key from her pocket and placed it on the ground under a pile of snow-covered leaves. "We realized it when we reached home and came back to search for it. What is your name?"

"Anja Steinberg." The woman pulled the youngest child closer to her breast, covering the child with the shawl as her son huddled against her side.

"You are German?"

"Danish. My husband is German."

Beth perched on the edge of the bench and waited. Each step that brought the possibility of discovery closer seemed to suck the breath from her until she thought she might faint.

The soldiers were now at the gate, but they barely paused before walking on without stopping. The baby stirred and whimpered. The leather heels clicking on the wet walkway came to a halt, and then Beth heard them moving back toward the park.

"*Ach*, here it is," she said in her normal voice as she rummaged through the leaves and produced the key just as the soldiers came through the gate and flashed a light over the scene. "It must have fallen out of my pocket when we were—"

"*Halt!*"

Beth heard the boy swallow a whimper and was surprised that her first thought was, *What kind of world have we made where a child of five or six knows better than to show his fear?*

She positioned herself in front of Anja and the children as the soldiers entered the park and moved toward them. "I know this one," she heard one say to his partner. "Professor—"

"Werner?" she ventured as she squinted up at one of the soldiers. "Is that you?"

Werner Ostmeir was the son of her uncle's downstairs neighbor. He'd just turned eighteen when Beth had first come to Munich. Beth had seen him march off to war side by side with his dearest friend—a boy her age who had been killed in battle. She had mourned that young man's passing and then rejoiced with Werner's family at his safe return. Just before the United States entered the war, she and the rest of the family had attended Werner's wedding.

"Fräulein," Werner replied shyly. Then he straightened to his full height, some two inches shorter than Beth, and glanced at the woman and children. "Who is this?"

God continued to shower blessings on the situation as the light snowfall escalated into a near blizzard. Beth seized the opportunity to pick up the boy, and as the soldiers bent their heads against the driving snow, she started past them. "A cousin visiting from Denmark. I dropped our house key when we brought the children here to play earlier." She continued to edge toward the gate, herding Anja along with her. "Perhaps your parents mentioned that my uncle and aunt are away and—Oh my, these children are going to catch their death. It was good to see you, Werner," she called over her shoulder. She hoisted the boy higher on her hip and wrapped her free arm around Anja's shoulders as she hurried away.

As they passed through the gate, she risked a look back and was relieved to see that the two men had taken refuge under an arbor. Apparently staying dry took precedence over questioning her and Anja. She gave a quick wave and hurried down the street and tried not to think about how she might explain this "cousin from Denmark" should Werner share that news with his parents.

~≋ CHAPTER 5 ≋~

Josef walked with the long, determined strides of a man on a mission. Fortunately the accumulated snow meant that the streets were fairly deserted and that his purposeful step raised no suspicions. He hurried on, anxious to bring Beth his news.

With the exception of one or two times when the two of them had been alone in the kitchen or sitting room, she had mostly avoided him. One evening he had returned to the apartment from a shift at the hospital to find the professor's study filled with people—people who the professor introduced to him as colleagues and former students. Josef had not been fooled. Students and faculty members they might be, but more to the point, these were people who were at the very least outcasts under the new regime and at the very most people with whom so-called *good* Germans no longer associated.

Still he had accepted Franz's invitation to join in listening to the poetry reading in progress and to stay for the discussion that followed. Beth acted as hostess in the absence of her aunt, who Josef later learned stayed in their bedroom whenever her husband insisted on hosting such a gathering.

Once the reading ended, the discussion deteriorated into stilted small talk. Josef was well aware that it was his presence in the room that had caused everyone to censor themselves. Beth was perched on the arm of her uncle's chair, sipping her tea.

"I have a concern," she said, as if the discussion of the poet's work had continued at the lively pace that Josef suspected was normal for the gathering. During the weeks he'd spent living in the house, Josef had learned that this was the Quaker way of introducing a troubling topic.

The professor cleared his throat, perhaps intending to warn her, but she continued speaking. The other guests gave her their full attention, expecting no doubt some commentary on the work of the poet.

"Is not the poet saying that all are created equal?"

Around the room guests offered nods and murmurs of agreement in response to her interpretation of the poet's words.

"Yet," she continued, "there are entire groups of people that are being singled out for harassment and open persecution—not just here in Germany but around the world."

"Even in almighty America?" another member of the group challenged, glancing at Josef as if to make it clear that he did not agree with Beth.

"Yes. Even there. My own family has written to me of the snubs of neighbors and the suspicions of local authorities simply because my mother is of German birth. And that bit of news was allowed to escape the black marking pen of the censor."

"Is that why you have not returned to America?" the young man asked.

"Why would she?" The speaker was a woman who was looking not at the young man but directly at Josef. "Things are surely so much better here."

A few people laughed, while others looked away. Franz struggled to find words to defuse the potentially volatile thread of conversation. "My niece has a point. The role of government is to serve all its peoples equally. Especially in those nations founded on the Judeo-Christian principles—"

"In any civilized society," Josef interrupted as he crossed the room to stand next to the professor's chair with the intention of showing his support for Beth and the professor. Beth had glanced up at him, and her smile was so tentative and uncertain that it had taken his breath away. The truth was that he was wracking his brain to come up with some way he might change the direction of the conversation. Regardless of the connections among those gathered, no one could be certain of another person's loyalties. The challenging student might well be working for the government to ferret out those who would dare dispute the Reich's absolute power.

"I wonder if I might share a poem a friend of mine has written. It's titled 'On a River Bank'," Josef continued. "Although my friend's work has not been published, I believe that it has some similarities to the work read earlier." To his relief, most of those in attendance nodded and sat back to listen to his recitation.

It was later that same evening that Josef had come down from his room in the attic to retrieve a book he'd left behind. The others had all left, but Beth was curled into the depth of one chair while Franz sat slumped in the other, his legs outstretched toward the fire.

"But child, you go too far," the professor was saying. "How can you not appreciate that as someone with no proper identification papers—as an American..."

"I know. I am so sorry, Uncle," she said softly. "Sometimes I don't know what gets into me. It's as if—"

She had looked up then and seen Josef standing in the doorway.

"I left my book," Josef had said, indicating a table just inside the room even as the incriminating phrase—*someone with no proper identification papers*—echoed in his brain. She had no papers? She was an American living in the midst of her country's enemy. She was in grave danger for that reason alone, and without the proper documents...

"Come in, Josef," Franz said, his voice weary and defeated. "How much did you hear?"

Josef pulled a third chair up to the fireplace. "Enough," he admitted.

"Can you help?" Franz asked.

Josef looked at Beth. "I will try," he promised her.

"Danke," Franz said as he turned his attention back to the fire.

Beth stood then. "You must not involve yourself in trouble that I alone am responsible for creating."

He had shrugged. "People lose papers from time to time—sometimes they are stolen, and other times simply misplaced."

He saw her exchange a look with her uncle and understood that he had not yet heard the true story. Once Beth had said her goodnights and left the room, Josef had turned to Franz. "If I am to help her, I have to know the whole story."

Franz had indicated that Josef should take the chair that Beth had vacated. The two men had talked long into the night, and by the time Josef returned to his room, dawn was breaking.

Later he lay on the single bed and stared at the rafters of the attic's ceiling. He was attracted to Beth Bridgewater in a way that might have been possible for them under other circumstances. But a German officer and an American who was stranded in Munich? That was inviting problems for each of them.

After that it was Josef who had avoided her. He would stay late in the research laboratory or beg off joining the others when he arrived home. The truth was that he was so smitten with the woman that he could not bear to be in the same room with her without blurting out his true feelings. But in the days and weeks that had passed since that evening, he had not forgotten his promise to the professor, and to that end he had finally gone to the extraordinary lengths of asking his father for help.

Of course he had not told his father the real story but instead had simply spoken of the papers being misplaced. But his father had seen through his efforts at nonchalance. "This young woman must be someone quite special if she has driven you to come to me," he had said. "I would like to meet her."

"Perhaps one day that could be arranged."

"It will be arranged," his father replied, "or there will be no replacement of the woman's documents."

The conversation was so very typical of the conversations Josef had shared with his father from the time he was a young boy. His father always established the ground rules.

And so tonight he had a surprise for her, a gift—the precious papers would be delivered to the apartment within the hour. He was excited to be able to bring her such good news, but he did so with some regret. He admired her courage a great deal, but the truth was that his feelings for her had moved well beyond simple respect. Any woman who could inspire him to ask his father for a favor was a woman to be reckoned with.

An inch or more of snow had covered the streets and sidewalks by the time Beth led Anja and the children to the rear entrance of the apartment building. She checked carefully to be sure no other tenants were around, then set the boy down as she used her key to open the door. But instead of following Beth into the dark hallway, Anja shifted the smaller child in her arms to remove the shawl.

"Thank you," she said in perfect English as she handed Beth the garment.

Beth smiled. As good as her German was, there was something in her accent that immediately identified her as a foreigner. "There's no one home," Beth assured her, leaving the door ajar as she stepped back into the small courtyard and whispered, "Come upstairs with me. We can dry your clothes and give the children something to eat and—"

"No. You have done enough. Thank you."

"Where will you go?"

"I . . ." Anja's voice broke. "We will be fine."

Beth glanced toward the rows of windows above her. With the requirement for blackout curtains to be secured before any lamps were lit, it was difficult to know if their neighbors were at home. To reach her uncle's apartment would require leading Anja and the children through the building and up past two other apartments on the second and third floors to the apartment on the fourth—the apartment with the extra attic room. She leaned her head back to look all the way up to the small attic window. Of course there was no way of knowing if Josef had come back.

"At least step into the hallway here out of the snow," she urged. "No one will come this way at this hour of the night. You can wait here while I get you some bread—a little cheese." Beth wrapped her arm around Anja's thin shoulders and guided her inside. The woman was shivering, whether from the weather or fear or sheer exhaustion, Beth could not say. Probably all three.

Once they were all safely inside, Beth secured the door and checked to be sure the blackout curtain was properly in place. Then she switched on the light—a single wall sconce that did a better job of casting shadows than lighting the way.

The boy sneezed.

"Oh, Frau Steinberg, we really must get him and the baby some dry clothes. If you'll come upstairs with me—just for a little while, we can at least hang their coats by the kitchen stove and. . ." Beth told herself that what she was offering was simply a part of what God had already led her to do in rescuing this woman and the children.

To her relief, Anja nodded, but it was not a gesture of acceptance. Rather it was an act of surrender. The woman looked utterly defeated.

"Good," Beth said with forced cheerfulness.

The trip from the back entrance to her uncle's fourth-floor apartment was blessedly uneventful. The younger child was asleep in her mother's arms, and the boy followed Beth's whispered instructions to be "as quiet as a mouse" with a sigh of resignation that told her this was not the first time he'd had to play this adult version of the game of hide-and-seek.

Once they were inside the apartment, Beth led the way to the kitchen. "You get those wet outer clothes off them and your own coat as well. I'll start some water to warm. We can mix powdered milk for the children and some tea for you and me."

Within minutes the air was permeated with the scent of damp wool. Beth placed half a loaf of bread and a carving knife on the table, then grated cheese and stirred up the last of the powdered eggs. "I have an extra coat you can have," she said, thinking aloud. "Forgive me for saying so, but you are fair enough to pass for Aryan. Perhaps if we—"

"I am Aryan," Anja replied as she carved a paper-thin slice of the loaf of bread and handed it to her son.

"Then why. . . ?" Beth could not stop herself from glancing toward the yellow star sewn to Anja's coat.

"My husband is Jewish. I was raised in the faith of the Freunde."

"Me too," Beth said. "American. Society of Friends." The teakettle whistled, and Beth reached for it after pouring the egg mixture into the hot skillet. "Wait a minute. Your husband and the children would be protected by your status as Aryan."

Anja gave Beth a wry smile. "That protection was removed when I stood with my husband in a protest against the government."

"Where is your husband now?" Beth asked and noticed the boy's eyes fix on his mother's face with interest.

"This afternoon he was taken for questioning."

"But not you?"

"I was returning home with the children when we saw the—saw him leave." Her eyes begged Beth not to ask more.

"Here we are," Beth said with a heartiness she didn't feel as she placed a plate of eggs and a mug of thin, watery milk in front of the boy. "And because you have been so very brave and good, I have a special treat for you."

As Beth had intended, the boy's focus immediately turned from the fate of his father to her. She went to the cupboard and brought back a single small square of chocolate. The boy's eyes sparkled with excitement as he glanced at his mother, and she nodded her approval.

"Thank you," he whispered in German.

"I am Elizabeth, but friends call me Beth." She extended her hand to the boy.

"I am Daniel. My friends are all moved away." He placed the piece of chocolate on a side of his plate as if it were the most precious of possessions and slowly ate his eggs, savoring each bite.

Beth prepared a second plate and set it before Anja. "The baby's name is?"

"Rachel. She's eleven months, but small," Anja said as she held a cup of the warm milk to her daughter's lips.

The child was more than small. Beth would have thought her to be perhaps six months old. "Stay here while I get the coat," Beth said and hurried down the hall to the bedrooms. She was well aware of the risk she was taking and just hoped that this would not be a night when Josef decided to stop by for the book she'd found for him while cleaning her uncle's study.

In the bedroom she shared with Liesl, Beth pulled the coat from the back of the wardrobe. Then she took a spare shawl and pair of mittens down from the shelf. She caught a glimpse of the sleeve of a coat that her cousin had outgrown and pulled it from its hook. Inside the pockets was a pair of mittens. Both would do for Daniel.

As she approached the slightly open door of the kitchen, she could hear Anja crooning softly to the baby. Beth wondered at the woman's courage. Her husband was gone—more often than not being taken for questioning was no more than a euphemism for *under arrest*. And Anja's home was no longer safe. She was alone on the streets of Munich with two small children. How would she manage?

Beth clutched the coats to her chest. Surely if there had been the opportunity to take this matter up with the Friends, any clearness committee would agree that she had to do whatever she could to help these people—these innocents caught up in a world gone mad.

By the time Josef approached the professor's block, the snow was letting up, but a blustery wind had taken its place, blowing the powdery snow into drifts that pressed against doorways. Josef turned up the collar on his overcoat and hurried on. He passed the deserted bookstore and heard movement and laughter. He realized the door was standing open, and inside he saw a group of youths vandalizing the place, tossing books onto the floor and breaking up the shelving. The front window was painted with the words *Juden Raus* and similar offensive epitaphs. The sight was hardly uncommon, but it was one that made Josef despair for this country that he loved—a country that had always prized its writers and poets as well as musicians and philosophers.

It would do little good to try and stop the vandals. The damage had been done, and no one was coming back to run the shop. The owners had been taken away along with several other Jewish families and shopkeepers in the area.

He cut through the narrow passage between two buildings to avoid the youths and used the rear entrance to the building. When he reached the fourth floor, Josef heard water running and the clink of dishes through the closed front door and knew that Beth was home. His heart beat a little faster as he used his key to enter the apartment, realizing that she would not hear his knock with the kitchen door shut and the water running. Once inside he slipped off his shoes, and, incredibly, he thought he heard a child speaking.

"It is Josef," he called as he unwound his scarf and hung it with his overcoat on one of the hooks. But when he pushed the kitchen door open, the scene before him stopped him cold.

Sitting at the table was a woman he'd never seen before, holding a child on her lap as she shared a piece of bread with another child sitting next to her. Beth was just coming back from the bedrooms at the end of the hall. She held a bundle of clothing. But it was the crude yellow star on the frayed woolen coat spread over a chair near the stove that dominated the room.

In that instant a fear unlike anything Josef had known plagued him. Even his father could not help with this. To even consider offering comfort—let alone sanctuary—to Jews was a risk of such outrageous proportions as to be unfathomable.

Surely you cannot possibly be so naive, he thought as he turned to Beth, ignoring the woman and children. "Are you insane?" His words came out on a hiss of breath.

She bristled, and her full lips hardened into a straight line, a stubborn slash of rose across her beautiful pale skin. The baby whimpered, and the mother tightened her hold. The other child—a boy—continued to eat, although his eyes were fixed on Josef.

"This is Frau Anja Steinberg," Beth said in a tone overly bright and social. "And this is Daniel and his sister, Rachel." She put the clothes on the bench opposite the one that the woman shared with her children and then dished up the few remaining eggs and handed Josef the plate. "This is Dr. Josef Buch," she added.

The woman nodded warily and fed a piece of egg to the girl even as her ice-blue eyes darted around the kitchen, seeking avenues of escape. Josef realized that once again Beth had allowed her impulsive nature to override her common sense. But the deed had been done—the woman and her children were here. Now he had no choice but to help Beth find a way to get them to safety.

"Elizabeth, a word?" he said as he set the plate on the counter, then gently removed the spatula from her hand. He motioned toward the sitting room, and just before exiting the kitchen, he reached over and turned the woman's coat so that the yellow star was hidden.

Beth waited for Josef to leave the kitchen entirely, then smiled reassuringly at Anja, ruffled Daniel's hair, and followed the doctor into the barely heated room where a radiator clanked in protest to the demand for it to produce more heat.

He had turned on her uncle's gramophone, and strains of an Italian opera filled the room. He raised the volume to cover their words. The room was cold after the steamy heat of the kitchen, and Beth crossed her arms over her chest, resting her hands on her shoulders. "I had no choice," she whispered.

"As you had no choice but to give away your visa?" he asked. "There is always a choice," he said wearily.

"Tell that to her," Beth said, jerking her head toward the kitchen, biting out each word. "Tell it to those children who watched their father being hauled away. Tell it to—"

"You had a choice, Beth. What were you thinking? Bring her here and what? What if your uncle and aunt had been here? Then what?"

"I would not have come here," Beth replied with the kind of self-assured logic she had learned was often a source of confusion if not exasperation for many Bavarians. "I would have—"

"What?" Josef pressed his point, his face inches from hers as he snapped out the question.

"She's in danger," she argued.

"*You* are in danger."

Beth stepped away. "It's all moot. My aunt and uncle are away until the end of the week. I brought her here. No one saw us. I prepared food for her and the children and—"

"And the food. We had three eggs to last the month. And the cheese—"

"I used only a little of the cheese, and the eggs are powdered," she said, hating that she was defending herself over food rations when the real issue was that Anja and her children were homeless, hungry, and in danger.

"And now what?" he demanded.

Beth wasn't about to admit that she hadn't thought that far ahead. She was on shaky ground here both in the face of his accusations and her own growing doubts that instead of acting within the tenets of her faith she had once again acted on pure instinct. How many times when she was growing up had her parents despaired over her inclination toward making rash, on-the-spot decisions?

Josef paced the confines of the room. He stopped at the chair where her uncle usually sat, while she stood opposite him, clutching the back of the chair she often occupied. In the slice of light that filtered through the crack under the kitchen door, she could see that he was far more unnerved by this than she might have imagined he would be, and it was her turn to register a guess as to why he should be so upset.

"Something has happened." She took a step closer, intending to bridge the distance between them, but he waved her away. "Something has happened to make you overreact to something that is easily remedied."

His laugh was a bark that held no hint of mirth. "You think having that Jew in your kitchen is 'easily remedied'?" he argued.

"How dare you speak like that of another human being? She is an innocent woman who is only trying to protect her children. Her religion should matter no more than do her politics."

Josef had the decency to look abashed. "I didn't mean it that way. I only meant—"

"Besides, she is not Jewish," Beth interrupted, her voice deadened by her disappointment in this man she had begun to believe might be different from other Germans in uniform she had met. "She is Danish and also a Quaker like we are. She married a *German* citizen who follows the Jewish faith, and because she chose to stand with her husband, she has been labeled as well, stripped of her rights as he has—as they all have." She watched Josef's features soften slightly, and the reaction only made her angrier. "Oh, so now that you know she's not Jewish you have some sympathy?"

"That's not fair," Josef answered, his voice hoarse and weary. "Why the star then?"

"Apparently she had the audacity to participate in a protest rally that the authorities found to be objectionable, and they all have suffered the consequences."

Beth slumped into the chair as the magnitude of what she had brought on them hit her. Josef was right. Jewish or not, Anja and the children were in danger, and so was anyone who tried to help them. "I could go to—"

Steps in the corridor outside the entrance to the apartment made both of them freeze. The doorbell sounded, followed by a firm knock.

"Are you expecting someone?" she whispered.

Josef nodded and motioned for her to stay quiet. "It's my father," he said. Beth started for the kitchen. Other than climbing out a fourth-floor window, the front entrance was the only way out of the apartment. What were they to do? Josef grabbed her arm to stop her just as there was a second, more insistent knock.

"It's not what you think," he whispered. "I have not betrayed you, Beth. I would never. . .your uncle. . ."

"Tell me what to do," she pleaded, glancing toward the kitchen and then back toward the front door.

Josef motioned for her to get the woman and children and take them upstairs to the attic. Beth gathered the clothing drying near the stove and the dry things she had gathered for the family and handed them to Anja as she pointed to the stairway that led to the attic.

A third knock, this one rattling the frosted-glass in the door.

"Coming," Josef called and glanced around the kitchen, his focus settling on the half-eaten food Beth had prepared for Anja and the children.

"Give me a moment," she instructed as she reset the table as if the two of them had been sharing a meal. She motioned for Josef to answer the door and steadied her nerves by refilling the kettle and setting it to warm on top of the stove. When she heard Josef greeting his father, she knew she must go into the hallway herself.

"Oh, hello," she said, extending her hand to the older man dressed in a business suit and black overcoat. "I am Elizabeth Bridgewater."

Josef hurried to complete the introductions. "This is my father, Beth. Herr Detlef Buch."

"So you are the professor's *American* niece," the man said, placing the emphasis on her nationality. She had spoken to him in German, but like every native he had seen through that. What had she been thinking to trust Josef? She felt what was becoming a familiar lump of pure fear tighten around her lungs.

"Won't you join us, Father? We were just finishing our supper."

"Yes, please," Beth said. "I think we have one last jar of the pickled tomatoes that my aunt puts up every summer, and we have enough powdered—"

"Your mother is waiting supper for me at home, Josef. A nice *Schweinebraten* with those potatoes you like so much and red cabbage," the older man replied, his eyes focused on Josef. "It would please her greatly if you would agree to dine with us from time to time."

Beth glanced at Josef as, through the slightly open door leading to the sitting room, they heard the phonograph needle scratching out a rhythm on wax now that the record had ended. Josef hurried to lift the arm and set it on its rest.

"I'll just leave you two to visit," Beth said, backing down the hall toward the kitchen.

"Actually it is you I have come to see, Fräulein," Josef's father said as he reached inside his coat and produced an envelope. "I believe you have been waiting for this to be returned?"

Beth opened the envelope and pulled out the contents. "My visa," she whispered. "Thank you, Herr Buch. Thank you so much."

"May I suggest you put that to use at the earliest possible moment? I have made arrangements for you to leave the country by the end of the month. Please do not make me regret taking such an unusual interest in your situation."

Before Beth could respond, Josef's father had turned away, replaced the shallow-brimmed loden-green hat so popular with Bavarian men on his carefully groomed silver hair, and opened the front door. "Josef," he said as he brushed past his son.

"Danke *sehr*," she heard Josef murmur, and she did not miss that it was gratitude his father refused to acknowledge.

"You did this?" Beth asked as soon as Josef had closed and locked the front door. "Why?"

"The professor rightly recognizes the importance of getting you out of the country as soon as possible. My father has made the necessary arrangements."

"*Pfui Di Good.*" Beth could barely form the words that expressed more than simple gratitude—words intended to show appreciation to someone who had gone to great lengths. "Thank you, Josef, and may God bless your father for his kindness."

"Consider it an early Christmas present." Josef turned toward the kitchen, then paused and looked back at her. "We are not all monsters, Beth."

As she met his eyes, so fervent and yet empty of any other emotion, Beth realized that going to his father on her behalf had cost him a great deal. Her uncle had mentioned Josef's estrangement from his father when she asked why he had moved in with them and not his parents. His break with his father over their divergent political views was why Josef had gone to Boston to complete his studies. It was why now that he was back he went to see his mother only when he knew his father would not be at home.

Beth was so overcome with emotion that she had trouble putting everything she was feeling in proper perspective. Guilt over her doubts about Josef. Relief that she held in her hands the means to go home to her family—her country. Thankfulness that God had shown His mercy. Overriding all was the unsettling idea that there were others who could make better use of this document than she could, people whose very lives depended on their getting out of the country. And the teachings of her faith demanded that if possible she stand up for those who could not stand up for themselves.

"Let me get Anja and the children," she said. "This calls for a celebration."

She was halfway up the stairs to the attic when Josef called out to her. "Beth? You cannot give Anja this visa. You will go to prison if you do not leave as my father instructed."

"I know. That's why we must find another way to help them."

Impossible woman, Josef fumed. Impossibly stubborn. Impossibly beautiful. Impossibly brave and naive.

In spite of any objection that Josef could think to offer, Beth persuaded Anja to stay in the attic with the children for the night. "Tomorrow," he heard her promise the woman. "There will be time enough for you and the children to leave tomorrow."

But the following morning as he made his rounds at the hospital, a nurse called for him to take an urgent phone call.

"Our friends," Beth began, her voice was shaking with panic.

"Have arrived?" Josef replied, his own voice far too hearty to be considered normal, hoping that she would understand that others were within earshot of his side of the conversation.

Thankfully, Beth played along. "No. They are not here. . .yet."

"I'm just finishing rounds. I'll be right there," he promised, and then he laughed as if she'd said something funny—as if she'd said anything at all.

The minute that Josef entered the apartment, Beth reached for her coat and scarf. Josef grabbed her arm to stop her. "Did you not hear what my father said?"

Beth paused—one arm in the sleeve of her coat, the other in his grasp. "I heard him. End of the month—we have almost three weeks. So there is time, and we have to find Anja and the children and get them to safety."

"How? They might have been gone already for hours. For all you know, they left last night the minute Anja heard you close your bedroom door. How will you find them? And even if you did find them, what then?"

"We could. . . ." She glanced around as if seeking out a proper hiding place. "We might be able to. . ."

"We?" He gave her a wry smile. "Are you not forgetting that I am your enemy, Beth?"

"I have no enemies," she replied as she pulled free of him and continued putting on her coat.

"Anja does," he reminded her.

"Then help me find her so she will not fall into the hands of those she cannot fight on her own."

Josef realized that in getting her the precious visa he had earned her trust. In that moment he would have happily moved mountains if such an act would please her. "You stay here," he said. "I will go. Just let me change into my uniform, and I promise you that I will do what I can."

"You'll find them and bring them back with you," she instructed.

"That's not—" He saw that she would take no less than his promise to do just that. "All right. Just give me your word that you will stay here and wait for me."

"Yes, but there's no time for you to change. You must go now before—"

"Beth, my uniform is a way for me to move through the city without being stopped and questioned. If you want me to find them, then. . ."

"Yes, of course you're right."

To his surprise she touched his cheek with her fingers. "Hurry, please. They must be terrified and so very cold. She did not take the clothes I left for her, although she did leave those horrid stars behind. I burned them in the kitchen stove."

Her eyes filled with tears, but he knew that she would not let them fall. To do so would show fear and weakness, and she would permit neither. "Just let me get changed," he said as he hurried up to the attic.

He didn't bother with more than his military jacket, cap, and boots. They would do, and time was of the essence. No telling where Anja had decided to run.

Sure enough, he was barely outside the front entrance when he was confronted by a trio of soldiers coming out of the bakery. They started toward him.

"Doktor," he announced, pointing to his medical insignia.

The ploy worked. The soldiers stepped aside without further question as he hurried past them and on down the boulevard. Along the way he scanned his surroundings for possible signs of the woman and her children. Where would she go with two small children? Where could she hide now that it was daylight? At least the boy had eaten something. But the truth was they could be anywhere. Munich was a large city, and he could hardly cover every street.

"Anja," he whispered whenever he spotted a potential hiding place. It was foolhardy to call for her even in a whisper, but perhaps she would be so startled to hear her given name that she would reveal herself.

The snow had started up again. She might be easier to track in fresh snow—her own small footprints and next to them the boy's.

He thought about the stories he'd heard from Willi Graf and his friends after they returned from the Russian front. On their way there, they had been in Warsaw for a brief layover. Willi had told him of German soldiers beating Jewish men working outside the ghetto, of the malnutrition they had seen among the few Jewish Poles allowed outside the walls. And he spoke of news from others who had seen the mass executions, who knew of thousands lined up and murdered, discarded in open graves.

As the war had progressed, few Germans could doubt the fate of those people that the authorities found objectionable—political adversaries, the mentally ill, Poles, and Jews, the most hated of all. Josef could no longer pretend that he—and anyone who really considered the situation—didn't know the fate that awaited Anja and her children. If caught she would be either killed on the spot or taken to one of the network of concentration camps that had been established across Eastern Europe. Rumors claimed that several of those camps were meant for more than incarceration. Some of them had been specifically designed to be facilities for extermination—death camps.

Josef quickened his pace to a run, desperate to find the woman. Not just to save her but to show her—and her children—that not all Germans agreed with the tactics of the current government. "We are not all monsters," he had told Beth the night before. But he had to wonder if Anja would ever believe that.

He paused to allow a convoy of military trucks pass. Each truck was loaded with people—people whose pleas for mercy and protests of innocence lingered in the air like exhaust fumes once the trucks had passed. If Anja had been picked up—if she and the children were now on one of those trucks—he could do little for them. But he ran toward the train station anyway. He had no doubt that this was where the trucks were headed, and if Anja was on one of them. . .

These days the cattle cars were loaded in plain view of anyone who cared to watch. Josef had noticed that most people either turned away, busying themselves with something else so as not to see, or they stood by and watched. To his shame and utter disbelief he had even heard that some people taunted the prisoners and applauded their captors.

It was still fairly early, and the station was not yet as busy as it would be later in the day. By the time Josef arrived, the trucks had come to a halt, and all the passengers were being ordered to proceed to the freight train that sat waiting on the track closest to the platform, its engine huffing and wheezing.

"Schnell!"

Up and down the long platform, the order was repeated again and again. Sometimes it came with a blow of a rifle butt or the snapping and growling of a barely restrained dog.

Josef walked quickly along the length of the train, peering into cars that had already started to fill, and then moving on even as behind him he heard the slam of the sliding doors and the wails of the people inside.

And then he saw her.

CHAPTER 6

Anja was lifting her son into the waiting arms of a man already on one of the cattle cars. The man was clutching the baby close to his chest. He held out his hand to Anja as she tried to avoid the crush of others who were determined to get aboard ahead of her. Common sense would dictate the importance of finding space close to the door in order to have fresh air. If you had to go—and no one here had a choice—you might as well fight for the best position. Even freezing fresh air was preferable to what the stench inside that crowded car would be within a few hours.

"Halt!" Josef shouted. The guard charged with loading the car Anja had just climbed into looked up. "That woman," he shouted. "Stop her."

Roughly the guard grabbed Anja's arm and pulled her back from the car. She fought him because the rest of her family was already aboard. The guard struck her hard across her face with the back of his hand, and she crumpled to the ground.

"The boy and the man," Josef said as he reached the guard and forced himself not to even glance at Anja. "*Alle!* This family is not to go until they are questioned by order of the Gestapo," he added, having learned the magic of those words. "Get them out of there. Now." He saw the boy huddled next to the door, his eyes riveted on his mother, who remained lying on the ground.

"You there," he ordered. The boy recognized him but showed no relief at Josef's presence. His eyes were wide with pure terror. "Come down from there at once. And you," he added, pointing to the father, who was trying to calm the wailing baby.

Josef grimaced as the guard roughly grabbed the boy's thin arm and swung him to the ground next to Anja as if he were no more than a sack of potatoes. "Stand back," Josef ordered and was relieved to see the guard obey. "Get up," he ordered Anja. "Schnell." He made a motion as if to strike her, and she scrambled unsteadily to her feet. The boy immediately clutched at her coat as the man climbed down from the cattle car and stood helplessly by.

"*Kommen Sie!*" Josef barked out the command. Fortunately the chaotic scene around them—dogs barking, children wailing, people begging for mercy, and guards shouting out orders—gave Josef the cover he needed to get Anja and her family safely away, but when Anja and her husband hesitated to follow his order, the guard raised his rifle.

"Nein!" Josef shouted as he stepped between the guard and them.

Anja started to cough, and Josef wondered if her hacking was the result of being too long in the cold or a ploy to help him rescue them. But when she looked up at him, he saw only fear in her eyes. She did not trust him even though he had moved to protect her from the soldier's bullet. She thought of him as no different from the others. Her cough was real.

"*Gehen Sie, los,*" he ordered and pointed toward the other end of the train—the long line of cattle cars with doors slamming shut like the prison cells that they were.

With her shoulders hunched as if to ward off any further blows, Anja took her son's hand as her husband sheltered his daughter with his arms and upper body. She gave Josef a sideways glance as they started to trudge back down the platform toward the station. Everything in their posture told Josef that at any moment they expected to be shot or perhaps simply thrown with their children beneath the train that was now moving slowly away.

He locked his hands behind his back in the manner that he had seen his father do on numerous occasions and moved closer so that he was not quite walking with her but was near enough for her to hear him. "Just keep walking," he said quietly. "If anyone approaches, say nothing. Let me handle it."

Anja's head bobbed once, and she glanced at her husband and nodded again. Josef hoped that was her sign that she had heard him and wasn't about to do something foolish. He wouldn't be able to stop the guards along the platform from shooting the entire family if they tried to run. "Do not try to escape," he added loudly for the benefit of the guard and also as a special warning to the husband, who refused to look at him.

Anja placed her free hand in her husband's and held onto him. The train moved past them, the cries of its cargo echoing down the track as it gathered speed.

Then there was silence. The soldiers hurried back to their trucks and left, taking their dogs with them. Momentarily the platform was deserted.

They walked past two soldiers armed with rifles who apparently were assigned to patrol the area. Farther on, two burly men waiting at the entrance to the station were watching them. The men wore the garb common to the Gestapo, their hands jammed into the pockets of their trench coats. Their felt fedoras pulled low over their foreheads. Their shoulders hunched against the bitter wind.

"Mama, you have blood," the boy said, pointing up at Anja.

Sure enough, as they neared the station entrance Josef saw that Anja was bleeding around her mouth where the guard had struck her. "Cough," he hissed. "Cough into this like you are sick." He thrust a handkerchief into her hand.

Anja followed his orders to the letter, going so far as to double over and gasp for air between hacking coughs.

"Doktor?" One of the secret agents stepped forward and looked at the insignia on Josef's uniform.

"I have orders to take this woman and the rest of the family. I need to examine them, and unless there is a need to quarantine them owing to the woman's coughing up blood, they are to be questioned—a matter involving her husband." He jerked his head in the man's direction.

The mention of quarantine had the desired effect of making the agent step back, opening the way for Josef to hustle the family into the station. "Keep your mouth covered, I told you," he ordered harshly as Anja started to cough again. The blood stains on the white cloth were obvious, but the agents had followed them inside and were now conferring. It was clear that one of them had his doubts.

"Stay back," Josef barked at the stationmaster and waiting passengers. They were attracting far too much attention, but he didn't know how else to get away from the agents. He shoved Anja and her husband, who still carried their daughter, through the door that led to the street, then roughly pushed the boy after them and closed the door behind him.

To his relief a streetcar headed in the direction that led to the hospital was just pulling to a stop across the street. "Hurry," he urged the family. "If they come after us, we will get off at the hospital. You'll be safe there."

It was a lie intended to get them moving when upon seeing the agents following them from the station, the husband froze.

Anja herded her son onto the car, soothing him as he finally gave into the stress of the last several minutes and began to shake with fear. Josef shoved the father, and the man handed Anja the baby as he found a seat and wrapped his arms around his son. Josef stood in the aisle, blocking them from the view of other passengers and hoping the agents would take his position as one of authority over them. His mind raced as he tried to come up with his next move. This was insanity. Why was he risking everything for these strangers?

Anja continued to cough, and Josef knew that she was no longer faking to fool those around her. A few of the passengers sitting nearby began to edge away from them and kept their eyes averted. One man cast a furtive and worried look toward Anja and murmured to Josef, "She sounds sick."

Josef ignored him. They were nearing the next stop, so Josef leaned over and touched Anja's arm. "We'll get off here," he said. They were just across the street from the hospital.

Once the streetcar had continued on its way, Josef checked to be sure no one was paying any attention to them. As usual people were going in and out of the hospital, but no one seemed especially interested in them.

"I have rounds," Josef explained. "Can you find your way back to the apartment?"

Anja nodded.

"I will get you some medicine for the cough, but—"

"We understand," Anja's husband said. "Thank you for your kindness to my family."

Josef shook hands with the man, then turned his attention back to Anja. "Beth is waiting for you. Walk three blocks in that direction, and you'll come to the alley that leads to the rear courtyard. Wait there until you see that it's safe to go inside."

Josef could only hope that Beth would be watching for any sign of him, knowing that he would come back through the building's rear entrance. If the family could make it to the professor's apartment, they would be safe—at least for now.

Beth looked up from the silent prayer she'd engaged in from the moment Josef left to find Anja and the children. Oh, how she wished there was someone else praying with her. Even one person would help. This was not the way she had been raised. Quakers placed enormous importance on taking the time necessary to come to a consensus. But no one had ever prepared her for something like this—when there was simply no time for gathering and contemplating and waiting.

A sound from the corridor startled her. Was that a knock or simply her imagination? She edged toward the door.

There it was again. *Tap. Tap. Tap.*

"Who's there?"

Her answer was a baby's full-throated cry, and she flung the door open and stepped back as Anja stumbled into the foyer with Daniel, the baby, and a man dressed in tattered clothing. Blood covered Anja's face around her mouth and chin. "This is my husband, Benjamin," she managed.

"The doctor?" Beth asked, peering out the half-open door.

Anja shook her head, and Beth's heart actually skipped a beat. "Arrested?" she asked, even as she could not bring herself to ask the question uppermost in her mind—the question of whether or not Josef was dead.

"No. No," Anja assured her. "He is well. He is—" A harsh cough drowned out the rest.

"He is at hospital," Benjamin explained.

"Come," Beth said as she ushered the family into the kitchen. She helped Daniel out of his coat and lifted him onto a bench so that she could remove his shoes and socks. "A glass of warm milk would be good, no?" she asked, and he nodded. "And then you can all spend the day here, all right?"

The boy glanced at his parents, both of whom seemed to have lost the energy to protest anything that Beth might propose.

"There's water in the kettle," Beth told Benjamin as she lifted Anja's daughter from her mother's arms and carried her up the stairs. Daniel followed her.

"Mama?" He paused on the stairway.

"Coming," she replied, her voice as weak as her smile. Benjamin turned on the gas under the kettle and then sat on the edge of the kitchen chair that Beth had been sitting in, his large hands dangling between his knees. "Go on," he murmured to his wife.

When they reached the attic and the children collapsed onto Josef's narrow bed, Beth realized that dried blood wasn't the only thing marring Anja's beautiful face. Tears ran down her cheeks, and when she looked at Beth it was a portrait of failure such as Beth had never seen before.

"We can do this," Beth assured her as she wet a cloth in the basin of water she'd brought to them the night before. "For today we can do this, and then tomorrow..." She had no idea how to finish that sentence.

Anja drew in a deep shuddering breath as she wiped away her tears with the backs of her hands and bent to help Daniel get undressed. "Tomorrow," she said firmly, "we will begin again."

At the end of his shift, Josef practically ran all the way back to the apartment from the hospital. There was no sound coming from inside, but still he knocked at the front door. After several long minutes and a second knock, he heard someone coming.

No light went on, but he saw the shadow of a woman.

"Beth?" He heard the latch turn, and she opened the door a crack. "Are they here?"

"Ja."

"We can get them out now that it is dark."

"They are sleeping. They are exhausted, Josef."

It was the first time she had used his given name without her uncle—or him—reminding her to do so. He permitted himself only a moment to savor the breakthrough, and then he pressed closer to the door. "Beth, they cannot stay here."

"I know, but tomorrow will be soon enough. They will be safe until then."

"And what will you do tomorrow?"

"I will think of something. Good night." She closed the door and clicked the latch.

Josef stood in the dim corridor, staring at the closed door. He recalled how during his years in Boston he had been constantly taken aback at the certainty with which Americans approached life. They simply assumed that somehow they would find answers to whatever challenge they faced. Beth's comment that she would come up with a plan showed that she had no idea of the lengths the authorities would go to in hunting for Anja and her family once they realized they were not on that train. He had no doubt that the guards knew precisely how many prisoners had boarded the train, and at the end of their journey, each one of them would be counted. Of more immediate concern was that he had no way of knowing if the guard or the agents in the station had reported Josef's actions to their superiors.

He raised his hand, prepared to knock again and try and reason with Beth. But knowing she was unlikely to change her mind and too tired to argue, Josef trudged down the stairs to the street and waited for the last streetcar to come. He had taken a terrible risk in rescuing Anja and her family. What if someone had recognized him? What if his father had been at the station? He could have been. These days it was not unusual for high-ranking Gestapo agents to take a personal interest in the kind of round-up that had occurred earlier that day. Eduard Geith, one of his father's more vicious colleagues, actually enjoyed bragging about his brutality during raids.

Unable to sleep once he reached the small apartment near the hospital where another medical student had offered him a spare bed, Josef didn't wait for the first rays of dawn to streak the sky. He dressed and headed for his lab at the university. He might as well get some work done. He had taken far too much time away from his studies and research these last days while he tried to come up with some way to get Beth's visa replaced. Now there was this new and far more dangerous situation that needed a solution.

He strode across the square, barely hearing the chiming of the Rathaus-Glockenspiel—the clock with its little figures putting on a show that as a boy he had so loved to watch. A trio of black sedans that had become synonymous with the government rumbled into the square, going so fast that if Josef had not stepped quickly into a doorway he would have been hit. As the cars roared away, Josef slumped against a pillar and looked at the buildings surrounding him. This was his home—the place where he had been born, gone to school, spent so many happy hours with his friends. But it all seemed so different to him now. Something sinister permeated the city these days—something that bordered on pure evil. Josef grieved for the country he loved.

Weighed down by despair, he walked the rest of the way to the university and unlocked the door to the laboratory that he shared with three other medical students. He had just switched on the lamp when he noticed the folded paper on the floor near the door. It brought back the memory of the first time he had found a copy of one of the leaflets calling for resistance and written by the group known as the White Rose. Now as then, notes left by unseen messengers were more often than not missives of bad news or words that could cause a person no end of trouble should such a document be found on his person. After the day and night he'd had, Josef decided the last thing he needed was to get caught up in something that could lead to more trouble for him or others. He ignored the paper and set to work.

But barely half an hour later he gave up any pretense of focusing on his work. He picked up the paper and spread it flat on his desk. The type was so faded that the words were almost unreadable. Josef held the paper closer to the desk lamp. He was barely past the opening sentence when he realized what he was reading.

This indeed was a copy of a White Rose leaflet—different from the one he'd read in the summer before he and his fellow medical students had left for their military assignments. Reading that original paper, he had been stunned and more than a little excited to realize that whoever had written those impassioned words shared his feelings about the current state of politics in their homeland. That essay had been a call to action—not to save the Jews and others designated as undesirable by the Third Reich, but rather to save Germany from Hitler and his Third Reich.

He turned his attention to the paper in his hand. This time the author or authors had taken a more strident tone:

There is an old proverb that children are always taught anew: Pay attention or pay the consequences. A smart child will only burn his fingers once on a hot stove.

    In the past few weeks, Hitler has registered successes both in Africa and in Russia. As a result, optimism grew among the people on the one hand, while consternation and pessimism grew on the other hand—and this with a rapidity that is unrivalled [in a nation known for] inertia. On every side among the opponents of Hitler—that is, among the better part of the nation—one heard plaintive calls, words of disappointment and discouragement, which often ended with the exclamation: "But what if Hitler really. . . ?"

    In the meantime, the German offensive in Egypt has ground to a halt. Rommel must hold out in a dangerously exposed position. And yet the march eastward continues. This apparent success has been at the expense of the most ghastly sacrifices, so that it can no longer be described as advantageous. We therefore must warn against every form of optimism.

    Who has counted the dead, Hitler or Goebbels? Probably neither. Thousands fall every day in Russia. It is the time of harvest, and the reaper approaches the standing crops with all his energy. Mourning returns to the cottages of the homeland and no one is there to dry the tears of the mothers. But Hitler deceives the ones whose most precious possession he has stolen and driven to a senseless death.

Josef read the words quickly, not because he feared being discovered but because he was in complete agreement with the author. The last line of the piece was especially compelling.

    "We will not keep silent. We are your guilty conscience. The White Rose will not let you alone!"

Josef leaned back in his chair and realized that his breath was coming in short gasps of excitement as if he had run a race and crossed the finish line ahead of his competitors. Given the events referred to in the document, the leaflet had been composed sometime after July—possibly just before the White Rose leaflets had simply stopped. He had assumed the author or authors had been caught. But if that was true, their cause had been taken up by others. This document—written months earlier—had been copied and left for someone like him to find—just as the original leaflets had been. Whoever had left this was still fighting for the Germany that Josef loved. He felt the sting of tears—tears of relief. Tears of hope.

Since returning from his military duty, he had been stunned by the changes in Munich. Beneath the surface of gaiety and holiday festivity ran an undercurrent of fear and caution that permeated everything. He thought about that autumn day when he'd first seen Beth Bridgewater. That day she had come into the apartment so full of vitality. He had thought of her high spirits as American, but now he realized that in some ways she had displayed the openness and energy of Bavarians as they had been before the war—before Hitler came to power, before everything changed.

Beth.

It had taken weeks for him to secure the precious document that could assure her safe departure. Of course, his father had named his price—to deliver the document himself and meet this American woman. Josef had had no choice but to agree, and he had hurried back to the apartment to prepare Beth for his father's visit. His plan had been to coach her on what to say—and more to the point what *not* to say. But then he had walked into the house and come face to face with Anja and her children, setting off a series of events that he could not have imagined.

Outside the laboratory door, he heard footsteps and froze. He glanced at the paper still clutched in his hand and crushed it into a ball as the doorknob turned.

"Ah, Herr Doktor Buch," the custodian said. "You are here earlier than usual."

Josef glanced at the wall clock and ran his fingers through his hair. "I could not sleep."

Instead of leaving and apologizing for disturbing Josef, the custodian rolled his mop bucket into the room.

Irritated at the interruption, Josef wrapped his fingers more tightly around the wad of paper clutched in his palm. "I'll likely be here for at least another hour before I leave for class," he said, hoping the custodian would move on down the hallway to clean another room.

"We all have our duties, Herr Doktor. I won't take long." He set his mop into the sudsy water and began moving around the room, swiping the wet mop under lab tables and desks, pausing only to move or empty a wastebasket or retrieve a fallen piece of paper.

Josef turned back to his work, glad that once he'd decided to abandon any possibility that he might be able to concentrate he hadn't packed up his papers and books. All the while he considered how he might best dispose of the incendiary leaflet still gripped in his hand. A metal wastebasket was close enough that he could certainly drop it there and then tear off sheets from his notebook and add them to the refuse.

He glanced over his shoulder to see what the custodian was doing and saw the man emptying a similar basket into a larger container that he had dragged into the room along with his mop bucket. But it was the way he emptied the contents of the trash that gave Josef pause. The man did not simply upend the smaller receptacle into the larger one. He pulled out the contents one paper or wadded ball at a time, setting the crumpled papers aside in a separate bucket as he tossed the others into the garbage bin.

Josef stealthily worked the incriminating leaflet beneath the cuff of his shirt and then stood and stretched as he reached for the uniform jacket draped over the back of his chair and shrugged into it. The custodian looked up.

"I just remembered that I need to stop at home before class," Josef said as he gathered his papers and thrust them inside his briefcase.

"Sorry for interrupting your work, but. . ." The janitor smiled but did not return to his work.

"*Kein Problem,*" Josef said as he left the room. But there could definitely have been a problem—a huge one if the custodian had come in and caught him reading that paper.

He was halfway down the hall when he heard the custodian call out to him.

"You must have dropped this paper, Doktor." He was holding up a page that had clearly been crumpled into a ball and smoothed out again.

Josef felt the start of panic but realized that he could feel the leaflet he'd hidden in his sleeve scratching against his arm as he moved. Whatever the custodian was holding, it was something else. Josef took the paper the man held out to him and held it up to the light spilling into the dim hallway from the laboratory. It took less than a second for him to realize that this was another copy of the leaflet he had hidden in his sleeve.

The custodian watched him closely. The man was testing him.

"Where did you get this?" Josef demanded, waving the paper in the man's face. He saw at once that he had effectively turned the tables. The custodian was now the one on the defensive, having realized too late that in giving such a document to Josef, he had raised questions of his own involvement in distributing such seditious literature. "I could report you for this," Josef added for good measure.

The custodian backed away, his hands raised in protest even as sweat leaked from every pore of his balding head. "Nein, Doktor. I. . .I saw the paper on the floor near where you were working, and I thought perhaps—"

"Get back to work," Josef ordered. "I'll take care of this." With that, he turned on his heel and strode down the hall, taking the second copy of the leaflet with him.

Outside he drew in long deep breaths of the cold morning air. How many of these papers were there? The originals had been printed on a mimeograph machine. This one as well as the copy hidden in his shirt sleeve had been typed. There could not possibly be many copies. It was possible that he had in his hands the only two.

He knew that he should simply burn the papers and forget about them. But somewhere people felt as he did. They were afraid for the future of their beloved country as he was and had decided to try and reach out to others who shared their concern. If they all banded together, perhaps they could change the course the Third Reich had set for their beloved fatherland. They could make a difference. *He* could make a difference.

I have a concern. . . .

He thought of the evening when Beth had uttered that phrase—the night when he had learned the true story of her missing visa. The night their lives had become intertwined.

Beth Bridgewater had taken actions every bit as risky and courageous as the author of the call to action against the Third Reich that Josef had hidden in his sleeve. She had done so not because of her love of country or even because of any special connection to the woman she'd given her visa—or for that matter Anja and her children.

She had been faced with a choice between doing what was safe and doing what was right, and on at least two occasions that Josef knew of, she had chosen the more dangerous but noble path. In so doing she had shown more courage than any soldier Josef had ever encountered on the field of battle.

He pulled the leaflet from his sleeve and folded it with the one he had taken from the custodian. Somehow he would find the author or authors of these papers—and once he did, he would join them. For the first time in weeks, he felt a kernel of hope sprout inside him, and he was determined to help it grow.

CHAPTER 7

For two days and nights Beth managed to keep Anja, Benjamin, and the children safe. She slept in her own bed, alert for any sound coming from the attic. In the evenings Josef joined them, and in spite of the meager supper Anja helped Beth prepare, their time together was filled with discussion and laughter and the rudiments of building friendships. They took turns telling the children stories until they fell asleep. After that the four adults would sit in a corner of the attic and talk about their lives before the war—places they had traveled, plans they had made for their future, people they had known in common.

While Anja asked Beth about life in America, her eyes shone with excitement when she imagined one day she and Benjamin might take their children and live there. "In peace," she always added quietly.

On these occasions, it seemed perfectly natural that Beth should sit with her head resting on Josef's shoulder as Anja stretched out so that her head was on Benjamin's lap. Josef would gently stroke her hair as he and Benjamin talked about sports—the 1936 Olympics in particular. Beth would link her fingers with Josef's as she told them about her life in America.

"Perhaps one day," Anja would murmur wistfully, "we will go there with the children and live in peace."

But they all understood that these idyllic evenings could not last. On the third such night Beth reminded them all that her aunt and uncle were due home in just two days. This would be their last night together for a while because the following night Anja and Benjamin and the children would have to leave.

It was that night that Josef excused himself, went up to his room in the attic, and came back a moment later with a small radio. He plugged it in, and to their amazement through whistles of static they heard the unmistakable voice of Winston Churchill addressing the people of Great Britain. As the four of them sat with their heads bent toward the radio, trying to catch every word, they took hold of each other's hands, forming a circle of solidarity around the radio. And when the static finally drowned out the British prime minister's voice, they remained sitting in silence, drawing strength from one another as they considered their futures. Beth did not know what the others prayed for or thought about during those moments. For her there was but one thought: getting Anja and her family to a place where they would be safe until this horrid war could be brought to its end.

With no idea how she and Josef might manage that, the following day she bought some peroxide and told Anja as a first step to lighten Benjamin's and the children's dark hair. Anja already had the golden-blond hair and Aryan features preferred by the current regime—even though most Bavarians, not to mention Hitler himself, had brown hair. Still, if the entire family were fair-haired, they might be able to move around more freely.

She had left them to this task while she went to the market and stood in the long line of people waiting to see what they might be able to buy with their ration stamps. Across Germany food was becoming increasingly scarce, and usually Beth felt fortunate to be able to trade the family's food stamps for a few potatoes and black bread, sometimes a small stunted onion, and if she was very blessed a beef salami sausage. The wait was over an hour, and Beth came away with very little—a small loaf of stale black bread, five small potatoes, and one orange.

"Happy Christmas from der Führer," the woman distributing the oranges announced, presenting each small, hard, green piece of fruit as if it were the gold laid at the manger by one of the three kings.

As Beth trudged home, she mentally ran through what supplies were still in the pantry that she might be able to give Anja for the journey ahead. Then as she approached the bakery, she heard someone call out to her.

"Beth! We're back!" She looked up to see Liesl leaning over the shallow balcony outside the apartment's kitchen. "We brought a present for you. I'm coming down. Mama says we can buy something at the bakery."

Beth's mind was racing along with her heart as she waited for Liesl to reach the street. She glanced up at the attic window and thought she saw the curtain move. Was that Anja or Benjamin? She saw Liesl exiting the street entrance to the apartments. Her cousin ran to meet her, taking her hand and dancing alongside her, her eyes sparkling with excitement as they walked the rest of the way together.

"You weren't due back until tomorrow," Beth said, glancing toward the attic window again, and this time she was certain that the curtain moved. Either Anja or Benjamin had to be keeping watch. Hopefully they recognized the problem and would take up their place in the closet Beth had shown them behind the trunks and boxes of off-season clothing that Ilse kept stored there.

"Mama says we have ever so much to do to prepare for Christmas. She is feeling much much better," Liesl said. "And Mama says I mustn't expect that you will have presents for us but that's fine because Mama says presents are not important. Our best present is that we are all together and safe and. . ." She frowned. "But Mama says this might be our last Christmas with you for a while."

Beth's mind was so focused on what to do about Anja that she was barely listening to her cousin's chatter until this last statement caught her attention. "Why? Are you going somewhere?"

"No, silly. Mama says you have to go back to America and the sooner the better," she added. "She says it's not safe for you here now that we're enemies and all." She sighed. "I so wish we could be friends, Beth."

"You and I are not enemies, Liesl," Beth reminded her as they entered the bakery.

"I know *we're* friends—and family, Beth. I meant our countries—Germany and the United States." Liesl pressed her hands to the glass display cases as she admired the pastries.

"That one," she announced, pointing to a Christmas *Stollen* fat with dried fruit and frosted with a white sugary confection. Once the purchase had been made, Beth took her time climbing the stairs to their apartment. She needed every second to think through how she might manage the next several hours before her aunt and uncle went to bed and she could somehow get Anja and the others out of the house.

Liesl ran up the stairs and down the corridor. "She's here," she shouted. "Beth is here."

Beth's heart caught in her throat when she walked into the kitchen to leave the bag of food and saw her aunt coming down the stairs from the attic. "What on earth has that man been doing up there?" she said testily. "It smells of something horrid—some chemical—this towel reeks of it."

She was holding one of the blue bath towels that had hung next to the sink. It was clearly damp and stained where the peroxide had splashed and distorted the color.

"I am sure that—"

"I thought I had made it clear that he was not to be here while we were gone," Aunt Ilse continued as she studied the towel more closely. "Some experiment, no doubt. Well, Herr Doktor Buch needs to understand that we can't easily replace things like towels and clothing and such."

"Is Uncle Franz here?"

"He went to the university." Aunt Ilse reached for the bag that Beth had carried home from the market. "*Das ist alles?*"

"I'm afraid so. I'll go back tomorrow. Perhaps with Christmas coming they will have more. There's an orange that might ripen if we save it for Liesl's stocking," she whispered, hoping to distract her aunt from the other contents of the bag. She might be able to manage to take at least half the bread and perhaps two of the potatoes and give them to Anja if Aunt Ilse did not unpack the food. "I'll just put these things away," she said, taking the bag back from her aunt. "How are Marta and the family?"

Aunt Ilse actually laughed. "My sister was intent on making sure we returned with enough milk and cheese to last through the month. I think she must have bought one farmer's entire supply and. . ."

Barely listening to her aunt's chatter, Beth gripped the edge of the sink and bowed her head. Everything was wrong here. It was wrong of her to keep secrets from her aunt and uncle. It was wrong of her to make such an important decision without first seeking counsel from her Quaker family. Yet to admit that she was hiding a Jewish family in the attic would surely send her aunt into a fresh cycle of the hysteria that for the time being she seemed to have overcome.

"Beth, come up to the attic," Liesl shouted as she started up the stairs. "I want to show you the presents I made for everyone—well, not yours, of course, but—"

"Let's do that in our room," Beth hurried to suggest. "There was a spill in the attic, and it smells up there."

"Ja." Liesl agreed as she reached the top step and sniffed the air. "But I want to hide the presents. Mama will never think to search up here."

Beth forced a laugh even as her heart pounded so furiously that she thought she might not be able to breathe. "Your mother is standing right down there in the front hall and now knows your plan," she said. "Let me help you find a better hiding place."

To her relief Liesl ran down the stairs and on down the hall to their bedroom. For the next half hour, Beth admired the crudely woven pot holder that Liesl had made for her mother and the rock she had painted for her father. "It's a paperweight," Liesl confided.

"It's wonderful," Beth assured her.

"And this is for Dr. Buch," the girl said as she held up a peppermint candy cane. "Aunt Marta brought it from Switzerland for me, but I'd rather give it to him. Mama doesn't like him, but I think that he's awfully nice—don't you, Beth?"

"I do, and I think he will like your present very much."

"Do you think he will have something for me?"

"That's not important, Liesl."

Her cousin sighed. "I know. That's what Mama keeps saying. 'It's not the gift but the giving.' But I do so love getting presents."

Outside their closed bedroom door, they heard the front door open and shut. "It's Papa," Liesl whispered. "Quick, we have to hide these."

Beth helped the girl find hiding spots for all three gifts and then followed her out into the hallway. Her uncle and Josef were standing in the foyer. Josef was hanging up his coat and putting on his slippers while her uncle told him some news he'd heard about new regulations at the university.

"I have a secret," Liesl announced in a singsong voice, and both men smiled at her. "And it's something to do with you, Herr Doktor Buch."

He crouched down to her height. "Would this secret have anything to do with the coming of Christmas?"

Liesl giggled and nodded. "You'll never guess—not in a thousand years."

"Well, I have a secret as well, and it has something to do with you." He tweaked her nose and got to his feet. He glanced toward the ceiling and then at Beth.

She could only offer a half shrug in return. It would appear that *their* secret was safe, but she could not really be sure until she went to the attic to check. What if Anja and Benjamin had decided to slip away as soon as they saw her uncle's car arrive? But she had seen the curtain move. Still, her aunt had been in the attic when she and Liesl entered the house. Could she have been the person at the window? And if so, where were Anja and Benjamin and the children?

Beth was still trying to think of some excuse for returning to the attic when Aunt Ilse stepped into the hallway from the kitchen. She frowned when she saw Josef.

"Herr Doktor Buch," she said in a quiet formal tone that was not at all the way she usually addressed him.

"Welcome home, Frau Schneider," Josef said. "It sounds like you and the professor and Liesl enjoyed the skiing."

Aunt Ilse ignored his attempts at small talk. "I believe this belongs to you," she said, handing him a small book. "I found it in our niece's bedroom." She wrapped her crossed arms with the skirt of her apron and waited for his explanation.

Beth looked more closely at the volume and recognized it as a book of medical terms that Josef had brought for Benjamin to study after Anja had told him that her husband had one day hoped to attend medical school. Beth had suggested that Anja and Benjamin study in her room while she and Josef got the children settled for the night in the attic.

"I. . .it. . ." Beth began. She did not wish to lie to her aunt, but what explanation could there be other than that Josef had been in her room and here was the proof?

"Frau Schneider, I had intended to speak with you and the professor later this evening, but this. . ." He glanced at the book and then back at Ilse. The man was actually offering Beth's aunt a sheepish smile. "You see, the fact of the matter is that I have become quite fond of your niece. I know that in many ways you and Professor Schneider still think of her as that teenager who came to live with you after Liesl was born, but to me she is. . . ."

He paused and allowed his gaze to rest on Beth. "To me, she is the one true beautiful reality in the midst of all that surrounds us. Her courage alone inspires me—her determination to stay here where she is needed when anyone else might have thought first of herself."

"It is not our way to think of ourselves before others," Aunt Ilse murmured as she glanced from Josef to Beth and back again.

"Are you going to marry Beth?" Liesl asked.

Aunt Ilse startled like a horse caught unaware. "Liesl, this is an adult conversation. Go into the kitchen." She cast about for some way to soften her reprimand when Liesl's eyes filled with tears. "Go on. Beth brought you a surprise from the market today."

As soon as the child had run to the kitchen and they heard her squeal of delight when she obviously discovered the orange, Aunt Ilse turned back to Josef. "You still have not answered the question of how you came to be in my niece's room, Doktor."

"Your niece is a twenty-five-year-old woman, Frau Schneider—an adult. If she were living in her own apartment, would you deny her the pleasure of guests?"

"Guests, of course, but—"

"We were talking about the future, and I mentioned that I had thought of perhaps one day becoming a nurse," Beth interrupted. This was the truth. "Josef brought the book after that." Again the truth although not exactly the whole of it.

"And you could not hold these conversations here in the study or kitchen?"

"I think we both felt safer in the back of the apartment away from the street," Josef said, as if the thought had just occurred to him. "We spend enough time in the cellar during the air raids, and the kitchen can be oppressive with the reminder of so little food. And you asked that we not heat the other rooms unnecessarily," he reminded her.

"He's right, Ilse," the professor said. "The radiator in the girls' room is by far the most productive in the entire apartment."

"We did nothing but talk, Tante Ilse," Beth added.

Her aunt fixed her gaze on each of them in turn. "From this day forward any 'talking' will take place in any room of your choice in the front of the house," she instructed. "Is that very clear?"

Josef and Beth both nodded, and Aunt Ilse turned on her heel and marched back down the hall to the kitchen.

"I warned you," Uncle Franz said with a grin as he shook his finger at Josef. "My wife misses nothing." He sobered and locked his gaze with Josef's. "We will talk later on that other matter?"

Josef nodded, and when Uncle Franz left them to return to his study, Josef moved a step closer to Beth. "Do you think they left?"

"I don't know. I hope not. It's still light and. . ." She felt a lump of pure fear close her throat and for one incredible moment realized that she understood how her aunt felt much of the time. "Oh Josef, what will they do? What can we do to help them now?"

He took her hand between both of his. "First things first. Go make sure they are still here. Then trust me. I have come up with a plan."

Reluctantly she pulled her hand free of his and touched his cheek. "I am sorry I ever doubted you, Josef."

"And I meant what I told your aunt, Beth. You are the single ray of beauty in all of this ugliness surrounding us." He put his fingers to her lips. "You give me great hope—and courage I did not know I possessed."

As soon as her aunt went into her bedroom and closed the door, Beth ran up to the attic while Josef went into the study.

Supper that evening was more strained than usual. Liesl was oblivious, still caught up in the excitement and anticipation of what Christmas Eve might bring. That was when they traditionally opened gifts. Ilse ate her supper with her head bent but her eyes occasionally shifting between Josef and Beth. The professor was his usual preoccupied self, leaving Beth and Josef to communicate with glances and wordless signals.

He had determined through her barely perceptible nod that the family was still on site. He had given her a signal that she took to mean eight o'clock and then said something to the professor about possibly taking Beth to Frauenkirche later for a concert—a performance of Handel's *Messiah*. "Some friends have invited us to join them for the concert, and perhaps we would all stop at a *Gasthaus* afterward," he added, turning his attention to Ilse.

The woman glanced at her husband. "You will be back before curfew." It was a statement, not a question.

"Of course."

They finished their meal with Liesl chattering on about her classmates and their plans for Christmas and her understanding that these were war times but still did her father think perhaps there might be at least one present for her to open? Josef could not help noticing that on this night it was Beth—not her aunt—who was nervous, and he thought he might explode if the child did not cease her whining.

"Are you finished, Uncle?" Beth asked, standing and beginning to clear the table.

"Ja."

"Let me help." Josef was immediately on his feet. He took his plate and Liesl's and followed Beth to the sink.

"A concert with friends?" she whispered, letting the water run to cover their conversation.

"Yes, my friends Anja and Benjamin," he explained. "The professor has a meeting he must leave for right after supper. I'll tell your aunt I'm going to get my friends, and then you must get Liesl and your aunt occupied in another part of the apartment. That way I can get Anja and the others down from the attic and out to the courtyard. At the proper time, the three of us will call for you."

"What about the children?"

"They'll wait in the courtyard. We are truly going to a concert, Beth. All of us."

"Well, I understand that, but so you get them to the courtyard—then what? It's freezing, and they hardly have the proper clothing and—"

"It's also nearly Christmas, and times are hard for everyone. Who would question a family going to church?" He tucked a strand of her hair behind her ear. "Trust me, Beth. It will all work out."

"Turn off that water," Ilse demanded, bringing them the rest of the dishes. It was evident by her frown that she had seen Josef's tender gesture.

Josef did as Ilse asked and then grinned at her. "Lovely supper, Frau Schneider," he said. "You seem to be able to work miracles with very little food."

Ilse snorted, but Josef could see that the compliment pleased her.

"Did the professor leave for his meeting?" he continued.

"He did," Ilse replied with a puzzled glance toward the front door. "He seemed in such a hurry."

"Perhaps he's not going to a meeting at all, Frau Schneider." He lowered his voice to a conspiratorial whisper. "Perhaps he's been trying to find some time to go shopping for gifts for you and Liesl."

This time Ilse's smile was warm with nostalgia. "We used to have the most wonderful Christmases," she said wistfully.

"Those days will come again," Josef assured her. "I seem to recall several boxes of Christmas decorations in the attic. Shall I bring them down for you?"

"That would be very kind of you," Ilse replied, and it was obvious that she was warming to him. "While you and Beth are at the concert and my husband attends his meeting, Liesl and I can go through the boxes and get the apartment ready for Christmas."

"I don't know what I should wear," Beth said. "Tante Ilse, would you come help me choose something?"

"Me too," Liesl shouted as she led the way to the bedroom.

Ilse dried her hands on a dishtowel and prepared to follow the others but then turned back to Josef. "Well, Josef Buch, if you intend to take my niece to this organ concert, I suggest you bring the boxes down now so that you can collect your friends and be on time for the concert."

"Ja *wohl*," Josef replied, giving Ilse a crisp military salute that actually made her smile.

Josef's plan worked brilliantly. When a stair tread creaked, Beth was sure her aunt could hear Anja and her family moving stealthily down the uncarpeted stairs. Then she was equally certain that Liesl's keen hearing would detect the opening and closing of the front door, but the truth was that her aunt was intent on lecturing her, and Liesl was intent on listening.

"You do understand that any idea that you and the doctor might ever. . .could possibly. . ."

"We are friends, Tante Ilse. Nothing more."

"A man who sees himself as a mere friend rarely speaks in terms of beauty and courage and such," she huffed. "He is attracted to you, and in these times such an attraction is not wise. Not wise at all."

"It's harmless." Beth could see that her aunt's anxiety was beginning to blossom now that she was back in the reality that came with living in Munich.

"It is not harmless, Beth. Have you forgotten your circumstances? Your country is now at war with Germany. Your uncle told me you have no papers. You. . ."

"I have papers," Beth said quietly. "Josef got them for me."

"How?"

"He asked his father to get them for me." She saw that instead of her response reassuring her aunt, it had only made matters worse.

"His father?"

"Yes. I am to leave the country by the end of the month. It's all arranged."

"No!" Liesl shrieked. "You can't go. I won't let you."

Beth turned to the girl. "I have to go, Liesl. The government here in Germany has said I have to, and you know what your teacher told you."

She hated the way the little girl obviously struggled between her loyalty to her country and its government and her love for Beth. "But. . ." she sniveled.

"There, there. No more tears. There will be time enough for our tears after Christmas." The reminder of the coming holiday had the desired effect on Liesl. Through the slightly open window that Aunt Ilse insisted on for fresh air even on the coldest of days, Beth heard a child's voice and knew that Josef was leading the family out into the rear courtyard. "Let's sing a carol," she said and launched into "Silent Night."

Liesl folded her thin arms defiantly across her chest and pressed her lips together.

"*Stille Nacht*. . . Come on," Beth urged, and to her relief not only Liesl but also Aunt Ilse joined in.

Half an hour passed before a knock sounded at the front door, and then suddenly Josef, Anja, and Benjamin were standing in the kitchen.

"Frau Schneider, these are my friends August and Maria Buegner," Josef said as calmly as if he were introducing Aunt Ilse to his own family. He turned to Beth. "You look lovely, Beth. Shall we go?"

"Yes." Beth was having trouble finding her voice as she tried not to stare at Benjamin—his hair now blond under a military cap that topped the military jacket he wore. Beside him, Anja was dressed in the coat and scarf that Beth had given her that first night.

"Beth, you have a coat just like that one," Liesl announced, pointing at Anja.

"I do," Beth managed. "We must shop at the same place, M–M–Maria." She stood between her aunt and Anja as she promised that they would not be late and then led the others into the front foyer, where she got her coat and scarf while Josef opened the front door.

"So nice to meet you, Frau Schneider," Anja said softly, offering Aunt Ilse her hand. Benjamin echoed the gesture, and finally they were outside.

The cold night air had never felt so wonderful. Beth sucked in a deep breath and blew it out. Then she hooked arms with Anja and started down the street. "Come on, Maria. We don't want to be late," she said, keeping her voice loud in case her aunt might be listening—and watching—from a window above them.

They walked for three blocks before doubling back down side streets and alleys to reach the courtyard. There they found the children waiting in a shelter of evergreen branches that Josef had constructed for them. They wore warm clothes, and Josef handed Anja a cloth bag filled with food and first-aid supplies. All the while he gave her and Benjamin their instructions.

"When we reach the church, you will take seats on the far right aisle near the confessionals while Beth and I go to the opposite side. In time a woman wearing a red coat will enter the church and kneel next to the pew where you are sitting to cross herself. That's your signal."

"I do not understand," Benjamin said.

"It is the signal you need to know that it's safe to take the next step. When the woman is seated, take Daniel as if he needs to use the toilet. Someone there will give you directions. The process will be repeated, Anja, this time with a man wearing a navy-blue jacket in the Bavarian style and a red lapel pin. He will kneel next to you and then sit with the woman in red. That's when you take little Rachel to the toilet. A woman there will give you directions."

"And then?"

Josef shrugged. "That's all I've been told. It's too dangerous to give any one person too much information." He glanced at Beth. "I do know this. You must say your farewells now. When we reach the church, we can't acknowledge in any way that we are acquainted."

Realizing that after everything they had been through this might be the last time that Beth would see her friend, she embraced Anja tightly.

"Thank you, Beth," Anja whispered repeatedly, prolonging the hug as if she could not bear to let go.

"Take this," Beth said, pressing an envelope in her friend's hand. She heard Josef suck in a breath. "It's not my visa if that's what you're thinking," she assured him. "It's a greeting card. When you are safe, drop it in a mailbox, and that way I will know to stop worrying."

"I will," Anja promised.

"We should go," Josef said, his voice husky.

At the church everything happened exactly as Josef had said it would. He and Beth took places on the far left-hand side of the church where they had a view of Anja and Benjamin and the children but no contact. The concert began, and the historic church swelled with the majesty of Handel's brilliant *Messiah*. After twenty minutes or so, Beth caught a glimpse of red and saw a woman start down the aisle near

Anja, pause to cross herself and genuflect, and then move on to a seat on the aisle several rows in front of them. Shortly after that, Benjamin stood and took Daniel by the hand as they walked back up the aisle.

A short while later, the process was repeated with the man in blue, and Anja and Rachel left. When Beth would have turned to follow her friend's departure, Josef took hold of her hand. He held onto it, their fingers intertwined until the concert came to an end.

After the concert Josef introduced her to Willi Graf and one or two other performers.

"I think we have time for a beer," Willi suggested.

"There is always time for that," Josef agreed, and the three of them set off for the Gasthaus.

Being with Willi and listening to him and Josef talk about their medical studies, Beth's thoughts turned to Anja. She wondered where the family was. While she was sipping beer and laughing at something that Willi had said, where was Anja?

As they walked home, Beth placed her gloved hand in the crook of Josef's arm and rested her cheek against his shoulder. "I don't understand you at all," she said sleepily.

He chuckled. "Then we finally have something in common, Beth." He stopped under the shadow of the bakery's doorway and pulled her into his arms. "The question I have is whether or not you might be willing to search for even more shared traits?"

"I have to leave Germany in just a few weeks," she reminded him. "But now there's a part of me that wishes I could stay."

"Because of me?"

She laughed. "Yes, all right, that's part of it."

"And the rest?"

She tried to read his expression in the shadows surrounding them. Could she trust him? Anja and Benjamin had. Of course, what choice had they had?

"Tell me, Beth. Is it your aunt?"

She shrugged. "I worry about her—about them all. But tonight I was thinking more about Anja and Benjamin. If we truly helped them escape, Josef, perhaps there are others that we could—"

He wrapped his arms more tightly around her. "These are dangerous times, Beth. Why risk your safety when you are in as much peril as anyone else?"

"Not anyone. I might be arrested—deported, but no one is going to shoot me or order me killed."

He was quiet for several long moments.

"You would stay?"

"Oh, Josef, look what we did for Anja and Benjamin and their children. What if we could do that for others?"

"You should go home, Beth. Home where you can be safe and away from all this."

"And what if I wish to stay?"

"To help more people like Anja." It was not a question. His tone—slightly disappointed—told her that he already knew the answer.

"That and because I am confused by my feelings for you." She was suddenly shy with him. "We should go up," she said, reluctant to leave the comfort of his embrace.

"I promised Willi that I would meet him after I had seen you safely home. I'll be back later, and tomorrow. . ."

"Tomorrow?"

"Tomorrow you and I will begin to work through our mutual confusion when it comes to our feelings for each other." He tightened his hold on her, resting his chin on her head. "Are you sure about this, Beth?"

"I am."

"Then I will speak with my father."

"I can't ask that of you. Let me go to him."

"No. I will speak with him."

"If he refuses to extend my visa—even if he agrees—we don't know how long we will have."

"Then let's not waste any of that time," he murmured, lowering his face to hers as she rose onto her toes to meet his kiss. And when the kiss ended, he did the one thing that Beth had never quite understood about Bavarians who were dating.

He shook her hand before turning to go.

Over the next several days, Beth moved in the haze of the wonder of that shared kiss. *Admiration and respect*, her head instructed. *Love*, her heart replied.

Less than a week later as she was still wrestling with the paradox that she—like her father—might have fallen in love with a German in the middle of a war, she received an even greater gift.

"There's mail for you," her uncle told her as he collected the letters and bills that had been shoved through the brass slot in the front door. "Odd, that looks so similar to your handwriting," he commented, handing her the small envelope.

An envelope that she recognized. An envelope that she had been praying to receive ever since she'd had her last glimpse of Anja at the church. She clutched the precious item to her chest and hurried out the door. "I'll be back," she called as she ran down the street and caught a departing streetcar just as it was pulling away.

At the university she asked directions and then ran all the way to Josef's laboratory, wanting to share her news with the only person who could possibly understand its true significance. She opened the frosted glass door to the sterile room, held up the unopened envelope, and breathlessly announced, "It has come. The card from Mary."

In her excitement she had failed to allow for the fact that Josef might not be alone as she had expected. He was standing at his desk with a man Beth recognized instantly to be his father.

"Ah, Fräulein Bridgewater, my son and I were just speaking of you."

CHAPTER 8

Beth took her time weaving her way past the lab tables lined with racks of test tubes and the other paraphernalia that Josef and his colleagues used in their research. Herr Buch watched her as he removed his hat and held it lightly in one hand. He wore the same black wool overcoat and leather gloves that he'd worn the night he'd come to deliver her visa. And for one incredible moment, Beth could not seem to put out of her mind the Saturday matinees she and her brothers had watched back in their hometown where the hero could always be easily identified by his white hat.

And the villain always wore black—and in this case a loden-green Bavarian hat with a red-tipped feather in the hatband.

"Apparently you have some good news to share with my son," Herr Buch said, glancing at the envelope she had all but forgotten she still held clutched in one hand.

"Yes, some friends. . ." She was suddenly at a loss for words. What to say that would not raise this man's suspicions?

"A young family that Beth knew—knows—left recently for a holiday, but the way things are today, there is always the concern that they might get delayed or caught in an air raid," Josef explained. "She was understandably worried." He took the card from her and read

Anja's short message. Then he placed the card back in its envelope and was about to pass it back to Beth when his father took it from him.

"Postmark is too blurred to read," he observed as he studied the envelope, turning it over twice as if he expected to find something new. "Where precisely did your friends go on this holiday, Fräulein?"

"They—"

"Bad Pyrmont," Josef said. "I suggested it as a good place for them to visit. There are still a few Quakers living there, and of course it's a wonderful place to go for the baths and mineral waters." He plucked the envelope from his father's fingers and handed it back to Beth.

"That's right, and the castle there is—"

"Speaking of travel, Fräulein"—Herr Buch continued placing his hat on Josef's desk and then tightening the fingers of his gloves as if in preparation for leaving—"I assume your plans are in place?"

To Beth's surprise, Josef chuckled and stepped closer to her, taking her hand in his. "My father is teasing you, Beth. I have asked if he might extend your visa."

"That would be. . .my aunt is still quite. . ."

"My son has requested this extension for purely selfish reasons, Fräulein. He tells my wife that he has grown quite fond of you. She is a romantic and has asked that I once again intercede on your behalf."

Beth glanced from Herr Buch to Josef. "I don't know what to say."

"It is, of course, your choice, Fräulein. I would only suggest that you consider the consequences of making such a choice. I will do as my wife and son have asked, but if you stay, there will be nothing more I can do for you." Herr Buch put on his hat. "Josef, your mother expects you to bring this young woman to supper tonight."

He nodded politely to Beth as he headed for the door. Josef took her hands in his, but she understood that the gesture was more of a warning to say nothing than a sign of his feelings for her. Herr Buch turned when he reached the door and focused a quizzical gaze on Beth. "Of course, it occurs to me that neither Josef nor I have heard your thoughts in this matter. Would you like to stay, or would you prefer to leave at the end of the month as scheduled?"

With everything that had happened since her aunt and uncle had returned, Beth had given little thought to the passing days. Her concern had been for Anja and her family, and once they had left the church, Liesl had claimed all of her attention with her plans for Christmas.

"I. . .this is all very. . ."

"Never mind, Fräulein. You can give us all your decision when you come for dinner tonight."

As soon as the door closed behind Herr Buch, Beth turned to Josef. "You spoke to your mother about extending my visa?"

He released her hands and walked quickly to the door, opening it and glancing up and down the corridor before closing it again. "I thought this was what you wanted."

"But your mother—how is she involved?"

He ran his hands through his thick hair. "I was. . . . It's complicated."

"I have all day." She suddenly realized that there was a great deal going on with Josef that she knew nothing about.

"You can still leave if that's what you want."

This should have been a moment for them to share. A time for joy and celebration that Anja and her family were safe, that Beth would be able to stay, that they could do more for those in need. Instead they were very close to arguing.

"Forgive me, Josef. It's just that everything is happening so fast, and well, I realize things between you and your father have been. . .difficult."

Josef snorted a derisive laugh. "Difficult is putting it mildly."

"Did you really tell your mother about me?"

This time his smile was genuine. "I did. And on that one topic, my father and I are in complete agreement. My mother is a romantic to her core. Let one word about some woman I find interesting pass between us, and she practically has us married with children on the way before I can finish the sentence."

"Even an American? Your enemy?"

"She would say that people can be either friends or enemies

depending on the political climate of the day. But in her opinion when it comes to romance, politics must not enter into the equation."

Beth laughed. "I think I will like your mother."

"You'll come to dinner then?"

"It did not seem as if your father offered a choice." She lowered her eyes as she formed the question uppermost in her mind. "Josef, you do understand that my main purpose in wanting to stay is so that perhaps I can do for others what we were able to do for our friends?" She held up the card from Anja. "Anything between us. . ."

"I understand, and I might have found a way that you can help others without endangering your own safety—at least not to the degree you have before." He glanced around at the empty room as if someone might have come in without their noticing. Then he slipped a paper out of his briefcase and handed it to her.

"I have seen these," she admitted as she scanned the words. "I saw one in the park last summer, and another was left on the seat next to me when I took Liesl to the movies several weeks before you came to stay with us." Her eyes widened in shock. "You wrote this?"

"No. No. But I now know who did. They are medical students like me, and they have asked me to join their cause." His eyes shone with excitement. "I want to do this, Beth, and I thought you might—"

"How did you find them?"

Josef looked away for a minute. "Willi."

"Willi Graf?" She tried picturing the mild-mannered, unassuming musician and medical student as a revolutionary and failed. "You are mistaken."

"Then it must be his twin who introduced me to other members of the group the other night. I am to go there for a meeting tonight—the final one before everyone goes away for the holiday."

Beth looked at the paper again. *The White Rose* was the only signature—the only clue to who might be behind such a revolutionary act. She sat down on one of the high stools next to a lab table. "Do you have any idea of the risk you are taking? You could be sent to Dachau or worse," she whispered. Still she could not ignore the way her pulse beat with excitement that just maybe they could do something to make a real difference.

"Beth, this is no different from what you did for Anja. What you want us to do for others." He refolded the paper and placed it back inside his briefcase in a compartment that was stuffed full of folders, notebooks, and other papers. "What is happening in Germany and throughout Europe is wrong—this war, the actions being taken against ordinary people are so very wrong. How can I make you understand that Germany is my country and I despair for the direction things are taking under this regime of Hitler's?"

"I do understand that, Josef. I'm just so. . ." By showing her the paper and telling her about his involvement and Willi's, Josef had taken an enormous risk. "You further endanger yourself and Willi by even telling me all this." Her head was spinning so much that she leaned against one of the lab tables and closed her eyes. "I am so afraid for you."

"Don't you see? If we can get others to stand against the Reich, then we can save dozens—perhaps hundreds—of lives. I have seen your courage, Beth, your fierce determination to do the right thing even to your own detriment. I do not have your courage, but I think together we could make a difference—a real difference."

"I have done nothing."

He picked up the card and waved it in front of her. "You have given Anja and Benjamin and their children back their lives, Beth. You have given them the opportunity to start over, to find safety and a new home. That is not nothing." He hooked his forefinger under her chin and forced her to meet his impassioned gaze. "Think of it. We could make that kind of difference for others."

"By writing little treatises like that one?" She jerked her head toward his briefcase.

"Exactly. That may appear to be no more than words on paper to you, but for true German patriots, those words are a signal. They are not alone, and the time has come for them to remain silent no longer in the face of the travesty this regime is making of our nation."

He was whispering now, glancing furtively at the door whenever there was the sound of voices or footsteps in the corridor. "And we are not alone, Beth. The White Rose has had contact with others in Berlin who were part of another group—larger and more direct in their actions. The government labeled them the 'Red Orchestra' because of what they believe to be the group's communist leanings. Many of them have been arrested. But there are still some. . . ."

With each new fact that Josef flung at her, Beth's head spun with the implications and the sheer madness of everything he was telling her. People who opposed the Third Reich were dealt with harshly— even Josef's so-called *good Germans*. This was not the same as helping a single person or family now and then. This was *treason*. Yet. . .

"I have to go," she muttered as she stepped away from him and held up her hands to prevent him from coming any closer. "I have to think. I have to pray. I have to. . ."

Josef nodded and remained standing near his desk even as she backed away from him. "Will you come for dinner?"

"I don't know, Josef. Please. . ."

He hastily scribbled something on a piece of paper and laid it on the lab table that separated them. "This is my parents' address. I won't pressure you, Beth. My mother will expect you at six. If you are not there, I will simply tell my parents that you have decided to return to your home in America."

He sat down heavily in his desk chair facing away from her, his shoulders slumped in defeat.

"How can you be two places at once? You said you intended to attend that meeting and—"

"I will go there later."

"And if I decide to come for dinner?"

He did not say anything for so long that she thought perhaps he had not heard her. Finally he turned and looked at her. "Then hopefully you will allow me to walk home to the professor's with you, and you will then tell me what you have decided staying will mean."

"Either I stay and join you and the others or. . . ?"

"Or you stay to care for your aunt and Liesl because surely now you understand that Ilse's fears are very real." His gaze locked on hers. "And whatever your primary reason for remaining here in Munich, hopefully you will stay because you wish to be with me as I wish to be with you."

After she left Josef, Beth walked for hours trying to think through all that he had said. To stay or to leave. Going home was a tempting possibility—no, it was something she could actually do. Josef's father had seen to that. But when she thought of Siggy and especially of Anja and the children, she knew that she would never be content to be safely back on the farm while there had to be hundreds—perhaps thousands—of people like Siggy and Anja just that tiny step away from living without fear.

And then there was Josef.

From the day she had first seen him standing in the doorway of her uncle's study, she had felt the power of his personality. His quiet certainty. The way he had looked at her with those deep-set eyes as if seeking answers only she might have. And now all these weeks later, what she felt for him was so much more complicated. She had never truly been in love, but if wanting—needing—to be where he was no matter the circumstances was love, then there really was no choice.

It was true that she could go back to America and work to save people like Siggy and Anja. But Josef would not be there. He would be here trying to save the country he loved by distributing essays that could eventually get him arrested and tried for treason.

The very idea that she might never see him again—might never hear his laugh, feel the touch of his hand on hers, feel his very nearness in the dark of an air-raid shelter—was simply unacceptable.

She would stay. The sense of peace and calm that settled over her made her certain that she had listened to God's still, quiet voice guiding her from within.

Dining with Josef's parents was several steps higher on the social ladder than the informal and simple suppers with plain, hearty food that Beth was accustomed to sharing with her German family. From the moment she arrived at the address Josef had given her, she was well aware that she was about to enter a world that was so very different from the one she had come to know since moving to Munich.

Certainly she had seen houses like the Buch mansion before. Unlike the apartment-over-shop structures that crowded together in her neighborhood, the homes in Harlaching sat separated from one another by expansive lawns and flower gardens. The gardens were dormant and covered in snow. But even the snow seemed a cut above the gray piles turned to slush that shopkeepers had shoveled away from their doors. The snow here was pristine—untouched by a human footprint and as white as. . .well, snow, Beth thought.

She smiled and felt herself relax slightly as she continued her way up the front walk toward the double doors of the front entrance to the house. As she would have expected, the windows were dark, the blackout curtains and shades blocking any light that might have ebbed out onto the lawn. But the night sky was clear, and a three-quarter moon provided enough light so she had no trouble at all making her way up the stone steps to a covered portico.

In the distance a clock chimed six. She was precisely on time, and somehow she thought that might actually impress Josef's father. Before the last stroke of the clock, she pressed the bell. As she waited for someone to open the door, she touched her hair and the collar of her coat to be sure both were reasonably presentable.

She was about to press the doorbell a second time when she heard footsteps coming toward her from the other side of the heavy door. She folded her hands in front of her, clutching her purse, and pasted a smile on her face just as the door swung open.

"*Guten Abend*, Fräulein Bridgewater." The man welcoming her was not Josef or his father but rather a servant—or at least she thought he must be a servant. He looked like a character out of a Rosalind Russell movie, and he treated her as if she were royalty. He helped her remove her coat and placed it over his crooked arm. She glanced around for slippers so she could leave her shoes by the door, as was the custom in every German home she had ever visited.

"Your footwear will be fine," the man said in a voice so quiet that Beth thought she might have actually willed him to reassure her. She wiped her shoes on the small rug anyway.

"If you will follow me," the man said and actually gave her a little bow before leading the way up a wide staircase to the main floor. When they reached a pair of beautifully polished wooden doors, the servant slid them apart to expose a room that took Beth's breath away.

It was easily the size of her uncle's sitting room, study, and kitchen combined. The high ceiling was striped with heavy dark wood beams, and from one of them hung a chandelier of black wrought iron with lights shaped like candle flames. A table surrounded by a dozen heavy mahogany chairs dominated the center of the room, but a matching sideboard was almost as impressive. The table was covered in a beautiful ivory-colored lace cloth, and places were set for the four of them with crystal stemware, china in a delicate floral design, and flatware that Beth had to believe was actual silver. Two matching candelabra with lighted candles had been positioned on either end of a low centerpiece of multicolored roses.

"Fräulein Bridgewater," the man who had answered the door intoned. All eyes turned to her.

The woman crossed the room, her high heels clicking on the wooden floor. "Danke, Gustav," she acknowledged the man, and as he nodded and left the room, she turned her attention to Beth. "So you are the young lady my son has been telling us about." She took Beth's hand and gently tugged her into the room. "I believe you have already met my husband."

"Guten Abend, Frau Buch. Herr Buch," Beth murmured.

"Fräulein," Josef's father replied. "May I offer you a glass of *Weihenstephaner Hefeweissbier?*"

"A fine Bavarian ale," Josef explained as he came to stand next to her.

"Yes, our son insists we cling to the old ways," Frau Buch said with a fond smile at Josef. "He's Bavarian to the core, this one."

Herr Buch handed her a tall glass filled with a golden liquid crowned with an inch of cream-colored foam. "Heil Hitler," he said, his eyes never leaving her face as he raised his glass in a toast.

"Oh for heaven's sake, Detlef," his wife said, her smile now forced. "Must we bring politics to the table tonight?" She turned to face Beth and raised her glass. "To Elizabeth Bridgewater," she said, "the woman who seems to have captured my son's heart."

"Mother, you're embarrassing Beth," Josef said, but they all drank to her—even Herr Buch.

"Thank you," she said after taking a sip of the beer and hoping she didn't now have a foamy mustache lining her upper lip. "It is my honor to be in your home."

Gustav entered the room with a small silver tray balanced on one open palm. "*Obazda?*" he said as he offered a small china plate with the cheese and herb concoction.

"It looks delicious." She juggled the plate and a napkin along with the glass of the ale. But the plate tipped, and in her haste to right it, the appetizers spilled off the plate onto the Oriental rug and under the large table. "Oh," Beth squeaked and set her plate and glass on a corner of the table as she bent to retrieve the food. The truth was that she was so embarrassed that she would have happily crawled under the massive table and remained there for the duration of the evening.

"Never mind," Josef's mother said immediately. "Our dog is more efficient than the best vacuum cleaner when it comes to searching out and devouring whatever ends up on the floor." The way she delivered this news made Beth feel as if food rolling off plates and onto the floor was a regular occurrence, and she realized that she liked Frau Buch very much. "Do you have pets, Beth?"

As she raised this question, the hostess placed a duplicate appetizer on Beth's plate and handed her that and the napkin, leaving the beer sitting where Beth could easily reach it.

"Back home," Beth began and saw Herr Buch's thick eyebrows narrow. "In America," she added, "our family has always had a menagerie of cats and dogs and once a rabbit in addition to the livestock we keep as part of the farm."

"Chickens and cows and such?"

"And horses," Beth said. "I have my own horse—or I did when I—"

"Beth has been here in Munich for eight years," Josef said.

"Why you must have been a mere child when you arrived," Frau Buch said.

"I was seventeen."

"By now you are practically a native then," Frau Buch said. "Isn't that right, Detlef?"

"If you and our son say so," he replied with an enigmatic smile at Beth.

Josef's mother continued to direct the conversation, asking Beth questions about her parents and her brothers and their families. "You must miss them all so very much," she sighed.

"I do."

"And yet you have remained here in spite of the changing times," Herr Buch said.

The man was baiting her, waiting and watching from his place in the shadows where the light from the chandelier did not quite reach.

"My aunt is not well." Beth turned her attention to Frau Buch, ignoring Josef's father. "She has been ill for several years now since the birth of her daughter. I would very much like to go home to my parents and siblings, but in our faith we place the greater good of the group ahead of our own personal wants."

"You and your family follow the traditions of the Religious Society of Friends, do you not?"

"That's right." Beth wondered if it was Josef or his father who had provided this information.

Josef's father took a step toward her. "From what I know of your beliefs, it would appear that they have much in common with Herr Hitler's doctrine of Service before Self."

"I don't understand."

"In your faith," he continued, "do you not place the needs of the entire community above the needs of the individual?"

"That is not exactly—"

"I'm sure we could debate the semantics of the matter, Fräulein. But the fact is that our philosophies are similar. We Germans are dedicated to placing the good of our country above our own personal and selfish desires."

"Oh my goodness, Detlef," Frau Buch said without a trace of embarrassment, "come down off your soapbox. It is just us—no need to crow the party line here."

Beth was shocked at the woman's directness and even more shocked when she saw Josef's father smile as he took a sip of his beer.

"Frau Buch, you have such a lovely home," Beth said, trying to come up with some topic of conversation that held little possibility of leading to further debate about her religion or politics.

Josef's mother smiled wistfully. "When I was a girl, we were so very poor even before the war—that war," she amended with a flicker of a glance at her husband. "It's because of my past that we have all of this," she added, waving her hand to encompass the fine furnishings of the room. "It's shameful, I know, especially when there are so many people who are struggling but..."

Her voice trailed off, and for the first time all evening, she seemed less than sure of herself. Herr Buch stepped to her side and put his hand on her cheek. "You deserve beautiful things, my dear."

But did she? Did anyone when, as Josef's mother had pointed out, there were others suffering? Beth thought of Anja and her family, and suddenly she felt as if the expansive walls with their fine paintings were closing in around her. She gripped the high back of the nearest dining chair.

"Are you all right?" Josef asked as he relieved her of the glass that was in danger of tipping. Once again all eyes turned to her.

"We should eat," Herr Buch announced. He had a way of speaking that left little room for discussion or debate. He did not raise his voice, and yet his words were delivered with undeniable authority.

"Of course," his wife said and signaled the servant to clear away the plates and glasses from the appetizers. "Beth, please take this place across from Josef."

Josef pulled the chair away from the table for Beth while his father did the same for his mother. Beth studied the array of polished sterling flatware lined up to either side of her plate. She knew enough to realize that every utensil represented a separate course for the meal. Across from her she saw that Josef was also looking at the elaborate place setting and lavish meal set out for them.

"I don't know, Mother," he said with a grin, "if we eat all of this, what are the chances that we'll be able to move for hours? We don't want to be the cause of Beth being out past curfew."

Where Beth's aunt would have taken the comment for criticism, Josef's mother simply smiled. "I happen to have influence with someone who can extend the curfew for our guest if it suits him to do so," she said and winked at her husband.

The look of pure adoration that Herr Buch gave his wife was something that Beth had never seen pass between two people other than her parents. For all of his stern demeanor, Josef's father adored his wife. And if he was capable of such utter devotion for one human being, might he not find it in his heart to have compassion even for those he did not know?

As he did for me in getting me a new visa?

Beth's spirits swelled with hope rather than the usual dread she felt in the presence of persons of authority in the Third Reich. She understood now why God had led her to this table with these people.

She was meant to stay in Munich and continue the work she had begun when she rescued first Siggy and then Anja.

She relaxed for the first time all evening. She even engaged in the conversation led mostly by Josef's mother as they worked their way through each course. Finally when dessert had been served and real coffee poured, Beth cleared her throat and turned to face Josef's father.

"Herr Buch? If you agree, I would very much like to extend my stay in Munich to care for my aunt and my cousin." She could feel Josef's eyes on her and knew that he understood that she had made her decision. But her true reasons for wanting to stay went well beyond her desire to help her uncle and aunt. She would stay so that she could continue to seek out others in need and help them. She would stay because to return to the safety of the farm in Wisconsin knowing there were people like Siggy and Anja—terrified, hungry, destitute with no place to turn—would be unthinkable.

The silence that greeted her request was far more deafening than if Herr Buch had suddenly stood up and begun to shout at her the way Herr Hitler seemed inclined to do.

Josef's mother glanced from her son to her husband to Beth. "You wish to remain here when you could have safe passage home to your family in America?"

"I do. And earlier today, when he extended the invitation for dinner, Herr—"

Frau Buch smiled. "Well, well, well," she murmured softly. "Isn't that romantic?"

"You are an American, Fräulein," Herr Buch reminded her. "You must understand that the very fact that our country and yours are at war makes everything more difficult."

"Freunde do not believe that war is an answer," she said and remembered her aunt mocking her when she had made a similar comment the first night that Josef had moved into the attic.

"To be sure I am hearing you clearly, Fräulein, you wish to extend your stay because of your aunt's health issues in spite of the risk you take for yourself?"

"That's true."

"Really, Detlef," Josef's mother murmured, "you said yourself that she's been here long enough that she's practically a native. Her mother *is* a native, and surely that counts for something. Besides she is little more than a child herself—surely you cannot believe she poses any sort of threat to the Reich."

Herr Buch smiled at his wife as if she were the child. "You would be amazed at the kinds of mischief these so-called children can manage, my dear."

"That may be, but does not the government offer protection for Jews married to one of our own? And if we would do that for those people, then surely a good German. . ."

Beth cringed at the way the woman spoke the words *Jew* and *those people* as if such words left a bitter taste on her tongue. On the other hand she was certainly making the case for Beth to stay on in Munich. The debate between Josef's parents continued as Josef and Beth concentrated on eating. She realized that he was nearly as uncomfortable as she was, and that surprised her. It was the clearest evidence yet of how far his views about the war and the role of Germany in the world were from those shared by his parents.

"And what about Josef?" Frau Buch said quietly after a silence had fallen between her and her husband.

"What about Josef?" Herr Buch replied.

"I'm sitting right here."

Beth saw Josef's mother cast a look at her son—a look that instructed him to let her handle this. "Detlef, war or no war, these young people are attracted to one another—they may even love each other."

Josef ducked his head, and Beth blushed.

"They have only known each other for—"

"And tell me how will they know each other better if you send her back across an entire ocean?"

"I told her earlier today that I would look into the matter once she was absolutely certain of her decision."

"Well then, what are we debating?" Frau Buch raised her glass. "Clearly she has made her choice, and frankly this calls for a celebration."

Everyone raised the china cups that Gustav had just filled with coffee—*real* coffee that Beth could not help but savor. "To Beth and her dedication to her Bavarian family," Frau Buch said.

Beth focused on Josef's father. "Danke," she murmured, and the man acknowledged her gratitude with a slight nod.

Josef stood up. "It's getting late, and Beth needs to get back." He placed his napkin next to his coffee cup and bent to kiss his mother's cheek as he came around the table. "It was a lovely meal," he said, pulling Beth's chair away from the table so she could rise as well.

The elder Buchs stood when she did, and once again Josef's mother took hold of Beth's hands. "Do come back any time."

"I would like that," Beth replied and realized that she meant it. She turned to Josef's father. "I do appreciate all that you—"

"I will take care of the matter, Fräulein. In the meantime may I suggest that you prepare your Munich relatives for your departure? In case I cannot work miracles."

"I understand." Standing so close to Josef's father, she could not help but notice that the eyes she had thought cold and aloof were in fact lined with weariness. She understood that in spite of his sumptuous surroundings, the access to luxuries such as coffee, and the power to determine another person's future, this man had paid a toll for his involvement in the war. "Thank you both."

Downstairs in the large foyer, Josef held her coat for her before putting on his overcoat and accepting the gloves the servant handed him. Gustav switched off the lamp so that when Josef opened the door there would be no light spilling from the house.

Outside Josef took hold of her hand as he ushered her down the front walk. "There's still time, Beth, if you change your mind. It will only get more difficult for you," he warned.

"Are you staying?"

"I live here."

"And for the time being so do I. And I intend to make the best of that."

CHAPTER 9

Franz Schneider stayed close to the buildings as he made his way down the blocks of shops and apartments. If he saw anyone he knew, he could always duck into a doorway until the person passed by, or if confronted he could always claim that he'd gone out on some errand. It was well known in their neighborhood that Ilse suffered from a nervous condition that sometimes required him to seek a refill of medication from the chemist when the hour was this late and her condition was severe.

He turned up his collar and clutched his briefcase more tightly as he reached the street that would lead him home. The contents of that briefcase could get him arrested and probably killed. Yet he was willing to take that risk—for his family and for his country. For on this night, Franz had cast in his lot with the members of the White Rose. His former students, Hans Scholl and Christoph Probst, as well as Josef's friend Willi and Hans's younger sister, Sophie, were all part of the core group responsible for writing, printing, and distributing the leaflets.

He had also learned that his colleague Professor Kurt Huber was considering joining the group. The man was a vocal and devout supporter of the Nazi Party's platform. But perhaps he had come to understand—as others were finally beginning to—that Hitler and his men were renegades who did not feel obliged to follow the platform that had brought them to power.

At the meeting Hans and Sophie had argued in favor of expanding the operation beyond the distribution of their impassioned essays. There had been talk of joining forces with others involved in similar activities in Berlin. Some were members—those who had not yet been arrested—of a larger, more dynamic group that the Gestapo had labeled *Das Rote Kapelle* or the Red Orchestra. Hans had actually met with Falk Harnack, the brother of Arvid Harnack, one of the primary leaders of that doomed group.

News had reached those in the White Rose that Arvid and his American wife, Mildred, had both been arrested. At the meeting that Franz had just left, Hans had reported that he had learned that day of the brutal murder of Arvid Harnack. The man had been strangled and his body hung from a meat hook by the Gestapo. Further reports were that Mildred had been imprisoned.

Hearing that last news, all Franz could think about was Beth. Beth and the way she had given that young woman her exit visa without a single thought for her own safety. Beth, whose natural bent toward the American way of speaking her mind was increasingly dangerous in the current environment. Beth, who had sacrificed some of the best years of her life in order to stay in Munich and care for his wife and daughter.

That had decided him. He had to make certain that he saved her—even if he could not save his country. He owed her that much. He owed his sister that much.

"Ilse?" he called as soon as he entered the apartment. He set his briefcase on a stack of books in the foyer and hung up his overcoat and hat before changing into his slippers. From behind the closed door of the sitting room, he could hear music—a waltz. It was a good sign. If Ilse had turned on the gramophone, usually that meant that she was feeling better and perhaps even having a good evening.

When he entered the room, the only light was a small reading lamp on the table next to his chair. Ilse was in the other chair, her eyes closed, her mouth softened into a smile as if she might be enjoying a sweet dream. In sleep the stress and strain that had aged her beyond her years disappeared, and Franz stood looking at her for several long minutes.

He thought about the draft of a leaflet that he'd started to work on in hopes that perhaps the others in the White Rose might find it worthy of distribution. He thought about the dozen copies of an earlier leaflet that he'd offered to distribute. Just having those items in the house endangered them all. He must get rid of them, throw them into the fire of the kitchen stove. He was about to retrace his steps when Ilse stirred.

"Franz?" She blinked up at him sleepily. "What time is it?"

"It's late," he replied, setting the gramophone arm onto its resting place and switching off the machine.

"Is Beth home?"

"I don't know. I just came in."

"How was your meeting?" She smiled at him, one eyebrow cocked in that funny way she had of letting him know that she did not for one minute believe that he had attended a meeting at all.

"My meeting was fine," he reported. "Why are you so skeptical about where I was this evening?"

She shrugged. "I thought perhaps you had gone Christmas shopping in the market."

Franz chuckled. "You know full well that I do all my shopping on the twenty-third when I go to get our tree."

As Quakers they did not hold with many of the more secular trappings of the holiday. But Liesl's schoolmates were not Quakers, and they were always filled with excitement about the trees they would decorate or the gifts they would receive. For this and other reasons, Franz and Ilse had adopted the tradition of a decorated tree and opening gifts on Christmas Eve.

Ilse stretched her arms high above her head and then covered a yawn. And in that simple gesture, Franz saw the girl he had married— the beauty who had captured his heart.

He turned the gramophone back on and held out his arms to her. "Waltz with me, Ilse."

"Here? Now?"

"If not here, then where? And if not now, then when?"

With a shy smile she rose from the chair and came to him. She rested her head in the crook of his neck as they moved slowly in time to the music. Only when he felt moisture on the fabric of his shirt collar did he realize she was weeping.

As they walked back to the professor's apartment, it seemed only natural that Josef should take Beth's hand. She was wearing wool mittens that she had told him her mother had made for that first winter she'd spent in Munich. The mittens were of thick soft wool that was wearing thin after so many winters. He could feel the shape of her slender fingers nestled inside them.

"So you have decided to stay to care for your aunt and Liesl, have you?"

"That is one reason," she admitted.

"There is more?"

"I believe that helping people like Anja and her family is the true reason that I was sent here. Oh, at first I've no doubt that God's intention was for me to help my aunt and uncle and be a companion for Liesl. But now—I mean why would God have put me in contact with Siggy and then again with Anja and her family if it were not His plan that I should help others like them?"

"You could help them from America as well."

"How? The need is immediate. Siggy never would have been allowed to enter the United States without my visa. And Anja and her family had no time to wait for some agency to come to their aid."

"Sometimes you mystify me, Beth. You would risk your very life for these strangers?"

"We are all children of God, Josef."

They walked the rest of the block in silence, but as they approached the bakery—closed and shuttered for the night like all the businesses on their street—Josef stopped walking and rested his hands on Beth's shoulders. "My father cannot protect you, Beth. Even if he succeeds in getting you the extra time you want, you have to know that you will be under even greater scrutiny than you are now—the entire household will be."

"I know, and that is why you must help me keep them out of it—my aunt and uncle must know nothing of what I did for Anja or what I might be called on to do going forward. Promise me, Josef. Promise me that you will help me protect these good people—good Germans loyal to their country. Please, if you care at all for my uncle, say you will do this." She rested her gloved hand against his cheek.

Josef cradled her face in his hands and leaned in close. "I will do this not for your uncle, although I admire him a great deal. I will give you this promise, Beth, because when you asked my father to extend your visa and I realized that you had decided to stay, I thought my heart would quite literally take flight." He grinned at her. "To use an adage of the season, I was filled with great joy."

"Why should it matter so much to you?"

"My mother is a wise and observant woman, for I am in love with you, Beth. I have tried hard to restrain those feelings for some time now. I have told myself again and again that if I love you I should want you to be safe. But safety also meant that we would have to be an ocean apart—perhaps we would never see each other again. I admit that I am not so noble as to be willing to let that happen."

"So earlier when you told your father that you had feelings for me. . .that was not a lie?"

Instead of answering her, he kissed her, wrapping his arms around her and rejoicing in the realization that she was clinging to him as well. When reluctantly he pulled away, he ran his forefinger along the features of her face. "It was not a lie," he said and kissed her again. "*Ich liebe Dich.*"

"I. . ."

He silenced her by placing his finger against her lips. "You need time," he told her. "We are from different worlds, you and I, and right now our countries are locked in a bitter war that will have repercussions for decades to come no matter the outcome. So do not speak in haste, Beth. It is sufficient for me to know that you trust me enough to seek my help in keeping your family here safe."

He pulled out his key to the outer entrance to the building and was surprised when Beth giggled.

"What?"

"Well, you have now kissed me twice, but where is my handshake?"

"I forgot," he admitted. "I got so caught up in—"

This time she was the one to stop his words with a kiss, and immediately after she held out her hand for him to shake. He opened the door, and they stepped inside the building where they kissed again and then shook hands. They smothered their giggles as they climbed the stairs, stopping at each floor to repeat the ritual until they reached the fourth floor.

Josef unlocked the door to the apartment while Beth admonished him to be quiet. "They might be sleeping," she whispered, but she was still giggling and did not resist when he shut the apartment door and then pressed against her for one final kiss in the cluttered foyer before they went inside.

Caught off balance, Beth sent a pile of books and her uncle's briefcase tumbling to the floor. The contents spilled out, and as they both bent to set things right again, Josef spotted the leaflets bearing the distinctive style of the White Rose. As he hurriedly gathered the loose papers and stuffed them back inside the briefcase, he realized that there were pages of writing—several versions of the same topic—a call for all Germans to take a stand and join the White Rose.

If the professor had decided to join forces with the resistance group, how on earth was Josef supposed to keep his promise to watch over Beth?

"You go on inside in case they are still awake," he told Beth, relieving her of the papers she had retrieved before she noticed what they were. "Your aunt will worry that I am taking unfair advantage of your innocence," he added, hoping to restore the lightness they had shared on their way up the stairs. "I'll take care of this," he added as he stuffed the leaflets and notes back inside the briefcase.

The problem was that between Beth's determination to seek out more people in need of her help and the professor's decision to join the group and carry out some of the work despite a tendency toward absentmindedness, Josef had serious doubts that he could take care of anything.

Beth heard the closing strains of a waltz coming from the sitting room and then the scratch of the needle and amazingly her aunt's girlish laughter. She tapped at the door before opening it. "We're back."

Her aunt and uncle turned to her, and Aunt Ilse's smile faded at once. She stepped away from Uncle Franz, and Beth realized that they had been dancing. "I didn't mean to interrupt."

"Not at all," Uncle Franz said as he turned off the gramophone and indicated that they should all sit down. "How was the dinner?"

"Quite. . ." Beth searched for the best word and finally settled on, "interesting."

"Who was there?" Aunt Ilse asked.

"Just Josef and his parents."

"And where is Josef?"

"I am here, Herr Professor," Josef said quietly as he stepped into the room and handed Uncle Franz the briefcase. "I thought you might want this. You left it in the foyer."

Suddenly there was a tension between the two men that Beth could not identify. She knew only that all trace of the light-hearted laughter she and Josef had shared had evaporated. And the romantic moment she had obviously interrupted between her aunt and uncle had disappeared as well.

Uncle Franz took the briefcase and briefly fingered the closings before setting it on the floor next to his chair. "I heard the music and discovered this lovely lady waiting for me to ask her to dance," he said. But his smile was forced, and his gaze remained locked with Josef's.

"Beth was just about to tell us about the evening she shared with your parents," Aunt Ilse said.

"Your niece certainly charmed my mother," Josef replied, turning his attention away from the professor.

"And your father?" Aunt Ilse asked.

Beth could not have been more shocked if her aunt had asked Josef if he had in fact moved in with them to spy on them.

Josef smiled. "My father is not so easily captivated," he admitted. "Yet I believe that it would be fair to say that he admires Beth and her devotion to you."

"I have news," Beth added. "It is not yet official, but I asked Josef's father if he could help get permission for me to stay in Munich for a little longer."

"How long?" Uncle Franz asked.

"That's difficult to say." Beth shrugged.

"I don't understand. You have permission to leave—to go home to America—and you have requested. . .you have asked this man. . . ." Ilse could barely find her voice much less the words to express her shock.

"Tante Ilse, I am worried about you—and Liesl. You have lost weight, and you aren't sleeping, and—"

"Do you not see that in asking this man for a favor you have—"

Uncle Franz cleared his throat loudly, drawing Aunt Ilse's attention to the fact that Josef was standing there.

"My father is a good German—a good and decent man, Frau Schneider," Josef said as he opened the door that led to the front hallway. "I have another appointment, so I will wish you all a good night," he added just before the door closed behind him and they heard him leave the apartment, the echo of his shoes on the stairs outside fading away.

The silence that followed obliterated any evidence of the rare respite from the strains of life in a war zone that they had all enjoyed earlier.

"Why are you doing this?" Aunt Ilse asked Beth.

"Because you would do the same for me."

"Still to make such a request of Herr Buch—to do such a thing without first seeking the counsel of a clearness committee. . ."

"There is no one left to serve on such a committee," Beth reminded her aunt. "You, Uncle Franz, and me—the others have all gone elsewhere."

Aunt Ilse chewed on her lower lip as she stared into space. Then she looked up at her husband. "Nevertheless we should consider this in prayer and silence—the three of us. We should seek guidance. After all, even if Josef's father is successful in getting Beth the extension, that does not mean she cannot change her mind and go, does it?"

"I'm afraid if Herr Buch goes to the trouble of—"

"Herr Buch is not God," Aunt Ilse interrupted. "We must not allow ourselves to be guided by his decisions."

"I agree," Beth replied. Her aunt's face was splotched red, a sure sign that she was working herself into an episode that might well require medication to control. "Let us consider the matter together and in silence."

For the next few hours the three of them sat in their separate chairs, their eyes closed, their hands either folded or lying open on their knees. Once Aunt Ilse rose as if to speak, stood for a long moment, and then sat down again. Beside her Beth's uncle rested his elbows on his knees, his head bowed.

As the hours wore on, Beth was aware that Josef had returned and gone straight up to his room. She could hear the creak of a floorboard as he apparently paced back and forth. The clock on the mantelpiece ticked off the minutes and hours as they waited for clarity in the matter of Beth's decision to stay or to go.

As the first rays of dawn found their way through a small pinpoint hole in the blackout curtains, Aunt Ilse stood. This time she spoke without any hesitation. "I am considering that, with Beth's help, over the next few months I might find my strength again—enough so that she could be safely returned to her parents and brothers. It is for me that she has stayed so long. She has practically raised Liesl, and I have allowed this. It is not—as I had first thought—her American rashness that keeps her here. What keeps her here is her kindness and concern—and my weakness."

She sat down again and resumed her posture of silent prayer and meditation. After several moments had passed, Uncle Franz stood. He spoke as if to a group of several people and as if their Quaker family were still all together instead of scattered across Europe.

"I cannot deny that it gives me great comfort knowing that Beth is here when I am away attending to my duties at the university. These are unsettled and unsettling times for us all, and we have come to rely on Beth's indomitable spirit to help us keep in mind that the challenge of making difficult choices is a part of every life. I believe that Beth has considered carefully this difficult choice and that she has been led to this decision—not by others but by God."

Normally the clerk of the congregation would wait for everyone who was moved to speak to do so and then either announce a consensus of opinion about the matter before them or—if there was no agreement among the group—table it for further discussion at some future time. But there was no clerk—no one designated to declare a consensus. Beth waited in silence. The pacing above them had ceased without her being aware of its absence until now, she realized. She hoped that Josef had finally gotten some rest.

Her uncle cleared his throat. "Then it is decided. Assuming Herr Buch can make the necessary arrangements to extend the expiration of her visa, Beth will remain here with us for the time being."

Beth took in a deep breath and slowly blew it out. She had not given them the whole story of why she had decided to stay. But God knew why she wanted to stay on, and she had to believe that if that had not been His plan for her then her aunt and uncle would have come to entirely different conclusions when they spoke.

"Let's start some breakfast," Aunt Ilse said, taking Beth's hand. "Liesl will be up soon, and Josef mentioned something about the need to arrive early for his morning rounds."

As Beth reached for the aprons she and Ilse kept on hooks behind the kitchen door, her uncle opened the blackout curtains, filling the room with the sunshine of a new day.

~≋ CHAPTER 10 ≋~

Later that day after Josef returned from his rounds at the hospital, the professor invited him into his study. Josef prepared himself for the man's usual excitement over some reference or study he had discovered that might help Josef in his research. The last thing he expected was that Beth's uncle would hand him a copy of the incriminating leaflet that had fallen out of his briefcase the night before.

Franz pointed to the paper that Josef held. "Seeing these in my briefcase last night is the reason you so carefully repacked the contents and presented the briefcase to me. I got the message." He sank into a chair and sighed heavily as he drummed his fingers on the threadbare arm of the overstuffed wingback. "So, what are we to do? I want so much to take a stand, yet I am so obviously bad at subterfuge."

Josef's mind raced as he imagined all of the ramifications if the wrong person had discovered the contents of that briefcase. "Tell me how these papers came to be in your briefcase in the first place."

A wry but weary smile passed over the older man's lips. "You have learned your lesson well, Josef. First consider the facts. . . ."

"You taught me that lesson. Assume nothing until you have gathered all the evidence. Only then make a diagnosis. I am simply following your instruction."

"You want evidence then. Very well. I attended the meeting. The others were busy preparing to leave for the holidays, but they were also full of talk about expanding the scope of our distribution. I offered to take several leftover copies of an earlier leaflet and place them in strategic locations."

"And the notes?"

The professor studied him for a long moment. "I have been working on the draft of a new leaflet—jotting down some thoughts."

"Surely you know the danger, Professor—not just to you but for your family, for Beth."

Franz shrugged. "It is for them that I have joined this cause—for them and for my country." He picked up another copy of the leaflet. "And unless you are the spy in our midst that my wife fears you to be, you agree that the work is important—vital for the future of Germany?"

"I do."

Franz smiled and got a faraway look in his eyes. "Do you know what I find most appealing about these young people?"

"Their enthusiasm? Their certainty?"

"There are those things, of course. But it is the lack of appointed leaders that is the greatest part of their appeal. We Freunde also do not have a hierarchy of official or even unofficial posts." He looked at Josef and leaned forward so that they were very close together. "And will you involve my beloved niece in our cause—is that truly the reason she has decided to stay?"

Josef was surprised by the professor's sudden shift in topic. But he respected the man far too much to dance around the question. "I have asked her to work with me mostly so that I can keep her safe. If she is distributing leaflets, then she cannot be doing things such as giving away her visa." He stated this with the firm assurance that there could be no argument with his reasoning.

Again the professor smiled. "Ah, but Josef, you do not yet know her. She knows no bounds when it comes to her concern for those she feels are weaker and unable to help themselves. She is brave to a fault."

"But surely you would not allow—"

"I cannot stop her, and neither can you. For that reason alone you must think carefully about any decision you make to take action against the government that involves her. For she is falling in love with you, Josef, and whither thou goest so will she."

Josef knew that Franz was right. He stared unseeing at the words on the paper he held. "There was a book I read once," he mused. "*Les Miserables* by Victor Hugo. His story was set in France—a group of students...."

The professor nodded. "I know the story. They believed the people would rise up and overthrow the corrupt government. In the end no one came to fight with them. In the end most of them died for their lost cause." He folded the leaflet he held into precise thirds. "One can only hope that in reality the outcome will not be the same. Although there is evidence that it could be worse—so much worse...." He told Josef about the news of Arvid Harnack's grisly death. "And Josef, they have imprisoned that man's wife—an American from Beth's home state of Wisconsin." He did not need to say more.

Josef picked up the slim stack of leaflets. "Let me take care of these while you destroy any notes you've made for a new leaflet."

"I volunteered to deliver...."

Josef smiled and held onto the papers. "My Christmas gift to you. And speaking of Christmas, I was going to ask Beth to go with me to the market today. It's the perfect opportunity to get these delivered and out of your possession. We could take Liesl along as well."

"No, not Liesl. If someone—"

"You're right. But holiday or not, we need to get these out of your possession as soon as possible. Even in today's Germany, one has to hope there is still a soft spot in even the hardest of hearts for a man and a woman in love out shopping for the holidays."

Franz nodded and then grasped Josef's forearm. "Be careful."

Beth felt a rush of pleasure when Josef invited her to go with him to the Christkindlmarkt, Munich's popular Christmas market.

"Me too," Liesl shouted.

"Nein, Liebchen," Franz said before Beth could agree. "I have a special job I need your help with. We must get a tree today."

"But I want to go to the market," the girl whined, her lower lip beginning to quiver.

"Now, Fräulein Liesl," Josef said, "think about it. If you come with us, then how am I supposed to find that surprise I promised would be for you under the tree tomorrow night?"

Beth noticed that he did not cater to the child. Instead he just kept eating his lunch as he made his point, speaking to her as if she were mature enough to understand the situation.

Liesl's lower lip was still extended in a sullen pout, but she was no longer on the verge of a tantrum. "I could close my eyes while you shop," she suggested.

Josef appeared to give this serious consideration, but then he shook his head and went back to eating. "No. There will be packages, and you might guess from the shape of them. And well, as much as I would be delighted to have you along, I just think not this time."

Beth's aunt and uncle waited, their eyes on their plates, and Beth assumed that like her, they were anticipating a flood of tears and wailing from Liesl.

"Next time then?" the girl bargained.

"How about tomorrow?" Josef proposed. "You can help me choose a gift for your cousin here. After all if she is with me today I can hardly—"

Liesl broke into a wide grin. "I know just the perfect thing," she assured him in a stage whisper, and she actually winked at the man.

"You certainly have a way with children," Beth said later as the two of them set out for the market. "In eight years of being around Liesl, I have never seen anyone disarm her the way you did."

Josef grinned. "You women are easily disarmed," he teased.

"Oh, really? You are casting me in the same league with an eight-year-old child?"

"You, your aunt, my mother. . . You simply want to have your way. The trick is to find the path that allows that without surrendering the principle at hand."

She laughed and punched his arm playfully. "I knew you were arrogant, Herr Doktor Buch, but this goes beyond. . ."

He lowered his voice even as he smiled at other shoppers they passed along the way. "Take you, for example. Your primary reason for wanting to remain in my country is because you believe that you can help others—your aunt and Liesl, of course, but also people like Anja and your friend Siggy."

"You are changing the subject." She did not want to lose the lighthearted spirit of the conversation.

"I am because it proves my point. In principle I do not agree with your plan to continue to risk your life to help people who are virtually strangers to you. And so I have proposed an alternate plan, the same way I did with Liesl earlier."

"You are speaking in riddles, Josef," Beth said and hated the tone of petulance that colored her words. Who was sounding like a spoiled child now?

"I am not. I have already pointed out to you that there is a way that you could help others—a great many others—that would not carry with it the danger you risked in helping Anja and her family."

Beth felt the familiar shudder that went through her every time she considered how many times over the course of their interactions with that family that they all might have been arrested, taken for questioning, imprisoned. . .or worse. "I know what you want us to do, Josef, but. . ."

"We have our first assignment."

"You mean. . . ?" She knew better than to repeat the name of the group aloud. Even in the crowded marketplace, anyone might overhear her utter the words *White Rose*. "And that is?"

Josef glanced around where shoppers pressed close to them, examining the wares. "It's cold. How about some *Glühwein*?" Without warning he veered away from the bustling stalls of the market and headed instead toward the Gasthaus they had gone to with Willi after the concert. Once inside he took her coat and waited for her to be seated at a table. Then he hung their coats on hooks near the door and placed the newspaper he'd been carrying from the time they left the apartment on the windowsill behind the coat rack. After the waiter took their order and left them alone Josef leaned in close, his fingers tenderly stroking her cheek.

"Listen carefully," he said, his voice low and intimate, but in his eyes she saw that same fierce intensity that she had noticed that first day she met him. "Underneath that newspaper is a copy of that item we were discussing—the one in my lab? When we have finished our wine, we will leave, but the newspaper will remain here."

He continued to stroke her cheek, leaning back only when the waiter delivered their order. Beth was speechless and glad for the interruption. Once the waiter left, she wrapped her fingers around the mug filled with the fragrant spiced liquid and murmured, "So while the others have all left for the holidays you. . ."

"I am helping a friend."

"What kind of friend?"

"Your uncle."

The idea that mild-mannered Uncle Franz might do anything so brazen as to join forces with some rebel group was so ridiculous Beth laughed. "Now you are teasing me and it is cruel to—"

His expression told her he was speaking the truth. She gasped. "What can he be thinking? Aunt Ilse. . . Oh Josef, we cannot allow. . . ."

Suddenly Josef was smiling, and his eyes actually twinkled mischievously. "Drink your wine. We have shopping to do." Now he was speaking in a hearty and normal tone as if he wanted others to hear him.

"Will you buy me a present then?" she asked, her own voice loud enough that patrons at neighboring tables glanced their way and smiled.

Josef caressed her cheek. "Presents—lots and lots of them," he promised.

"Then we'd best get started," she teased as she made a show of finishing her wine and stood up.

Josef followed her lead, finishing his wine and then helping her on with her coat. They linked arms and left, but the newspaper stayed where Josef had placed it. Not one of the patrons or staff seemed to notice.

"Do you think someone will find it—the leaflet?" Beth asked as soon as they were safely on their way to the market.

"We can hope so. Furthermore we can hope that whoever finds it will read it and feel inspired to take a stand—perhaps copy the words and pass them on to others. That's the only way this will work, Beth."

They held hands as they strolled along looking at the various wares in each booth at the market. Josef bought gifts for Franz, Ilse, and Liesl and then led the way to a nearby park where they could speak more freely.

"I understand why you might wish to get involved in all this, Josef. You love your country and you—"

"But you are wondering why I have involved you?"

She nodded.

"Two reasons. If you and I distribute these leaflets, then your uncle won't have to." He sighed heavily. "The professor's inattention to small matters—the way he left his briefcase lying open in the foyer the other night as one example—is bound to catch up to him eventually."

She could not deny that. "You said there were two reasons."

"I believe that, politics aside, you hate this war as much as I do. What if we could help bring it to an end, Beth?"

"We are two insignificant players in this time and place, Josef. All we can do is—"

"Pray? Does God not expect His people to act on those prayers? Does He not lead us to follow His way to make a better world?"

She took her time before speaking again. Obviously her uncle had considered very carefully the action he had taken in agreeing to unite with this band of resistors and join in their work. Quakers were not political, and he would never do such a thing unless he had prayed long and hard on the matter. "Very well, I will join you in this work. But there is one thing you need to understand, Josef Buch. I am not a child that you can manipulate as you did Liesl. I can do this *and* save someone like Anja again should God see fit to bring that person to my attention."

On the morning of Christmas Eve, Liesl was awake before dawn, her excited chatter filling the small room she shared with Beth.

"It's snowing," she crowed triumphantly. "I prayed that it would, and look, Beth." She pulled back the blackout curtain, exposing the small window that overlooked the courtyard below.

Beth stood behind her cousin, wrapping her arms around the girl's thin shoulders as together they watched fat snowflakes drift past the window and turn the scene outside to a wonderland. The radiator hissed and clanked but put out little heat.

"Let's get dressed and go outside," Liesl said. "We can be in the middle of it all before others can walk through and spoil it with their footprints and shovels."

"What about *our* footprints?" Beth teased, tweaking her cousin's nose.

Liesl paused, then began pulling her snow pants on over her pajamas. "I hadn't thought of that." She frowned, but she brightened at once. "But we will still be the first to leave footprints."

Beth laughed and hurried to get dressed. "We must be very quiet," she whispered when they stepped into the hallway. "Your parents are still sleeping."

They tiptoed past the kitchen, and Liesl stopped. "Let's go wake Josef," she whispered, and before Beth could object, the girl had bounded halfway up the stairs to the attic. "Josef!" she hissed. "Josef!"

"Shhh," Beth said as she tugged at Liesl's sleeve. "Let him sleep. He was so late at the hospital last night."

"Who is that making such a racket?" Josef mumbled as he leaned over the banister, his chin showing the stubble of whiskers, his eyes heavy with sleep. But he was grinning down at them, and Beth realized that she was thinking that this is the way he would look if they were married and woke up together. She ducked her head to hide her blush.

"It's snowing," Liesl said in her normal voice, and then she giggled and softened her tone to a whisper. "Right this minute. Come on." And assuming that Josef would do her bidding, she hurried back down the stairs and on to the front door. "Schnell," she urged as she squatted on the floor and pulled on her boots.

By the time she had them on and fastened, Josef had joined them. He hopped on one foot and then the other as he pulled on his military boots, hooked Liesl's ice skates over his shoulder, and then held out his arms, inviting them to link theirs with his. "Ladies, shall we go?"

The three of them made their way down the four flights of stairs to the courtyard, giggling and whispering all the way. Liesl set the tone with her questions and guesses about what the package with her name on it from Josef might contain.

"I think I know what you got for me," he teased.

"You'll never guess in a million years."

"Oh, I might. It's long and thin. . . ."

Liesl glanced up at Beth with a worried frown.

"I'm pretty sure it's a giraffe," Josef announced.

"A giraffe? Where would I get a giraffe?"

"It's not a giraffe then?"

"No. That's just silly."

"Oh, you have gotten me something serious then." Josef pretended to consider the possibilities, stroking his chin. "Could it be a book?"

"No. It's too thin to be a book," Liesl reminded him.

The game continued as the three made their way through the deserted streets to the park. All the while Beth kept recalling how wonderful Josef had been with Anja's children, telling them stories, tucking them into bed the three nights they had spent in the attic. He would make such a wonderful father.

She shook off the thought. What was the matter with her? First she was thinking about them married and waking up together, and now she had advanced their future to include children. It had to be the season and the surroundings, for certainly the snow falling on deserted streets, covering the rooftops, and sparkling in the rising sun made everything seem as if they were walking through a fairyland—living in a fairy tale where happy endings were assumed.

But this was Germany in 1942 with a war that was slowly turning against Josef's beloved fatherland if reports heard in secret from the British Broadcasting Company could be believed. This was reality.

When they reached the park, Josef helped Liesl with her skates and then swept the snow off a park bench at the edge of the rink so that he and Beth could sit and watch her. It always surprised Beth to see what an accomplished skater her cousin was. Off the ice her movements were awkward and ungainly, but on the ice she seemed to take flight, her face raised to the sky, her arm outstretched, and her lips parted in a smile.

"Look at her," Beth said to Josef. "She's so graceful."

Josef nodded. "The picture of innocence," he agreed, but there was an undertone to his words that made Beth turn to him.

"That's good, isn't it? I mean she's still so very young and perhaps once the war ends. . ."

"Once the war ends, Beth, she will still be German, and she will pay the price for our government's arrogance and cruelty to others the same as every other German regardless of their age for generations to come."

"You think Germany will lose?"

He shrugged. "Even if we should be victorious, we have already lost." He took hold of her hand. "But we will not speak of such things on this day. It is Christmas Eve. *Frohe Weihnachten*," he said, his voice husky as he leaned in to kiss her.

His lips—chilled by the winter cold—warmed quickly, and as he held her close and lightly kissed her cheeks and eyelids and nose, she surrendered herself to the fantasy of a life with Josef. "Merry Christmas to you as well," she whispered when he pulled away.

"I have something to ask you," he said, his cheek resting against her temple as she sat huddled close to him, and together they watched Liesl skate. "I have thought about this a great deal—all through last night—and I don't want you involved in the White Rose after all. Just take care of your aunt and Liesl. Just be here so we can be together. The other? It's far too dangerous and. . ."

She sat up and stared at him, searching his eyes for answers. "You're giving up?"

"That's not what I said. It is dangerous for you—doubly so because you are American and no doubt being watched whether you know it or not. I am also going to try and persuade the professor to—"

"But you will continue to take the risks and place yourself in danger?"

He sucked in a deep breath and slowly blew it out. "I have thought this through carefully, Beth. I will have Christmas with you and your family and then move out after the New Year. By that time, Willi and the others will have returned from their holiday and the plan is—"

"No. And by the way, you said you had a question. Yet you are not *asking* me anything. You are telling me that this is what you want."

"Be reasonable. I am doing this for you—and the professor. For Frau Schneider and for Liesl. Surely you understand that."

"What I understand is that we are already involved—my uncle and me. What I understand is that you cannot protect us, so do not deny us the opportunity to do what we can to bring peace." *What I understand,* she thought but could not bring herself to say aloud, *is that I love you and want to be where you are no matter the danger.*

"You Americans can be so stubborn—and so naive," he muttered, his eyes now focused on Liesl without really seeing her.

"Do not go throwing around labels, Josef Buch. You Germans are every bit as determined to have your way or our countries would not be at war with one another."

Liesl glided across the ice and came to a stop in front of them. "Are you going to marry my cousin?" she demanded of Josef.

"Why do you ask?" It was evident that he was still upset with Beth but trying hard not to pass his emotions on to the girl.

"You kissed her. I saw. And Mama says when people kiss they are either married or about to be."

"Sometimes people kiss because they are good friends and happy to be together, Liesl," Beth said. "Because they want to be together no matter what." This last she added hoping that Josef would hear it for the remorse she felt at having quarreled with him.

Josef reached over and took her hand. "And sometimes," he added, "it's because the people have argued and need to make up. Like this." He leaned over and kissed Beth's cheek.

Liesl looked doubtful. "Before you kissed her on the mouth," she pointed out as she plopped down on the bench to remove her skates and put on her boots.

"So I did," Josef replied, and before Beth could stop him, he kissed her full on the lips. At the same time he gathered a handful of snow, and when he broke the kiss, he tossed it in Liesl's direction.

She giggled, and the snow fight was on, each of them finding protection behind a tree or the park bench as they hurled snowballs at each other. Before Beth realized it, Josef joined forces with Liesl, and the two of them came toward her, taking turns pelting her with the weapons that barely held together, so light and powdery was the snow.

"I surrender," she finally shouted, but when Josef turned to congratulate Liesl on their joint victory, Beth had her revenge. She scooped up snow and dumped it on his head. "We Americans," she said with a twinkle in her eyes, "are not only stubborn. We are also ingenious when it comes to winning." She took off running, knowing that Josef and Liesl would follow. After giving chase for several minutes, the three of them collapsed breathless in the snow.

"This is the best Christmas Eve I ever remember," Liesl said with a satisfied smile. "And the very best part? It's only just begun."

"Ja," Josef said as he took hold of Beth's hand. "I agree. The very best."

⟶⟩⟩ CHAPTER II ⟨⟨⟵

The almost-magical feeling surrounding the day continued well into the evening. Perhaps it was the fact that the streets were mostly deserted and the shops closed early. Perhaps it was the fact that there were no sirens or the drone of planes overhead. Perhaps it was the calming sound of church bells calling worshippers to evening services.

Whatever the explanation, the family embraced the calm that had settled over the city as they gathered for a special Christmas Eve supper. Aunt Ilse had placed favors—inexpensive miniature toys she had purchased at the market—at each person's place. A tiny doll dressed in Bavarian costume lay at Liesl's place; a book not much bigger than a postage stamp with the opening of Dickens' *A Christmas Carol* waited for Uncle Franz; and Beth found a small-scale American flag by her plate.

"Wherever did you find this?" Beth asked.

"I have my sources," Aunt Ilse replied with a smile. "Josef, there's a favor for you as well," she said.

Josef unwrapped the small package at his place to reveal a wooden train—each car no bigger than an inch and the engine, passenger car, and caboose all linked together with string.

"A train?" Uncle Franz said as he examined Josef's favor.

"Every boy loves a train," Aunt Ilse said, unable to restrain her natural defensiveness.

"I always wanted a train—as a boy," Josef said. "My father believed in more practical gifts."

The adults around the table fell silent. They were all a bit mystified as to why Josef had chosen to spend this special evening with them and not his own parents.

"I'm going to name my doll Lily," Liesl announced as she pretended to walk the tiny doll across the table. "Unless," she added with a sly look at her mother, "perhaps there might be another doll under the tree?"

"First we eat," her mother informed her. But she was smiling, and she ruffled her daughter's hair as she went to get the platter of sausages and cheeses that she and Beth had prepared for the meal. In addition, they enjoyed potato salad and applesauce and fat, yeasty pretzels that could be dipped into a special spicy mustard that their landlords in the bakery had sent.

"I could not eat another bite," Franz exclaimed after they had devoured the meal. He leaned back and patted his stomach as he gazed fondly at his wife.

"Me neither," Liesl announced, mimicking her father's actions and making them all laugh.

"Well then I suppose that I will simply have to throw out the *Guglhupf*," Aunt Ilse said. "I made your favorite with chocolate and nuts, and it won't keep until tomorrow."

"I have plenty of room," Josef announced.

"Me too," Beth agreed.

"And me," Liesl shouted as she hurried to clear away the dishes and bring bowls for the dessert.

"There is always room for your Guglhupf," Franz added.

Once they had eaten their dessert and the women had washed and dried the dishes while Josef and Franz made a fire in the sitting room, it was finally time to open the gifts that Liesl had been pinching and shaking most of the afternoon.

The small sitting room was made even smaller by the presence of a fragrant fir tree trimmed with a dozen tiny, white candles, each housed in a small brass holder that clipped to a branch of the tree. Precious glass ornaments from Aunt Ilse's youth and the silver tinsel that she carefully saved from year to year completed the decorations. As the youngest, Liesl had the job of handing out the gifts.

"This one is for you, Josef," she said, handing him a long, skinny package.

"Ah, my giraffe."

Liesl giggled. "It's not a giraffe—I told you."

Josef tore off the brown paper that Liesl had drawn pictures on for decoration to reveal the candy cane she had brought back from their skiing trip. "I love peppermint," Josef announced. "And all this for me? It's very special, Liesl. Thank you."

Liesl frowned. "You could share," she suggested, and everyone laughed.

"Tomorrow," Aunt Ilse said when Josef seemed about to begin breaking the stick candy into pieces. "We've had enough sweets for one night."

Liesl did not protest but turned back to the small stack of wrapped packages. "Papa," she said and handed him a gift—a pair of thick wool socks from his wife.

There followed the gifts that Liesl had chosen for her parents, a new hat for Beth from her aunt and uncle and Liesl, a package of tobacco from Beth for Uncle Franz, and a lavender shawl for Aunt Ilse. For Josef there was a fountain pen from Uncle Franz—"My father's," he told Josef. Aunt Ilse had made him a set of handkerchiefs with hand-rolled edges. And from Beth there was a beer stein painted with winter scenes.

"It will always remind me of the time you, Liesl, and I spent together this morning in the park," he told her.

There was only one present left.

"It's for me," Liesl said, her eyes glowing with anticipation as she ripped off the paper from the large package to reveal a small but detailed dollhouse. "It's Lily's house," she declared and ran back to the kitchen to retrieve the tiny doll.

While the family admired the dollhouse, Beth noticed that Josef had slipped away. She heard him climb the attic stairs and considered going after him, thinking that the closeness of her family had made him sad. But almost as soon as he left the room, he was back and juggling four packages—crudely wrapped in paper he must have gotten from the butcher.

"Fräulein Liesl," he said, presenting her the first gift with a courtly bow. She tore the paper off to reveal three new books.

"Look, Beth. Oh, just look," she cried as she slowly turned the pages of the first book.

Josef handed Aunt Ilse the next package. "It's less than you deserve," he told her, "but it comes from a heart filled with gratitude for your many kindnesses."

She carefully opened the hinged box. Inside was an enameled green brooch. "Oh Josef, it is far too dear," she murmured even as she pinned the jewelry to the front of her dress.

For Uncle Franz there was a new pipe that he filled immediately with some of the tobacco Beth had given him and lit in spite of Aunt Ilse's protests.

"There's one more." Liesl pointed to a slender gift box. "And I know what it is because I helped Josef pick them out."

Josef handed the package to Beth. She could not hide her blush as she untied the ribbon on a package that had been professionally wrapped and opened the lid. She pushed aside the tissue to reveal a pair of soft leather gloves the color of honey.

"Try them on," Josef urged. "I had to guess at the size, but the clerk..."

"They are perfect. Just perfect."

The whole day had been perfect, and Beth wished it would never end.

PART 2

MUNICH
JANUARY—FEBRUARY 1943

~≋ CHAPTER 12 ≋~

As the New Year came and went, Josef could not help but wonder what the next Christmas would bring. The one thing he knew for certain was that he wanted to spend whatever time he had in this life with Beth. But how to do that and make sure that she was safe and did not suffer once the war ended?

They had finally come to a compromise regarding her participation in the activities of the White Rose. Or rather he had agreed that she could continue to work within the group so long as she promised never to try to distribute the leaflets without him by her side. But he was well aware that she was always on alert for an opportunity to do more.

In early January the members of the White Rose returned to Munich with renewed determination to expand their efforts. Josef had told Willi about his discovery of the leaflets in Franz's unattended briefcase, and everyone had insisted that Franz could help with the printing but was never to have any of the incendiary papers in his possession again.

So by mid-January they had all settled into a routine. Most evenings Josef and Beth would leave the apartment after supper, saying they were meeting friends at the Gasthaus or seeing a film at the movie house or attending a concert. This was all true. What they did not say was that they often shared these evenings with their friends from the White

Rose. Less often Franz would claim some meeting he needed to attend and leave Ilse at home with Liesl. It all appeared to be working perfectly until Ilse got it into her head that she should invite Josef's parents for Sunday dinner.

"It seems only polite," she said one evening as they were finishing their supper. "After all Josef and Beth are. . .seeing a good deal of each other. Josef, will you ask them?"

"Sunday?" Josef was stalling for time. He had to think. The very idea that his father might sit at this table or perhaps share a *schnapps* with the professor in his cluttered study—who knew what might be lying around in there?

"Nothing fancy," Ilse added. "We're plain people after all." Her voice shook slightly. Josef had learned that this was a sure indication that she was beginning to have second thoughts about her invitation.

"I'm sure it would be a lovely occasion," he said. "It's just that my father is quite busy these days, called into headquarters at all hours of the day and night to hear my mother tell it."

"Of course. I wasn't thinking."

"But we should set a date anyway," Franz announced. "And if it falls through, then we can set another. This Sunday, Josef?"

Josef glanced at Beth. They both understood what Franz was doing. Ilse had been doing so well. She had even begun to accept the relationship between Beth and Josef. If Josef made some excuse—especially a transparent one—it could be enough to undo all the progress that Ilse had made.

"I'll call them today. And if this Sunday does not work, perhaps a week after?"

Ilse gave him a genuine smile—a rarity when it came to the way she usually interacted with him. "That would be fine, Josef. Thank you."

Of course his mother was delighted to accept. "It's about time we had the opportunity to meet Beth's family," she told him. "Call it a mother's intuition, but I sense that you and that young lady have moved well beyond the stage of being just friends."

"Now, Mother, it's a simple invitation for Sunday dinner. Don't make more of it than—"

"She's lovely, Josef, and in spite of her background, this war surely cannot last forever. You deserve your happiness, and it is evident to me that Beth makes you happy."

He couldn't argue that. "All right, Mother, I admit it. She. . .I. . . we. . ."

His mother's laughter interrupted his stumbling attempt to put his feelings for Beth into words. "Apparently this delightful young lady leaves you speechless," his mother said, and Josef had to smile.

"She does indeed," he admitted. *And breathless as well.* "I'll let the Schneiders know to expect you this Sunday right after church."

That night at the meeting of the White Rose, Josef stood across the room from Beth, turning the crank on the mimeograph machine to print more copies of the fifth and latest leaflet. This time they were producing thousands instead of dozens, and the heading was new: *Leaflets of the Resistance Movement in Germany: Call to All Germans!* It was indicative of the group's determination to present a more pragmatic and less idealistic message. The contents bluntly stated that the war was lost—Hitler could not win it. He could only prolong it.

The words of the new leaflet thrilled Beth with their democratic— even American—flavor. *Freedom of speech. Freedom of religion. The protection of the individual from the caprice of the criminal, violent States— these are the bases of the new Europe.*

"We need someone to go to Eglofs," Hans Scholl's sister, Sophie, announced.

Silence. Everyone glanced around the room and realized that most already had their assignments. "Or perhaps we could combine—"

"I'll do it," Beth said. All eyes in the room turned to her. "My aunt's sister lives there," she explained. "I can say I'm taking my cousin to visit."

Josef saw Sophie and Hans exchange a look. He was well aware that they had their doubts about Beth—an American. They had accepted her only because of Willi.

"I can go as well," Josef said. "After all, we live in the same apartment, and I am practically considered a member of the family. It would be perfectly natural for Frau Schneider's sister to want to meet me."

"But the child," Sophie protested. "I mean you've told stories of her. . .precocious nature."

"She will be fine," Beth assured the group. "Trust me," she added, her eyes meeting Sophie's.

Sophie nodded and turned to her brother, who began telling them about plans to meet again with Falk Harnack in early February. Josef barely listened as he worked his way closer to Beth.

"Why did you do that?" he asked.

"Somebody has to, and no one was volunteering. Besides it's a perfect assignment, don't you think? If I volunteer to take Liesl to visit Aunt Ilse's sister. . ."

"And what if your aunt wishes to come along?"

He could see by her frown that this was one possibility she had not considered.

But when told of their plans, Ilse seemed glad for them to go as long as they took Liesl with them. "It will give me peace and quiet for planning Sunday's dinner for Josef's parents." The date had already been postponed twice, and with each cancellation Ilse's nerves frayed a little more. It was now nearly February. "It will be spring before we persuade your parents to visit, Josef," Franz had teased.

Ilse packed them a lunch for the train and filled a second bag with clothing that Liesl had outgrown and that Ilse thought her sister's children might be able to wear. "Where is that coat, Beth? You know the one Liesl wore last winter? The blue one?"

"I. . .one day while you were out, some refugees came to the door, and there was a child, and I. . ."

Josef could tell by the way that Beth avoided looking directly at her aunt that she was not telling the entire truth. Then he remembered Anja's son, Daniel, and the ill-fitting blue coat he'd been wearing the night the family escaped.

"We should get going," he said quietly.

"Yes. I'll go see what's keeping Liesl."

While Beth went to get her cousin, Josef helped Ilse finish packing the clothing. "Your niece is a generous and kind woman, Frau Schneider," he said. In all the time he had lived with the family, he still found it impossible to call the woman by her given name.

To his surprise, she placed her hand lightly on his wrist. "I have been looking for the opportunity to speak with you, Josef. I wish to thank you."

"I don't understand."

Her weariness showed in her eyes as she looked directly at him. "I am not a fool, Josef. I know that my actions may have given you cause to doubt my concern for Beth and my husband and child, but I assure you that I would walk through fire for all of them. Yes, even Beth."

"You are confusing me, Frau. . .Ilse."

"My husband does not seem to have nearly so many meetings these days. Yet at the same time he is unable to rest until you and Beth are safely home when you go out in the evenings." She turned back to the packing, refolding several items so that she could fit still more inside the case. "So I thank you because I believe that you have somehow taken my husband's place in whatever he was doing."

"I. . ."

"What I must ask you now is to think long and hard before you continue to involve Beth in this effort—whatever it is. She has a streak of the adventurer in her, and while she may have grown into a mature young woman, the rashness of her youth has not changed. I know what happened to her visa, Josef. I also know that given the opportunity she would repeat that act without a second's thought for the consequences."

Josef was having a hard time grasping what he was hearing. Both Beth and the professor had worked so hard to protect Ilse, to keep her from worrying, and here she had known everything. Well, not everything. So far there was no indication that she knew about Anja.

"I love Beth, Ilse."

"And she loves you. The thing is, Josef, sometimes love is not enough—not nearly enough." She closed the lid to the suitcase and snapped the latches before handing it to him. "I am trusting you to take care of my family, Josef."

Before he could think what to say, Liesl burst into the kitchen, her eyes shining with excitement. "I want to sit by the window," she announced. "Going and coming home again."

Josef laughed and ruffled her short hair. "It will likely be dark when we come home. There will be nothing to see."

"But I will know what's out there," Liesl explained. "I will have seen it on the way to Tante Marta's house."

Beth picked up the picnic basket. "You'll be all right?" she asked her aunt.

"I will be all right. Now go before you miss your train." She followed them to the front door of the apartment, and just before she closed it, Josef looked back at her. "I promise," he mouthed. She nodded.

But knowing the true purpose of their journey and feeling the weight of the leaflets they were to deliver hidden under the lining of the case he carried, Josef was not at all sure that this was a promise he could keep.

The rocking of the train made Liesl nauseous, and she spent much of the trip to Eglofs with her head on Beth's lap instead of taking in the passing scenery.

Beth's thoughts were taken up with the people she'd met in the White Rose. She admired Sophie. It was difficult for her to believe that someone so young—just twenty-one—could be so intense when it came to any discussion of politics or philosophy. Hans's sister certainly could hold her own when her brother and his friends bemoaned the current state of affairs and what they might do to change things.

When Beth had first begun attending gatherings of the group, she had mistakenly thought that their only mission was to save their country. But she soon learned that for many of them, their concern went even deeper. Traute Lafrenz—Hans's former girlfriend, for example, had in 1937, when she was only seventeen, taken risks to care for and protect her Jewish neighbors.

Seventeen, Beth thought. That was the same age she had been when she first arrived in Munich.

Then there was Alexander Schmorell—*Shurik* to those close to him. He was handsome, aristocratic, and part Russian. Every week he would dress in a Russian peasant's shirt and take food to a group of Polish and Russian laborers serving out sentences of hard labor in the city. More than once Beth had heard him speak of his dream of living out his post-war days in Russia.

But the single thing that struck Beth most was the bond of friendship that had formed between these men and women of the White Rose. They loved each other as if they were family—in some cases more deeply than family. They were a group not unlike Beth's Quaker family back home in Wisconsin. But this group did not sit in silence and wait for guidance. Instead they debated and argued and sometimes even shouted at one another until they reached a consensus.

As the train approached the station in Eglofs, Beth was looking forward to meeting Sophie's friend, who would meet the train. The plan was for there to be a mix-up in the cases, and then the friend would come racing after them to exchange cases, signaling that she had removed the leaflets from behind the lining in the top of the suitcase.

But as they stood in the rail station, no one approached them, even though Josef went through the prescribed motion of setting down the suitcase and pretending to make a phone call.

Several of the pamphlets were already in stamped, addressed envelopes and only needed to be dropped into a mailbox. That part was easy. But at least two hundred copies were intended for distribution in the usual manner. Some would be left in phone booths, others in movie houses or posted on bulletin boards or taped to shop doors under cover of darkness.

"We can't do it ourselves," Beth murmured to Josef while a kind stationmaster tended to Liesl. He had suggested some carbonated water and soda crackers to help settle her stomach. Beth and Josef were following Liesl and the stationmaster to his office. "We have to come up with an alternate plan." She did not even want to consider why the contact had not shown up as scheduled.

"You take Liesl and go on to her aunt's. I'll manage the rest." He was carrying the suitcase containing the hidden leaflets. "I'll be right there," he said, raising his voice so that the stationmaster heard him. He pointed toward a sign that read TOILETTE. "Feeling a little queasy myself," he added.

When he joined them in the stationmaster's office, Beth saw that he was still carrying the bag but his clothes looked different—bulkier. Surely the stationmaster would notice and demand to know what he was hiding.

But as it turned out, Liesl saved the day. "I'm feeling better," she announced, hopping down from the stool she'd been sitting on. "Let's go. I have cousins who live here," she told the stationmaster.

"What do you say, Liesl?" Beth prompted.

"Thank you." Then she turned to Josef. "You look different, Josef. You should have a cracker. It will settle your stomach."

They all laughed as the stationmaster handed Josef a cracker and then ushered them from his office. Outside the station Josef asked for directions and then led the way to the nearest streetcar stop. "I'll join you after I've finished my business," he told them, handing Beth the suitcase.

Beth had not wanted to leave him, afraid that he would be caught and arrested. But what choice did she have? They had Liesl to consider. So she boarded the streetcar, and as the vehicle wound its way round a curve in the road, she saw Josef stuffing several envelopes into a mailbox.

When she and Liesl reached Marta's apartment, a half-dozen children—three of them Liesl's cousins and the other three neighbor children—greeted them. "I care for them during the day while their mother is at work," Marta explained. "Their father is serving on the Russian front," she added in a whisper. "I assume you have heard the terrible news?"

Beth nodded sympathetically. It was not exactly news that serving on the Russian front was the worst possible assignment a soldier could have. Thousands of German soldiers had died there already, yet Hitler continued to push for victory.

"But why am I spoiling the day with such gloomy thoughts? Come, let's see what Ilse has sent." Marta took the suitcase and picnic basket. "Leave it to my sister to pack enough food to feed half the town."

"She sent clothes for the children as well," Beth said, pointing to the other suitcase. "Shall I help unpack that for you?"

"I'll do it later. For now let's ration out this food so that you'll have something for the train ride home."

"I couldn't."

"You could and you will," Marta instructed. "I understand you and a certain doktor have become—close?"

"We are. . .well, that is. . ."

"I thought I was going to have the chance to meet this man who has—according to my sister—so captivated you that you passed up an opportunity to return to America." She grinned. "This must be one gorgeous man."

Beth could not get over the difference between Marta and her sister. Where Ilse was always looking for the darker side of a situation, Marta seemed to take everything in stride. She was a large woman who laughed loud and often and seemed completely unaffected by the fact that she now had seven children racing through her apartment, shouting and squealing at the top of their lungs.

"Josef will be here later. He had some business he needed to attend to. I'm not sure how long it will take," Beth added apologetically.

Marta shrugged. "All the more time for us to catch up. *Kinder*," she shouted as she clapped her hands together to gain the attention of the children. "Could you manage to keep things down to a proper roar before the neighbors assume that we are under attack?" The woman even found humor in the fact that she was living in the middle of a war.

They prepared lunch for the children and themselves, with Marta keeping up a one-sided conversation about her husband—a chemist in the village—her children, and her sister. Beth did a lot of nodding and smiling, allowing Marta to carry the burden of the conversation. Every few minutes, she checked the clock that hung on a wall behind the kitchen table. *Where was Josef now?*

The afternoon wore on as the clock clicked off the seconds, and the children were persuaded to settle down for the quieter pastimes of playing a card game and drawing pictures for Liesl to take home with her. The neighbor came to fetch her children and was persuaded to stay and share a cup of ersatz coffee with Beth and Marta.

"Remember real cream?" Marta said with a sigh as she sipped her coffee and made a face.

The neighbor laughed. "Remember real coffee?"

The talk turned more serious when Marta asked if there had been any news from the front and the woman had to admit that she had heard nothing for weeks. "Since before Christmas," she said, her voice breaking. "Nearly two months now."

"We will hold him in the Light and pray for his safe return," Marta told her.

"We could pray now," Beth suggested, suddenly knowing that taking time to put aside all of her fears for Josef and for this woman's husband was exactly what was called for.

"I am not of your faith," the neighbor said. "I don't know—"

"Just close your eyes and empty your mind of all worries and thoughts," Marta instructed. "You are waiting on God, just waiting, not asking for anything or questioning anything—like why on earth we are involved in this horrible war in the first place. Just close your eyes, and let clarity come to you."

"May I pray my rosary?" the neighbor asked.

"If that's what works for you," Marta agreed.

The street noises faded, and the room went absolutely still except for the rhythmic clicking of the woman's fingers moving over the beads of her rosary. Beth was also aware of the children quietly talking as they worked on their drawings. She focused all of her thoughts on Josef—willing him to be safe, to come back to her.

When Marta touched her arm, Beth opened her eyes and immediately glanced at the clock—this one standing on the mantel above the fireplace. Half an hour had passed. Marta was grinning as she drew Beth's attention to the children. They were sitting in a circle, their hands resting on their knees and their eyes closed—the perfect picture of a Quaker meeting for worship.

Beth's eyes welled with tears, and she saw that she was not alone. Both Marta and her neighbor were dabbing at their eyes as they gently prodded the children back into action. "Time to go," the neighbor said softly, and without protest her three children presented Liesl with their drawings and followed their mother to the door.

When they opened it, Josef was just coming up the stairs, and Beth thought she might fall into his arms with relief. He looked utterly exhausted, but he smiled when he saw her.

Introductions were made, and Marta ushered him into the small apartment, insisting on making him a cup of tea. "You look all done in," she said. "Children, put away your games," she instructed, and to Beth's surprise, even Liesl did as she was asked without question or protest.

"How was your meeting?" she asked Josef as she hung his coat on a hook in the hallway.

"We made a start, but there's still work to be done," he replied with a nod toward his coat.

Beth saw the tip of a familiar envelope peeking out from an inside pocket and quickly arranged the coat to hide it. So Josef had not been able to distribute all of the leaflets. Her mind raced with ideas for some way they might complete their assignment before they had to board the train.

"Beth? Bring me that suitcase," Marta called. "My sister is not the only one who has clothing she no longer needs."

Beth glanced at Josef. They were alone in the hallway. The suitcase had been left by the front door. As if he read her mind Josef opened the case and Beth held it while he stuffed the remainder of the supply of leaflets beneath the lining. Whatever had happened to their contact, Josef had done what he could. As he snapped the latches and handed Beth the case, he stroked her cheek with his forefinger.

"We have to go soon," he said.

"I know. Come, have your tea while Marta packs the bag, and then we can leave."

At the rail station they struggled against the crowds to make it to their train on time. Josef led the way, carrying the picnic basket and suitcase, and Beth followed, fairly dragging a weary and cranky Liesl along with her. "We can't be late," she said when Liesl protested that she needed to rest.

All around them Beth was aware of soldiers—storm troopers in their brown shirts and the even more frightening Gestapo agents, members of Hitler's elite and all-powerful secret police. Of course these men were not secret at all. They were easily recognizable. They wore another sort of uniform—trench coat and black fedora hat with the brim pulled low so that their faces—especially their eyes—were always in shadow. Yet they gave the appearance of seeing everything.

"We're almost there, Liesl," Beth said, her breath coming in short gasps brought on by the need to rush and her fear of being stopped.

Josef boarded the train and set down the cases, then turned to pull Liesl and then Beth aboard just as the train began to move. As she reached for Josef's hand, Beth saw two of the agents boarding the next car.

Josef kept a watchful eye on the doors connecting their car to the one where Beth had seen the agents board. She had finally dozed off while a revived Liesl kept up a running monologue about the passing scenery that she could not possibly see because it was pitch black outside the train's windows. Josef made what he hoped were the appropriate sounds of interest to keep the girl occupied.

They were less than half an hour from Munich when he saw the agents crossing into their car. He nudged Beth and nodded toward the door, open now and announcing the new arrivals with a rush of cold wind. Liesl's chatter stopped as she turned to observe the new arrivals.

"Papers, bitte," one of them said as they started up the aisle, each taking a side and moving slowly along the car, examining identification cards and travel documents, asking questions, testing passengers with little tricks like suddenly smiling and switching to English or Russian in order to entrap someone faking his or her German heritage.

Josef, Beth, and Liesl were at the very back of the car. "Just stay calm," he said as Beth squeezed his fingers so tight he thought she might actually break the bones. "You have the proper documents. There is nothing they can do."

She glanced up at the suitcase in the rack above their heads. "What if..."

"I'm hungry," Liesl complained.

"Me too," Josef agreed and he pulled out the picnic basket from under the seat across from them and opened it. "Look at this, Liesl. There's chocolate cake."

"Tante Marta put that in there," Liesl confided. "She told me that it was a surprise and the cider as well. It's for you and Beth to celebrate with. What are we celebrating, Josef? Christmas has already been, and my birthday—"

"Papers."

Josef presented his documents as well as Beth's to the agent. The man looked briefly at Josef's before handing them back. "Herr Doktor," he murmured as he turned his attention to Beth's visa. Then he nudged his cohort and handed him the papers to examine. Both men focused their attention on Beth.

"We're having a picnic," Liesl announced. "I don't know what we're celebrating but it's something. Do you like chocolate cake?"

The men ignored her, their eyes going to the suitcase in the rack above them. "Does this case belong to you, Fräulein?"

"It does not," Liesl protested. "It belongs to my mother."

"We were visiting the girl's aunt in Eglofs, and her mother sent along some clothing that Liesl here has outgrown." Beth took care to speak to the agents only in German.

"I'm eight. My cousins are much younger," Liesl announced. "Except for Beth, of course. She's much older than me."

"And you are related to this woman?" the agent persisted, directing all of his questions to Liesl.

"This is Beth," Liesl said with a huff of frustration. "She is also my cousin. She takes care of me and my mother, who is sometimes very sick and needs to stay in her room." She looked at the man as if he weren't very bright. "Can we have our cake now?"

"We would not wish to disturb your celebration," the agent said, but he was still holding Beth's visa, tapping it lightly against his palm. "What is the occasion?"

"I don't know," Liesl whispered. "Josef was just about to tell me."

The agents and just about everyone in the railway car turned their attention to Josef. Beth sat by his side, and she was shaking so much that he thought surely the agents must see how nervous she was.

He grasped her hands between his. "Elizabeth Bridgewater, will you marry me?" he blurted. Everyone in their compartment erupted in excited commentary as the news of Josef's proposal was shared. Soon other passengers had left their seats and crowded into the aisle for a view of the young couple.

"Yes," Beth whispered, her gaze locked on his as if needing to be sure that she was giving him the correct answer. "Yes," she repeated, her voice a little stronger as an uncertain smile played over her lips.

"*Küssen die* Fräulein, *Dummkopf,*" the agent closest to them ordered, but he was smiling.

Josef leaned in to kiss Beth, and the car exploded with joy. A businessman pulled down his valise and extracted a bottle of champagne. The agents only laughed when he popped the cork and took a long swallow before passing the bottle on to others around him.

"Can we have cake now?" Liesl shouted above the turmoil surrounding them.

"We can have cake," Josef assured her, and when Beth received her precious visa along with the agents' congratulations, he gestured toward the empty seats facing theirs, inviting the two men to join them.

"Nein, danke. *Glückwünsche*, Herr Doktor."

As Josef accepted their congratulations and the agents moved on to the next car, he could only hope that the following day's dinner with his parents and Beth's aunt and uncle would go half as well.

CHAPTER 13

Sunday dinner with the Buchs had all the makings of a complete and utter disaster. Beth was certain that it would be weeks before her aunt's distress over the whole event could ease enough so that the woman did not burst into tears at the mere thought of it.

The trouble began almost the moment they arrived home from the visit with Aunt Marta. Liesl began telling her parents all about the agents on the train.

"They took your papers?" Aunt Ilse asked.

"They examined them and gave them back," Beth explained. "Everything was in order. There was nothing they could do." She knew that wasn't true, and so did her aunt, but neither of them said so. "Why don't I help Liesl get ready for bed?"

"Josef and Beth are getting married," Liesl announced as she headed for her room. "He asked her right there on the train, and everybody was so very happy."

Now it was Josef's turn to calm Aunt Ilse. "It was the only way I could think of to take their attention off the fact that Beth is American, and it worked."

It worked?

"You didn't mean it then?" Aunt Ilse asked, her relief evident.

"Because Josef, I know you care for our niece and she for you, but a union between you in these times. . ."

"I know, Ilse." He glanced up at Uncle Franz. "I had to think of something that might draw their attention away from her."

Beth saw her uncle nod and grip Josef's shoulder in approval. Then she hurried after Liesl and took her time getting the girl settled for the night. She gave in to every request for one more story and even stayed sitting next to her cousin's bed long after Liesl had fallen asleep.

By the time she returned to the sitting room, she could hear Josef and her uncle talking in low tones behind the closed door of Franz's study. Aunt Ilse was standing in the middle of the room, studying the furniture. "Perhaps we should move that chair here and place the—"

"Do you have something in the oven, Tante?"

Aunt Ilse's hands flew to her mouth as she dashed into the kitchen and threw open the oven door. Black, acrid smoke poured into the room. "Oh, it's ruined," she cried as she fanned away smoke with the skirt of her apron.

Beth turned off the oven and grabbed a dishtowel to serve as protection while she reached for the pan inside. Whatever the contents had been, the food was now charred and inedible. "We can make it over again tomorrow."

"Do you think sugar grows on trees?" Aunt Ilse snapped. "That was to be our dessert. It took me hours to adjust the ingredients so that it would be perfect. Now look at it. And that pan. I need that pan tomorrow, and it will never be clean."

"We can soak it overnight, and by morning—"

"Ruined," Aunt Ilse moaned and ran from the kitchen, her sobs echoing down the hall.

"What has happened?" Uncle Franz said, opening the door at the sound of his wife's distress. "And what's burning?"

"Go to her," Beth said wearily. "I can manage this."

She did not hear Josef come into the kitchen because of the water she was running and the steam rising from the burnt pan. So when he placed his hands gently on her shoulders, she jerked away from his touch.

"Let me help," he said.

"I can do it. You should get some rest. It's been a long day." She could not look at him, the memory of his words still ringing in her ears. She knew that she had foolishly allowed herself to believe that his proposal had been sincere and not simply a ruse to distract the agents on the train. But the fact was that she was in love with Josef, and the next logical step for any woman in love was to imagine a life together.

"For you as well, Beth. Let me scrub the pan for you."

"It will do no good to scrub it now. It needs to soak overnight," she snapped. "Now please just go to bed."

She was relieved when he said nothing and moved away. But instead of hearing his step on the attic stairs as she had expected, she heard him pull out a kitchen chair. When she turned he was seated at the table, his arms folded across his chest. "What's going on?" he asked.

"It's nothing. I'm tired, and Aunt Ilse is upset, and a great deal needs to be done before your parents come tomorrow and—" She couldn't help it. She burst into tears. *And you said you loved me*, she wanted so much to add.

"Beth?" He came to her and wrapped his arms around her as she leaned against the sink, sobbing into the dishtowel. "You're safe. Those men. . .it's over now. Everything will be fine."

"Will it? Will anything ever be fine again, Josef?"

When he pulled her into his embrace so that his cheek rested against her hair, she understood that he had no answers. They were caught up in a time and place that neither of them had had a hand in creating but nevertheless a time and place that was in complete control of everything they said or did.

Beth had things well in hand by the time Aunt Ilse came to the kitchen the following morning. With Liesl's help, she had set the table using

Aunt Ilse's best linen tablecloth and napkins and her good china and crystal. She had managed to get the pan clean and had seasoned the special pork roast that Uncle Franz had secured for the meal with the last of their monthly ration coupons.

"Where's Liesl?" Aunt Ilse asked as she put on her apron and began paring potatoes to boil.

"Josef took her out to see if they could find some evergreens for a centerpiece."

"We have no dessert to serve."

"Yes, we do. Marta sent you some gingerbread. She said it's always been your favorite. If we cut the slices very thin. . ."

"Josef's parents will think that we are—"

Beth sighed. "Aunt Ilse, it does not matter what they think of us. It is highly unlikely that we will see any of them again—including Josef— once this war has ended."

"How can you say that? I thought that you and Josef. . ."

"We are friends, but once the war ends, how can we possibly sustain such a friendship? One of us—perhaps both of us—will have a price to pay and—"

"Do not speak of such things."

"I'm sorry. I did not mean to upset you. Did you see the table? Is it as you would want it?"

"It is lovely," Aunt Ilse replied as she fingered a plate. "These dishes belonged to my great-grandmother, and my mother embroidered the cloth and napkins herself."

"You should mention that to Frau Buch. She seems to me to be someone who likes to hear such things."

"Perhaps. . ." Aunt Ilse murmured. "Perhaps it will be all right after all."

But it wasn't.

Just half an hour before the Buchs were scheduled to arrive, Josef's mother called to say that her husband had been called away for an important meeting and they would not be able to come. Josef had taken the phone from Franz and spoken to his mother in low tones for several minutes. In the end he had announced that he would be back—with his mother—within the hour if Ilse could please hold dinner. He would also send word that his father should join them for dessert if at all possible.

Josef had a dual purpose in going to his parents' house to escort his mother to the professor's for Sunday dinner. On the one hand he did not wish to see Ilse any more upset than she already was. On the other, he was curious to learn why his father was suddenly spending so much of his time in secret meetings and why he had been called into headquarters on a Sunday. Such information could be invaluable to his friends in the resistance.

Granted, the more deeply involved Josef became with the activities of the White Rose, the more paranoid he grew. He fully understood that he and his father stood on opposite sides of the political fence. But his first concern had to be for Beth and her safety. He was doing what he did for the love of his country, while she was risking everything to distribute essays that—as much as he prayed and hoped otherwise— admittedly had little chance of getting the citizens of Germany to rise up against Hitler.

He was also well aware that she continued to look for ways to do more. Her concern was for those being persecuted. People whose only crime was that they held beliefs and attitudes that the present government did not like. She did not believe in war—or politics for that matter. To her—and the professor—people were people. "We are all God's children," she had once said to him, and for Beth that was the crux of the matter. He was quite sure that for Beth loving someone— anyone—meant that she would move mountains for that fortunate person.

He was completely consumed with thoughts of Beth as the streetcar rolled along, its bell dinging out stops and starts for more passengers to exit or come aboard. Before he knew it, he had left the professor's neighborhood of shops and apartment buildings crowded close together on narrow streets. Now the streetcar made its way along a snow-covered boulevard lined on either side by impressive homes set on spacious grounds. His parents' neighborhood was only a few miles but worlds away from where Beth lived.

After exiting the streetcar, he walked the half block to the circular drive that marked the entrance to his childhood home. He stood for a long moment, looking at the heavy columns that stood sentry outside the front door, the large stone planters that his mother filled with red geraniums and trailing vines every May, the front lawn where his father had taught him the finer points of navigating a soccer field. They had been so happy then.

Josef headed up the driveway. A large black sedan was parked in front of the entrance to the house, the uniformed driver standing at the ready next to the passenger side of the car. Josef nodded to the man as he entered the house he had once called home.

"*Mutti?*"

His mother came down the wide staircase, her coat over her arm as she pinned her hat into place. "Your father sent his car and driver," she said.

"So he will not be joining us?"

"I don't know, Josef," she said impatiently. "He was called to headquarters, and you know how these things are. It could be hours before he can get away."

Josef held her coat for her and could not help but compare the fur-trimmed garment that was obviously new to the thin wool coat that Beth wore—had apparently worn for some time given the way it had been mended around the collar and cuffs. "Nice coat," he murmured as he watched his mother check her appearance in the gilded mirror that filled one wall of the foyer.

She smiled and stroked the fur collar and cuffs. "It was a Christmas present from your father," she said, and then she frowned. "Do you think it's too much—I mean for today? For this occasion? I wouldn't wish to offend or. . ."

"It's fine. Shall we go?" He opened the front door, and the driver immediately snapped to attention. "This meeting at headquarters. . ." Josef began once he and his mother were in the car.

"Please do not ask questions, Josef. You know I could not discuss matters of state with you even if I had any information myself."

"It just seems to be rather sudden. I don't ever recall—"

Again his mother interrupted him, but this time she was laughing. "Oh, Josef, as if you have been around enough to know when your father has business he must attend. We barely see you."

"I do have duties of my own," Josef reminded her. "Shifts at the hospital, not to mention my classes and research."

"And of course there is Beth," his mother said, her voice softening. "Do you make time for her?"

"We live in the same place. I share meals with the family. I—"

"There is no cause for defensiveness, Josef. I am simply attempting to make conversation and find out what is going on in your life."

"I have asked Beth to marry me."

As he expected, his mother hid her shock well, but not so thoroughly that she could fully disguise her disapproval at such a notion. "Do you think that wise, Josef? I mean in times like these to make such a decision. . ."

"I love her," he replied.

"Romeo loved Juliet, and look how that turned out." His mother pulled a cigarette from a case in her purse and handed him the lighter.

"That was fiction. This is real." He lit her cigarette and handed her back the lighter.

"Precisely," she said as she blew out the first puff of smoke. "You are in love with your enemy."

"Beth and her family are Quakers—they have no enemies."

His mother's laugh was brittle, and he saw the driver cast them a glance in the rearview mirror. "If they believe that—if *you* believe that— then you are all fools." She turned away from him and stared out the window, and he realized that her eyes had filled with tears.

He took hold of her gloved hand, but she waved him off and took a long drag on the cigarette. Josef did not recall a time when he had seen his mother look so miserable.

"Beth, come see," Liesl shouted.

Beth and Aunt Ilse both hurried into the front room, where Liesl was perched on the window seat that overlooked the street. Outside sat a large black car—a Mercedes like those used by the Gestapo. Beth heard Aunt Ilse suck in her breath.

"It's just Josef and his mother," she assured her aunt as she watched Josef get out of the car on one side while the driver hurried to open the passenger side rear door for Frau Buch. "I'm sure that Herr Buch had his driver bring them."

"But the neighbors. . .they will think. . . ."

It was true, of course. The arrival of such a vehicle on any street at any time of day or night was an ominous sign. "The neighbors know Josef. They will see him and think no more of it."

Beth hoped she was right, but across the way she saw curtains move in several neighboring apartments and knew that people were watching and speculating. She was momentarily pleased that Josef's father had not come, for surely the sight of him in his black trench coat would have stirred up even more gossip. "Look how lovely Frau Buch looks," Beth said, hoping to turn her aunt's attention to something more pleasant.

"She has a fur coat," Liesl said, her eyes widening in wonder.

"Well, there is certainly fur on the collar and cuffs," Beth agreed. She turned to find Aunt Ilse pulling off the apron she had worn all morning.

"I should change," she muttered. "This dress. . ." She fled down the hall, and the next thing Beth heard was the slam of the bedroom door.

"What's happened now?" Uncle Franz asked, coming out of his study at the sound.

"Josef and his mother are on their way up."

"Mama went to change her dress," Liesl added. "That's her very best dress though, so. . ."

"I'll go check on her," Uncle Franz said, already halfway down the hall as the buzzer sounded, announcing their guests had arrived.

"Liesl and I will take care of this," Beth assured him, turning to welcome Josef's mother. "*Wilkommen*," she said as she opened the door and stood aside to allow Josef and Frau Buch to enter the foyer.

"Oh my, what is that delicious smell?" Frau Buch asked, focusing her attention on Liesl.

"It's a pork roast," Liesl replied. "I'm so glad you came. It's been so long since we had anything so grand as a pork roast. Is that real fur?"

"Shot that bear all by myself just this morning," Josef joked, and Beth saw that his mother blushed.

"It is, Liesl." She offered the girl a chance to caress the cuff of her coat. "The coat was a Christmas gift. Did you get any special gifts?"

"I did. Come on, I'll show you." She took Frau Buch's hand and led her down the hall to her bedroom.

"Is everything all right?" Josef asked as soon as they were gone.

"Not really." Beth explained about Aunt Ilse seeing the car and then the coat. "My uncle is with her. I'd best tend to dinner."

"Let me help."

Lying awake the night before, Beth had forced herself to face reality. Josef was a good and decent man intent on protecting her and her German family. When he proposed on the train, that had been his motivation, nothing more. He might be fond of her—even in love with her—but Josef was a practical man. The very idea that they might marry given all their differences was ludicrous.

"Will your father be coming later?" Beth asked as together they finished preparing the side dishes for the meal.

Josef shrugged. "I don't know. I tried to get some information on the drive over, but all I truly understand is that my mother is worried."

"About what?"

Again the shrug. "Things are changing, Beth. Not just for you and me and your family."

"Surely your parents are—"

From the hallway they heard voices. Uncle Franz greeted Josef's mother while Liesl kept up a running conversation about Frau Buch's beautiful coat and how their special guest had said that the color of Liesl's new dress was a perfect match for the girl's eyes. "Frau Buch is going to give me a scarf that she doesn't wear anymore. She's going to send it with Josef the very next time he visits her," she announced as the three of them entered the kitchen.

There was still no sign of Aunt Ilse. When Beth raised her eyebrows, questioning her aunt's continued absence, Uncle Franz simply shook his head and indicated a chair at one end of the table.

"Shall we enjoy this wonderful meal?" he asked. "I'm afraid my wife has taken ill and won't be joining us today. Beth, will you serve?"

"Of course." She set the roast in front of her uncle, along with a carving knife, then placed each side dish on the table before taking her place next to Liesl and across from Josef.

"We say grace in silence," Franz told Josef's mother once everyone was seated. "Will you join us?"

Frau Buch folded her hands in her lap and bowed her head. And when Beth noticed the small circular stain on the front of the woman's burgundy dress, she realized that Josef's mother was crying. Her uncle must have noticed as well, for he prolonged the silent prayer until Liesl became restless.

"Forgive me," Josef's mother said as Uncle Franz stood and began carving the pork roast. "I don't know what's come over me." She dabbed at her eyes with a lace-trimmed handkerchief that she pulled from her long fitted sleeve.

"It's an emotional time," Uncle Franz said, continuing to carve thin slices of the precious meat and place them on each plate as it was passed to him.

"My mother sheds tears for the smallest things," Josef said, taking hold of Frau Buch's hand and grinning. "I had this puppy once, and. . ."

By the time Josef had finished his tale and Beth had told of the family of kittens that she and her brothers had rescued from the pound and tried unsuccessfully to keep secret from their mother, everyone was laughing. Just then Aunt Ilse entered the room. It was evident that she had been crying for some time, for her skin was blotched and reddened and her eyelids swollen.

Uncle Franz was on his feet at once. "Ah, Frau Buch, may I present my wife, Ilse?"

"I apologize for—"

"No, my dear Frau Schneider, it is I who must apologize for my tardiness and the absence of my husband. You have gone to so much trouble."

Uncle Franz guided Aunt Ilse to her place at the table next to Josef. "You're feeling better?" he murmured.

She nodded, but Beth saw that her hands were shaking as she accepted the plate of food Beth handed her.

"Tante, tell Frau Buch about the china," she said, seeking any possible topic of conversation that might lift the sudden shift in mood that had occurred with Aunt Ilse's sudden appearance.

It worked. Ilse told how her great-grandmother had saved for the china until she had a full set and then how it had passed from one generation to the next.

"And one day when I marry, it will be mine," Liesl said, and then she gave her mother a worried frown. "You won't give it to Beth, will you?"

"Of course not. Why would she?" Beth asked.

"Because when you and Josef get married, then—"

"We are not getting married," Beth said quietly, and she did not miss the look that passed between Josef and his mother.

Frau Buch looked at her son. "But I thought—"

"What about on the train when we had cake?" Liesl protested.

"Josef lives here in Germany, and Beth will one day return to her home in America, Liesl," Aunt Ilse said with a nervous laugh. "You know that."

"But—"

"Eat your potato salad," Aunt Ilse snapped, and once again the mood around the table disintegrated into an uncomfortable silence with the only interruption being the occasional clink of flatware on the fine china.

∼⩾ CHAPTER 14 ⩾∼

A stretch of clear sunny days in February finally broke the oppressive damp and cold that had held the city prisoner since Christmas. Unfortunately the improvement in the weather did little to lift spirits or improve the situation of anyone involved in trying to bring the war to an end.

After the surrender of the Sixth Army to the Russians on February 2, 1943, Hitler was so infuriated that he declared a national day of mourning. The declaration was not meant to honor and grieve for the hundreds of thousands of soldiers killed, maimed, starved, frozen, or captured over the long campaign in and around Stalingrad. Rather Hitler's rage was directed at the shame he felt his generals had brought upon Germany.

Shortly after this act, the dictator turned the full force of his wrath toward anyone who was suspected of opposing his government's policies. The news that Mildred Fish Harnack, the American wife of Arvid Harnack who had himself been tortured and killed in prison, had received a six-year prison sentence for her part in her husband's activities further enraged Hitler. He ordered her brought to trial again, and this time the sentence was death.

Franz was horrified when he heard this news and vowed to sever all ties with the White Rose and to make sure that Beth and Josef also had nothing more to do with the group. If Hitler was taking such a personal interest in his enemies, what chance did any of them have of keeping Beth safe?

For several weeks he had been deeply disturbed by the turn that matters had taken with the White Rose. His colleague and friend, Professor Kurt Huber, had finally agreed to join the group. Unfortunately Kurt and Hans Scholl were at polar odds about the direction they thought the group needed to take. Hans and others favored joining forces with Falk Harnack's Berlin group. Kurt found their approach far too left-leaning and radical for his taste.

A few nights earlier the situation had disintegrated to the point where Kurt had walked out. Then after the news of the Stalingrad defeat was made public, Hans, Alex, and Willi had decided to celebrate the fact that the tide was turning against Hitler. They painted anti-Hitler slogans such as *Down with Hitler* and *Hitler Mass Murderer* on the sides of buildings along Ludwigstrasse—the main thoroughfare leading to the university. Sometimes they added a crossed out swastika and the word *Freedom* in bold letters.

To Franz, such reckless disregard for the obvious dangers they put themselves and the rest of the group in was tantamount to giving the Gestapo a roadmap to find them. The young men staged these raids under the very noses of police and others patrolling the streets. The action was blatant and far more dangerous than anything the group had done to date.

One morning in mid-February after the third such raid, Franz saw city workers covering the graffiti with butcher paper in an attempt to hide the defamatory words until the walls could be scrubbed and repainted. But the oil or tar used to mix the paint was deliberately chosen because it bled through the paper, making the words readable to anyone passing. That same morning Franz observed Hans and Alex passing one of the covered signs and then smiling as they continued on their way. They were becoming far too overconfident that the leaflets with their rally cries for the people to rise up were finally having some effect.

Of course, Franz understood their confidence. On January 13—a day few associated with the university would ever forget—a high-ranking Bavarian official had called a special assembly to address all university students.

Not only did the man chide female students for wasting time and funds by insisting on getting an education, but he further insulted the women by lecturing them on their true duty—to provide sons for their beloved *Vaterland*. And if that weren't enough to enrage the women in the audience, the official actually offered them the services of studs if they were not alluring enough to attract a husband. When many female students attempted to leave the hall in protest, the official had them arrested.

Chaos reigned as several male students, many of them in uniform, rushed forward to form a protective circle around the women until the arrest order was rescinded. The news spread quickly throughout the city, and it was understandable that such a student outcry along with news of the devastating defeat at Stalingrad gave reason for the core members of the White Rose to feel confident that at last the people were prepared to take a stand.

But in the apartment above the bakery, the news of the riot at the assembly, the death of the American woman by Hitler's direct order, and the crushing defeat on the Russian front had an opposite effect. Ilse walked through her days barely touching her meals, her eyes haunted and shadowed from lack of sleep. Although Franz tried to soothe his wife's anxiety by pointing out that the war was winding down and would soon be over, she refused to be consoled.

"And then what? We start again as we did after the last war? And the world turns against us, and we are cast into poverty, and. . ."

These days she did not dissolve into tears. Instead she would simply break off her tirade in midsentence and sit staring at nothing as if in a trance. With the increase in air raids—or at least the warnings that sent them all scurrying to the cellar—Liesl had developed terrible nightmares and often awoke screaming, waking the entire household. And while Josef continued to make sojourns by train to distribute the leaflets of the White Rose in nearby towns and villages, Franz was relieved to see that Beth no longer accompanied him.

Wearily Franz crossed the lobby and climbed the stairs of the building where he had spent years of his life lecturing and meeting with students and shepherding them along. He had a lecture to deliver in less than an hour. He liked to arrive before the students so that he could go over his notes one last time. He was a good teacher—and a popular one.

When he entered the large, empty room that would soon be filled with the chatter of students, only a single lamp burned at the lectern. It took a moment before he noticed a man sitting on the aisle of the first row.

"*Guten Morgen, mein* Herr," Franz called out as he made his way past rows of empty desks. "*Kann ich Ihnen helfen?*" He felt his heart rate increase as he realized that this was a Gestapo agent.

As if worn down by exhaustion, the agent rose and turned to face Franz. The man was Josef's father—Detlef Buch.

"Ah, Herr Buch," Franz said with a heartiness tempered by uncertainty. Josef's father could be here because he wanted to talk with Franz about his son, or he could be here in a more official capacity. "Please sit. Sit. I have some time before the students arrive." He indicated the chair that Herr Buch had vacated, but the man remained standing.

"I will not keep you. Your family has been kind to my son and my wife, and I appreciate that a great deal."

"Josef is a gifted physician. He was one of my finest students."

Buch waved away the compliments impatiently. "You and your family—your niece especially—should consider leaving Munich. I believe your wife has a sister in Eglofs?"

"She does, but I cannot leave my work here at the—"

"Later today—if it has not already happened, Herr Schneider—your work at the university will be terminated. It is not my habit to share such information, but as I have said, you and your wife are people my son respects and holds in the highest esteem."

Franz found that he could no longer stand. He slumped into a chair, dropping his briefcase as he did. So many times he had imagined this moment, had dreaded opening the mail he received through the slit in his office door. He realized that he had been waiting for weeks—months—for the letter saying his services were no longer required. The moment was here, but in a way he had never imagined.

"How do you. . .why would you. . ."

"I was at a function last night, and I overheard a conversation between the head of your department and university chancellor Wust. Naturally when I heard your name mentioned, I paid attention."

"Did they say why?" It was a foolish question. No reason was needed—at least not one that showed cause.

"They did not." Detlef Buch put on his hat and pulled on his leather gloves, taking time to make sure each finger fit precisely into its designated space. "And I have said more than I should. Thank you and Frau Schneider for the care you have given my son. *Auf Wiederschauen*, Herr Professor."

He walked to the exit, his normally erect posture marred by the slump of his shoulders and the slowed pace of his step. Franz heard the click of the door closing. Almost immediately it opened again as the first of the students arrived and took their places. Franz pushed himself up from the chair and retrieved his lecture notes from his briefcase.

His last lecture.

He stared blindly at his notes, the words swimming before his eyes as he heard the hall fill with students, so full of life with their laughter and chatter. When the room grew quiet, he continued to stare at the water-stained papers before him. He allowed himself one moment of fantasy in which he imagined telling the students of his impending dismissal and envisioned them rising up and marching as one to the office of the chancellor to demand his reinstatement. The very idea of such an insurrection actually made him smile through his tears.

Then reality took charge. He stacked his notes and tapped them into alignment on the edge of the lectern before putting them back inside his briefcase. He switched off the lamp over the lectern and looked up at the students for the first time.

They all watched him, their expressions rapt with curiosity and interest. He had achieved what every professor dreams of—the undivided attention of this assembly. He could feel their eyes following him as he made his way to the exit, briefcase in hand. When he reached the door, he turned and looked back at the lectern that had been like a stage for him—a place where he had known his worth.

"Class dismissed," he said softly and left the room.

The minute she entered the apartment after collecting Liesl from school, Beth knew something had changed. Instead of being in his study preparing a lecture or researching something for an article he intended to write, Uncle Franz was in the kitchen, standing by the open window, a bottle of milk in his hand.

In the winter the family often used the small balcony outside the window as a makeshift second refrigerator, setting the milk and butter and eggs out there to allow more space in the actual refrigerator for other things. But they had not needed to store anything out there for weeks. What food they had fit with room to spare. Times were hard—even harder than they had been before the holidays.

"Uncle?"

The glass bottle slipped from his fingers and shattered in the sink as his shoulders slumped and then shook violently. His tears came accompanied by audible gasps and moans.

"Papa!" Liesl screamed and ran to him, wrapping her arms around his legs.

Beth pulled the girl free. "Go to the bathroom and get me a wet cloth," she instructed, trying to hold back her own fear. "Your father has cut his hand. Go."

Once Liesl had left the room, Beth guided Franz to the nearest chair. "Let me see," she said, taking hold of his hand. "It doesn't appear to be too bad." She looked at him then—at his red-rimmed eyes, his thin hair standing up in tufts as if he had repeatedly run his hands through it, his wire-rimmed glasses askew on his forehead. "Now calm yourself. Where is Aunt Ilse?"

"I sent her to the market. I told her. . . ." He drew in a shuddering sigh. "I lied to her. I gave her money and told her they were selling oranges."

"What has happened?"

Liesl came running just then with a cloth soaked and dripping all over the floor. "Here," she said, thrusting the cloth at Beth and then immediately climbing onto her father's lap and wrapping her arms around his neck. "It will be all right," she assured him. "We can put a bandage on it until it heals."

Beth took the cloth to the sink to wring out the excess water and wondered if the sound her uncle made was an attempt at laughter at his daughter's unintentional analysis of their new situation. Outside the still-open kitchen window, a clock chimed the hour. Four thirty. Beth mentally ran through the usual schedule. On Thursdays, Uncle Franz had a late-afternoon lecture—a lecture that began at four o'clock. She turned to face him. Their gazes met, and he nodded in answer to her unspoken question.

"Liesl, why don't you go into the front room so you can watch for your mother? We don't want to upset her when she gets home and realizes that your father has cut himself."

"I'll tell her that everything is going to be all right so that she is not scared like she gets," Liesl announced as she hurried off to the front room, closing the door behind her.

"Tell me," Beth said as she tended to her uncle's cut.

He released a shuddering sigh and then told her the story.

"Josef's father? But how. . . ?"

"He overheard a conversation at some social gathering he was attending. The fact is that he came to warn me because of Josef—out of gratitude. He also made it clear that we should go away—he suggested moving to Eglofs and living with Marta."

"But Munich is your home." She tied the ends of the gauze bandage and glanced at him. "Is this because of me? Is that the reason for. . . ?"

He cupped her cheek. "Nein, Liebchen. You mustn't think that. No, what I believe that Herr Buch was trying to tell me is that my activities are being observed. They may have even discovered my association with. . ."

"If they know about you, then they surely know about Josef." Her heart hammered with a level of fear that she hoped never again to experience. "That is why Herr Buch came to you. Josef is also in danger, and he believes that if we leave Josef will follow us."

"I believe that what he was telling me is that we are all in danger, Beth." They heard the front door to the apartment open and close and Liesl's excited but muffled voice telling her mother about Franz's cut hand. "But he is fine. Beth bandaged it, and the bleeding has stopped, and. . ."

Beth prepared herself for her aunt's collapse into hysteria as the door to the kitchen opened and Liesl burst in and ran to her father.

Aunt Ilse calmly set a small paper bag on the table and slowly began removing her gloves. "Beth, please take Liesl to the park," she said quietly, then turned to Liesl. "Your father and I need to talk privately."

It was evident that Liesl was as taken aback by this unexpected change in her mother's demeanor as Beth was. "I'll get my coat," she said and left the room without a word of protest.

"It has happened?" Aunt Ilse said, looking from Uncle Franz to Beth and back again.

"Ja. Not officially but then I did not stop at my office. I am certain there is a letter waiting there."

"We can speak with Josef," Beth said. "It was his father who—"

"Beth, please attend to Liesl," Aunt Ilse interrupted. "Your uncle and I need to consider what options lay ahead for us."

"But—"

"Enough," Ilse hissed, clenching her fists at her sides. "For once just do as I ask."

Reluctantly Beth left the kitchen only to discover Liesl huddled in the foyer dressed for the winter's day in her coat, hat, and mittens. She sat with her hands wrapped tightly around her knees as she squatted next to the door. "I'm scared," she whispered. "I wish Josef was here."

"So do I," Beth agreed as she put on her coat. "I'll tell you what. It's almost time for his shift at the hospital to be over. Why don't we go and meet him—surprise him?"

As she had hoped, the girl's mood brightened immediately. "Let's go," she said as she leapt to her feet and flung the door open. "Josef will know what to do. He's a doctor."

But Josef was nowhere to be found—at least not any place that Beth felt she could take Liesl. Someone at the hospital told them he had left as soon as his shift ended. "Seemed in a terrible hurry about something," the man added. And Beth remembered there was a meeting of the White Rose friends set for that evening.

"We should go home," she told Liesl. "Your parents will wonder where we are."

The two of them walked through the marketplace, taking the shortest route back to the apartment from the hospital. Beth was lost in thought and anxious to get Liesl home so she could make some excuse and go to the meeting and warn Josef and the others. She barely noticed that Liesl was also unusually quiet.

"Beth?" The girl's voice shook. At first Beth thought it was the cold, but then she saw how Liesl looked up at her, her face puckered into a worried frown. "Is something really bad going to happen to us?"

"Of course not," she replied, stunned at the child's perception of the events that had unfolded that afternoon. "It has just been a difficult day for your father and—"

"Something has happened, and I know that it made Papa very sad. Even when the bombs fall, Papa is never sad. He is always singing and telling me stories and holding tight to Mama and—"

Beth stopped and knelt down so that she and Liesl were looking directly at each other. She placed her hands on the girl's shoulders and told her the truth as she knew it at that moment. "Liesl, we may be going away for a while—all of us. We may go to stay for a while with your Tante Marta and your cousins. You would enjoy that, wouldn't you?"

Liesl looked doubtful but nodded, even as her eyes filled with tears.

"I mean think about it. There are almost never any bombs in the country. No need to be afraid when the planes come. No need to hide in the cellar. You can play outdoors with your cousins and—"

"But Papa cannot come, can he? He has to be at his work and—"

"No, Liesl. He is going to find another job."

Her eyes narrowed with suspicion. "Why? Why will he find a new job?"

"Because if we move to the country—"

"He has been dismissed. My teacher said. . . ." Her eyes widened in horror, and she began to howl like an animal caught in a trap.

Beth pulled her close as much to muffle her cries as to comfort her, for they were beginning to attract the attention of passersby. "Liesl, it will be all right. You'll see." She hoped that she was not lying to this child who had become as dear to her as a sister.

"It's my fault," Liesl wailed.

"No."

"It is. My teacher said that the professors at the university sometimes did not teach what they should, and I told her that Papa was not like that. But then she asked me all sorts of questions about what he taught and what he said about Herr Hitler and whether or not at home we. . ."

Again she dissolved into tears, and she clung to Beth so tightly that Beth lifted her into her arms and carried her down the street. "Shhh," she whispered soothingly, even as her heart raced with this new evidence that Liesl's teacher had possibly—probably—reported her uncle to the authorities.

"I hate my teacher—and Herr Hitler," Liesl said, her voice rising in tandem with her fury.

Beth glanced quickly around. They had turned onto the block of shops where the bakery was. They were almost home. She set Liesl down as she rummaged through her purse for the key to the entrance leading to the apartments. "You must not say such things," she told Liesl. "You are a Friend and as such have no room in your heart for such feelings."

"I wish we could just go away from here and never come back. I wish we could go live in America with you. I wish—"

"Be still now," Beth instructed as she followed Liesl up the stairs. "It is not the time to speak. It is the time to listen." *And to pray.*

CHAPTER 15

The following morning while Aunt Ilse packed and Uncle Franz spent time in his study going through his papers—burning some in the kitchen stove and ripping others to shreds—Beth tried to concentrate on Liesl's incessant chatter. Having apparently decided overnight that a move to the country was a good idea, she talked without ceasing about what they might expect.

"I suppose I will share a room," she said with a sigh.

"You share one now—with me," Beth reminded her. She stood at the window, watching for any sign of Josef. He had not come home all night, and the last any of them had seen or heard of him had been the previous morning when they had all naively believed they were safe.

What if he had been detained for questioning? Arrested? Or worse?

As Liesl's high voice pierced the air, Beth forced herself to make what she hoped were the appropriate sounds of agreement or listening, but her mind was on Josef. Where was he?

"Beth?" Her uncle had come into the small bedroom without her realizing it. "Could you do something for me?"

"Of course. Anything."

"I need you to go to the university—to my office. I believe that I may have left something there—some important papers."

Her eyes widened in fear. Josef had told her of her uncle's determination to author the next leaflet. Now she saw how his hand shook as he handed her a key. "Do you know where they might be?" she asked.

"Under the blotter on my desk."

Beth nodded and hurried to put on her coat and hat.

"If someone stops you or interrupts you or if they have changed the lock or already—"

"I understand," Beth assured him. "Don't worry."

"You must hurry," he reminded her. "Our train leaves. . . ."

"I know." She was halfway down the first flight of stairs when she turned and saw her uncle standing in the open doorway of the apartment watching her. "If I am not back in time, go without me," she instructed. "Josef and I will get a later train." They were scheduled to leave just after two, and it was already approaching ten o'clock. By the time she got to the university and reached her uncle's office without attracting attention and then made it all the way to the train station, it would be nearly time for the train to leave.

"I—"

"Promise," she whispered, coming back to stand near him in case any neighbors might be listening. "Because once I am done with your errand, I am going to find Josef."

He touched her cheek and grasped her hand in his. "I don't know how we would have survived without you, Beth," he said, his voice breaking. "They may come for me yet, and if they do. . ."

"I will make sure that Aunt Ilse and Liesl are safe," she promised. "But you must get on that train if you can. It's your only chance." She did not wait for his answer but pulled her hand free of his grip and ran down the four flights of stairs to the street.

She wanted to run the distance to the university, but she also did not wish to draw attention to herself. Instead she walked as quickly as possible down the narrow cobblestone streets, across busy squares, slowing to a normal pace every time she saw soldiers or Gestapo agents so as to not draw attention to her haste. When the university was in sight, she broke into a run, keeping her eyes fixed on the massive building with its high arched windows and stone statue sentries that lined the rooftop as if looking down on her with disapproval.

It was already after ten o'clock. There was no time to waste.

In the lobby she saw Willi Graf on his way to class. Traute LaFrenz was with him, and Beth waved to them both. She remembered then that he and Josef both attended Professor Huber's lecture at that hour, so she stopped in the atrium of the building, hoping to see Josef hurrying to class as well.

When there was no sign of him, Beth started up the wide stairway past a pair of life-sized white marble figures to the floor above. She stopped long enough to peer into the lecture hall where Professor Huber was about to begin his class to make sure that Josef was not there. She saw lots of men in uniform but no Josef. As she made her way along the corridor, one by one doors closed as classes began. Beth was relieved to realize that she was alone except for the custodian sweeping the stairs. With a nod to him she hurried past, hoping that he would assume she was simply late for class. Her uncle's office was down a narrow side corridor.

Reaching her uncle's office, she fumbled in her pocket for the key before realizing that the door stood slightly open. She stood frozen outside the door, listening for sounds of movement inside. After a long moment she cautiously pushed the door all the way back and stepped inside.

The room was a chaotic mess. Drawers open, files scattered, and the blotter stained with a spilt bottle of black ink lay on the floor along with a broken desk lamp, the plaster cup that Liesl had made in school and given to him to hold his pencils, and the nameplate that identified him as professor of natural sciences.

It took time to sift through all the papers and file folders scattered around the room, but she was fairly certain that whoever had searched the office had already taken any incriminating documents. She glanced at a wall clock and saw that it was nearly eleven. Classes would be letting out soon, and the halls would be filled with students. She picked up the heavy black receiver of the telephone that sat precariously on a corner of the desk and dialed the apartment.

As soon as her uncle answered, she uttered two words and quickly hung up the phone. "Go now," she whispered, and she knew that he would understand.

Knowing she needed to get away from his office without being noticed, she stepped into the hallway and looked both ways before setting the door open to the degree it had been when she arrived. She could go down a back stairway, but she still hoped that perhaps Josef had arrived late for Professor Huber's lecture and she could warn him so that he could get to safety.

On tiptoe to keep her leather heels from echoing on the tile floor, she ran to the end of the hallway and edged close enough to the balustrade that she could see the floors below her and the main lobby. A few students were leaving their classroom as others began drifting in for their eleven o'clock lectures. Willi and Traute were just leaving the building. Beth called out to them and again they waved but left the building without stopping to visit.

A moment later she saw Hans and Sophie enter the large reception area below her. One was carrying a suitcase she recognized as one they used to store leaflets and the other carried a briefcase. They started up the stairs and headed along a corridor, leaving leaflets outside classroom doors. Then together they ran to the very top floor of the building.

Beth had little time for worrying about Hans and Sophie. She had her own problems. She hurried across the lobby, intent on catching up with Willi and Traute. Josef and Willi had the same class schedule, and she knew that their next class was in a building closer to the hospital. If she could just catch the same streetcar that Willi and Traute were no doubt catching, she could find Josef and go with him straight to the train station. There was still time to meet up with her aunt and uncle and Liesl. There was still time to escape Munich.

There was still time.

But just as she reached the main floor, a shower of white papers rained down around her and the other students. She caught one and glanced up in time to see Hans and Sophie shaking the last of the latest White Rose leaflets from the suitcase. Immediately the custodian that she'd seen sweeping when she arrived raced up the stairway toward them, shouting for them to stay where they were. At the same time, uniformed students automatically took up positions blocking the exits. There was nothing she could do for Hans and Sophie, so she ran for the one exit that was still unguarded.

As other students crowded into the hallways on all floors, straining to see what the commotion might be about, Beth glanced back once at Sophie and Hans. Amazingly they had made no attempt to flee but rather stood patiently waiting for the custodian to reach them. When Beth looked back, the exit was blocked.

An eerie silence punctuated only by the shrill whine of arriving police and Gestapo vehicles settled over the crowd. No one spoke except in whispers as everyone watched the brother and sister being marched into a nearby office. Police began pouring into the building, followed by a phalanx of storm troopers. Near her, Beth saw some students pick up a copy of the leaflet and then drop it instantly as if it might scald them. A few others took the leaflet, scanned it, and then quickly hid it inside a book or pocket before heading for the exit. Next to her the policeman stationed at the exit pushed forward to collar one such student, and Beth saw her chance to slip away from the building. But before she could, a storm trooper stepped in front of the door.

Outside the whine of arriving Gestapo and more police vehicles drowned out any attempt at conversation. Those students and faculty who had been intent on getting away as quickly as possible could now only wait and watch as Gestapo agents strode into the building followed by an entourage of SS officers. In the hushed silence that followed the agents' entrance, somewhere outside a clock chimed the half hour.

Beth scanned the crowd. She had to believe that Josef had not attended the lecture, for surely he would have left earlier with his friends. On the other hand he could still be here. Above her she saw Professor Huber. She moved slowly through the crowd but saw no sign of Josef. *Where are you? Why weren't you with Willi and Traute?*

Careful not to draw attention to herself, she worked her way back up the stairs to the top floor, deserted except for a lone police officer who did not see her. He moved from room to room—trying doors that were locked, opening those that were not, and rounding up any students inside. Still no sign of Josef.

She hid behind a column until the policeman passed and then edged her way back to the main floor so that she could disappear into the crowd. She had just spotted another member of the White Rose— Gisela Schertling, Hans's current girlfriend—when the tenor of the whispered conversations around her shifted into silence.

Beth edged around a gathering of students and saw Hans and Sophie being led away. As they passed, Hans called out to Gisela, "Tell him I won't be coming this evening."

Beth recalled that this was the day Hans was supposed to meet with Falk Harnack to discuss the two resistance groups joining forces. As Hans and Sophie were led away, several students made a show of taunting them while others cheered the arrests. Beth could not help thinking how foolish they had all been to think that these students—some of them no doubt the very ones who had protested against the government only weeks earlier—would stand with them now.

And still they were held captive inside the building. Beth realized it could be hours before they were allowed to leave. She saw her former neighbor Werner guarding a side door and edged her way toward him. She gave him a weak smile and then sat down on the floor nearby, holding her head as if in pain.

"Fräulein?"

"I'm all right," she assured him, then grimaced. "I have these headaches, and unfortunately noise and crowds only make them worse.

Werner glanced around. "Go," he said, opening the side door barely a few inches.

She got the last seat on a crowded streetcar that she knew would take her to the railway station. If there were no delays, she would reach it in time to say good-bye to her uncle, aunt, and Liesl and assure them that she and Josef would follow.

But the car was filled with students all whispering about the events some of them had observed and others were eager to learn more about. The car stopped often, and by the time it reached the station, Beth was only in time to see the train pull away from the platform. She waved in case Uncle Franz or Aunt Ilse or even Liesl might be watching, and then she collapsed onto a wooden bench.

It was all too much for her. What was she to do now? The way her uncle's office had been searched was evidence enough that it would not be safe for her to return to the apartment. She did not know where Josef might be, and because she had spent most of her time caring for Liesl and in the company of friends of her uncle's—fellow Quakers, university faculty, and students who had long ago left Munich—she really had nowhere to turn.

A train chugged into the station. Up and down the way, the doors to each car slammed open, releasing a stream of passengers. Half-a-dozen Gestapo agents prowled the platform and the main station. A young priest emerged carrying a small suitcase and looking around as if trying to get his bearings.

Beth studied every face—looking for what? A potential ally? A familiar face perhaps from the White Rose? Josef?

She was becoming as bad as Aunt Ilse at seeing things that were not there. She forced herself to move away from the station, along familiar boulevards and streets, past places she knew as well as she had once known her small village back in America. She walked for hours, aware but not comprehending the passing of the hours. Exhausted, she wandered into the small park where she had first encountered Anja and the children.

She sat down on the concrete bench, planted her feet firmly on the frozen, snow-covered ground, and closed her eyes as she prayed for guidance.

Josef had spent the night at the hospital and stayed on through the day working a double shift as much because he simply needed a place to be as because he wanted the extra work. Just before his second shift ended, he heard other medical students just arriving to begin their shift talking about the arrests and knew that it was only a matter of time until names would be revealed and more arrests would be made.

Beth.

She was already of interest to the authorities. Only his father's power had kept her safe until now. But if it came to light that she knew Hans and Sophie and the others...

He was running by the time he reached the hospital's exit. He went first to the apartment and stood across the street from the bakery under the tattered awning of the abandoned bookstore, watching as men went in and out of the entrance to the apartments. When they finally got into their car and drove away, Josef went around to the rear courtyard and entered the building. The door to the Schneiders' apartment stood open, and he could see that the place had been searched.

For once he did not remove his shoes as he entered the hallway and noticed the doors to every room standing open. Ridiculous as it was, his first thought was how upsetting that would be to Ilse.

There were no coats hanging on the hooks in the foyer. No neatly aligned pairs of shoes showing that the professor or Ilse or Beth or Liesl were home—only their slippers kicked aside in the foyer. He walked quickly down the hall to the bedrooms. The double mahogany doors to the wardrobe in the professor's room stood open, revealing only a cluster of empty hangers and a single forgotten woman's shoe.

In the room that Liesl shared with Beth, Liesl's clothes were gone but not Beth's. Hers were stacked on one of the two single beds next to an open suitcase. He fingered a blouse that he recognized as the one she'd been wearing the night he had proposed to her, then grasped it to his face, inhaling the scent of her.

He heard a step outside the doorway and turned. The baker's wife stood holding out an envelope to him. "They left this for you and this one for their niece," she told him. "But. . ."

"I will see that she gets it," he promised, stuffing the one addressed to Beth in his jacket pocket and buttoning the flap to secure it. "Thank you."

Without another word, the woman retraced her steps down the hall and shut the front door to the apartment quietly behind her as she left.

He sat on the edge of Liesl's bed as he tore open the envelope addressed to him. Scanning the contents and reading between the lines, he understood that Beth had gone to the university—to the professor's office—and that she had called them from there to warn them. They were on their way to catch the train to Lenggries.

Lenggries? What about Eglofs and Marta?

Spurred to action, Josef placed some of Beth's clothing in the suitcase and then ran up to the attic to retrieve some of his clothes as well. He barely paid attention to the fact that his room had also been searched but not nearly as thoroughly as the professor's study. Downstairs he finished packing and snapped the latches of the suitcase closed.

This time he left by the front entrance, stopping at the bakery to buy some rolls and casually mentioning that he was going to visit friends. The baker's wife nodded and refused to let him pay.

Now he had to find Beth. The professor obviously knew nothing of the arrests, but Josef was certain that Beth had heard the news even if she had managed to be away from the university when they occurred. She would know better than to return to the apartment, but where would she go?

Unconcerned by the understanding that he could be in as much danger of being arrested as she was, Josef roamed the neighborhoods that he knew she frequented. He went to Liesl's school and half expected to see Beth waiting with others for a child. But she was not there—and of course, assuming that the professor had gotten on that train, neither was Liesl. He went to the restaurant in the marketplace where they had spent hours together, talking and laughing and worrying about the future.

He walked and walked until he felt as if he could not take another step and as if the suitcase held bricks instead of clothes. Finally he sat down on the steps of the church where they had taken Anja and Benjamin that night. He closed his eyes at first in weariness, and then he realized that he was silently praying for God to lead him to her. *Help me find her.*

In a perfect world, he would have opened his eyes and seen her crossing the street, but Munich in February 1943 was far from perfect. When he opened his eyes, it was growing darker and colder, and there was no sign of Beth.

Please.

He stood and picked up the suitcase again but left the rolls behind. The bread would be stale by the time he found her—if he found her. For reasons he couldn't understand, he found that he was thinking more about Anja and Benjamin as he walked than he was about Beth. That irritated him, and he tried to force his thoughts back on Beth.

Instead he wondered where they were now. He thought about the boy—so bright and perceptive. He thought about the night that he and Beth had introduced Anja and Benjamin to her aunt and uncle as his friends while the children hid in the rear courtyard.

Suddenly he knew where Beth would be.

Beth was so cold she was shivering. In her haste to leave the apartment and retrieve her uncle's incriminating papers, she had grabbed only a heavy sweater from the hook in the front hall. It was a sunny day, and the weather had been mild for February all week. But with dusk coming on and no sun to warm her as she huddled inside her hiding place, she could feel the damp chill down to her bones.

She was well aware that some of her shivering came not from the cold but from fear—the abject terror she had felt when she'd come back to the apartment building and seen two black sedans parked outside. If they happened to look out the window, they would see her. She had to hide.

Where? Acting on sheer instinct she had made her way to the rear courtyard, seeking a place she could hide until the agents left. She had glanced around at the piles of snow and bare spots where some of the snow had melted. She had first considered hiding in the cellar, but the door opened at ground level and had to be pulled closed by a pulley system that would surely attract someone's attention. Besides, it was heavy and awkward to operate, and what if she didn't have the strength?

So she had rejected the idea of the cellar and resumed her visual search of her surroundings for any possible place she might hide—at least until dark. She edged along the garden wall toward the rear gate. Perhaps beyond that gate. . .

Then she saw the perfect hiding place. It had certainly worked once before and surely would again. It was the temporary shelter that Josef had managed to cobble together to shelter Anja's children while their parents were inside the apartment pretending to be people they weren't on their way to a concert.

She had crawled beneath the low lean-to made of a cast-off trellis covered with evergreen branches the gardener had trimmed and left to be stripped and cut up for kindling in the spring. The place smelled of damp earth and the faint remnants of cedar berries. Once she sat down with her arms wrapped around her knees, she filled the space entirely.

At first she had listened intently, trying to identify every sound. She had heard the Gestapo agents leave the building, the slam of their car doors, the roar of their powerful car engines. She had heard neighbors enter the courtyard and share the news. "Did you hear? I told my husband that it was only a matter of time before they came for her—an American living right out in the open."

Sometimes she recognized the voice as someone her aunt considered a friend, someone to be trusted. Sometimes she did not recognize the voice at all and realized how isolated they had become, staying to themselves—especially her. She rested her forehead on her knees. How very lonely her life had become. For months her contact had been mostly limited to her uncle, aunt, and Liesl.

And Josef, she reminded herself sternly. And the contacts she'd made in working with the White Rose—Traute and Sophie, Alex, and Willi, and the others. How she had looked forward to the meetings and the times spent cranking out leaflets and stuffing them into envelopes in the small rented rooms that Hans and Sophie shared. For the first time in months—no, years—she had felt as if she were living a normal existence among people her own age. And the work was thrilling, especially when news came of the student uprising after some official lectured the female university students about wasting time and money going to school when they should be finding husbands and having babies—preferably male babies. A faint smiled tugged at her lips as she recalled how incensed Sophie had been over that whole business.

But Sophie had been arrested along with Hans and who knew what others. Everyone was well aware that the government had their ways of getting people to tell them what they wanted to know. In this case they would want the names of anyone remotely involved in the movement.

What if they had arrested Uncle Franz? She had seen the train leave but had no idea if he and Aunt Ilse and Liesl were actually on it. And what about Josef? Would his father be able to warn him—protect him? She prayed for it to be so.

Somewhere a clock chimed six. She would wait for the chime of seven before making her move. All the shops would be closed by then, and most people would be home behind their blackout curtains for the night. The streets would be deserted, especially in residential areas. Of course there would be patrols of police and storm troopers, but if she took care, she could avoid them.

She closed her eyes. Now after hours in this position she felt as if she might never be able to stand up straight again. She was so very tired. . . so very cold. . .so very frightened.

CHAPTER 16

Josef found Beth exactly where he had thought she might be. She was sound asleep, her face covered with lank tendrils of her blond hair. He could smell the decayed leaves and garden refuse along with the dank wool of her sweater.

"Beth," he whispered. "Beth, it's me—Josef." He touched her shoulder, and she startled awake and shrank from him. "I'm here." He knelt so that she could hear him more clearly and perhaps make out his features in light from the half moon reflecting off the snow. "It's all right."

Clumsily she crawled toward him and fell into his arms. "Josef," she said, her voice a painful rasp. She touched his face, his hair, his shoulders as if trying to reassure herself that he was not some dream. "Oh, Josef, what are we to do?" She buried her face in the crook of his neck, muffling her sobs.

"Come," he urged, half lifting her with him as he got to his feet. "Let's get you some dry clothes."

"No. The Gestapo. . ." she hissed when she realized where he was leading her.

"They won't come back—at least not tonight."

He understood that she did not have the strength to resist. She could barely walk, so cramped were her muscles from staying in one position for however many hours. He wrapped his coat around her shivering shoulders and helped her to the front of the building, then up to the door of her uncle's apartment. Inside the moonlight came through the windows, for there had been no one to close the blackout curtains until now. "Sit," he instructed as he shut the door and moved from room to room, closing the curtains.

When he returned to the front room where he'd left Beth half-reclining on the sofa, she was not there. His heart racing, he headed for the front door and then saw her standing in her uncle's study holding the professor's pipe in her hand. "Why wouldn't he have taken this with him?" she asked. "He loved this pipe."

"He was in a hurry. We can take it to him." He eased the pipe from her ice-cold fingers. "Come, I'll make a fire. We'll have some tea."

After he had built a fire in the wood stove and prepared tea and filled a plate with a stale pretzel, some mustard, and hard cheese and set it before her, Josef went to her room. He had abandoned the suitcase in the courtyard so he could help Beth. Now he sorted through the remaining clothing on her bed and found a pair of wool slacks, a long-sleeved blouse, a sweater, and a pair of heavy socks. "Here are dry clothes," he said, laying the clothing on the bench next to the kitchen table. "I'm going up to the attic to get an extra jacket."

She remained sitting, staring at the floor. She had not touched the food or the tea. "Beth, we have to get out of here as soon as possible—now change and then eat something."

She stared up at him unseeing. "Don't leave me," she whispered.

He knelt next to her. "I won't leave you, but you must get out of those wet clothes and into something warm and dry, and your aunt would have my head if she thought I had been in the room while you changed."

His ploy worked. The mention of her aunt brought the hint of a smile to her lips, and she took a sip of the tea before setting the cup on the table. She peeled off the sodden sweater. "Well go on," she said. "We wouldn't want to upset Tante Ilse."

Josef ran up the attic stairs. He rummaged through his trunk until he found a sweater vest, which he pulled on over his shirt. Then he put on a wool military jacket over that. They would leave the suitcase—it would only slow them down and draw attention. They were fugitives and needed to spend the night on the run. They might spend the next several days and nights on the street—but better that than in a prison cell.

When he came downstairs, Beth was dressed and seemed somewhat recovered. She was packing whatever food she could find into a knapsack that the family had carried on picnics in happier times. She wore her coat and hat and the leather gloves he had given her.

"Where are your mittens?"

"I prefer these."

He took her hands. "These will not keep you warm enough."

"Then I will wear my mittens over them," she informed him and continued searching for food to add to their supply. If he hadn't been so filled with panic, he might have smiled. This was the Beth he knew—and loved.

It was clear to Beth that Josef had no better idea than she did of where they should go next. By the time they sneaked away from the apartment the next morning, it was stunning how quickly options they had once taken for granted were no longer available to them. They could not risk traveling by streetcar or buying a train ticket. The train station was teeming with men in uniform—police, storm troopers, Gestapo. Just walking down the street they might be stopped at any moment and asked to show their papers.

"Perhaps they are not looking for you," she suggested as they walked as quickly as they dared so as to not attract attention. Josef turned down a street where he had heard of a man willing to create forged documents.

"We can't take that risk."

The man was not home. "He left," a neighbor across the hall informed them. "I have pen and paper if you want to leave a note."

Josef grinned broadly at the woman and slapped his forehead.

"Dumkopf, I got the day wrong," he told her and then took hold of Beth's elbow and steered her back down the stairs.

"Now what?"

"Lilo," he said, already walking away.

Lilo Ramdohr was a friend of the White Rose—especially close to Alex Schmorell—but she had stopped short of becoming fully involved in the group's activities. If anyone could help them, it would be Lilo. Beth hurried to catch up to Josef. Lilo's apartment was on the other side of the city. It would be late by the time they got there.

Lilo opened the door to her apartment as if she had been expecting them. She served them a thin potato-and-red-cabbage soup as she told them what she knew of the events of the last twenty-four hours.

"We passed by Willi's place but. . ."

"Willi left yesterday to have dinner with his cousins in Pasling. He got home around midnight and was immediately arrested along with his sister."

"And Hans and Sophie?"

"The Gestapo found the typewriter and some of the envelopes and stationery in Hans's apartment. They are both still being held at Wittelsbacher as far as I've been able to learn."

Beth did not have to be told that Wittelsbacher Palace was headquarters for the Gestapo. She shuddered. "And Alex?"

"Everyone is in danger. We have no idea what they have done to our friends or what names they've been forced to reveal. They are also looking for Christoph. They found his leaflet in Hans's pocket. He tried to get rid of it but failed. No one can say for sure what will happen now."

"Won't there be a trial? I mean, they've been arrested and presumably charged," Beth pointed out.

Lilo gave her a smile that spoke volumes about her opinion of that wishful thinking. "This is not America, Beth. A trial is at best a formality."

"But if the students rise up—"

"As they did when Hans and Sophie were taken into custody? I understand some actually cheered."

It was true. Beth had seen that for herself.

Lilo turned to Josef. "I cannot help you. You might have some chance if you ask for mercy from your father—perhaps he. . ."

Josef stood and laid his napkin next to his plate. "Thank you, Lilo. We will find a way," he said as he held out his hand to Beth. "Take care."

Beth understood that Lilo had no choice but to let them go. She could only pray that this dear brave woman would be safe and that someday perhaps when this horrible war was finally over they could all. . .

It was better not to think beyond this moment. She and Josef were fugitives and needed to find a place to hide. As they stood outside Lilo's building buttoning their coats and fumbling in the pockets for gloves and mittens, Josef pulled two envelopes from his pocket.

"I forgot I had these," he said. "The professor left you this note." He handed her the envelope. "He left a message for me as well."

"What did yours say?" Beth asked, frustrated at the awkwardness of her mittens as she tried to open the tightly sealed envelope.

"They got your call. They were sure they could make the train to Lenggries in time. We should join them as soon as possible." He turned the paper over as if expecting more. "Why there? Why not to Marta's in Eglofs?"

"Perhaps they had to change plans," Beth said as she finally pulled off one mitten and ripped open her envelope. Her message was even more brief than Josef's had been, and the words written in her uncle's familiar flowery scrawl struck fresh fear into her heart: *Josef has betrayed us.*

Beth's face had gone pale as she read her uncle's message, but when Josef reached for the note, she crumpled it and shoved it into her pocket. "He says—that is, it says the same as yours."

A military transport truck rumbled by.

"We should go," Josef said and reached for her hand as he glanced around for the safest route. "This way," he said and realized that she had not taken his hand. Indeed when he turned to her, she was backing away from him, her hands stuffed into her coat pockets, her shoulders hunched.

"I think perhaps we would be safer if we split up. After all, people know we are often together, and Lilo said that Willi had been arrested. If he gives them our names. . ."

"Willi would never. . . ." He could see that she was terrified but thought her fear was understandable given everything she'd had to face over the last two days. He took a step toward her. It was only when she turned from him that he realized that what she feared most at this moment was him.

"Beth," he said, stretching out his hand to her.

She ran to board a streetcar just pulling away from the curb. As she reached up to grab onto the door post, the crumpled paper fell from her pocket. Josef ran alongside the car as she made her way toward a window seat, but although he continued to run until he could no longer match the streetcar's speed, not once did she look at him.

He stood in the middle of the street, paralyzed by confusion as he watched her disappear. Then he walked back to where he'd seen the note fall and picked it up.

Josef has betrayed us.

How could the professor believe such a thing? How could Beth believe such a thing? He loved her. He would gladly sacrifice his life for hers. Suddenly nothing mattered—not his rage at what Hitler was doing to his beloved homeland, not the work of the White Rose, not even the arrest of his friends and the likelihood that he would be among them soon if he didn't find a way out of the country.

The only thing that mattered was that Beth believed that he had deceived her. If it was the last thing he did, he had to find her and convince her that he had not.

Beth rode the streetcar to the end of its route and found herself in Harlaching, where Josef's parents lived. Because she had only been in this part of the city that one time, it was definitely unfamiliar territory. As she exited the streetcar, other passengers crowded on—men and women headed home from work or shopping, wanting to be back in the safety of their houses or apartments before dark. Not one of them smiled. Ever since the defeat at Stalingrad, it was as if everyone had suddenly realized that Germany was vulnerable and that history might repeat itself. Those who had lived through the first war were all too aware of what could happen if once again Germany went down in defeat.

On the other hand, everyone's preoccupation with the future meant that they paid little attention to her. Dressed as she was, Beth might pass for someone on her way home after a day in the country. She walked quickly along the busy street, barely glancing left or right as if on a mission to reach her destination. Anyone passing her would never guess that she had no idea what that destination might be.

As she left the shopping district behind and walked down the streets lined with homes very like the one where Josef's parents lived, twilight settled over the city. Beth's panic became real. A wind from the north promised a cold night despite the sunny day just passed. Without once breaking stride, she considered every park and garden gate she passed as a possible place she might hide until it got dark and she could move about the city more freely.

At the same time, she could not get Josef or her uncle's message out of her mind. How could she not have known? How could it possibly be true? Perhaps it was Uncle Franz who had been fooled. Perhaps somehow he'd been led to believe that Josef had betrayed them when all along...

She hunched her shoulders and shoved her hands deeper inside her coat pockets, feeling all the while the soft leather of the gloves that Josef had given her clinging to her fingers and hands. It was almost as if Josef himself were touching her, linking his fingers with hers as he so often had these last weeks. She should have given him the opportunity to explain. She should have trusted her love for him—and his for her.

Oh, Josef, what am I to do?

Then she saw the church, its spire half-gone and one wall of what had once been the sanctuary reduced to rubble where the bombs had struck. She climbed over piles of brick and stone until she reached what had been the interior. Rows of pews covered in dust faced an altar that sagged badly on one side.

Beth made her way to a far corner of the church and sat down in one of the pews. She closed her eyes and opened her heart as she settled into the tradition of silent waiting that was the very heart of her faith.

Eventually she slept, and when she woke just before dawn, she realized that someone had been there, for she was now curled onto the pew and covered with a rough blanket. Panicked, she sat up and felt for her purse. It was still there, worn bandolier-style across her body. She checked to be sure that her papers and the small amount of cash she had were still inside. Her knit hat had come off in the night, and her hair lay in damp clumps around her face and shoulders.

Kneeling in front of what remained of the altar was an old woman wearing a babushka with her head bowed. Four small candles burned on the steps to the altar. As quietly as possible, Beth folded the blanket and laid it over the back of the pew. Then she removed her mittens and gloves and combed through her hair with her fingers. Shaking with the morning cold, she pulled her hair over one shoulder and braided it, then used a length of string she found on the church floor to tie off the plait. Her hat was sodden and would be useless to keep her warm so she stuffed it into her pocket.

She slid to the end of the pew and considered her escape route. If she left the way she'd come, she was bound to make a racket climbing back over the rubble. But the other way led deeper into the interior of the church, and who knew what awaited her there?

"*Gut geschlafen*, Fräulein?" The woman in the front row was coming toward her. She was short and stocky and dressed in a man's heavy coat, galoshes that flopped around her ankles, and a wool scarf.

Beth's mind raced with possibilities. She glanced around, half-expecting to see the familiar brown shirts of a team of storm troopers come to take her away. "I—did you bring the blanket?" she asked even as she edged closer to the aisle that was opposite the path the woman was taking to reach her.

"I did. My name is Helga, and you are?"

"Beth—Elizabeth." Beth had ascertained that there was a corridor just behind her and hoped that it might lead to an exit and escape.

Helga sighed heavily. "Please do not run from me. I am far too old and far too fat to chase after you."

"You are with the..."

"I am with no one. Not the government. Not the underground. Not the church. I am quite alone in this world, and it would appear you are as well."

"I have a family—an uncle and aunt in Eglofs—and if I could just..."

"You are a long way from Eglofs, my dear." She pulled something from the bag she carried over one arm and held it out to Beth. "Eat something."

Josef had been carrying the knapsack of food when she'd run from him, so it had been several hours since she'd last eaten. As Beth accepted the hard roll that Helga offered her, the woman sighed and pulled a second roll from the bag, plopped down on the nearest pew, and took a bite. "So here we are."

"Where is your family, Helga?" Beth was not used to addressing a stranger by her given name, but then the woman had offered no other information.

"Dead," she said. "My husband in the last war and now all three sons in Stalingrad. Every morning I light a candle for each of them."

"You live nearby?"

"I live here." She nodded toward the recesses of the small church that Beth had considered her escape route. "If you want to stay until you can figure out your next move, I don't mind."

"I don't know this area. How far is the train station from here?"

Helga laughed. "Not far, but being a fugitive as I suspect you are, that's the last place you want to go. Don't you have any friends you can contact?"

Beth could not have been more surprised when the words that came from her mouth were, "My friends have either been arrested or—like me—are trying to escape."

The woman studied her more closely and then nodded. "That business at the university the other day? Those are your friends?"

Beth thought of denying the woman's assumption, but how could she? These were indeed her friends. "Ja."

Helga clicked her tongue as she shook her head. "Those children are no different than my children," she murmured more to herself than to Beth. "All of them fighting for what they thought would be best for Germany. You can be sure that the authorities will make an example of them."

"They'll be sent to Dachau?"

Helga's laugh was guttural and completely without humor. "They'll sentence them to death like they did that American woman and her husband. They like to make the most of the flashy stories like this one."

Josef.

Beth was on her feet at once. "I have to go. Thank you so much for your kindness—the blanket, the roll."

Helga waved off her gratitude. "Going to get yourself arrested, are you? And what good will that do?"

"I'm going to try and save a friend. His parents live in this area." She gave Helga the address and asked for directions.

"He's Gestapo—Detlef Buch," Helga whispered as if to merely state the fact placed them in more danger.

"I know that, but his son is not. And I have to believe that Josef's mother will do anything to protect her child and that even his father..."

Helga nodded and stood. "Come on," she said, leading the way through what was left of the church to the street. Once there she gave Beth the directions she needed to reach the Buch home. "I hope this young man's mother has more luck saving him than I did saving my boys," she said. "You tell her that I said that enough of our brave boys have died for this senseless war. You tell her. . . ." She broke down and sobbed, but when Beth would have stayed to console her, Helga pushed her away. "Go. You have work to do and not much time to do it."

~≋~ CHAPTER 17 ≋~

She was too late.

When the servant answered the door, she saw the way he hesitated and glanced toward the stairs before greeting her. "Fräulein Bridgewater," he intoned. "May I help you?"

His tone and expression were funereal, and Beth felt her heart lurch into a gallop of panic. "Josef?"

"Who is it, Gustav?" Frau Buch's voice trembled with fear as she came to the door. "Oh, Beth, my dear, come in. Come in."

Beth did not miss the way that Gustav glanced uneasily toward the street as he opened the door just wide enough for her to enter. The aura inside the grand house was so very different than it had been the night she had come for dinner. Even though the late-morning sun streamed through a series of large windows, the feeling was one of solemnity that bordered on grimness. Josef's mother looked as if she had not slept in days. Her eyes were swollen with the aftermath of crying, and her hair was a wild bird's nest around her face.

"Did you hear? Do you know anything? Anything at all that can save him?"

The woman peered closely at Beth as if expecting to find answers by simply looking into her eyes.

Beth turned to Gustav because it was evident that Josef's mother was on the verge of a complete breakdown. "What has happened?"

"He was arrested last night." The servant did not have to call Josef by name.

"Where have they taken him?"

"Headquarters," Gustav replied. "Herr Buch has gone there to see—"

"And they'll arrest him as well," Frau Buch moaned as she sank onto one of the carpeted steps leading up to the main floor. "What are we to do?"

Somewhere in the bowels of the house, a telephone jangled. Gustav left to answer it. Beth sat on the step next to Josef's mother and put her arm around the woman's shoulders. "Surely. . ."

Frau Buch looked at her. "Don't you understand? He was one of them—those students arrested day before yesterday. They are to be tried today." She edged back from Beth. "You knew. You *know*."

Gustav returned, carrying Frau Buch's coat, hat, and gloves. "That was Herr Buch's secretary. He is sending a car for you, and I told him of Fräulein Beth's arrival. He said that she should come as well."

"Josef?"

"Herr Buch has retained the services of an attorney—a trusted friend of the family. Josef will not be tried with the others." Gustav held the coat for her, and once she put it on, he handed her the hat and gloves. "But. . ."

Both women gave the servant their full attention.

"What?"

"He will be tried."

They all turned at the sound of a car arriving. Gustav held the car door for them while the driver kept the engine running. "Hurry," Frau Buch murmured when he started slowly down the drive.

"I have an idea," Beth said in a low voice. She saw the driver watching her in the rearview mirror and cupped her hand to prevent him from seeing her lips. "Please, Frau Buch, when we arrive let me speak with your husband privately."

"You foolish girl," Frau Buch hissed. "We have no idea if my husband. . ."

"But he sent the car," Beth reminded her.

"Did he?" The wild-eyed look Frau Buch gave her struck terror in Beth's heart. Josef's mother was nearly hysterical with fear.

There was little to be gained by trying to reason with her, so Beth leaned back and stared out the window as she searched her brain for some way she might save Josef. She was completely spent. This is what Germany had become—a nation of people afraid of their own neighbors, terrorized by their government, and nearly hysterical with having to face a future they could not imagine. She closed her eyes and willed herself to shut out everything and everyone for the duration of the ride.

After reading Franz's message, Josef had been so intent on finding Beth that he'd done the one thing he should have known would be the worst thing he could possibly do. He had gone to the railway station.

The place had been relatively quiet—making it feel even more ominous than if there had been hundreds of people around. He checked the timetable for departures to Eglofs, having realized that Franz had been trying to deceive him in saying the family had gone to Lenggries. The last train for the day had already left, and there was no sign of Beth. He was about to continue his search when someone tapped his shoulder.

"Sergeant Josef Buch?"

If the SS agent had addressed him as "Herr Doktor" he might have had the wits to deny his identity, but his military training was ingrained, and so he turned expecting to see someone from his former unit.

The SS agent did not smile. "Come with us, bitte." He nodded to a second agent, who fell into step next to Josef. A few people glanced at the trio as they passed and then immediately turned their attention to other matters. Everyone knew that the arrests of Hans, Sophie, and

Christoph had set off a massive hunt for anyone else who might have been involved in the activities of the White Rose.

Outside the station the two agents led Josef to a Mercedes similar to the one his father used going to and from his office. "I would like to let my father know—"

"Your father knows," one of the agents said as he waited for Josef to climb into the rear seat.

While Josef was trying to digest this information, the second agent got behind the wheel of the car and glanced over his shoulder. He was grinning at Josef. "Who do you think sent us to look for you?"

Surely they were joking—the kind of graveyard humor that those loyal to Hitler and his party seemed to enjoy. Josef did not return the man's smile.

He spent that night in a cell with one other prisoner. His fellow inmate spent much of the time they were together trying to get Josef to confide in him. Josef was certain that he was either a Nazi mole disguised as a prisoner or he was actually a prisoner and had been promised a lighter sentence or more food rations or some other reward if he could get Josef to talk. Either way the man was clearly dedicated to his assignment and, along with the lights left blazing in the cell round the clock, Josef got little sleep that night.

Before daylight found its way through the slit that passed for a window high on the wall of their tiny cell, guards came and took Josef to a windowless room. He sat at a metal table on a cold metal chair and waited. . .and waited.

Hours passed. Finally the door behind him opened and closed with a soft but distinct click. Josef waited for his interrogator without turning to acknowledge him. The man stood by the door for several minutes, but Josef could outwait him. He folded his hands on top of the table and stared at the blank wall in front of him. Then he closed his eyes and counted the footsteps of his interrogator.

Step. Step. Pause. Step. A deep sigh and then silence.

Josef opened his eyes.

Standing in front of the blank wall was his father.

Franz and Ilse had waited on the platform next to the snorting train until it was almost too late to board. Liesl had been in a foul mood—whiney and impatient to be going but at the same time fussing about the absence of Beth. The conductor had already given the first call to board, but Franz was certain that if they just waited a little longer, not only would they make the train but also Beth would arrive in time to join them.

He wondered if the baker's wife had managed to deliver his messages—especially the one to Beth. If not and if she located Josef and followed him instead of coming to the station as planned, she could be in serious trouble. And what if she'd been seen in his office at the university? What if she'd been arrested? What if...

"Franz, we have to go," Ilse said, tugging at his sleeve and glancing back at the conductor, who was checking his pocket watch. "She'll come on the next train—with Josef."

Franz had not told his wife about his belief that Josef had to have been the one to tell his father of Franz's activities with the White Rose. Franz had no proof of course, and he didn't want to believe it, but who else could have betrayed him? He knew how Josef longed to find some way to prove himself to his father, to show him that he was every bit the loyal German that his father was. How many times had he and the young doctor sat in his study, talking about the matter?

"Franz, the train will leave without us," Ilse pleaded even as the engine released a blast of steam and a long blare of its horn.

There was no choice. He helped Ilse and Liesl aboard as the train slowly moved away from the platform. The conductor offered him a hand up and then turned his attention to Liesl. "Well, Fräulein, and where are we off to today?"

"We're visiting my aunt, but my cousin..."

"She'll be on the next train," Ilse hurried to say, and she smiled at the conductor as she herded Liesl down the aisle to an empty seat.

When they arrived in Eglofs, they were surprised to see Marta waiting at the station for them. She sat behind the wheel of an old model car, and her three children were in the backseat. "Get in," she ordered tersely as soon as they approached the car.

Ilse and Liesl climbed in back with Marta's children while Franz took the front passenger seat. The door was barely closed before she took off.

"Where's Lucas?" he asked.

"He'll meet us there," Marta replied without looking at him as she navigated through the narrow streets of the village, past the building where she lived, and on out of town.

"Tante Marta," Liesl said, "you passed your house. Aren't we going to your house?"

"No, darling," Marta said, glancing in the rearview mirror and pasting on the phoniest smile that Franz had ever seen. "Surprise! We are going on holiday—to Switzerland."

"But Beth is coming later, and she won't know," Liesl said, and she began to wail. "How will she ever find us?"

"Now, stop that. Remember my neighbor—the one whose children you played with that day?"

Liesl sniffed and nodded.

"She will tell Beth where we are."

Franz knew that Marta was making up answers as she drove. She could not possibly have known that Beth would not be with them. He stared at her.

Marta continued to focus on the road, her hands clutching the steering wheel so tightly that her knuckles were white. "We do what we must," she said quietly, and Franz was not sure if her words were meant to reassure him—or her.

~⌁~

As soon as Josef's mother and Beth arrived at headquarters, they were escorted into a room furnished with comfortable club chairs arranged around a fireplace and told to wait. An hour passed, during which Frau Buch either stood staring out the window or paced back and forth occasionally murmuring to herself. Beth sat with her eyes closed and concentrated on taking deep, steady breaths. She wished that she were in the company of others who would join her in this silent reflection and waiting, but she was alone.

She blocked out the movements and sighs of Josef's mother, the sounds that came to them from outside the closed door and from the street. For that was what those of her faith did. "*Be still and know. . . .*" She deliberately left off the rest of the verse, finding strength and solace in the instructions to sit in silence until the knowledge she needed came to her.

An idea had been forming in her mind just as the car pulled up to Gestapo headquarters and she'd been aroused from her meditation to follow Frau Buch inside. Now she tried to reclaim the germ of that idea. Thoughts of Josef filled her mind. Where was he now? Why had she not trusted her love for him and his for her? How could she have believed her uncle's message when she had seen Josef take chances that could have gotten him shot? How could she have doubted him after listening to him speak of his deep love for his homeland and his deep fear of what Hitler and the Nazis were doing to destroy that? Always her thoughts returned to the love they shared—the bond they had found in being with one another.

Her eyes flew open. That was the answer. Of course. They were meant to be together—no matter the consequences.

She stood up and went to the door of the reception room. It was heavily carved and almost twice her height.

"They told us to stay here," Frau Buch said, her voice quavering with the fear that had only increased during the time they had been kept waiting.

Beth opened the door, and immediately a uniformed guard blocked her way. "I wish to speak with Herr Buch," she said and was amazed at how firm and steady her voice was. "I have information that may be of interest to him."

The guard frowned. "Wait here," he said.

As much to indicate her willingness to cooperate as anything else, Beth stepped back inside the room and closed the door. "Someone will come soon," she said.

Within minutes they heard the click of leather boots on marble flooring. "So, they will come now for us, you stupid, stupid girl," Frau Buch hissed. She drew herself up to her full height and faced the door, prepared to meet her fate.

Beth had a moment of doubt that she had done the right thing when, instead of Josef's father standing in the doorway, she saw the guard. "This way," he instructed.

They followed him across the lobby and down a stairway, then down another narrower stairway into a corridor lined on either side with doors. *Is Josef behind one of these doors?* Beth listened carefully for voices—his voice. But she heard nothing as she continued to follow the guard and Frau Buch through a maze of hallways that seemed to be leading them farther and farther into the depths of the building.

Finally the guard stopped outside a door and tapped lightly.

When the door opened, Frau Buch fell into the arms of her husband, sobbing uncontrollably. Herr Buch dismissed the guard with a nod as Beth pushed past him to reach Josef. She knelt next to his chair, taking his hands in hers. "Forgive me," she whispered. "Please forgive me."

He pulled his hands free of hers, and her heart sank. But then he cupped her face. "I love you, Beth." He pulled her to him, kissing her face as he murmured again, "Never doubt that. I could not go on if..."

"Shhh," she whispered as she stroked his hair. "We'll get through this together."

She was aware that Josef's father had calmed Frau Buch and led her to the only other chair in the room. He handed his wife the glass of water that sat in front of Josef. "Take a sip," he instructed.

She did as he asked and then released a shuddering sigh as she focused her attention on Josef. "This has all been a terrible misunderstanding," she assured him. "Your father will. . . ."

ANNA SCHMIDT

Josef's father cleared his throat and held out his hand to Beth. "Fräulein. I understand that you have information that could be of help?"

Beth accepted his assistance in getting to her feet. She stood next to Josef's chair, her hand resting lightly on his shoulder. For the first time since entering the room, she was aware of a man seated at a desk in the corner of the room, a stenographer's notebook open before him and pen poised to record whatever she might say.

"I had thought—"

"This is an official interrogation of the prisoner, Fräulein," Herr Buch said. "You have information?"

Josef stood up. "Leave her out of this."

"Sit down," his father ordered.

"Detlef," Frau Buch protested.

Her husband ignored her. "Well, Fräulein?"

Beth tightened her grip on Josef's shoulder, hoping he would accept her signal to stay quiet. "Your son—"

"Sergeant Buch," the father-turned-Gestapo-agent corrected her with a glance at the stenographer.

"Dr. Buch has asked me to marry him, and I have accepted." She had no idea where those words came from. She had intended to take full responsibility for their involvement in the activities of the White Rose. "Given the current situation, we wish to marry as soon as possible."

Buch raised a hand to stop the stenographer from writing more. He walked over to the man's desk and picked up the pad, ripping off the most recent entry and crumpling it into a wad. "Give us a moment," he said, and the secretary scurried from the room.

Suddenly everyone—except for Beth—was speaking at once. Josef's mother stood up protesting and then embracing the announcement. "Of course, Detlef. This is the perfect solution. Josef marries Beth, and they are both deported, and—"

"Fräulein, I do not believe you fully appreciate the seriousness of the charges against this man."

Josef had turned to face Beth. "Stop this now. Already you have placed yourself in serious jeopardy by coming here and—"

Beth chose to focus on the words of Josef's father. "*This man,* as you have referred to him more than once, is your son, sir. He is not some unknown prisoner that you have been given to interrogate. He is your son."

Herr Buch's lips moved, but no sound came out. He turned his back to her.

It was Josef who spoke. "My father is only doing his job, Beth."

"Sergeant Josef Buch has committed acts of high treason against the government," Herr Buch reported in a monotone.

"In America his acts are known as free speech," Beth replied, and when the elder Buch half-turned to protest, she held up her hand and added, "and if my history is correct, such acts would once have also been considered the right of a free citizen here in Germany."

"Detlef, you must do whatever it takes to stop this madness. Our son—our only child. . ."

Josef's father released a sigh of pure exhaustion and defeat. "I cannot stop it. He will be tried and sentenced later tomorrow. At best he is facing a life sentence or perhaps the opportunity to *volunteer* on the Russian front. At worst—"

"No!" Frau Buch grasped her husband's arm. "He is innocent. He has done nothing wrong. He is a soldier and a loyal German. He—"

"I have confessed," Josef said. "I distributed literature that spoke against the government."

"And I helped him," Beth said. "So if Josef is to be tried and sentenced, then I must be as well. We were equal in our actions."

"You will name the others?"

"I will not," Beth replied resolutely.

"Not even if I can arrange for your safe return to your family in America?"

"I have come to consider Germany as much my home as Wisconsin is." She realized that this was true—that she had not returned to America when she could have because she felt some tie to the culture and people of Germany. "If Josef and I were to marry, we would surely have made our home here."

"I do not understand you, Fräulein."

For the first time in days, Beth felt a genuine smile cross her lips. "That is not the first time I have been told this, Herr Buch. Your son has also mentioned that I often confuse him."

"You could face death," he said to Josef.

"Then allow him to do so as a married man," Beth pressed.

"It might help if they were married," Frau Buch said, clearly clutching at any straw. "I'll call Father Schwandt."

"No," Josef said softly. "Beth and I are peace-loving people, and if we cannot be married in her faith—as Freunde—then we will have a simple civil union. Father, I am asking you for one last favor—expedite the paperwork so that we can be married immediately."

~~≋~~ CHAPTER 18 ~~≋~~

Shortly before Josef was to appear before the judge, his father took them to his office and introduced an older man. "Josef, you remember your grandfather's attorney, Dr. Karl Bretholz?"

Josef stood at once. "How are you, sir?"

"I am still here," the man replied with a wry smile.

Josef turned to Beth. "May I present my fiancée, Elizabeth Bridgewater?"

"So you are our little American troublemaker," Herr Bretholz said, taking Beth's hand and continuing to hold it as he looked around the room. "I suppose this will have to do, Detlef."

"Time is of the essence," Josef's father replied.

"I don't understand," Beth said.

"Dr. Bretholz was a judge of the court under the Weimar Republic. With the change in leadership, he decided to retire. He has been advising me on various projects since then."

"I still have the authority to perform marriages," Bretholz said. "Now then Elizabeth, suppose you tell me a bit of how this would go were you being married in the traditions of your faith—Quaker, is it?"

"Yes sir. Simply put, we believe that the success or rightness of a marriage depends on the two people involved rather than on any external service or words. The ceremony is performed in the presence of family and friends by the couple."

Josef saw his mother frown. "Surely there is some. . .process?"

"In normal times, Josef and I would have written to the clerk of my Meeting—my congregation—either here in Munich or back in Wisconsin. The clerk would read the letter in a meeting for business, and a clearness committee would then be appointed. Those Friends would consider whether or not there were external obstacles to the union—especially because Josef is not a Quaker."

She smiled at him.

"Well then, who do we contact for you here?" his mother asked.

Josef saw Beth hesitate. "I'm afraid, Frau Buch, there is no one left of the Meeting here in Munich. Everyone—except for me—is gone."

"Oh, this is a disaster. I am calling for Father Schwandt."

"Now now," the judge said, "let's not be so hasty. Elizabeth has said that in the end the decision is between the man and the woman. You are both of legal age?"

"We are," Josef replied.

"Then Quaker or Catholic is not the point. I perform civil ceremonies and as long as both parties are of age and there are no impediments—you aren't hiding a wife somewhere, are you Josef?"

For the first time in days, Josef actually laughed. "No, sir."

"Then there you have it. Shall we all gather nearer the fire?"

Josef took Beth's hand. They stood facing the judge, the fire's embers glowing behind him. Josef's parents stood to his right. But there was no one to stand with Beth. "Mother?" He gestured, and his mother shifted positions so that she was standing next to Beth. "Ready when you are, sir."

The judge smiled and from memory delivered the words of the civil ceremony. When the time came for giving Beth the ring, Josef realized that he had nothing to give her.

"It's all right," she murmured. "It is not our custom to have external symbols such as rings and flowers and such."

Behind her, Josef's mother slid a thin silver band from her finger and passed it to Josef. "It was your grandmother's ring," she told him. "She would be pleased."

"I really—" Beth started to protest.

His mother laid her hand on Beth's cheek. "Please indulge me, Beth. It is our custom to pass a special ring from one generation to the next."

Beth nodded, and the judge continued with the ceremony. When it was evident that he was about to pronounce them man and wife, Beth interrupted. "I would like to say something to Josef."

"By all means."

Josef thought he had never seen Beth quite so serene as she spoke in a strong, clear voice. "In the presence of God and your parents and of friends and family absent but present in spirit, I, Elizabeth Alice Bridgewater, take thee, Josef. . ." She hesitated, and they both realized she did not know his full name.

"Klaus Otto," his mother prompted.

"Josef Klaus Otto Buch, to be my husband. I promise with divine assistance to be unto thee a loving and faithful wife so long as we both shall. . ." Again she hesitated, and tears filled her incredible blue eyes. "Shall live."

Outside the door they heard footsteps approach and a murmur of voices, then a knock at the door before it opened. The guard looked in and announced. "It is time."

The judge completed the ceremony with the prescribed closing words. "You may kiss your wife, son."

Josef cupped his hands around Beth's face. "And I promise you, Liebchen, that when this war is ended we will have a proper Quaker ceremony with everyone we know in attendance."

Her tears ran freely down her cheeks, and as he kissed them away, his father took hold of his arm. "We must go now." Reluctantly Josef followed his father and the former judge who would defend him from the room.

Grateful that Josef's father had somehow managed to keep her from being arrested in spite of all she had revealed to him, Beth watched the trial with Josef's mother from the galley. Shortly before entering the courtroom, the news had reached Josef's father that Hans, Sophie, and Christoph had been given the death sentence. That sentence—death by beheading—was to be carried out later that same afternoon.

The news nearly drove Frau Buch to hysterics, but Josef took hold of her shoulders and pulled her into his embrace. "I love you, Mother, with all my heart. You and Father have made me the man I am today—a man proudly standing up for the country he cherishes. Take care of Beth."

His mother emerged dry-eyed from his arms and linked her arm with Beth's. "Be strong, my son."

Josef's attorney called a string of witnesses—people whom Beth had never seen before or heard Josef mention. All testified to his character—his devotion to family and country. None mentioned his involvement with the White Rose unless the prosecutor brought that up, which he rarely did. It was almost as if both the prosecution and the sitting judge had already determined the outcome.

Beth felt as if her heart would surely explode, so frightened was she for Josef. When the judge seemed about to pronounce sentence, Beth interrupted him by standing in the galley. Her hands planted on the railing, she called out to him in flawless German. "Your honor, if it please the court. . ." She really hoped the language she had picked up from watching movies was appropriate.

A guard moved toward her, but the presiding judge held up his hand. "Who are you?"

"I am the wife of the accused."

"American?"

"I am."

The judge signaled the guard to bring Beth from the galley to the courtroom floor. Despite her fear she walked to the elaborate desk where the judge sat high above her and raised her face so that she was meeting his gaze directly.

"Well?" he demanded.

"Herr Doktor Buch has served his country with great devotion and honor—"

"He is a traitor," the prosecutor shouted.

The judge silenced him with a look. "Continue."

She continued to use only German to state her case—her second language rolling easily off her tongue as she listed each point. Josef was a man of medicine. Surely there was a need for his services somewhere perhaps on the front or in one of the work camps the Reich had built in Poland. She was not a trained nurse but had years of experience caring for others. "Could we not better serve the Reich by caring for the wounded and the infirm?"

"You are offering to be sentenced with your husband?"

The sly gleam that sparkled in the man's eyes only added to her terror. "I am," she replied. "Because whatever his crime may be in the court's eyes, surely I am as guilty."

"Sergeant Buch has admitted to distributing literature and taking part in other activities of the group known as the White Rose. Are you saying that you also participated in such activities?"

"Beth, no," she heard Josef say.

"That is precisely what I am telling you, sir."

"You are an American spy?"

"I am no spy. I am a Quaker—a believer in no man's war. I do what I do to try and bring peace to those around me."

Again the smile. "Sit down, please."

Beth started back toward the steps that led up to the galley, praying with every step that she had not made matters worse for Josef.

"Not to the galley, Fräulein. Sit *there*," the judge ordered, pointing to a chair at the defendant's table next to Josef. "I will deliver sentence in one hour."

An hour passed, then two and then three. A guard brought water for Beth and Josef. As the clock over the exit ticked off the minutes and the courtroom emptied, a clerk closed the blackout shades and turned on lamps on the judge's podium and the prosecutor's and defendant's tables. The room filled with shadows, but Beth barely noticed as she clung to Josef's hand.

"I only wanted to help," she said. "I am so very sorry for. . ."

"Shhh. My brave girl. Whatever happens, we have each done our best."

Beth turned to Josef's parents—his father pacing back and forth, his mother having taken a seat just behind her son.

"Frau Buch? I believe that both Josef and I will be sentenced, and in that event, I would like for you to keep this." She removed the ring and handed it back to her mother-in-law. "It is likely to get misplaced where we are going."

Frau Buch accepted the ring. "I will keep it safe until you return to us."

Josef squeezed and released Beth's hand and then stood up and faced his father.

"I want you to know, sir, that I have always looked up to you—respected your honesty and integrity and belief in what you were doing. I only hope that in time you might come to see my side of things."

For a moment it looked as if Herr Buch might simply turn on his heel and walk away. Beth's heart broke for Josef. Then the elder Buch did something so unexpected that even his wife gasped in surprise. With tears running down his cheeks, he embraced Josef, and Beth heard him murmur, "I am so very proud to call you my son, Josef Buch. Your courage and, yes, your patriotism put me to shame."

The two men stepped apart as the presiding judge's clerk entered the courtroom and called for court to resume. Herr Buch returned to his place next to his wife as the lawyer sitting with them indicated that Beth and Josef should stand and face the judge.

"Josef Buch, I hereby sentence you to be stripped of your rank and citizenship and all privileges attendant to that and to spend the rest of your natural life imprisoned at SS-Sonderkommando Sobibor."

Behind them Beth heard Frau Buch break down in sobs—whether

relief that her son's life had been saved or despair that he would spend the rest of his days in prison, Beth could not have said.

"Frau Elizabeth Buch," the judge said in a singsong teasing way that made her blood run cold. "You may or may not know that a countrywoman of yours was convicted as a spy recently and hanged." He deliberately paused to take a long drink of water. "Still your plea that you should share in your husband's fate has moved me. Therefore, I sentence you to spend your life in SS-Sonderkommando Sobibor as well."

"Thank you," Beth blurted and immediately realized how foolish that must sound.

The judge looked down at her, and a hint of sadness colored his gaze. "Oh, do not thank me. In time you may both well wish that I had given you the easier way out—that I had sentenced you to die."

PART 3

SOBIBOR, POLAND
FEBRUARY—DECEMBER 1943

CHAPTER 19

The trip from Munich across much of Poland seemed endless and still was over far too soon. The judge had ordered them transported by truck rather than train because the trip would take less time. Beth had heard Josef's father say that the judge was having second thoughts about his unorthodox decision and wanted to get them to their assigned prison as soon as possible. Trains routinely were sidetracked for hours or even days while troop trains took precedence.

Behind them lay a situation they knew and could possibly navigate. There were people—like Josef's parents—who might be able to keep them safe even if they spent the rest of the war serving a prison term. There was always the possibility that the war would end sooner rather than later, that the Allies would come marching into Munich and they would be free.

Just a month earlier, Hans Scholl had assured Beth that the Americans would take Munich by the end of February 1943, and now Beth wished his optimism were warranted. She comforted herself on the trip by closing her eyes and imagining American soldiers stopping the transport truck in which she and Josef were riding and declaring them free to go wherever they pleased.

What lay ahead was a complete mystery—one where the clues were nothing more than gossip overheard through the years about a series of forced labor camps built by the Nazis in Poland for the purpose of using prisoners to produce whatever supplies might be needed for the war effort.

"Sobibor?" The guard escorting them had raised his eyebrows and exchanged a look with his companion. He had studied first her and then Josef closely. "You don't look Jewish."

"That's because I am German," Josef had snapped irritably and earned for himself a slap from the guard.

But Beth had thought about the guard's comment long after they had climbed into the rear of the transport with half-a-dozen other prisoners and Josef had fallen asleep next to her. The way the man had said those words: *You don't look Jewish.*

It was widely known that the Jews were being rounded up along with others—clergy and professors who dared to speak out, homosexuals, Jehovah's Witnesses. But it was the Jews who seemed to bear the brunt of Hitler's anger toward any group he deemed to be "subhuman." It was also widely rumored—though Beth had no actual proof—that Jews and others were being sent to special extermination camps in eastern Poland. The label assigned to such facilities told the story of their fate.

The sun was high as they approached the camp. The day was unusually warm for late February. Through a slit in the canvas that covered the truck, Beth saw that they were in a rural area, and she could hear a train approaching across the fields. She closed her eyes and called to mind a summer's day when she had gone to the foothills of the Alps for a day in the country with her aunt and uncle and Liesl. They had picnicked in the meadows and hiked the trails, singing Bavarian folk songs as they climbed. They had gathered wildflowers, and Aunt Ilse had made flower crowns for Liesl and Beth. But that had been years earlier when Liesl was still a toddler and Uncle Franz carried her easily on his back or shoulders as they climbed.

Where were Aunt Ilse and Uncle Franz and Liesl now? Beth couldn't help but wonder. She prayed that they were safe. Perhaps they had managed to cross those mountains into Switzerland. Perhaps they were even now sitting at a café, enjoying a cup of real coffee with Marta and her family. *Please hold them in Your light,* she prayed silently as the truck rocked from side to side, throwing her against Josef on her right and an older man on her left.

Throughout the entire journey, Josef had said nothing. Instead he either slept or sat with his arm around her shoulders, his feet planted resolutely on the littered floor of the truck, his eyes closed.

Finally the truck rumbled to a stop. A man wearing the uniform of the SS stepped forward and spoke to the driver. Behind him near a railway siding that ran directly into the camp stood several more soldiers with guns, some of them also restraining snarling dogs. Nearest to the track stood men in dark blue coveralls wearing caps with the "BK" insignia for the railroad station detachment or *Bahnhofkommando*. In the distance the train whistle sounded.

"They leave nothing to chance," Josef murmured as they waited their turn to leap from the truck to the ground. "Keep your eyes lowered," he added as they inched forward toward the opening. "If you look ahead, you will be looking into the sun, and if you raise an arm to shield your eyes the dogs might attack."

He was right, and Beth could not help but wonder how he knew. As she leapt from the truck, she heard a man cry out as a dog charged him and was barely held in check by its master. Slowly her eyes became accustomed to the light, and she cautiously took stock of her surroundings. They were just inside what she assumed were the main gates to the compound surrounded by a barbed-wire fence at least nine or ten feet tall. A very tall watchtower stood opposite a building marked ADMINISTRATION. Shorter watchtowers were arranged around the perimeter of the camp, and in each of them stood guards with guns, including machine guns.

Beth and Josef were standing in the midst of a cluster of buildings— most of them arranged in a square in one corner of the compound. She was able to identify some of the buildings as barracks, a garage, a barbershop, and a kitchen. There was one villa amongst those buildings that bore the sign SCHWALBENEST—Swallow's Nest. Closer to where she and Josef and the others waited was a two-story villa—a simple country home down to the early spring flowers some prisoners were tending in the front yard. Over the front door hung a sign—HAPPY FLEA.

Strange.

Her eyes fully used to the bright sunlight, she realized that there was not just one barbed-wire fence but three of them—one within the other. Between the one nearest her and the middle one, guards patrolled the perimeter. The outermost fence was entwined with evergreen branches. But if their wardens thought this touch would make the place seem less intimidating, they were wrong as far as Beth was concerned.

Through her work with the White Rose, Beth was well aware that as early as 1940, the Nazis began establishing forced-labor camps in the Lublin district of Poland. Most were set up in existing structures such as schools or factories, but not the Sobibor extermination camp. Beth had overheard the two guards driving the transport talking and learned that this camp had been built by Jews taken from ghettos in the area. The guard had also told his partner that rumor had it that as soon as construction was completed, the laborers were shot.

"Stand here," a guard said and led them to a spot off to one side of a platform where the SS officer who had met their truck now conferred with another man—the man in charge by the looks of things. Then another soldier turned on a phonograph, and the music of a Strauss waltz sounded throughout the compound.

The train huffed its way slowly along the siding, stopping in front of a barricade that marked the end of the track. The railway detail that had stood at attention facing the track now went into action, unlatching and sliding open the doors to five cattle cars. Beth watched in horror as dozens of men, women, and children pressed forward, squinting into the sunlight and accepting the helping hands of the BK as they leapt to the ground. Some of the men wore business suits. Some of the women wore coats trimmed in fur and hats with feathers or in one case a fashionable half veil. Some adults carried or held hands with a child.

They all spoke at once, calling out to one another as families separated during the journey were reunited. They were told to leave their luggage where it was—it would be delivered later. Immediately they were herded away from the train to an open assembly area outside the administration building. The soldier guarding Beth and Josef and those they had arrived with indicated that they should follow.

They wound their way through a barracks where they were told to deposit any hand luggage, purses, wallets, or papers that they might be carrying. At first the order was delivered as a polite request, but when a few resisted or questioned, they were pulled from the line and struck by a guard's fists or the handle of a whip.

Outside they came to another open area where an SS officer stood on a balcony above one of the buildings. The music had stopped. The man stepped to a microphone and called for silence.

He seemed genial enough. He even smiled as he addressed the new arrivals. "Wilkommen," he shouted, and the din quieted as all eyes turned to him. "I am SS-Oberscharführer Hermann Michel, and I wish to apologize for any inconvenience you may have suffered in your journey. I assure you that it is our intent to see that you get the rest you have earned as quickly as possible."

He appeared to be sincerely concerned for their welfare, and around her Beth saw several people visibly relax. She wondered at her inability to trust this man who certainly looked and sounded like someone who had their best interests at heart.

"However, I regret to inform you that there has been an outbreak of typhus recently in the area, and since your new home here was constructed on what was originally a swamp, we cannot take chances. For this reason we have asked you to abandon your belongings, but be assured that the porters will take care of delivering them to you after you have showered and been properly disinfected."

Murmurs through the crowd. A baby howled. The officer frowned. "Please, be quiet so that we can get this done in as orderly a manner as possible. The way to freedom lies in your ability to follow orders and work hard. If you do that, you will live in peace with your families until the war is won."

Next he asked them to separate into two groups—women and children on one side and men and boys over the age of fourteen on the other. Beth saw some of the men from the railroad detail pushing a couple of large wooden luggage carts through the compound. The guards began selecting people who were elderly or disabled or just unable to walk and helping them onto the carts. She saw one old woman gently pat the cheek of her helper. The guard brushed her hand away and turned to help the next person.

It broke Beth's heart to see the way people clung to family members as next the guards stepped in and began shoving and prodding and shouting at them to follow the officer's order.

"Excellent," the man standing on the roof said once the new arrivals stood in separate areas. "Now before you go, we need some volunteers for special assignments. Seamstresses, tailors, shoemakers, goldsmiths, mechanics?"

A few hands went up. Men in SS uniforms moved up and down the masses of people, questioning each volunteer and then choosing a few to stand apart as she and Josef were.

"*Sehr gut,*" the speaker said. "If you please. . ." He indicated that the women and children should proceed through yet another set of gates and down a long shaded path. Several of the women turned and waved to one or more of the men and boys waiting for their orders. Some of the smallest children skipped along or paused to pick up a stone. The carts carrying the infirm rumbled by, and last came the men and boys.

Beth studied their faces—some resigned, others lined with terror, and a few glancing around, their expressions seeming to say that they could do this—it would not be so bad.

"This way," a guard ordered as the gates closed behind the last of the male prisoners. Behind them the railway detail was now delivering luggage and other belongings to one of the buildings nearby.

It occurred to Beth that if the others were to be showered and disinfected, then why not those pulled aside as volunteers. She would ask Josef about that as soon as she got the chance.

Josef and Beth had traveled through the night to reach their assigned prison, and Josef was bone weary, thirsty, hungry, and determined to figure a way out of this place. As the others were led away, a bell sounded followed by the guards blowing whistles as, from every part of the compound, prisoners came running. Intent on gathering as much information as possible, Josef studied his fellow inmates. The women were all wearing dresses—the kind of housedress women wore at home when tending to the usual household chores. Some of them wore aprons and kerchiefs over their hair, but it was apparent that they still had their hair. The officer had told the women being sent for showers that—with apology—their hair would need to be cut for hygienic reasons.

As he and the others standing with him were shoved into the ranks, a guard ordered a man down the row from Josef to stand separate from the others and undress.

"Do not react," a voice behind Josef warned quietly. "And do not look away or show revulsion."

Josef did as he was told, but when the guard struck the man across his face because he was not undressing fast enough to satisfy the guard, Josef clenched his fists and made an involuntary move forward.

"You'll be shot," the voice said.

"Ukrainian bastard," another man next to him muttered.

The comment confirmed what Josef had been able to observe. The camp was run by a small contingent of SS men in charge of a larger group of Ukrainian soldiers—widely known to be even more brutal than their SS counterparts. Supporting both was a contingent of Jewish prisoners who had been given special status and privileges for their assistance in managing their fellow inmates.

Once the prisoner was undressed, he stood facing his tormentor, his hands at his sides, leaving his nakedness visible to everyone. "Stand there," the SS man growled, and then he turned to the others. "This man is accused of the crime of speaking out against our beloved Führer. For the benefit of our newest arrivals, let me be very clear about the punishment for such a crime." He turned around, pulled a sidearm from its holster, and shot the man at point-blank range.

Josef heard Beth gasp.

"Back to work," the man on the balcony shouted, and everyone scattered, running to their posts in various places around the yard.

A guard grabbed Josef's arm, pulling him away from the group.

"No!" Beth's protest rang out above the sounds of the others racing to their posts. The guard turned on her and raised his hand. He surely would have struck her had a man of obviously higher rank not stepped forward and stopped him. "Herr Doktor Buch?"

Josef came to attention, but he did not offer the Hitler salute.

"*Ich bin Kommandant* Franz Reichleitner," the man said. He spoke to Josef as if the two of them were alone. "I hope your father is well?"

"Ja. Danke, Kommandant."

The commandant turned his attention to Beth. "And this is your wife? The American?" He spoke to Josef in German but kept his eyes on Beth.

She stood a little straighter and met his stare directly. "I am," she replied in perfect German before Josef could say anything.

"*Schön,*" the commandant said even as he signaled one of the prisoners designated as a Kapo, or prisoner with privileges and responsibilities, to step forward. "Take Frau Buch for processing and then on to the sorting house." He turned back to Josef and indicated that Josef should walk with him as they followed Beth and the Kapo through yet another set of gates into a third compound.

Here the Kapo took Beth inside one of three identical buildings while Josef and the commandant continued across the yard toward a small building with a cross on it. "Unfortunately your predecessor made a serious error in judgment," Reichleitner said as they walked together.

"He attempted to escape and had to be shot. I trust that you—and your wife—will be more gracious and appreciative when it comes to accepting our hospitality."

Without waiting for Josef to reply, the man opened the door to the small building. "I wanted to show you this place. It is the last stop for those who are so infirm that they have no possibility of recovery."

Josef stepped inside, and instead of the chapel he had expected, thinking the commandant was saying this was where the funerals were held, he saw that the room had been stripped of anything resembling a house of worship. Indeed the walls were scarred with bullet holes, and the floor was stained with blood.

"Now then," Reichleitner said, indicating that Josef should leave the house of God turned house of horrors, "as to your assignment, permit me to show you the way to the dispensary."

Josef followed the commandant back across the compound outside the administration building, past the tallest watchtower, and through yet another set of gates surrounded by more barbed wire. Along the way Reichleitner kept up a running commentary on the camp's facilities. "Shoemaker for the guards, residence for female prisoners, kitchen, two barracks for male prisoners, painters' shop, latrine, carpentry shop, mechanic shop, tailor, carpentry shop, shoemaker and tailor for the officers, and finally the dispensary. Welcome to Lager One," he said.

"Such lovely hair you have," the Kapo said as he twisted a lock of Beth's hair around his forefinger and gave it a hard yank. They were standing inside a warehouse filled with clothing precisely organized by category—children's clothing, men's suits, men's hats, women's blouses, women's skirts, sweaters, and on and on. One entire end of the large room was a wall of suitcases, stacked one on top of the other.

Just then one of the Ukrainian soldiers entered the building. He stood to one side as a female prisoner following him wordlessly searched Beth from head to toe—even going so far as to probe the inside of her mouth and other orifices of her body. Apparently satisfied that she had not smuggled in anything of interest, the guard nodded to the female prisoner, who scurried from the building. "Wait here," he ordered.

"But my husband—"

The slap came out of nowhere and was followed by the guard's hand wrapped around her throat. "Do not question me," he hissed and then tossed her easily against a floor-to-ceiling shelf filled with shoes. Without another word he and the Kapo left the building.

Beth tasted the blood from her split lip and grimaced with pain as she struggled to her feet. After a few minutes, she heard the measured sound of boots—one pair, heavy, slow. The person was taking his time. How she wished that Josef were with her—just his presence calmed her fears, although she fully understood that he could do little to protect her.

The commandant entered the building followed by the Kapo, and he was actually smiling until he saw Beth's face. "*Was ist los?*" he demanded, stepping closer to examine the cuts.

"I fell." Beth kept her eyes lowered, certain that this would be what was expected. "I tripped." She had little doubt that the commandant knew she was lying, but behind him she saw the Kapo regard her with something approaching respect.

Reichleitner frowned but held the door for her to precede him outside before heading for the next building. "Here in Lager Two we have storerooms for clothing, shoes, luggage, and other belongings," he said as he opened the door to the next building. Inside several women busily sorted through clothing. Others were seated at sewing machines. Although they all must have heard the door open and certainly heard the commandant's voice as he conducted his tour, not one of them looked up from the work.

"Will this do, Frau Buch?" Reichleitner prompted as if asking for Beth's approval of her assignment.

She nodded. Did she have a choice?

Reichleitner moved to a long table that held a typewriter and a thick ledger. "Frau Buch, can you manage *die Schreibmaschine?*"

"I can type," Beth replied quietly.

"Anja!" Reichleitner did not shout. Indeed he barely raised his voice, yet one of the women working at a sorting table immediately dropped what she was doing and scurried to his side.

Beth thought she must be seeing things when her friend stepped fully into view, but something in the look Anja gave her before turning to face the commandant told Beth that it would be dangerous to acknowledge they knew each other.

"I have brought you a new assistant. It would appear that you are overwhelmed already, and we have a new shipment being delivered nearly every day now." He glanced at the enormous pile of clothing and smiled.

"Nein," Anja protested. "That is, we can manage if this woman is needed elsewhere."

Reichleitner frowned, and Anja stopped talking. "She will work here. Perhaps you will be so kind as to orient Frau Buch?"

Beth cringed at the way the man dished out orders in the form of requests—as if Anja had a choice and could refuse or suggest an alternative plan.

"Kommen Sie," Anja said sternly, taking Beth by the arm and leading her away. "I will show you."

As soon as the door closed behind Reichleitner, Beth and Anja fell into each other's arms.

"How?" Anja whispered as she studied Beth's face and ran a light hand over her hair.

The events of the last several days hit Beth like a tidal wave. She had no words. She just stood there, shaking her head as she clung to her friend.

"Never mind," Anja said, leading Beth to a high stool and urging her to sit while another woman brought a damp rag to tend to her cut. "Thank you, Lena," Anja said, and the woman nodded and went back to her sewing. "I'll introduce you to everyone later," Anja said softly when she saw Beth glancing around, taking it all in.

"Benjamin?"

Anja shook her head and stared at the floor as she drew in a heavy sigh, let it out, and then faced Beth once again.

"The children?" *Not the children,* she prayed.

"Rachel...they..." Again the shake of her head and the sucking in of her breath as if to steady herself.

"And Daniel as well?"

To her surprise Anja smiled. "No, not Daniel. Remember the woman in red?"

Beth nodded. From outside came the sound of footsteps on gravel, and Anja glanced anxiously toward the door. "I'll explain later. He is safe...for now."

She led Beth to a table on which stood the typewriter, a ledger, and a small lamp. Beth saw one of the other workers standing at a window. She nodded to Anja and then hurried back to her work. The door opened, and an SS officer that Beth had not seen before walked in.

Anja opened the ledger, pointed to a recent entry, and began berating Beth for her stupidity. "Nein," she shouted, coming right up so that she locked gazes with Beth as she spewed words into her face. "Nothing is to be open and on the surface unless you are at the desk. You do not leave anything lying around, do you understand?"

"I do," Beth replied. "I apologize." She took a step back.

Anja dogged her. "Well?" she practically screamed the single word, and over her shoulder Beth saw the officer smile. "Can you write, or must I teach you that as well?" Anja demanded, thrusting the ledger from the desk into Beth's hands.

"My little tiger," the officer said fondly as he stroked Anja's cheek with his manicured forefinger. He took his time walking slowly up and down the long room, observing the women at work. "Carry on, Kapo," he said, smiling at Anja as he left the building.

Again one of the others ran immediately to the window and watched. Finally she nodded, and the others all visibly relaxed even as they continued to work.

"You need to work," Anja said firmly. "We have quotas that we must achieve or risk being replaced, and we must finish before the next roll call." She turned to the others. "Ladies, let's get to work, or we'll get no rest at all."

~≋ CHAPTER 20 ≋~

Josef was ashamed to find himself grateful for the relatively easy assignment. Certain that his father's influence was the cause, he was determined to form a bond with his fellow inmates. But it did not take him long to realize that because he was German and definitely not Jewish, no one in camp was willing to trust him. Clearly they suspected him to be a spy—another trick of their captors to learn whatever they could about the prisoners.

Every afternoon promptly at five, a whistle signaled the end of the workday. All the prisoners except those assigned to Lager III—the so-called area for showers—ran to line up outside the prisoners' kitchen to receive their meager ration of a hunk of stale bread and a cup of ersatz coffee. They then stood in silence in all kinds of weather to be counted for perhaps the second, perhaps the fifth time that day depending on the whims of the commandant. After that they returned to the barracks for the night.

The barracks were crammed with wooden bunks stacked three high with little space between them. The first night he spent there, Josef was surprised at the way the men joked, played games, sang songs, or talked quietly in small groups. It was no different than the nights he'd spent with his fellow soldiers. But he was never included in any of these interactions—until his second week in camp.

That night the old man he worked with in the dispensary sat down next to Josef on his bunk and offered him a tin cup filled with a green watery liquid.

"Dandelion tea," the man said. "One of the men found a patch today. Try it."

Josef took a sip as he warily watched several of the others move closer so that they had closed off any possible avenue of escape should he need one.

"I am Rabbi Moshe Weiss."

"Josef Buch." Josef nodded to the rabbi and then in general to the men around him. "I see you teaching the younger boys at night," he added, hoping to gain trust.

"Hebrew lessons—every Jewish boy takes such lessons."

Josef took another sip of the tea. It wasn't half-bad. "Thank you for this," he said.

"Tell us your story, Josef Buch," the rabbi urged, and then with a wry smile added, "You are our first non-Jewish roommate. We are naturally curious."

So Josef told them everything—that he was the son of a fairly powerful member of the Gestapo, that he had studied medicine and served on the western front and returned to Munich to complete his medical training, that he had met Beth. . . .

"Ah, the American woman who works with Anja Steinberg in the sorting rooms. You are a fortunate man, my friend. Your wife is not only beautiful, but also kind. Several of the woman and girls have mentioned that."

"She's a Quaker—a member of the Religious Society of Friends," Josef said as if somehow that explained everything there was to know about Beth.

"How did the two of you end up here?" the man occupying the bunk above Josef's demanded. These were the first words he and Josef had exchanged.

Josef told them about the White Rose. He named no names, but it hardly mattered now. With Hans, Sophie, and Christoph dead and the others arrested or on the run, he saw no reason not to sing the praises of his courageous friends. He told them about the leaflets that he and Beth had distributed, told them about the arrests and how Beth had been led to believe that he had betrayed her and her family. "Not unlike many of you who no doubt also believe that I am not to be trusted, I suspect," he added, fixing his gaze on each man in turn before continuing.

He told them of his arrest, of the reunion with Beth, of the trial and sentencing and how incredibly brave Beth had been through it all. "And I will not deny that, were it not for my father's position, certainly I would have been sentenced to death and perhaps Beth as well."

He fell silent then, drinking the last of the tea, gone tepid now, while the men watched him in the silence of their own thoughts. Finally the rabbi covered Josef's hand with his. Josef saw that the old man's fingers were knotted with arthritis. "Thank you, Josef Buch."

Then he and the others moved back to their own bunks as promptly at ten o'clock the lights went out.

The following day as they performed the morning ritual of making up their bunks, cleaning the barracks, and assembling for the first roll call of the day, it was as if overnight there had been a referendum regarding Josef. Whatever had transpired, there was little doubt that nearly all of the suspicion had been wiped away. Men spoke to him— some calling him Josef, others Buch, and a few calling him Doc. He was one of them now, and the simple pleasure he felt in that was like a gift.

Each evening before lights went out, Beth did her best to make herself presentable and then waited just outside the women's barracks for Josef. Their time together would be in minutes rather than the hours she longed to spend with him, but she would take what God offered and count her blessings.

They sat side by side on a rough wooden bench under an eave of the barracks in all weather—rain, snow, or mild moonlit nights. He wrapped his arms around her, and she nestled next to him, memorizing the way they fit together like puzzle pieces. They kissed and then talked of the day—what they had seen and heard, who they had encountered, and which of their fellow prisoners were in need of special comfort or attention. Before lights went out and they each had to return to their respective barracks, Beth had persuaded Josef to sit in silence with her, their hands joined, their eyes closed, their breathing steady.

All around them others might also be in the yard outside the barracks—often this included other couples seeking a dark corner where they could consummate their love or simply find solace in the body of another. But Beth had asked only one thing of Josef—not here in this place. And he had agreed.

One night about a month after they had first arrived in Sobibor, Rabbi Weiss asked if he could sit with them for a bit. They made room for him on the narrow bench. In a few days, by Josef's best calculations, March would turn to April. Already the evenings held the promise of spring—even in this place.

The rabbi stared at the orange glow that rose above the treetops in the area they knew was Lager III. "Elizabeth, I am curious. In your faith there is as I understand it no place for war or violence of any kind."

"That's right."

"Yet how do you reconcile your faith with that?" He motioned toward the orange sky where they all knew the fires of the recently completed crematorium were now running round the clock. A train arrived nearly every day, and each one carried more and more men, women, and children—all of them except a precious few walking down the lane that the guards called *Himmelstrasse* or Road to Heaven.

"It is not my place to explain such things," Beth replied. "In our faith we believe that God's spirit dwells in everyone regardless of age, gender, nationality. . .or faith. We are born with God's spirit already inside us."

"Beth often has to remind me that we are all God's children," Josef added.

"So this holy spirit—it is like any part of us—heart, brain, muscle?"

"Oh, Rabbi, I am not as educated as you are. You tell me."

"But what do you think, child?"

Beth could answer this easily, for both her parents had instilled the answer in her from childhood. "I think that if we do not feed and nurture that spirit in the same ways that we care for every other part of our being, then it will wither. . .and in some cases die."

The three of them sat for a long time staring at the glow of the fires and barely noticing anymore the stench of burned bodies that permeated the camp day and night. After a while Rabbi Weiss stood up. "You have given me renewed hope, Elizabeth, and I am grateful." He walked back toward the men's barracks, and Beth saw that despite his gratitude he still walked as if he carried the burdens of the world on his bony shoulders.

As each day and week passed with stupefying sameness, the man who slept above Josef scratched a mark into the side of his bunk. Using that as his abacus, Josef knew that more than two months had passed since he and Beth had arrived in the camp. The idea that they had been sent to this place to use their skills as doctor and nursemaid had long since been abandoned. Josef worked in the dispensary handing out medicines to their captors while Beth sorted through the mountains of clothing, shoes, purses, and other effects of the dead. Josef spent every waking minute thinking about how he and Beth might get out of this place. He took every opportunity to study the terrain beyond the wire fences. The area behind the barracks for men had been doubly secured with the tall fences and a deep ditch filled with water, but outside of Lager II near the main tower and opposite the main gate was a vegetable garden.

In spite of the fact that—even now that it was May—there was still the possibility of a frost, the onions and radishes and other vegetables the prisoners planted were beginning to flourish. Of course most of the produce went to feed the officers and Ukrainian guards. The prisoners still received their daily ration of bread and coffee, and on special occasions they might get a cup of watery soup. But when the commandant had called for volunteers to tend the garden during roll call a few weeks earlier, Josef had been the first to step forward. As he did, he had nodded to Beth and was relieved when she stepped forward as well. Then so did Anja and finally Rabbi Weiss.

"Well, well, well," Reichleitner had remarked. "So eager to help. Let me be clear that any one of you caught stealing so much as a kernel of corn will be shot."

But it was not the bounty of the garden that interested Josef. It was its position close to the fence. It was the fact that the space was partially blocked by the shoe warehouse and the stables. It was his observation that if he and Beth could somehow make it from the garden past the stables and on to the trees that ran along one side of Himmelstrasse, they might be able to cut through the three wire fences and make it to the woods beyond.

One evening as he took his time setting up a small trellis for the beans to climb, he stared at the trees beyond the fence, trying to estimate the distance they would have to run to take cover.

"Don't," a voice said softly. "Others have tried. You'll never make it, and others will pay the price."

Josef glanced sideways and saw that his counselor was a Kapo—one of the few that he knew the other prisoners trusted. The Kapo walked on, pacing around the perimeter of the garden, occasionally reprimanding the rabbi or Anja in a loud voice meant to assure the guard watching from the tower that he had everything under control.

The next day as they went off to their assigned jobs, the prisoners noticed a flurry of activity outside the triple fence on three sides of the camp. Earlier that week the train had arrived, but the passengers had not cooperated when ordered to assemble in two groups. Instead they had panicked and begun running in all directions, throwing themselves against the gates and fencing, crawling beneath the cars of the train, only to face more fencing.

Those working in the various shops and storerooms were ordered to remain at their posts away from windows. Outside they heard the staccato firing of multiple machine guns punctuated by the pop of individual bullets fired from a handgun or rifle and the shrieks of the newly arrived prisoners. It took less than an hour to restore order. Afterward the battered and wounded prisoners were shuttled through the usual routine and ordered to leave their belongings with no pretense that these items would be returned to them later.

That night the glow coming from Lager III had appeared brighter than ever, taunting them. As he now did every evening, Rabbi Weiss gathered the other prisoners together in the yard to say kaddish or the prayer of mourning.

"They are mining the fields around the camp with explosives," Josef's bunkmate told him that night. "Three sides."

"What about the fourth?" Josef whispered.

"I don't know—too close to the main railroad tracks and the road to the village maybe."

"I heard there were partisans in the woods, and that worries them," another voice added from the dark. "They don't want those who might come to our rescue to get close enough to do anything."

The next day, ordered to put on the blue coveralls of a railway worker and stand at the track for the next shipment of Jews to arrive, Josef focused all of his attention on the area that lay beyond the siding. He saw there were only two fences and a guard tower positioned at either end. Beyond that was the main track and the road. And beyond that lay farmland and woods. . .and freedom.

When Josef told Beth of his plan, she felt a fresh wave of fear. The stories of what happened to those who tried to escape were legend throughout the camp. Even if someone succeeded, the others paid a heavy price.

"Josef, even if we could do this, what of the others?"

"We can't save everyone," Josef argued.

"Then we cannot do this."

"Beth, we are prisoners of war—a war we had nothing to do with starting. A war we did what we could to stop, but nevertheless here we are. This is the price we all pay."

"And so it is all right that others should die so that I can be free?"

She knew that Josef did not understand her. She knew that he had thought she would be as excited as he was that he had come up with a plan.

She heard him take a breath, and then he tried again. "If one of the women you work with were to make it out, would you deny her that freedom? What if that woman were Anja?"

"It does not matter who the person is, Josef. I would be thankful for the deliverance from this horrid place. But I cannot do anything that I know will endanger the lives of others. Such an action would go against everything I believe, and other than you and my love for you, the only thing I have left is my faith."

"You would die here?"

"Josef, how do we know what God's plan is for any of us? Was there some purpose in the deaths of Sophie and Hans and the others? I believe that we live out our lives as a tiny part of a greater plan. I will not question that."

"I know that. It's just that if it had not been for me, you wouldn't be here. You could be home with your family safe in America. You *should* be," he added as his voice broke.

"And I had no say in this at all? What a short and selective memory you have, my husband."

"Some husband," he grumbled, and she understood that for the first time since she'd met him that Josef doubted himself. He was a man of action—a man dedicated to doing whatever it took to make things right.

From the open door of the women's barracks she heard Anja laughing. She took Josef's hand and stood. "Come with me."

She led him to the doorway where inside Anja and some of the other women were dancing to the music provided by one woman playing a battered violin. The dance was a Jewish folk dance—one that Anja and the others had taught Beth. They danced with abandon, their heads thrown back, their arms raised, their laughter only adding to the music.

"You did that," Beth reminded Josef. "Anja would not be alive today if you had not found her and Benjamin and the children."

"Benjamin and the baby are dead," he reminded her.

"But Anja and hopefully Daniel are alive."

"This is not living," Josef told her as he walked away. She shuddered at the bitterness in his tone.

Together they walked back into the darkness and took their places on the bench they had come to think of as theirs. Beth curled into the hollow of his side, inviting him to put his arm around her. When he did, she closed her eyes and waited for words that might reassure him, that might steer him from this dangerous path.

As the others began moving back toward their respective barracks, Josef stood up. He kissed her but did not move away. "I know that you believe that if we make it out they will make Anja pay the price."

Beth breathed a sigh of relief. Finally he understood.

"That's why we have to take her with us," he added as he kissed her again and then ran for his barracks to beat the curfew.

Now that Josef had the plan in mind, he realized that he had only scratched the surface of what it would take for him to execute it. So many details. How to get Beth and Anja and himself together at the same time to make their move. He would need wire cutters for the fencing. And the best time to go would be after dark. What about food and water and medical supplies in case of an emergency? In case one of them was shot or fell or was cut by the barbed wire and developed an infection?

With every new thought, his spirits plummeted. But each night after he sat with Beth, holding her hand as they closed their eyes and waited together for guidance from within, he felt a little more certain that God was indeed leading him to consider a plan for escape.

He was thinking about all of this one stifling late-July day when he had been sent to work the garden instead of his regular job. He had considered the shovel he used to dig potatoes as a possible substitute for wire cutters. The handle was already loose, and if he could secure the blade beneath his clothing somehow and bury the wooden handle in the garden, perhaps he could hack at the wire with the blade of the shovel. But that brought to mind the noise that metal on metal would make. He was beginning to feel a kind of desperation that was almost like a fever.

Suddenly the Kapo grabbed Josef's shovel and examined it. "You have ruined this," he shouted, waving the tool in Josef's face as he pulled the handle free. "Take it to the carpenter now," he ordered, thrusting the two pieces at Josef.

Josef knew better than to question the man. "Schnell!" the Kapo ordered.

Josef stepped into the shop where he saw Leon Feldhendler, a former mill owner and rabbi's son, sanding a board. "Doktor," he said politely as he relieved Josef of the broken tool and passed it to another man. He indicated that Josef should sit.

"Rumor has it that you are planning to try and take your wife and perhaps the Danish woman and attempt an escape."

Josef did not reply but kept his eyes on the man repairing the shovel.

"I am asking that you not do this thing," Leon continued. His tone was conversational, nonthreatening, and polite.

Josef glanced at him.

"I cannot yet say why I must ask this of you," Leon continued. "But you are an intelligent man, and I believe that if you consider my words carefully, you will understand."

"I know the dangers," Josef said.

"No doubt. You are not the first to consider such an idea," Leon said, and then he grasped Josef by the shoulders. "You will not be the last. I am asking you to trust me when I tell you that the time is not yet right for such a plan."

Josef shrugged him off and stood. The other carpenter was just completing the attachment of the shovel blade to the handle. "I appreciate the advice. I have to get back to work."

This time Leon placed his hand lightly on Josef's forearm. "The only plan that can work, Josef, is one that gives every prisoner the same opportunity."

Josef's froze. "That's insanity—there are nearly five hundred prisoners here." And as he said the words, he knew that even so this might be their only chance. If Leon's plan included everyone, then Beth would have to agree to go along with it. "How can I help?"

Leon glanced at the other carpenter, who nodded. "We will be in touch," Leon said as he walked with Josef to the door. "And Doktor? No one—not even your wife—can know."

"I understand."

Outside Josef felt as if he'd been looking at things through blinders. Never once had he considered the idea that they all come together to form some grand escape plan. This was the "family" that Beth always alluded to when she spoke of her Quaker faith—the importance of everyone looking out for everyone else, of always taking time to consider what was best for the greater good instead of the individual.

The Kapo was waiting for him and gave him a slap on the side of his head. "Get back to work," he ordered, and Josef shied away from the guard's raised hand, playing his part in the show they were staging for the guards watching them from high atop the main tower.

⇒ CHAPTER 21 ⇐

The small group of men continued to meet in secret through August and into September, and with each meeting Josef grew more and more impatient. He wanted action. He wanted results. The time for talking and ruminating had passed. If they took much longer to come up with a plan, cold weather would set in, and then they would be trapped—not that they weren't trapped now. But the leaders counseled patience, and because Josef had no choice, he waited.

In late September a transport arrived as usual, and as usual Josef was told to put on the railway uniform and stand by the tracks. But this transport was different. Among the people on this train filled with Jews from Minsk was a group of Russian prisoners of war. They still wore remnants of their uniforms, and they moved with the pride and confidence of soldiers. When the cattle cars were unloaded, the small group of POWs was pulled aside. Later Josef heard that they had been assigned to hard labor in the new Lager IV area where the camp was being expanded to include a munitions operation.

One night when he was called to a meeting with Leon and the small band that the former mill owner had assembled to plan the escape, Josef was surprised to see one of the Russians.

"Josef Buch, this is Sasha Pechersky," Leon said. "He and his men will be helping us."

Josef was immediately suspicious, but when he learned that Sasha and the other POWs were not only Russian but also Jewish, he understood why they would join forces with Leon. That night they discussed plans for the actual escape. Someone wanted to build a tunnel, but Sasha pointed out the time it would take not only to dig deep enough to go below the explosives in the minefields but also to move hundreds of people through the tunnel before it was discovered.

Someone else thought that mobilizing the young boys who served as servants to the Nazis and had access to their quarters to kill them while they slept. But that plan was also rejected for several reasons—the boys were not strong enough to overpower a well-fed man, and the act would need to happen in the mornings when the boys were sent to the quarters, meaning the escape would have to happen in daylight, hours from the protection that night time would give them once they reached the woods.

"Whatever we do, we must act soon," Leon said. "The transports have slowed, and I have learned that they are already beginning to dismantle some of the facilities in Lager III. No doubt they plan to convert or close this camp by the end of the year, and we all know what that means."

"They don't call it a death camp for nothing," one of the men muttered.

"Besides we need to act before the weather turns," another pointed out.

"So," Leon said with a heavy sigh. "All we need is a plan."

The group continued to meet whenever they could as the days passed. Early in October a transport arrived carrying Polish Jews—they were dressed in rags, looked as if they had not eaten in days, and carried very few possessions. It was more evidence that the round-up of Jews was reaching its zenith. Then two of the Kapos came to Sasha, telling him their suspicions that an escape was in the works. The leaders had a choice—include the two Kapos in the plan, or they would expose them. "We have privileges and can move prisoners like you from place to place without suspicion," one of them reminded him.

The two men were included in the next meeting of the conspirators. Sasha unveiled the plan. "During phase one," he explained, "we prepare—those with access to warehouses and sorting rooms will gather knives, axes, and other small weapons and deliver them here to our command post. Meanwhile we will take up our positions. This phase must be completed by four o'clock."

They all knew that in the late afternoon the Nazis were free to leave their posts for a coffee break or to take care of personal business such as picking up a new pair of boots at the shoemaker or trying on a new uniform at the tailor's. No one would think twice about not seeing a particular officer during this time.

"Each of the sixteen Nazi officers will be eliminated during this hour before roll call."

The assignments were given—the boys were to act as messengers, luring each Nazi stationed in Lager I to either the tailor or cobbler shops at an assigned time. An officer was to be executed every few minutes. In Lager II the SS men would be drawn into some ruse to come to the warehouse where the sorted goods from the transports were stored.

Meanwhile the phone lines would be cut and the generator that controlled the camp's state-of-the-art lighting system would be disabled. More guns and ammunition would be stolen and given to the leaders of the conspiracy.

Finally when the call for roll call sounded and all prisoners gathered in the main yard to be counted, the Kapos would march them toward the main gate because there were no mine fields between the gate and the forest beyond. The Ukrainian guards took their orders from the SS officers, but with all SS officers dead, the Kapos would simply say that they were under orders to move the prisoners through the gate. Once the gates were open, the prisoners would be told to run, and by the time the guards realized what was happening, it would be too late.

"We go on the thirteenth," Sasha announced, and Josef felt for the first time since arriving in the camp that freedom was within reach.

Ever since Josef had first spoken to Beth about trying to escape, she had worried that he might become desperate enough to do something foolish. But he had said nothing more about the idea. At the same time, however, she had noticed a tension that she could not explain whenever they were together. One night she told him about the rumor making the rounds that the camp was to be closed.

"You know what that means, Josef—they will kill us all."

"We will not die here, Liebchen. I promise you that."

"You cannot know that."

He turned to her then, taking hold of her face with both hands. "I know you have had cause to doubt me in the past, Beth, but please do not doubt me now. I need to know that you trust me and that when the time comes..."

"I trust you," she said. "Never doubt that, Josef, whatever happens. It's just that in this place we have no power."

"We have power, Beth. You have taught me that. If we will only be still and wait. Is that not what you have taught me?"

"Yes, but..."

"Be still and wait," he repeated as he kissed her and then walked quickly back to his barracks. "Soon," he called over his shoulder. "Very soon."

It sounded like a promise, but she had no idea what he meant, and she worried that he was once again planning something—something that would get them or others killed.

She confided her fears to Anja. But her friend was surprisingly unconcerned.

"Perhaps he is only trying to reassure you," she said.

"No, this is something different."

Anja shrugged and turned back to her work.

Later that day Beth saw Anja set aside two pocket watches from the latest shipment of prisoner belongings that they were sorting. As she slipped them into the pocket of her apron, she looked up and saw Beth watching her. Her eyes begged Beth not to question the action.

Of course Beth was well aware that many if not most of the women took things from time to time. They used the items to barter with the Kapos for extra food or other special favors. But she had never seen Anja take anything.

"It's not for me," Anja assured her later when the two of them were sitting together, eating their bread.

"It is stealing," Beth reminded her. "Whatever the reason you give yourself."

Anja glanced around to be sure she was not overhead. "Beth, we both know that the owners of those watches are dead—murdered by our jailers. Do you not think that if they were alive they would willingly hand over anything we might need to be free of such oppression?"

"I suppose—if it were for the greater good, but. . ."

"Those watches are for the greater good," Anja said. "In the end they will help everyone here, and that is all I will say on the matter. If you cannot condone my actions I understand, but let my punishment be the loss of your friendship."

Beth squeezed Anja's hand. "I would never desert you."

"Then trust me," Anja whispered as a guard passed close to them and frowned.

"Get back to work," he ordered.

Beth had grown immune to the feelings that had kept her awake nights when she'd first started going through the personal property of people she knew were already dead. Now she did her work as the other women did—almost as if they were working an assembly line in a factory. Every night as she and Josef sat together in silence, she stared at the orange glow of the crematorium fires and prayed for forgiveness.

Trust me, Anja had said before the guard passed by. The words echoed in Beth's brain as she continued to sort through mounds of clothing, cutting open linings and hems of garments where the doomed prisoners had hidden jewelry and gold and paper money. First Josef and now Anja. Something was going on, and she intended to find out what it was.

Spirits were high as the leadership gathered for their final meeting that evening. Leon had arrived with the news that SS officer Hans Wagner had left that day on vacation. Wagner was the single officer that the group feared the most—he was intelligent and suspicious and made a habit of showing up unannounced in the most unexpected places. He was also a large man and incredibly fit. Killing him would take strength and perhaps more than the homemade knives they had at their disposal.

Josef had made an excuse to leave Beth early so that he could make the meeting at nine. They had an hour before lights out to finalize their plans. Anja had given him the pocket watches that she'd collected over the last several days. He would distribute these to the others so they could synchronize their actions. Timing was the key to success.

But on the following day a car arrived with several SS officers from a nearby labor camp. Josef was working in the garden—harvesting potatoes and the last of the other vegetables, storing small potatoes in a special pocket that he had sewn into the leg of his trousers for them to eat once they escaped.

At first Josef and the others feared that their plan had been discovered. Then they heard the new arrivals and their Sobibor comrades laughing. Later they heard singing coming from the open windows of the SS quarters. Still the addition of several new Nazis had to be taken into consideration. Word spread quickly among the rebels, and the plan to act that day was scrapped.

That night as he sat with Beth and heard the drunken and bawdy laughter and slamming of car doors as the visiting SS men left the camp, Josef faced for the first time the dangers of what they were about to do. So many unpredictable details. What if the officer scheduled to be lured to the warehouse by the promise of a new leather coat refused to come? What if the man with the appointment to try on new boots arrived early while his comrade was being killed? What if. . .

"Josef?"

He turned his attention to his wife—this woman that he had come to love more than life itself. If he could just get her out of here. . .

"Tell me the plan," she said quietly.

"The plan?"

"I have seen you talking with the Russian and with Leon Feldhendler. Tell me what is going on."

He could not lie to her. "I have asked that you trust me," he reminded her.

"I do trust you. But I want you to also trust me—and I want to help."

"The danger is. . ."

"Anja is helping you, isn't she?"

Just then Sasha walked past them, his arm around a woman named Luka. The other women in the barracks had teased Luka—who was only eighteen—about her romance with the tall, handsome Russian. But Josef knew that Luka was acting as a decoy, giving Sasha and Leon and the other leaders opportunities for passing information right under the noses of the Ukrainian guards patrolling the alley between the fences that separated them from the garrison where the SS quarters were.

"Tomorrow," Sasha murmured as he passed, and then he laughed and pulled Luka closer to his side.

Adrenaline pumped through Josef's veins. He turned to Beth and grasped her hands. "Tomorrow when you dress for work, wear an extra sweater—a jacket if you can do so without drawing suspicion," he told her. "And your heaviest shoes."

"What's happening?"

"Please don't ask me anything more, Beth. Just. . .be ready."

The following morning as Beth prepared for roll call and the day's work, she noticed that Anja had also put on extra clothing. "Chilly today,"

Anja said, loud enough for the others to hear. "Best take your sweaters and jackets just in case the evening roll call is a long one."

The others nodded. They saw nothing odd in what Anja was advising. Too many times they had all stood for hours in a downpour or ninety-degree heat. It was always best to be prepared.

But the autumn day was warm and sunny and so routine that Beth began to think that perhaps something had gone wrong. The only difference was the sound of the Kapo's shrill whistle that signaled the evening roll call fifteen minutes early. As usual the woman in the sorting room stopped what they were doing and moved quickly to the assembly area. Beth was aware only of the absence of SS officers and a murmur spreading through the gathering like a brush fire.

"Revolt...escape..."

Rabbi Weiss stepped out of the men's barracks. He was wearing the prayer shawl that he wore every night when he gathered the others to say the prayer of mourning for those killed that day. He stood in the middle of the yard, swaying back and forth as he murmured to himself.

Suddenly the crack of a pistol shot rang out. The crowd turned as one and saw a prisoner fall as one of the SS officers who had just returned from a shopping expedition in the village holstered his sidearm.

Anja grabbed Beth's arm and held on. At the same time, Sasha climbed onto a table. He told them most of the SS officers were dead and reminded them that they were all part of a larger struggle. "Forward," he urged and added that those who survived must bear witness to these crimes against humanity. He delivered his speech in Russian, and all through his audience, others translated.

The Ukrainian guards in the towers waited for orders from the SS, their guns silent in spite of the nervous activity they were observing in the compound. They were too far from Sasha to hear his speech.

But all around her, Beth realized that others had taken up Sasha's cry. "Forward," they repeated as they moved toward the main gate. Then they were shouting it as one defiant voice.

Suddenly everyone was running—some toward the main gate and

others to the sides. "Here, put this on," Anja said as she thrust a heavy jacket into Beth's hands.

She turned to look for Josef and saw him standing with Sasha and Leon and other men, aiming rifles they had somehow gotten at the watch towers. "Josef!" She started running toward him even as Anja pulled her away.

"Go," he yelled. "Go now."

Anja dragged Beth along with her as hundreds of prisoners stormed the barbed-wire fences. Some had garden tools and other weapons they used to try and hack through the wire. When that failed, they started going over the top. All around her Beth heard gunfire and explosions and shouting. All around her people fell. And still Anja urged her forward.

"Josef!"

"He'll meet us in the woods," Anja shouted. "Now come."

Anja started to crawl through a small opening others had created at the base of the fence as others decided scaling it was faster. Beth followed Anja. Just when Anja made it through, the fence collapsed, and Beth felt the sting of the barbs embed themselves in the jacket that Anja had insisted she wear. She was trapped, and the more she struggled, the more entangled in the fencing she became. She saw Anja turn back to help her. "Go!" Then she covered her head as others trampled over her.

The noise was deafening, and Beth was certain that she was about to die. She closed her eyes and forced her mind to ignore the tread of feet over her, the sting of the barbs making their way through the coat and into her skin, the shouting and the explosions and the shrieks of the dying.

It felt like forever, but then she felt someone tugging on her arm and opened her eyes to see Josef kneeling next to her. His eyes filled with tears of relief when she opened her eyes and looked up at him.

"Go," she urged, her voice choked by the dirt she had swallowed with her face pressed into the ground.

"No. Can you get free of the jacket?"

She slipped one arm free even as she noticed that with Josef there helping her, the others avoided stepping on her.

"That's it. Now the other arm?"

It was a struggle, but that arm also came free, and with Josef's help she was able to shimmy her way free of the wire. Josef helped her to her feet. He was no longer carrying the rifle. She was aware of fewer explosions and more people making it all the way across the open field to the haven of the trees. It was also beginning to get dark, and the lights in the camp had not come on.

Clutching Josef's hand, she ran as she had never run before, her eyes on the forest as behind them sporadic gunfire sounded and all around them the open field was strewn with the dead bodies of their fellow prisoners.

When they finally stumbled the last few feet into the cover of the pine forest, Beth collapsed into Josef's arms. "Are you all right?" she demanded as she examined him for wounds.

He brushed her hair away from her dirty face. "Beth, we are free," he said quietly.

"Not exactly," Anja reminded them both as she emerged from a thicket of bushes. "Now come on. We have to get as far away as possible because they will come after us."

"The river," Josef said. "We can tend Beth's cuts, and if they use dogs, they won't be able to track us."

But as their days on the run lengthened into a week and then two, Josef realized how badly he had underestimated the determination of their captors to hunt them down. They could travel only at night, and during the day it was essential that one of them stay alert at all times for the possibility of discovery by the network of soldiers, local police, and even local citizens who might spot them and turn them in. Their feet were blistered and bleeding, and the few potatoes and carrots that Josef had managed to smuggle out were gone.

The good news was that the focus of the hunt seemed to be toward the east. That made sense because the camp was very close to the Russian border. So Josef decided that the three of them should head north. If they could make it to the Baltic Sea, they might be able to get a boat or stow away on a fishing vessel and make it to Denmark.

Anja was in favor of this plan mainly because she had grown up on the Danish island of Bornholm, and as far as she knew still had relatives there in the fishing village of Gudhjem. Although occupied by the Germans, the island was used primarily as a lookout and listening station for tracking naval and submarine activity in the Baltic. But Josef was all too aware that such a journey meant traveling nearly two hundred miles—mostly on foot and while being hunted. He knew the Nazi mind. They did not like loose ends, and they would not give up the search until they had accounted for every last prisoner.

"Josef?" Beth took hold of his hand as the three of them sat together in a cornfield that had not yet been harvested. This late in the season it was more than likely that the farm it belonged to had been abandoned. The crop was field corn for the livestock, but it tasted like manna to them. "We need to come to consensus."

Next to her Anja nodded. The two women laid down their corn cobs and closed their eyes as they prepared for the Quaker ritual of sitting in silence and waiting for divine guidance. Josef was irritated that either of them thought that God was going to show them a way out of this. Did they not understand that he spent every waking minute planning for their safety?

"I need to think," he said and would have stalked off to some other part of the field were it not midafternoon with a sky that threatened to bring rain before nightfall.

"You can think here," Beth said without opening her eyes.

"Well, we'd all better pray that the Light dawns soon because we need to find shelter for the night," he grumbled.

Just before he closed his eyes and took a deep steadying breath as

Beth had taught him to do when preparing for worship, he was sure that he saw Anja smile.

Quakers. It was one thing to be married to one and quite another to be outnumbered.

After a few minutes, Beth spoke. "I am thinking that we need to find the best way to bring all three of us to safety," she began and paused. "Perhaps this island—even if it is occupied—is at least a place we can begin."

Silence.

Anja spoke. "If we travel as far as possible through each night..."

"Do you not understand that we are in territory we don't know and we have no map?" Josef had had enough of the silent meditation.

The two women remained stone still, their eyes closed, their breathing even.

Josef squeezed his hands into fists, his frustration like a weight inside him. What other options did they have? He intended to wait out their silence and so focused his attention on alternate possibilities. So far they had made fairly good time. While the search parties focused mostly on the eastern end of the Bug River, he had been able to rescue an abandoned rowboat, and by using a branch from a pine tree as a pole and following close to the river banks, they were now west and north of Warsaw.

He knew that they were past Warsaw because he'd seen a sign for a village that he knew was north of that major city. He also knew that rivers flowed to larger bodies of water—a bay or gulf and then on to an open sea. If they followed the river... "All right, we'll go to Gudhjem."

"We have consensus then," Beth said softly.

Josef did not think he would ever understand these Quaker ways, even if the three of them were fortunate enough to survive. But the way both women looked at him with such conviction of the rightness of this decision, he could not help feeling that there was something to this whole waiting-in-silence thing.

—≋ CHAPTER 22 ≋—

At night as the three of them made their way through fields and forests, crossing streams and dodging tree roots, Beth developed the habit of following Josef's steps in complete silence. They could not risk talking—even in a whisper. The farms and villages in this part of Poland were close together, and who knew when a local might be nearby? Instead she placed her thoughts on Josef, imagining the future they would share—the home they would make for the children they would raise.

She never put a name to the location of that home, but she saw it in her mind as clearly as she saw the moon above her on starry nights. A house with a garden. She thought about how Josef had found refuge tending the garden at Sobibor. She'd been surprised to hear him talking about how the various plants were developing as they sat together each summer night on that rough bench outside the women's barracks. He had found such hope in tending those plants.

And it would be a house with a fenced yard where the children could play safely, especially when they were young. Children that she pictured like Anja's Daniel and Rachel. Such beautiful children. Such thoughts would make her wonder where Daniel was now and how Anja could possibly stand not knowing. Her friend had never really spoken about the capture of her family, the deaths of her husband and daughter, and the burden of not knowing where her son was or even if he was alive. How did she manage to keep going day after day?

Josef held up his hand and stopped walking. He motioned for Beth and Anja to crouch down, and after dozens of similar incidents, they obeyed without question. Beth heard male voices and laughter. They had been following a dirt road for several miles. In the east the sky was starting to lighten. They had come to the end of another night of travel and would soon need to find somewhere to hide for the day. She crouched a few feet away from Anja and felt the chill of the night held deep in the rocks that formed a wall at their backs seep into her bones. The voices came closer.

She saw two men in silhouette as they rounded a curve in the road. One of them was smoking a pipe, and the scent of the tobacco almost made her weep for the memory it carried of her uncle. Where were he and Aunt Ilse and Liesl now? Were they safe? Were they still alive? Who could say?

Suddenly Anja gave an involuntary gasp, and Beth looked over to see a dog sniffing at her friend's shoulder. The men were nearly even with them. Beth signaled Anja to stay still and turned to see if Josef had noticed the dog.

But Josef was gone.

The two men were speaking in Polish, but by their tone Beth surmised that they had noticed the missing dog. One of them let out a sharp whistle. The dog turned its head toward the sound but remained with Anja. The man whistled again, and both men stopped walking and talking as they scanned the roadside.

Where was Josef?

The dog pawed at the dirt and then dropped a stick at Anja's feet. When she did not pick it up, the dog barked and pranced around her, nudging the stick closer. Anja huddled closer to the stone wall. One of the men grumbled something in Polish and turned toward them.

He gave a command to the dog, which the dog ignored. Up the road, rustling came from the brush. The dog turned to the sound, and so did both men. One of the men laughed and said something.

Beth knew almost no Polish, but she knew the word for *rabbit*—the SS officers had kept a rabbit hutch near the garden, and their cook was a Polish Jew. More than once she had heard the cook complain that the prisoners ate stale bread while the Nazis feasted on rabbit stew.

Again the rustling—this time farther into the field. The dog abandoned Anja and the stick and bounded back the way the men had come. Both men started after the dog—one of them clearly swearing and the other nearly bent double with laughter.

Suddenly Josef was there, his breathing coming in short spurts as if he'd run a race. He tapped Beth's shoulder and motioned for her and Anja to climb over the low wall while the men were distracted and hide on the other side. They did as he instructed, but now they could not see the men or the dog, and to make matters worse there was a ditch filled with water on that side of the wall.

After what seemed like forever, the dog ran back to where Anja had been and once again sniffed the ground, but this time when its master gave a whistle the dog gave up the search and followed the men down the road. Still, they stayed where they were for some time just to make sure they were safe.

"Come on," Josef said finally as the sky in the east grew lighter. The three of them ran across the field toward the safety of a cluster of trees. Beyond the trees was a farmhouse, smoke rising from the chimney and activity in the yard as the farmer's wife scattered feed for the chickens and the farmer and a boy about Daniel's age and size climbed aboard a hay wagon.

Anja began to sob. "I can't," she whispered, her words coming in broken syllables. "Can't do this one day more."

Beth's heart broke for her friend, who had lost everything. She and Josef still had each other, but Anja. . .

"We'll wait for the man and his son to head out to the fields then go to the wife. Perhaps she'll give us some food," Josef said. Beth knew that he was not ignoring Anja. This was simply his way. When faced with any sign of adversity or distress, Josef looked for ways to make the situation better.

"Let me go," Anja said, sniffing back her tears and swiping the back of one dirty hand over her eyes. "That way if something goes wrong..."

"We'll both go," Beth said. "Josef can keep watch and give a whistle if there's danger."

Early in their journey, they had worked out a system of signals to use should they get separated. It had been Beth's idea, and how Anja and Josef had laughed when she told them she had taken the idea from the Hollywood Westerns that she and her brothers used to attend every Saturday afternoon back in Wisconsin. But it had worked for them more than once, and no one was laughing now.

"All right," Josef agreed.

They waited, shivering in the cold morning air, as the farmer and his son left the farmyard and headed down the road. They stayed a while longer to make sure that no one else was around other than the housewife.

"Go now," Josef said.

Together Beth and Anja walked quickly toward the farmhouse. It was a plain house, but pristine in its orderliness. It was—Beth realized— not unlike the house she had imagined one day sharing with Josef.

They went to the back door. They could hear the woman inside humming to herself as she washed dishes. Beth knocked on the back door, and too late she wondered if the woman spoke or at least understood German. Perhaps they should have sent Josef. He could have presented himself as a soldier separated from his unit. How were she and Anja to explain themselves?

But the minute the woman opened the back door, her eyes went soft with pity, and she signaled to them that they should wait on the back stoop. Moments later she returned, her arms full of warm clothing— coats for each of them, hats, mittens, scarves. While they gratefully put the garments on, the woman once again disappeared. This time she returned with mugs of hot tea and a knapsack bulging with apples, potatoes, bread, and even a bottle of apple cider.

Both Anja and Beth thanked her repeatedly. She held up her hand once more and ran back inside the house. This time she brought with her two blankets and the most precious gift of all—a compass and a roughly drawn map. The woman pointed repeatedly to an area that she had labeled *die See*—the sea.

"Baltic?" Beth asked, pointing to the spot, and the woman nodded.

"*Funfzig*..." She broke off as from the road behind them they heard the sputter of the farmer's ancient tractor, and suddenly the woman's entire demeanor changed. "Gehen Sie," she urged, her voice filled with panic as she glanced toward the road. "Schnell!"

Beth hooked the straps of the knapsack over one shoulder while Anja took the blankets and compass, and they ran for the woods, where Josef waited.

Josef watched helplessly as Beth and Anja raced across the open yard and climbed the hill to reach the safety of the forest. Behind them the farmer had halted the tractor and was now standing on it as he pointed a pistol at the two women. He fired. The shot missed, but both women did as they had been taught and dropped where they were, covering their heads with their arms.

"Come on," Josef shouted, exposing himself to draw the attention of the farmer his way. "Get up. Run."

Thankfully they obeyed and had almost reached the line of trees when the farmer took aim and fired one last time. The crack of the shot echoed in Josef's head as Anja ran past him. He reached for Beth's outstretched hand to pull her to safety and saw her eyes widen in surprise as the bullet found its mark and blood spurted from her calf.

Josef lifted Beth in his arms, throwing the knapsack to Anja as they scurried deeper into the woods, the rantings of the angry farmer following them.

When they could go no farther for having come through the stand of trees to another open area on the outskirts of a village, Josef set Beth down so that he could examine her wound. As far as he could tell, the bullet had lodged in the bone, and without the proper instruments, the best he could do was stop the bleeding and bandage the wound.

Anja used the makeshift knife they had brought with them from Sobibor to cut one of the wool scarves the farmer's wife had given them into strips. It was the best option they had for a sterile bandage—their own clothing by now covered in dirt from their days on the run.

"The farmer will contact the local authorities," he said as he worked. "We need to get away from here as soon as you can walk," he told Beth.

"I can walk now," she replied. "Anja, go find something I can use as a crutch." She grimaced as Josef probed the wound, hoping to work the bullet loose and remove it.

Anja headed back into the forest. "The woman gave us a map and a compass," Beth said, nodding toward the knapsack. "We're only fifty-something—kilometers I expect she meant to say—from the sea, Josef. We can do this."

"When you can travel," Josef said as he wrapped the strips of fabric around her leg. "We'll give Anja the map and compass and send her on."

He couldn't look at her because he knew she would see in his face the real story. The likelihood was that they would be caught, and if they sent Anja ahead at least one of them might make it to freedom.

But when she touched his cheek, he raised his face to hers. "It's all right, Josef," she said. "We may fail, but we must try."

He had never loved her more than he did in that moment, for he saw in her eyes that she fully understood the ramifications of what had just happened. "We will go as far as we can, and if. . ."

He shushed her by placing his finger against her lips. "Rest now." He retrieved the bottle of cider from the knapsack and gave it to her. "Drink."

She took a long swallow, and her eyes widened in shock. "It's fermented," she managed to say as she choked down the liquid.

Josef grinned. "Good. It will help you sleep. Now close your eyes. We'll move again as soon as it's dark."

The cider and perhaps the lost blood did their job, and when Beth awoke she felt more rested than she had in weeks. But her leg had stiffened up and now throbbed with pain. The idea of standing on it, much less walking for miles, was hard to imagine.

Anja and Josef were leaning against a tree. Josef was scraping a long branch with their knife—their only weapon.

"What's that?" Beth croaked.

Immediately Anja scooted closer and handed Beth an apple—part of the food the farmer's wife had given them. "We're saving the potatoes," she said. "Maybe once we reach the sea we can actually risk having a fire and bake them in the embers."

"And this," Josef said as he stood and presented her with the smooth branch, "is your crutch. Try it on for size," he urged.

Anja and Josef helped Beth to her feet. The pain that shot up her leg the minute she put weight on it nearly made her cry out, but she bit her lip and anchored the crude crutch under her arm. It took only a few minutes for her to get the rhythm of using it in place of her injured leg. She made her way around a tree and grinned at them.

"Well, there's no need to go showing off," Anja teased as Beth increased her speed on a second circuit of the tree.

Josef was watching her closely, his handsome face furrowed into a frown.

"It's good, and it's almost dark, so let's get going," she said. Then she looked at him more closely. "What on earth are you wearing?"

He grinned sheepishly. "Anja made one of the blankets into a sort of poncho for me. Do you like it?"

"Very dashing," Beth said, and she realized that in spite of her injury she was filled with hope. For the first time in days they were all warm, they had food, and they had the map and compass. For the first time since they'd left Sobibor, she truly believed that they might actually make it to freedom.

"Ready then?" Josef hooked an arm through the knapsack and handed Anja the compass.

"This way," she said, and they moved away from the shadows of the forest and into the night that was blessed by cloud cover and the hint of rain.

Josef had estimated that, if the farmer's wife was right, it would take them three nights of travel to reach the coast. Of course that did not allow for the fact that by the end of the second night Beth's leg had become badly infected and she was running a high fever. The bandages were stiff with dried blood and pus, and they had no other clean rags they could use. He had to risk going into one of the villages for help.

The coat that Anja wore was a man's coat, far too large for her small frame. She and Josef had exchanged outer garments after they'd discovered how the oversized coat restricted Anja's movements that first night traveling. With the coat of a local and a cap he had found one night when scrounging for food behind a bakery in a town days earlier, Josef hoped that his appearance in the small village of Olsztyn would not draw attention. After all, as the war had raged on for year after year, people's circumstances had worsened to the point where many people looked like vagrants these days.

"Try to keep her still," he instructed Anja, handing her the remainder of the cider. "If anyone comes..."

"Go," Anja ordered. "I know what to do."

It was just after dawn when he entered the village. Few people were around at this hour, and he walked quickly toward what seemed to be the main part of town. He passed the butcher's shop, the fish market—a sure sign that they were close to the sea—the chemist's...

The chemist!

Josef didn't need a doctor—he was a doctor. He needed the tools to make Beth better—medicine and bandages and disinfectant and…

Thou shalt not steal.

But he had no money—nothing he could even barter for the goods he so desperately needed. This was his wife—the woman he hoped to spend the rest of his life with. If she died, what meaning was there for anything? For the escape? For everything they had been through?

He saw the shopkeeper unlock the door and go inside. The lights came on—necessary at this time of the morning and probably throughout the day given the overcast sky. He watched through the window as the man went about the business of preparing his store for the day—checking the cash register, opening the radiators to bring more heat, taking a broom from a corner.

Josef tried the door and as he stepped inside and shut the door, its bell jangling all the while; the chemist looked up. "*Sprechen Sie Deutsch?*" Josef asked politely as he approached the counter. The man was older than he'd appeared at first, his skin lined with the years, his hair thin and wispy. Josef knew that he could easily overpower the man and take what he needed before any alarm could be raised.

"Ja," the chemist answered and continued speaking in German as he asked, "How may I help you?"

Josef recited the list of supplies he needed even as he studied the calendar posted on the wall behind the counter. They had been traveling for days—weeks—but he'd had no idea that it was already nearly the end of October. Still the chemist clearly took pains to cross off the days, and there it was before him—October the twenty-ninth. As Josef placed his order, the shopkeeper immediately began gathering them and setting them next to the brass-plated cash register. "Will that be all?"

"I cannot pay," Josef blurted. "But I can work—I can sweep the shop for you and do anything you need for two hours." By then he calculated the town would begin to come alive with shoppers and the usual business of any village on a weekday.

The man stared at him for a long moment. "You are Jewish?"

"No," Josef protested, but immediately thought, what if he were?

What did it matter whether he was Jewish or Danish or Polish or American? "Please...my wife..."

The man turned away and reached for something. Josef edged toward the door. But when the chemist faced him again, Josef saw that he was adding items to the order. "Is she very ill?"

"Ja. Fever, chills. I am a doctor, but without..."

"She has been wounded?"

Since Josef had specified bandages and disinfectant and a pair of long tweezers as part of the order, he could hardly deny the man's guess.

"The bullet is lodged in her leg," he admitted.

"Take these for now and try to get the fever down. Then bring her tonight to the rear entrance—after midnight—you'll hear the clock tower chime the hour. You can operate here and remove the bullet." He finished, tying the string that held the brown paper around the package of supplies. He handed it to Josef. "Tonight," he said again and pointed to a rear doorway covered by a curtain. "Go."

Throughout the day Anja and Josef took turns caring for Beth while the other one slept. It occurred to Josef that the chemist might easily have reported him, that local police or even German soldiers might even now be on their way to search the woods.

He was beyond caring.

What he knew was that Beth was better—the fever was down, and he had been able to dress the wound properly. The bullet was still lodged there, but tonight...

He felt someone shake him. "Josef? It's time," Anja whispered.

He sat up and heard the village clock striking the hour. He shook off sleep and crawled over to where Beth had been lying on a bed of pine needles all day. Her eyes were open.

"Josef?" She slurred the word and smiled up at him.

He glanced over his shoulder at Anja. "I gave her the rest of the cider. I guess that along with the medicine might have made her a little..."

There was no way she would be strong enough to walk even with the crutch, so Josef gathered her into his arms while Anja packed up everything and made certain they left no evidence of having been there.

"Ready?"

"Lead on," Anja said as together they stepped out into the open and headed for the village.

But as they approached the chemist's shop Josef immediately saw that something was wrong. In the first place the lights were all on. In the second place a car was parked in front. He motioned for Anja to head down a narrow lane that ran between the butcher's and the fish market.

"Wait here," he whispered as he set Beth down so that she was hidden by several wooden barrels behind the fish market.

Cautiously he edged his way back to the main street to a position where he could see into the shop without being seen. The chemist was there looking older and more frail than ever as two large men in uniform stood over him. Obviously one of the men was shouting at him.

Josef's heart sank. They had to go, and the sooner the better. If only there were some way of transporting Beth other than carrying her. He searched the alley for ideas, and outside the back entrance to the chemist's he saw a three-wheeled cart—the kind they had used at Sobibor to transport the luggage left by the prisoners at the side of the train.

When he got close enough to examine it, he saw that it had been outfitted with bedding and blankets, and he knew the chemist had prepared it for him to take Beth away once he'd removed the bullet. He considered what he could do to help the poor man who was even now being questioned inside but knew he would only make matters worse for him if he interfered.

He stood with his hands poised on the handles of the cart and closed his eyes. He prayed for the chemist and his family and promised God that one day he and Beth would return here and thank the man for his kindness—and his courage.

CHAPTER 23

Beth faded in and out of consciousness. One minute it was pitch black, although she knew that her eyes were open, and the next she saw a sliver of a moon. One minute she felt herself being carried along on a bumpy ride, her body cushioned by padding to all sides as whatever conveyance she was in stumbled over cobblestone streets.

"Josef?" she whispered, but her lips were cracked and dry, and her throat burned for lack of moisture.

At one point she thought she heard Anja say that they were nearly there, and she wondered where *there* might be. She had no feeling in her leg, and she wondered if perhaps she would be crippled for life.

Life.

They were still alive—all three of them. Anja seemed to have recovered her indomitable spirit, and Josef—dear brave Josef. She could hear the now-familiar sound of his steady breathing and knew that he was the one pushing her forward. They were on the move—to freedom at last.

The terrain changed. They had left the cobblestones behind and were making the trek across a field of mud. It was raining hard, and suddenly they stopped.

"It's stuck," Josef said.

From close by, Beth heard what sounded like the cars of a train being hooked one to the other. "That door is open," Anja called. "Come on. We can make it. It's going north, and we can—"

Her voice was lost in a crack of thunder as Josef lifted Beth into his arms and started across the muddy field. She forced herself to focus on their destination, determined to do whatever she could to help make certain they reached the train in time.

She could see Anja scrambling aboard an open cattle car. She and Josef were still twenty yards away as he plodded through the mud.

"Put me down," she demanded. "Josef, put me down and let me lean on you so we can make it before it leaves."

To her surprise he did as she asked, and using him as her crutch, she hobbled the last few yards to the train. Overcome by the stress and fears of the last several weeks, she started to laugh.

"Don't," Josef said as he reached to lift her again.

She pushed his hand away as she continued to hop toward their destination. "I'm all right," she said but could not stop laughing. "It's just that. . ."

"She's delirious," she heard Josef tell Anja as he hoisted her onto the bare floor of the cattle car just as the train began to move.

"I am not," she protested, lying flat on her stomach, as was Anja, their arms outstretched to Josef, who was now running alongside the train.

As the train gathered speed, he made his move and managed to flop down next to them in the car.

"You want to tell me what was so funny back there?" he asked irritably as he brushed himself off and bent to examine her dressing.

"I just suddenly thought about a picnic our Quaker community has every summer back in Wisconsin," Beth said as she combed his hair back from his eyes with her fingers. "We always ran a three-legged race, and the way you and I were hobbling across that field. . ."

Anja giggled.

Josef frowned.

"Well, she's got a point," Anja said. "Under other circumstances the two of you would have made quite a humorous sight."

Josef still did not laugh—did not even smile.

Beth took hold of his face, forcing him to look at her instead of her wound. "Josef, I am going to be all right—we are all going to be all right," she said.

"How can you be so certain?"

"I don't know, but what would be the point of bringing us this far if there were no purpose?"

Josef settled himself next to her while Anja made a pillow for herself of the knapsack—almost empty now.

Beth laced her fingers with Josef's and rested her cheek on his shoulder. The pain in her leg that the medicine had masked was beginning to break through again. But they were on a train—not walking for miles and miles through all kinds of weather. They were dry if not exactly warm. They had food—for now. "I believe that we will be all right, Josef—all three of us. God has other work for us to do."

"I wish I had your faith," Josef murmured.

"You can—close your eyes, open your heart, and look inward, Josef. The answers are there inside you—they always have been."

Josef didn't have to be told that Beth's pain had returned. He was well aware that the effects of the medicine he'd given her could not last forever. In truth he had thought that once he'd been able to remove the bullet, the kindly chemist would have made certain that they left with everything they would need for her recovery.

But such plans had been dashed the minute he saw the soldiers questioning their rescuer. There would be no surgery, no sterile instruments he could use to take out the bullet. And there would be no more medicine. The fever and infection most likely would return. He was desperate to get Beth to a place where she could receive proper care. Time was the enemy. They had miles to go yet, and it was already the first of November. The temperatures would continue to drop, and their tattered clothing would not keep them warm once they faced nights below freezing.

To further complicate matters, they had to remain on constant alert, and now that task was up to him and Anja. While the train was in motion, they were all right, but when it stopped, they had to hide in the corner of the cattle car, and because there was no cargo or livestock to hide behind, they had to hope that no one would decide to check the empty cars. Worse, Josef feared that the empty car they occupied might be uncoupled and left behind before they reached their destination.

Even on the battlefield as he'd crawled from one wounded soldier to the next, Josef had not been as terrified as he was now. The stakes were so much higher—he had a wife and a cause that he believed in. The White Rose might have perished with the arrests of his friends, and it had been evident that the people would not rise up and take back their government. But the acts of courage and defiance that he had witnessed at Sobibor had inspired him. He could do more. He had to do more.

But first he had to get Beth and Anja to safety.

"Tell me more about your relatives in Bornholm," he said to Anja as Beth dozed and the train rumbled its way toward the coast.

"My grandfather is a fisherman—herring mostly. He and my grandmother have lived on the island their whole lives. As a girl I used to spend summers with them. I loved being there."

"The island is occupied?"

Anja nodded. "The last letter that Benjamin and I had from them before..." Her voice drifted off as it so often did whenever she thought about her late husband. But then she rallied and continued. "It sounded as if the Germans leave the locals pretty much alone—no roundups and no Gestapo—at least not then."

"That would have been how long ago?"

Anja calculated, counting out the months. "Over a year now," she said softly as if she could not believe so much time had passed. "They wanted us to go there and stay until the war ended. My grandfather said that he would train Benjamin in the fishing business. How Benjamin laughed at that idea. 'How can I go out to sea when I can't even swim?' he used to say." She was silent for a long moment and then said, "How I wish we had gone."

"We'll go now," Josef told her and felt the inadequacy of his words even as he spoke them.

Anja—never one to wallow in her fears—brightened. "When that woman took Daniel, I gave her my grandparents' address. Perhaps she was able to get Daniel to them—or at least she wrote to let them know he was all right. Do you think so, Josef?"

He would not offer false hope—there had been too much of that. "We'll have to wait and see, but the good news is that, unless the train gets sidetracked, I heard two of the railroad workers say at our last stop that we should reach Danzig later today."

Beth was well aware that the infection had returned. Her leg was swollen and tender, and whenever Josef removed the bandages to examine the wound, she could see the pus. The slightest touch was so painful that she had to bite hard on her lower lip to keep from crying out. The bedding that the chemist had lined the cart with and that Josef had wrapped around her when he was carrying her across the muddy field toward the train was useful now as the most sterile bandaging available.

She and Anja had torn the fabric into strips, which they had carefully rolled into balls and placed inside the knapsack. Whenever Josef changed her dressing, he discarded the old soiled bandage in favor of one of the clean ones. But Beth was well aware that they were almost at the end of their supply.

She could no longer stand or walk even by leaning on Josef and Anja without the pain feeling like a fire in her leg. So whenever she needed to move—away from the doorway of the cattle car to the shadows while they were stopped—she crawled, or Josef carried her. She was beginning to think that she might actually lose the leg altogether. But even if that happened, it seemed a small price to pay for freedom when so many others had paid with their lives.

Most of the time she slept—or pretended to sleep—so that Josef and Anja could concentrate on keeping watch. She discovered that if she used the time for silent worship, she was able to forget about the pain and discomfort. She gave herself over to the rhythm of the train rocking side to side as it sped through villages and past farm fields and thought only about the future she and Josef would build together once they reached their destination.

"Bornholm is not free," Josef reminded her one night as they sat together while Anja slept and Beth—weaker than she'd ever been with fever and hunger and pain—talked about the life they would have there.

Once while they were in Sobibor, she had begged him to promise her that he would always tell her the truth. Even in her state of near delirium, she knew that it would have been so much easier for him to assure her that all her dreams for them would come true. "Josef, will I ever see Bornholm?"

He was quiet for so long that, if it were not for the sudden tensing of his body, she would have thought he'd perhaps dozed off. "Josef? The truth?"

"If you are asking me if you are dying, Beth, then my answer is this—I will do everything in my power to make sure you not only live to see the island but fully recover once you are there." He leaned over and kissed her forehead. "Now get some rest."

Beth curled closer to him, and when he wrapped his arms around her, she knew that no matter where life took them, this was home.

Josef had worried for much of the train ride that he was making a mistake. The train was headed for Danzig, Poland's largest seaport and as such a place of supreme importance to the Nazis. The port was the gateway to the Baltic Sea with access to Denmark, Norway,

Finland, Sweden—and Russia. With the defeat at Stalingrad and the subsequent turning of the tide of war against Germany, he suspected that Danzig had taken on even more significance, and he was not surprised to see a strong presence of men in uniform as the train approached the station.

Anja had prepared everything for their departure from the train—packing up whatever they had left of the supplies they'd brought from the chemist and leaving no trace that they had been there. Beth was weak but determined to do her part. The plan was for them to jump as the train slowed down for the final approach to the station.

"Ready?" he asked the two women as the three of them crouched next to the open door, the cold damp wind whipping at their clothing.

"The fog is a blessing," Beth said as she waited for Josef's signal.

She was right. The heavy fog rolling in off the sea would give them cover in an area they did not know and where they might be seen. "Let's go," he said and made his leap.

Anja threw him the knapsack and Beth's crutch, and then she and Beth held hands and made the jump together.

Beth fought hard to hide the shot of pain she felt with the hard landing, but she could not keep the tears from welling. "I'm all right," she assured them. "Give me the crutch, and let's go."

Josef shouldered the knapsack, and the three of them started walking. With Beth setting the pace, it was slow going. Every step she took was obviously excruciating, yet she kept going.

"This way," Anja said when they came to a corner. "My grandfather would sometimes bring me with him when he came to sell his smoked herring here. The docks are this way; I'm sure of it."

Josef hoped she was right. He'd already seen soldiers stopping people on the street and demanding to review their identity papers. As escaped prisoners, they had no identity and no money with which to bribe a soldier willing to look the other way. If they were stopped, they might as well surrender.

"If we are stopped," Beth said as if her mind and his had been on the same topic, "I will pretend to faint into the arms of the soldiers. You and Anja must run."

"There will be at least two of them," Anja said.

Beth appeared to consider this and then smiled. "So I will fall on the one and use my crutch to trip the other."

"No one is going to fall on anyone," Josef grumbled. "And should we be stopped, I will handle things. Are we clear?"

He did not miss the way the two women rolled their eyes at each other before meekly nodding and trudging on through the fog and misty rain.

As they approached the docks, Josef saw several boats preparing to head out to sea for the day—some were larger ships loaded with goods and probably bound for some larger city. It seemed unlikely that any of those would stop at a small island. That was too bad because stowing away on one of those larger ships and making it to their destination without being discovered held more potential for success than taking a smaller craft.

Anja tugged on his sleeve. "I know that man," she whispered, pointing to a grizzled old fisherman who was readying a small boat that looked as if it might not make it across a small creek, much less across a sea that could turn rough at any time. "Wait here."

Before Josef could stop her, Anja called out to the man. The two of them carried on an animated conversation, with Anja doing most of the talking. But then the fisherman broke into a smile and began hugging Anja and babbling away in what Josef could only assume was Danish.

"Come on," Beth said when Anja motioned for them to step forward.

"It could be a trap," Josef muttered, holding Beth's arm to keep her from going.

"And it could be a blessing," she reminded him. "Either way we have no choice." She hobbled toward the fishing boat.

"This is Edvard Larsen," Anja said. "He is a friend of my grandparents."

Beth extended her hand to the man. "Elizabeth, and this is my husband, Herr Doktor Josef Buch." Anja translated.

Edvard stared hard at Beth's leg with its bloody bandage. He frowned, said something to Anja, and started walking away from them toward a cluster of buildings.

"He's been gone a long time," Josef said as they continued to wait for the fisherman's return.

Anja shrugged, but she looked worried. "He said something about getting help."

"It's too dangerous to just sit here waiting," Josef said, glancing around for possible escape routes. He had allowed himself to hope that their journey was at last coming to an end, but could they trust the fisherman? He didn't think so. They would have to keep moving in spite of a hint of snow in the air. In spite of the fact that they were all exhausted and hungry and Beth especially could not go on much longer. "Come on."

"No wait," Beth said, pointing toward the building Edvard had entered. The fisherman was coming out. He was carrying two satchels filled to overflowing.

"Now we can go," Anja translated as Edvard muttered the words to her and placed the satchels in his boat. He turned and offered his hand to Beth, helping her as if she might break, fussing over her comfort as he settled her inside the small galley area and handed her a lap robe to tuck around her knees. Then he did the same for Anja. Finally he turned to Josef and nodded.

Apparently Josef was on his own if he wanted to get in and out of the vessel. He left the seat closest to an ancient outboard motor free for Edvard and took a position on deck but close to the open galley door and Beth. He noticed that she was perspiring in spite of the chill and knew that her fever had returned.

Moments later they were on their way, floating slowly past the larger cargo ships, some tugboats, and several other fishing boats. The fog was still thick, and Josef wondered how the old man could be sure of where he was going. But as they cleared the busy harbor, they broke through the fog and faced a sea of gray that matched the gray skies so perfectly it was hard to find a horizon.

At Edvard's instructions Anja unpacked the satchels. One was filled with food—bread, cheese, smoked herring, and beer. The other contained medical supplies—medicines and salves and clean bandages. Edvard gestured to Josef as if to say, "You're the doctor—do something."

While Anja assembled their meal, Josef got to work. He unwrapped the soiled bandages and used the alcohol and gauze pads that Edvard had gotten to clean the wound. As he had feared, the infection was back. But to his surprise, as he probed the wound he realized that the bullet had worked free and moved closer to the surface. He pulled the tweezers the Polish chemist had given him from the knapsack. He handed them to Anja.

"Boil some water and sterilize this," he instructed. He was aware that in addition to navigating the boat, Edvard was keeping a close watch on their activities. He scowled at Josef whenever Beth grimaced or moaned. Eventually they would need to tell the fisherman the story of their escape. But right now the important thing was to let the medicine do its job, get some nourishment, and then try to remove the bullet.

While Anja sterilized the tweezers, Josef gave Beth some of the medications for pain and fever. He hoped he was reading the labels accurately. Finally she drifted off to sleep.

"I'll stay with her," Anja said, handing him a plate of food for himself and one for Edvard. "You go on." She nodded toward the fisherman.

To Josef's surprise, Edvard spoke enough German so that they could converse as Edvard guided the small craft through waters he obviously knew as well as another man would have known the road home. Josef gave him the story of their escape, and Edvard's eyes grew wide with disbelief and then respect at what they had overcome to make it this far.

"And what will happen when you reach Bornholm?" Edvard asked.

It was a question that had plagued Josef for hours now. The island was occupied by the Nazis. On the other hand, here was Edvard—a lifelong resident who must know exactly what dangers they might face. "What do you suggest?"

The older man rubbed his hand over his beard and stared at the horizon for several minutes. "Anja's grandparents live on the north side of the island—it's steeper there and more remote. The Nazis aren't as concerned about it as they are the south side around Ronne."

"But we can't do anything that might put Anja and her grandparents in further danger. We'll need to keep moving—get to Sweden maybe."

Edvard shrugged. "Your wife is in no shape to keep running, Josef. Give her time to heal while you put together a plan. I've got a little cottage I only use over the winter when I can't get out to fish. But my sister is always after me to come stay with her—she worries that I don't take care of myself. You and your wife can stay there in the cottage—it's isolated, and the Germans are not likely to bother you. By spring. . ." His voice trailed off.

Josef was suddenly overwhelmed with emotion. What would they be doing right now if this man had not decided to come to Danzig? If Anja had not recognized him? If he had refused to help them?

"Thank you," he said softly. "You have. . .I don't know what we would. . ." After days of worry over Beth and the constant need to stay one step ahead of the Nazis, Josef broke down.

He felt the strong grip of Edvard's hand clasp his shoulder. "You'll be all right," the old man said. "You're safe now."

But as the rocky shores of Bornholm came into view on the distant horizon, Josef could not help but wonder if they would ever be safe again. "I have to treat my wife," he said.

As they approached the island, the sea began to roil, and the little boat rocked from side to side, making it impossible for Josef to risk trying to operate, especially with nothing more than a pair of tweezers.

⫸ CHAPTER 24 ⫷

Beth opened her eyes at the sound of voices. She blinked several times as it dawned on her that for the first time in days her leg was not throbbing and she felt stronger. She pushed aside a blanket as she tried to get her bearings. Where was she? Where was Josef? And Anja?

She sat up and promptly bumped her head. Across from her was a compact kitchen area, and her immediate thought was that she was hungry—more than just hungry. She was ravenous. She saw a partial loaf of thick bread on the counter next to the sink and reached for it.

"Not too fast," Anja advised as she ducked through the low doorway and joined Beth. "Josef?" she called. "Come see."

In seconds Josef was by Beth's side, holding her as he peered into her eyes and then felt her forehead like a mother testing for fever. "Lie back," he instructed.

"I've slept long enough," she protested.

"I want to examine your wound."

She did as he asked.

"The infection is under control," he muttered, and then he grinned. "I think the patient will make a full recovery."

"Thanks be to God," Anja said.

Above them, Beth heard a great deal of commotion—men shouting out orders to each other in a language she did not understand, heavy objects being moved, and the smell of the sea. "Where are we?" she asked.

"Home—at least for now," Josef told her. "Do you think you're feeling well enough to get up?"

"Stop fussing over me. I'm fine."

But the minute she tried standing, she realized how weak she really was.

"Lean on me," Josef instructed.

Together they climbed the short stairway to the deck of the fishing boat. It was all coming back to her now: the train, Anja leading them up and down streets until they reached the dock, the kindly old fisherman—a friend of Anja's grandparents. But after that everything was a blank.

"Welcome to Bornholm," Anja announced, having followed them on deck.

Beth thought the sight before her must be a dream. The sky was a cloudless blue, and the water surrounding them was calm. Both were rare occurrences once the temperatures dropped and the first snow set in, according to Anja. The boat was tied to a wooden dock, and men were busy unloading large wooden barrels. Up a steep cobblestone path sat a cluster of houses and shops with tiled or thatched roofs, their half-timbered stucco walls sometimes painted a cheerful yellow. Surely after the gloom of Sobibor, this could not be real. When they'd left Danzig, it had been foggy with snow flurries.

"My leg feels better."

"That's because you are married to a surgical genius," Anja told her with a grin. "We had to ride out a storm last night, but as soon as the winds died and things settled, he went to work. The man has not slept a wink."

"He removed the bullet?"

"He did indeed."

Beth examined the clean bandages wrapped around her calf and noticed that the swelling had also gone down. She turned her face to the sun and took a long look at her surroundings. "Where are we?"

"Gudhjem on the island of Bornholm—welcome to Denmark," Anja said as Edvard walked down the dock toward them.

He spoke to Anja in Danish, all the while flicking his eyes toward Beth and smiling.

"Edvard has arranged for transportation to take us to my grandparents' farm," Anja explained. "The closest doctor is miles away, but the local midwife will bring whatever Josef needs to continue treating your wound."

Beth saw a couple of soldiers wearing German uniforms climbing the steep hill to the village. "We don't want to put your grandparents or the midwife in danger," she told Anja. "Perhaps. . ."

Josef pulled her closer against his side. "It's all arranged, Liebchen. Edvard has even offered us his cottage for the time it takes for you to regain your strength."

"And then what?" She had not meant to voice the question aloud, but there it was. "The island is occupied, and if anyone becomes aware of how we. . ."

"We're safe here for now, Beth. Let's just take the time we have to rest and get you well. Then we can think about what to do next."

A fresh wave of exhaustion washed over Beth, dampening her uplifted spirits. The reality was that in spite of the idyllic scene before her, they were not yet free from the fear that had dogged them for months.

As if sensing the change in her mood, Josef wrapped his arm around her and helped her cross the deck to the dock. "Come, let's go bring Anja's grandparents the good news that their granddaughter is not only safe—she has come home to them."

As it turned out, Anja's grandparents—Olaf and Ailsa—were the ones to bring the best news of all. Once introductions had been made and Anja had briefly told them what had happened to them—and to her late husband and daughter—Olaf handed Anja a letter.

"It came after we had lost all contact with you."

"Open it," Ailsa urged. "Perhaps it is good news."

Beth saw a Belgian postmark on the envelope and a return name and address. Anja began to weep as soon as she saw the return name on the envelope. "It is from the woman in the red dress," she told Beth. "The woman at the church who took Daniel." Her hands were trembling uncontrollably, and she sobbed. "I can't," she managed to say as she thrust the letter into Beth's hands. "You read it."

Beth slid her thumbnail under the flap of the envelope and removed the single sheet of paper inside. "It says, 'Your package arrived safely on the twentieth and is a wonderful addition to our garden, thriving and blossoming as you hoped.' It's signed simply 'Hannah.'"

Anja reached for the letter and scanned the contents. A smile of relief replaced her tears. "It's Daniel," she explained. "Hannah was taking him to Belgium to a convent outside Brussels where they run an orphanage. That's the garden and. . ." She peered closely at the date stamp on the envelope, and once again her features darkened. "When was this sent? Months ago now—nearly a year. What if. . ."

Olaf hugged his granddaughter until her wails of distress had settled into shuddering sobs. "We will find him," he assured her.

"Come," Ailsa invited. "Let's go inside. The midwife will be here soon, but we have invited some Friends to join us in silent worship—we have much joy in our hearts."

"Of course." Beth had almost forgotten that if Anja followed the faith of the Friends, it was likely that her family did as well. And if she had needed any more evidence that she and Josef were home—at least for the moment—the invitation to sit in silence with other Quakers for the first time in months was more than sufficient.

Josef and Beth settled into Edvard's small cottage. They passed the time reading aloud to each other, visiting with Anja and her grandparents, and planning the future neither of them could be certain they would ever know. As their days on the island lengthened into weeks and November passed and December brought more snow, Josef was surprised to find that the daily worship meetings with the Danish Quakers brought him a sense of peace and hope unlike anything he had ever experienced in his restless life. Even as a boy he had always felt as if he was expected to manage any challenge that came his way on his own. His father had insisted that Josef address any conflict without the help of his elders. It was a policy that Josef knew his mother had often disagreed with, but his father had been adamant. "How do you expect the boy to learn?"

The memory of that made the lengths that his father had gone to— even jeopardizing his own career—to save Josef and Beth even more remarkable. Often as Josef sat in silence with the others, his thoughts turned to his parents, and he wondered what price they must have paid when news reached Munich of the Sobibor revolt.

One day when he had gone down to the docks to sit with Edvard and mend fishing nets, he asked the fisherman if he would be willing to do him one more favor.

"One more. Ten more." Edvard shrugged.

"I would like to contact my parents and let them know that Beth and I are all right. It is too dangerous for me to write them directly, but if you..."

"Write your letter, Josef, the way you want me to put it, and I'll take care of it."

Late into the night as Josef and Beth sat beside the fireplace in Edvard's cozy cottage, they worked on the letter. What could they say? What should they not say? How much information was enough but not so much as to cause problems?

It was Beth who reminded him of the coded letter that Anja had received. The return address had been a general mail address that was not tied to any specific place, and the message had been brief and to the point. "Surely in his position your father is well used to reading between the lines, Josef."

In the end they decided to compose the piece as if it were a business exchange. *The two barrels of herring you requested are in storage for the winter.*

"Should we say where?"

"They'll know from the stamp and return address."

Josef ran his hand through his hair. "We need something more specific. My father will see this and simply dismiss it as a misdirected letter or a ploy to get his business."

"What if. . ." She frowned, unable to complete the thought. But then an idea occurred to her. "Josef, there must have been a time when you were a boy that your parents had some pet name for you. What was it?"

Josef sighed. "Can you honestly imagine my father calling me by any name other than the one he had chosen for me?"

"Your mother, then."

Josef thought for a long moment, and then he smiled. "*Sepp*—she called me Sepp. It drove my father to distraction, and I think that may be why she continued to do it from time to time even after I left home. It was always said with such affection. . . ." His voice trailed off as he remembered those happier times.

"But your father would recognize it?"

Josef shrugged. "I suppose. What are you thinking?"

"What if the letter said, 'The two barrels of Sepp herring you requested are in storage for the winter'? Perhaps we could put the name in quotes or italics or something to make it stand out."

"It's worth a try. And we could add a line—something like 'Please approve by return post.' Then if we get a letter, we'll know my father understood the message."

"And if we don't?" Beth hated to ask, but it was important to know how Josef would react.

"If there is no response, then either my father missed the reference, or he understood it and chose to ignore it."

Beth knew full well that in spite of Josef's attempt to remain stoic, the very idea that his father might ignore a message from him was devastating.

"He will respond," she said. "Think how he risked everything for you after your arrest. And he warned Uncle Franz and arranged for us to be married and. . ."

Josef cupped her cheek tenderly. "You have such faith, Beth—you always see the good in others. How do you manage that, especially after everything you've had to endure? Everything I've put you through?"

"I chose to be with you, Josef, so whatever came after that was part of that decision. I love you, and I would rather be with you in the worst of circumstances than separated from you under the best of conditions."

"But did you stop to consider what being with me meant? You are the daughter-in-law of a high-ranking Gestapo official, Beth. How can you make peace with that?"

"I did not marry your father—I married you. Besides I was raised to believe that the inner Light that guides us all dwells in every person. We have only to be still and wait, and eventually God will show us the way."

"Even men like my father?"

"Oh Josef, surely you can see that he is doing the best he can manage. Imagine how torn he must have been when forced to choose between loyalty to the country he loves—the country you both love—and defending your actions. Actions that went against everything he believes. And still he found it in his heart to forgive you and to stand with you in your darkest hour."

Josef studied the draft of the letter they'd been working on for hours now.

"Your father will most assuredly recognize your handwriting."

The idea seemed to inspire him. "We should include some mention of my mother—that will get his attention." He bent over a clean sheet of paper and started writing. A few minutes later he handed the paper to Beth:

Dear Herr Buch,

Per Frau Buch's instructions, two barrels of our finest "SEPP" brand herring have been placed in storage for the winter. Please confirm that these arrangements meet with your approval.

"It's perfect," Beth said.

Josef nodded, but Beth did not miss the way he read the words again as if searching for some flaw.

"And after we deliver the letter to Edvard, we will sit in worship and pray for God to hold your parents in the Light and lead us all to a day of reunion once this terrible war is ended."

The more Josef participated in the silent meetings attended by Beth, Anja and her grandparents, and a few of their neighbors, the more he found the kind of inner peace and understanding that he had sought almost from the day that Hitler had taken full power. At first his thoughts focused on regrets about the unfinished work of the White Rose. But then he considered the incredible courage it had taken to organize and execute the escape from Sobibor, and he began to see a connection. A positive connection, as if the road might be hard but it was indeed the right path.

The realization excited him, and at one evening's meeting for worship he found himself on his feet and ready to speak for the first time. In other meetings others had sometimes spoken aloud, their observations always followed by a respectful return to silence before anyone else spoke. Other times the group sat in silence for over an hour, and no one said a word. No one had spoken on this day, but Josef felt as if he had to say something.

"I am a stranger here," he began. "A stranger from another land and a stranger from another faith, yet I have never experienced such a sense of community—of friendship and caring and concern. I am so very grateful that I have come to this place. Beth has lived among Friends all her life, and it is through her that I have been brought to this Meeting." He hesitated, looking at the small circle of friends gathered around the fireplace in the fishing cottage while outside a northern wind whistled warning of a coming storm. "I do have a concern, and it is that Beth and I were not able to be married in the traditions of her faith. Even so, I ask that you hold us in the Light as we hold each of you in the Light to face whatever the future may bring."

He sat down, and as was their custom, no one spoke or reacted in any way. He closed his eyes. Part of him hoped he had not embarrassed Beth or spoken out of turn. And then he felt Beth's fingers close around his, and he knew that the instinct to speak out had come from within— and it was absolutely right.

Following the meeting for worship, Anja and Beth set out the covered dishes of food they had prepared and received from the neighbors. They worked in contented silence in the kitchen, which was almost as small as the galley on Edvard's fishing boat. The others remained in the sitting room, talking quietly—mostly in Danish.

"You know you could marry properly in the faith," Anja said as if she were continuing a conversation the two of them had been engaged in as they set out the food. "We could do it here."

"There is so much we have yet to consider," Beth replied. "Why add a wedding to the list?"

"Because it would do everyone good to be able to celebrate something normal. Think about it."

But when Beth mentioned Anja's idea to Josef, he had concerns. "I would like that as well, but I fear calling undue attention to ourselves and especially to our friends here. The island is occupied after all, and if the Nazis. . ."

"Josef, what are we to do? Anja is planning to leave for Belgium as soon as possible to search for Daniel. Perhaps we should go with her."

"And do what?"

"There are still people in desperate need of help—we could join the underground resistance there and continue the work we began in Munich. We could. . ."

Josef's eyes widened in surprise. "You would go back to that life? To always living in danger and fear?"

"Danger, yes, but not fear, Josef. Never fear. If we are doing God's work, then we have nothing to fear."

"You amaze me." He held her close and kissed her. "Marry me, Beth," he whispered before kissing her again.

"We are already married," she reminded him.

"But Anja is right—that wedding is not the one we want to hold in our memories to share with our children and grandchildren. Let's let Anja plan a proper wedding for us."

"I thought you were worried about drawing attention to the others."

"If they allow us to worship in peace, then surely they will take little note of a simple ceremony."

Beth felt her heart swell with joy. From the moment Anja had suggested the idea, she had been unable to think of much else. What if. . .

But her innate caution and concern for the community made her seek out Edvard later that day. The fisherman had delayed his visit to his sister and continued to live on his boat, leaving Josef and Beth the privacy of his cottage. Many aspects of Edvard and his character reminded her of her father, and she had found that spending time with him helped to assuage her homesickness. Also she had another reason for going to visit him that day—she wanted to get word to her parents that she was safe, knowing they must be worried sick by now.

"I can carry a letter for you when I go over to Sweden next week. It'll be my last run before full winter sets in."

It was the perfect solution. Because Sweden had maintained its neutrality, her letter had a far better chance of reaching her parents without the blacked out lines of the German censors. "I'll write the letter tonight," she promised.

"And as for this other matter, you and your young doctor deserve a wedding you can remember with pleasure. A wedding bound only by the love the two of you share. Let Anja put it together for you."

"But we don't want to cause trouble for anyone, and what if—"

Edvard smiled. "The people in this village have handled a lot more than any problems a simple wedding might cause. Besides the war's turned against Hitler and his gang. Word has it that some of those Nazis stationed here are already beginning to reconsider their futures. I expect we'll start to see the desertions any time now." He patted Beth's head as if she were a little girl. "You go on and plan that wedding."

"Will you be there?" she asked, feeling suddenly shy with him.

"Would not miss it for the world."

~≋ CHAPTER 25 ≋~

This time they took the time they needed to follow the traditions of the Quaker faith. As clerk of the meeting for business, Anja's grandfather Olaf read aloud the letter that Josef and Beth had given him announcing their wish to be married. Beth and Josef sat quietly among the circle of Friends gathered for the monthly meeting for business.

"He will appoint two or three Friends to form a clearness committee," Beth explained in a whisper.

"What's a clearness committee?"

"They will question us and point out potential difficulties we may encounter and then—"

"But we're already married," Josef reminded her.

"I know, but it's part of the tradition."

Anja and Edvard were appointed, and with a nod from Anja, Edvard stood and addressed everyone there. "Anja and I approve the proposed union and recommend that they be allowed to marry."

"So much for questions and potential problems," Josef said with a wry grin.

"Shhh," Beth whispered.

Olaf turned to the next order of business. "With the approval of the meeting, I would like to appoint my wife, my granddaughter, and myself to serve as the oversight committee."

Nods all around.

"Another committee? What's this one for?" Josef whispered.

Beth took hold of his hand hoping to calm him. "They will oversee the arrangements for the wedding—the wedding certificate, the food and place for the reception—everything."

"Oh." He was obviously relieved.

"Who will perform the ceremony?" Josef asked later as they walked back to Edvard's cottage together.

"We will."

"I don't understand."

"Friends refer to it as being married under the care of a Quaker meeting. When the time comes, we will stand before the gathering of friends and members of this meeting and speak our vows."

"No minister or priest or whatever you call the clergyman?"

"God is our clergy."

Josef was silent for the rest of the walk to the cottage, and Beth knew that he must be thinking how different this all was to the faith he was raised in with its ritual and robed clergy and ceremonial trappings.

"Would you rather not do this, Josef?" she asked as they stepped inside the cozy cottage and hung up their coats. "I mean we are already man and wife, and there's no—"

He laid his finger against her lips. "I want very much to do this. I like everything about it, especially the idea that it's just you and me coming before God to speak our vows. I love you with my entire being, and when I thought I might lose you—that the infection from the bullet..."

"Shhh. I am healed now and getting stronger every day. Why, the walk down to the docks and back up that hill every day has done wonders for me. I hardly limp at all."

"And I was going to carve you a walking stick for a wedding gift," he teased. He brushed her golden curls away from her face, and his expression turned serious. "I want so much to make you happy, Beth."

"Then you have what you want, for I am happier and more content in this place than I could ever have imagined."

"You must miss your family."

"Of course I do. But I feel more strongly than anything that God brought us to this place. I want to stay, Josef—for now. I want to stop running and stay here."

"Then that is what we will do. We'll find a cottage of our own. Maybe I can practice medicine among the locals."

"What will I do?"

Josef grinned, and Beth thought he was never more handsome than when his eyes sparkled mischievously and his smile lit up his entire inner being. "You, my love, will be busy raising our children."

Three days before Christmas Day 1943 Josef and Beth sat side by side next to Anja and her grandparents at the meeting for worship. The members of the meeting were all present. Edvard had even trimmed his scraggly beard for the occasion. After several minutes of silence, Josef took Beth's hand, and the two stood.

Josef spoke first.

"In the presence of God and this gathering of Friends, I take this my friend Elizabeth Bridgewater to be my wife, promising with divine assistance to be unto thee a loving and faithful husband so long as we both shall live."

Beth repeated the same words to Josef, and, still holding hands, they stepped up to a small table and signed the wedding certificate. Once they had again taken their seats, Olaf as clerk of the meeting read the certificate aloud. He sat down, and everyone returned to the silence of worship.

After a while Edvard stood and cleared his throat. "I was sitting here thinking about how these two young people are just at the beginning of their journey while some of the rest of us are coming to the end. May God hold them in the Light as He has blessed those of us gathered here today many times over."

Around the circle, the worshippers raised their hands in wordless praise and returned to their silence.

Anja's grandmother was the next to speak. She struggled to stand, her arthritic knees suffering in the damp and cold of the winter day. "These young people have already been tested in ways the rest of us cannot imagine," she said. "Let us all pray that they continue to find their way—hand in hand—through these difficult times."

Beth thought about all that she and Josef had faced together. She thought about the day she first met him and how she had looked at him with suspicion because he wore the uniform of a German soldier. How she had prayed that very night for God's forgiveness that she had judged this man for his outward appearance instead of getting to know the inner man beneath the uniform.

She thought about the train ride with Liesl when Josef had proposed to her, and she understood now that his proposal that night had been every bit as genuine as his love for her was on this day. But again she had doubted. And then she squeezed her eyes closed to hold back tears when she recalled the day she had read her uncle's note and in that single moment believed that Josef had betrayed them all.

She realized now that God had shown her the way back to Josef and had given her the strength to stand with him in his darkest hours as he faced the judge and the possibility of a death sentence. She took no pride in or credit for her actions that day, but rather saw the events that had led them both to Sobibor as a unique blessing because it had reunited them with Anja and had shown them that in the face of true evil, there were the blessings of friendship and courage and community.

Olaf reached over and shook Edvard's hand, signaling that the meeting for worship had come to its end. Several of those in attendance stepped up to sign the wedding certificate while Anja and her grandmother set out the refreshments. The room that had been so filled with silence only minutes before was filled with laughter and conversation and good wishes for Josef and Beth. The room and these people felt like family. . .like home.

Josef held onto her hand as if he intended never to let go of it as they received the congratulations of the others. The language barrier was hardly noticeable, as enough of those present spoke German that they could translate the Danish for the happy couple.

Beth saw Edvard remove an envelope from his pocket, and he smoothed out the wrinkles in it before stepping forward. "This came for you, Josef."

"It's addressed to you, Edvard."

Beth watched as Josef studied the handwriting. "It's from my father." His hands were shaking as he opened the envelope. She leaned closer so that they could read the short and simple message together:

> *Please keep the two barrels in your custody until Frau Buch and I can come to collect them. We are both so very thankful for your kindness.*

"They know you are both safe," Edvard explained. "They just couldn't risk saying anything that might. . ."

"I know," Beth said as tears streamed down her cheeks. "One day soon," she promised herself and those around her, "we will speak out loud all the joys and concerns that we have had to bear in silence."

She felt Josef's arms wrap around her, and she looked up at him. In his eyes she saw that same passion and fierce intensity that had first drawn her to him. And she knew that whatever the future held, they could ask no greater blessing than that of facing it together.

~ AUTHOR'S NOTE ~

As a history buff I am fascinated by all of the true but little-known stories of people facing incredible adversity with such courage and determination. I became aware of the White Rose when I visited the Holocaust Museum in Washington, DC, for the first time—the arrests of Hans and Sophie and Christoph took place on my husband's birthday; another trial and execution took place on my birthday; and still another on my father's birthday. Seeing three familiar dates that signaled such happy times in my life, I was of course determined to learn more about these brave young people. Similarly I stumbled quite by accident onto the true story of the escape from Sobibor.

In any story set in the midst of war, there will be characters—like Anja, Franz, Ilse, and Liesl—whose fate remains unresolved. It is not realistic to think that Beth would be able to discover what became of her aunt and uncle and cousin while imprisoned in Sobibor or on the run. That is why *All God's Children* is the first of three books in the Peacemaker series.

Book 2, *Simple Faith*, tells Anja's story (and continues the story of Josef and Beth). They will play out their lives in the very real world of what became known as "The Freedom Line"—an incredible underground system where locals helped American, Canadian, and

British airmen whose planes had crashed behind enemy lines get back to the safety of England.

And in Book 3, *Safe Haven*, Franz, Ilse, and Liesl will again play key roles. The story moves to America and upstate New York, where a boatload of refugees from Europe—mostly Jews—were allowed to live out the war in relative safety.

I hope you will be inspired to read all three books. In any case, please stop by my website (www.booksbyanna.com) to learn more about these actual heroes and events or write to me at P.O. Box 161, Thiensville, WI 53092, and share your thoughts. Until then may you—like Josef and Beth—learn to see the blessings of the difficult times and the wonders of those times when your cup indeed runneth over with joy and the Light!

All best wishes!
Anna

Anna Schmidt is the author of over twenty works of fiction. Among her many honors, Anna is the recipient of *Romantic Times'* Reviewer's Choice Award and a finalist for the RITA award for romantic fiction. She enjoys gardening and collecting seashells at her winter home in Florida.